Hummingbird

Hummingbird

James George

First published in 2003 by Huia Publishers,
39 Pipitea Street, PO Box 17-335,
Wellington, Aotearoa New Zealand.
www.huia.co.nz

ISBN 1-877283-66-5

Literary agency services provided by Dr Susan Sayer

National Library of New Zealand Cataloguing-in-Publication Data
George, James, 1962-
Hummingbird / James George.
ISBN 1-877283-66-5
I. Title.
NZ823.3—dc 21

Published with the assistance of

To A J M

And to all those who have never returned

Contents

Next he prepared his son. 'Take care,' he said,
'To fly a middle course, lest you sink:
if too low the waves may weight your feathers;
if too high the heat may burn them ...'

Ovid, *Metamorphoses*

I

Promises

Kataraina

There was a female cat that lived by a creek behind a bedsit I stayed at. She would sit there for hours, staring at the water. A weather-beaten old stray, like a frayed jacket that you never wear anymore but can't bring yourself to throw away. I was eight months pregnant by then, but I waddled down the slope, as quiet as I could, until I was close enough to see my shadow on the creek, breaking and reforming in the ripples. Then I saw the reflection of the cat's face.

I didn't move, just stood watching her ears for a flicker, some sign that she sensed me there. But she was lost in whatever she saw in the water. She raised a paw, began to wash, the cat in the river also raising a paw to wash. I sat back against the bank, watching the cat watching herself. No sound except for the whisper of the water. Just the two of us and our shadows, like them old paintings, the watchamacallit, Madonna and child.

My daughter was taken from me thirty seconds after she was born. I wanted it that way. I didn't want to see my face in her, see some tiny mark that would stick in my memory and keep coming back to me. Some hint in her eyes or a fall of an eyelid, the shape of her nose, even a little finger or toe. Anything I'd recognise, anything that would say, 'you and me, we're the same, eh.'

I mean … I couldn't keep a kid, how could I? I was seventeen years old. Hell, all the stuff I was sticking into me, up me. I was moving from one dive to the next. Anyway, I'd done right by her, I hadn't killed her. Hadn't flushed her down some sink and down into the sewer. No, she got to breathe. But I couldn't look at her, that bit I couldn't do. So I rolled over and stared at the wall.

But then I saw a metal dish all shiny in the operating-theatre lights. Sitting there on a table like a huge diamond. So I focused on it, tried to block out the sound of her voice by screaming inside. I'd got used to screaming inside. To them I must've looked like a stone someone had dropped into the middle of the room, but they didn't know.

Even through that, I still heard a nurse say, 'It's a girl.' I nodded my head, yeah, focused on my diamond again. I reckon I'd done right by her. Didn't flush her down some drain, no, I gave her life. Maybe to most people that wouldn't be enough, but it was all I had to give.

She got to breathe.

A couple of nights after I let them take my baby I got drunk and took this little two-dollar torch and my guitar down to the creek bed and sat on the dirt of the bank, my bare feet in the water. I lay the torch next to me, its tiny beam like a rip or tear on the surface. I flicked it off and sat in the dark. I wondered if I still cast a shadow. Just something that would say, 'you and me, eh. We're an *us*.'

I sat playing in the dark, singing along, singing to that unseen face in the river.

I did right by her, I gave her life. It was all I had to give. She got to breathe.

Ninety Mile Beach, September 1990

The old pilot looks up over the glass of the small cockpit windscreen to where the Tiger Moth's upper wings frame the sky. He looks back through the heat haze from the engine, the blur of the propeller blades. He flexes his thumbs against the handle of the control column, eases it to the left and watches the port wingtips bank against the coastline, against the ribs of surf far below. There is clear sky to the horizon.

Two, two and a half hours and he'll land the Tiger Moth for the last time. He glances at the gauges indented in the ornate wood of the control panel: air speed, altitude, oil pressure – all fine. Above his right knee is an original AM MKII compass rescued from a Hawker Hurricane. He glances at the crosshair pattern encircled with a ring of numbers. He takes his gloved right hand off the column handle and taps the glass of the compass face. Then he rights the Tiger Moth's balance, points it to the south-east.

Kataraina crosses the loose stones at the edge of the rutted metal track and steps onto the sand. She moves down to where the beach gives way to the rainbowed turquoise and emerald of the ocean. She slips off her sandals and walks across the wet sand to the surf where she clasps a fold of her dress between thumb and forefinger and steps into the shallows, taking the wave tips against her bare thighs. She raises her face to the wind, catching its touch on her cheekbones, and shutters her gaze, clothing the world with a slip of her eyelids.

How long has it been. How long has it been.

She turns and moves up over the ribs of sand, pausing to glance back at her footprints. She scuffs at one with her bare toes, then steps back into her own imprint, heel to toe. Rocking back and forward, engraving her mark.

She walks up into the softer sand and climbs the highest dune. There is an old jetty a couple of hundred yards to the north, a ragged troop of posts, half of them crumbling into the waves.

'There's not much of you left, is there,' she says.

To the east beyond the dunes a steep hill rises, its southern face half-missing now, broken off. Through a gap in the next spine of sandhills there is a hint of green – cut grass, not wild. She makes her way through an opening in the dunes, noticing now a faint tapestry of footprints beneath her own. She is surrounded by a ring of small cabins. They are much as they always were, perhaps a little more worn. Beyond them another circle, this time of pines. Beyond that, only the hill, carved against the sky. She stops in the circle's centre, a hub to its wheel, listening for voices beyond the wind in the leaves, the calls of gulls.

A peek into each silent cabin. She steps into the concrete kitchen building, squints through the sudden change of light at the ancient stove, the metal sink, the faded wood of the cupboards. She leans against the scratched and pitted table, her fingertips running across its face. There's a faint hint of voices, snatches of movement at the edge of her eyes. Glasses chink, a mother's grin, a father's cigarette-stained laugh. A brother's silent face. She steadies herself, closes her eyes and nods.

The old pilot jerks in his seat, jolted by a sudden skitter of shadows. He raises a hand to his goggles. He blinks through a wave of dirty hail, as if he has flown through shattered glass. The cockpit windshield is streaked with grey and red. He reaches over the top of it, wipes some clear space with a gloved hand. Feathers. He must have bisected a flock of gulls. He blinks again, hard, focusing on the circle of the propeller, regaining his bearings.

In the haze of the propeller glimpses of memory come to

him. The air suddenly thick with shadows. He loosens the chinstrap on his flying helmet and runs his tongue along his lips, tasting the wind. Then something else. He opens his eyes. A taste of oil in the air now. He listens to the motor, to the break in the rhythm, the pistons missing a beat. He checks the control panel, the air-speed gauge steady, but the oil-pressure needle stuttering. He reduces height, turning the ocean beneath him from distant glass to a more intimate, finespun fibre. Wave and trough and white caps.

Smoke on his lips now. Acrid. A dark soot peppers the cockpit windshield. The engine-temperature gauge rises against the oil-pressure needle's fall. The air intake must be clogged. He doesn't have two hours, not even close. Perhaps only a few minutes. He looks east, searching for flat land. There is none – except for a pale, thin strip of sand bordering the ocean.

He is dropping fast, almost too fast to control. He leans back, using all his strength to keep the nose at least halfway horizontal. The motor is a war of shudders, the Moth's body skidding in the air. He struggles to ease the left wing down, focusing on his makeshift runway, lining the nose up between high-tide mark and sea.

Kataraina looks up, interrupted by a sound she cannot place. A cry at first mechanical, then faltering like the heartbeat of something wounded. She strides across the grass and climbs the dunes and stands with an arm shielding her eyes from the sun. There, to the north, a small aeroplane. Two sets of wings, painted a mustard yellow. Skittering across the wind currents, a haze of dirty smoke coming from the engine. Its wheels hit the sand, kicking up a cloud, as if it has set the beach afire. The engine silences and it rolls towards the sand beneath her.

She descends the face of the dune, stands among a shoal of shells. Her hand reaches to touch a wingtip. In the rear of the two cockpits the pilot leans back, a leather helmet and a pair of antique goggles masking his face. He undoes a couple of snaplocks from the helmet's chinstrap, snaps the goggles up onto his forehead and steps from the cockpit, down onto one wing, then drops to the sand. He pushes the helmet right up over his scalp and Kataraina is surprised to see his metal-grey hair putting him perhaps twenty years older than she'd thought. He loosens a couple of buttons on his scuffed and faded jacket and stands looking at the smoking engine, shaking his head. He turns to her.

'Where are my manners,' he says. 'The name's Kingi Heremia.'

'Kataraina.'

'Are you from around here?'

'A thousand years ago.'

He glances at her. 'And yet you don't look a day over five hundred,' he says.

'I wear it well. Force of habit. Love the get-up, by the way. What'd you do, mug Biggles?'

A smile. 'You don't strike me as a reader of Biggles,' he says.

'No, but my dad was.'

'Good man.'

'You obviously didn't know my dad then.'

Kingi turns and stands looking at the aeroplane, a sorry drift of smoke wafting from beneath the forward cowling.

'Do you always jet in for your holidays?' says Kataraina.

'Holidays?'

'This is a camping ground. Most people just come here by car.'

'Rather hadn't intended to put her down here. Engine cut out.'

'A biggie?'

'Don't know. But she'll probably outlive me.'

'She.'

He raises his eyebrows.

'You call your aeroplane she,' says Kataraina.

'Force of habit.'

Kataraina smiles this time, then looks away down the beach. When she turns back he is unfastening a couple of latches on a metal flap behind the second cockpit. He opens the hatch and draws out a metal toolbox, sets it on the wing and opens its cantilevered drawers.

'I can make you a cuppa or something,' says Kataraina. 'If you want. I know my way around here a little bit.'

'From a thousand years ago?'

'Yep.'

'Thank you. Later perhaps.'

'OK. Suit yourself.'

She turns and walks down the beach, glancing back once to where he fiddles with the toolbox. She goes to her car and drives it up the hard-packed sand, steering it through the gap between the dunes and onto the ring of grass encircled by the cabins. She slides a handbag and sports bag from the back seat and goes to a cabin. She sits on the edge of a bed, opens a small jar of moisturiser and wipes the edges of her eyes, her forehead and cheekbones. She glances up to where the sun catches faint trails, speckled circles on the window pane. There is a suggestion of the hand that has passed over it with a cloth. She reaches into her handbag and lifts out an old diary, its face wrinkled, coming apart at the spine. The diary is tied together with a rubber band wrapped twice around its bulging girth. Magazine and newspaper cuttings spill from its edges. She peels off the bands and opens the cover, leafs through a handful of pages decorated here and there with faded pencil lines. Words, sketches, doodles. She finds a blank page, takes a pen and sits tapping its tip against the yellowed paper. Then she begins to write.

Auē.

That's what you used to say, Nan, remember? Whenever there was something you couldn't agree with, or just didn't understand. Maybe you'd just seen some stuff, even if you wouldn't talk much about it.

I reckon maybe I have, too.

Auē.

She looks back up at the window, discerning a hint of fingerprints on the glass. Two, three. She lays the diary on the bed, rests an elbow on the windowsill and stares into the prints, then through them to the dune beyond, with its thin papering of marram grass. She stretches her fingers across the glass, bisecting the spread of the ghost hand. The fingerprint maker's shadow is more recent than she had first thought. She lies down on the bed, her own hand raised, framed in the rectangle of the open door. Her nose is conscious now of the sweet scent of cut grass on the wind.

In a few minutes she is asleep.

Kingi lifts a blanket from the stowage hold and unfolds it on the sand. The tool box sits open on the lower port-side wing. He takes a pair of spectacles from his breast pocket, puts his gloves back on and peels the cowling away from the engine, baulking at the pungency of burned oil, the stench of metal fused upon metal. Oil drips from the interior of the cowling. He takes a rag from the toolbox and wipes some grease away from the engine housing, the metal still hot beneath the cloth. He lifts a feather from the entrance to the air intake, raises it against the sun.

The engine is a De Havilland Gypsy Major III: four cylinder, inverted inline, air cooled. One hundred and thirty horsepower at 2,650 rpm. Built in 1939, and rebuilt twice since; the last time in 1984, after Kingi purchased it from where the entire aeroplane sat gathering dust and cobwebs in a farmer's barn just out of Warkworth. He had spent months tracking it down via letter and telephone, then driven down from his home in a borrowed flatbed truck. He stood in the sundrenched doorway, blinking his eyes against the slatted light sieving through the broken boards. His eyes, perhaps also his memory, traced a schema of a Tiger Moth out of the shadows. Disassembled, strewn in the straw and against the walls, but almost complete. He spent the next two years reassembling it in his spare time, working from a few rough drawings and a cocktail of schemata and imagination. He had to build whole new cabane struts, elevator wire linkages and wing bracings, the originals having dissolved into fragile honeycombs of rust.

He selects a wrench from the tray and eyes the sizing, then sets it against one of the bolt heads fastening down the induction manifold.

By mid-afternoon he has various pieces of the engine laid out on the blanket, glittering in the sun like the catch of a fisherman. He holds each component against the light, then sets them down on the blanket and reaches back into the Tiger Moth's heart.

Kataraina wakes, squints her eyes at her surroundings. The small cot, the window, the door open to grass and sand. She swings her legs off the bed, picks up a sarong and moves to the door. Stillness. Silence. She walks out onto the soft grass, conscious of the sun on her bare shoulders. The sensation sets a tiny candle of a smile alight. The door to the concrete shower block is open. A scent of watered stone, a few blades of cut grass blowing on the floor. She reaches for the shower mixer and twists it, raising her eyebrows in surprise when, after a half minute or so, the spray warms in her outstretched palm. She undresses and draws the shower curtain behind her, pushes the handle beside the louvered windows to prise them open, her eyes blinking through the sun–dappled water. She opens her arms, stretching them out from her sides, the fingertips of each hand a few inches from the stone walls. Her body an aqueduct, an arch of water.

Kingi steps back from his work, wipes his hands on a rag then drops it on the blanket and walks down to the waterline. He removes his boots and socks and steps barefoot into the shallows. He looks up and down the endless stretch of beach where the grey horizon segues into mirage. He reaches into his pocket for his cigarette case, an elegant swirl of a signature across its mottled face. A flick of the lid to fish out a cigarette. A search of his other breast pocket finds an ornate lighter. He rocks forward and sinks his toes into the sand, braces his bare feet against the withdrawal of the waves. He glances up at the archipelagos of distant cloud, shakes his head.

On the island he had stood watching the rain clouds gather in what had been a clear, blue morning. But they weren't clouds. The distant drone of engines alerted him, drew the other men from their hiding places, walking at first, mugs of tea, pieces of toast in their hands. Then running. Shouting. The clouds that weren't clouds began to disperse like feather-down on the wind. It was when the shooting started from the machine-gun positions at the far end of the airfield that he realised the clouds were men suspended beneath the open palms of parachutes.

Kataraina clips the wet towel to the clothesline, looking over the encircling trees to the hill, its broken face bronzed by the setting sun. The thin wire of the clothesline is a false horizon between the world beneath and above. She wipes her wet hands on her sarong and steps beneath the trees.

She finds a trace of a path, her footsteps setting free a wave of rust-coloured leaves. She stoops and picks up a leaf, raises it against the fading sun coming through the branches. She tucks it down the front of the sarong, between her breasts, and walks out from beneath the canopy to the roots of the hill. The rising spirals of ancient terraces cut into its skin are stark in the retreating light, as if their makers have emerged and dug them anew. She uses roots, old branches to pull herself up, stopping only when the path ends in the air. She grips a root in one hand, leans a couple of inches above the sheer drop to earth. Fifty feet beneath her a small stream cuts through the sandy soil and on a small flat of dirt next to the stream sits an old boat, landlocked, propped up on blocks. She tries to place its shape, or colour, from her memory. Snatches of its shape flicker behind her eyes. She takes the leaf from where it lays against her skin and raises her hand out over the gap, letting the leaf fall, the wind turning its path aflutter, like the wings of a bird. She watches it dip and float, landing softly on the boat's deck.

Kingi reaches up between the support struts, into the starboard side of the engine cavity. There is oil all over the upper reaches of the exhaust. He brushes away another couple of feathers, glances to where they flit to the sand. He leans back on his haunches, looks between the dunes to where there is a flicker of movement against the hillside. He eases his glasses forward onto his nose and peers over the rims, watches Kataraina inch down the slope. She stops, her outline still enough to be carved on the hill's skin. Brushstrokes of toetoe frame her. He focuses on her footsteps. Despite her easy grace there is a hint of a lead weight inside her that she veils with her flippancy. Is she a seeker, like he, another pilgrim? Or just a sojourner here, a prisoner to the whims of the wind. He stands, pushes his glasses back up to the bridge of his nose, and she waves a hand. He returns her gesture, the two raised hands like each end of a bridge. Then he goes back to his engine.

Kataraina skirts the base of the hill, her footprints retracing an old sheep track. She navigates through the jumbled landscape: old boxes and tins, a rope line strung between the desiccated trunks of two dead trees. Wooden pegs clasping a couple of T-shirts, a pair of shorts, a pair of holed and faded jeans, to the frayed strand.

'Hello,' she says. 'Anyone about?'

No answer. She taps her knuckles against the boat's raised hull, hearing in the echo of the wood more snatches of her corner of its history drifting back to her. An old fisherman the children called 'Pōrangi Sam'. A laugh like the hiss of a match igniting. He was the patriarch of the 'tribe' that ran the land between the hill and the sandstream to the north. Te Awa was their name. There were hundreds of them, or so it seemed. When her family would make the twenty mile trek in her father's old Vauxhall Velox to this camp in the summer holidays there would always be a wave of wild Te Awa boys screeching across the sandpit, imitating the yelps of Hollywood Indians.

There is a small ladder against the boat's hull. She climbs it, peers through the glass of the cabin window, noticing – when she draws her head back – the same faint circles over the pane as in her hut. She steps through the door frame. There are the rudiments of life: a table, a small stove, a kettle and an over-turned cup. She lays her palm on the polished wooden bench, moves her fingertips across its face. A patchwork leather shirt lies draped over a stool, the stitching huge and jagged, its seams rough, knife slashes. She lifts it; its width dwarfs her. She lays the shirt back down, turns to where some steps lead down to an inner cabin where a jumble of bedclothes hints at a sleeping figure. She taps against the wall.

'Hiya,' she says. 'Didn't mean to bust in …'

Silence. She walks down the stairs, pauses a moment, then opens the blankets to reveal not a sleeper but the body of a guitar. Its body is carved with intricate patterns. The neck is inlaid with jewelled lettering, mother of pearl, spelling out the word 'Papatuanuku' from the twelfth fret to the second. She smiles, takes the guitar and sits, the roundness of its hollow body beneath her breasts. She runs her right thumb across the strings, her left hand forming a chord, a major, her head nodding at the purity of intonation. It has been tuned by a true ear. She lifts her left index finger, strums again, this time letting a major seventh ring. The memory in her fingertips returns, tone by tone. Her right hand stumbles through a jerky arpeggio and she raises it, stretching her fingers in the fractured light from the tiny windows, recalling the words of an uncle long ago, planting a delicacy in her strum. 'As you'll do with the touch of your first boyfriend,' he had said with a smile. She had crinkled her twelve-year-old's nose at the thought of a boyfriend. She ripples her fingers across the strings again, begins to play, distilling her movements, wrapping herself in a quilt of chords, retracing the outlines of passageways she has allowed herself to forget. She lies back on the bed, the guitar against her chest. There is a page of paper stuck to the ceiling. She tries to make out what it is. A reef, a cloud – water, perhaps? A figure, or just the head of a figure? It is too dim to make out any more. She lets her eyes close to it, her hands on the guitar strings guiding her through a stuttering serenade to the twilight.

She stands in the kitchen, stirring the contents of a tin in a bubbling pot. Kingi appears in the doorway. She raises her eyebrows.

'I followed the delectable aroma,' he says.

'Just plain ol' spaghetti on toast,' she says. 'But you're welcome to tuck in.'

'Best offer I've had all day.'

She sets some rudimentary cutlery and condiments out on

the table, lays out the toast then flips the lid on the spaghetti.

'Any sign of civilisation?' says Kingi.

'Place is pretty much deserted, except for …'

'For?'

'The old boat on the other side of the hill.'

'Moored?'

'Nah, just up on blocks like it always was. I don't reckon it ever actually floated.'

'These cabins are rather well taken care of though,' says Kingi. 'Must be someone keeping a hand in here.'

'Maybe someone comes by from the settlement. I mean, there's not an office or anything here. There never was. You just stopped by the homestead on the road in and told them how long you planned to stay.'

She butters another piece of toast, puts it on the edge of his plate. 'You planning on crashing here then?' she says.

He raises his eyebrows.

She grins. 'Oops. Lousy choice of words, huh.' She looks around the room, then back to him. 'Hey, what's it like?' she says, 'to fly?'

'You've travelled in aeroplanes?'

'Yeah, course. But it's not the same. My arse was always jammed back in economy class. I mean to *really* fly, you know, pilot the thing yourself.'

He raises a hand, as if to draft the shape of something in the air. But he doesn't. He lowers his hand again.

'It's like nothing else you can imagine,' he says.

'So where were you going?'

'There's a promise I have to keep.'

'A promise to yourself or to someone else?'

'Both, I suppose.'

Kataraina stretches her legs beneath the table. 'Don't reckon I was ever much one for making promises,' she says.

'I venture it's not the making that counts,' says Kingi, 'but the keeping.'

In the evening Kingi leans back in the aeroplane's cockpit, a folder of papers and a torch in his lap. Kataraina has made a bed for him in one of the cabins, but he doesn't seek the solidity of a mattress, the weight of blankets tonight. He would rather have the frame of his Tiger Moth and a few feet of air between his old bones and the ground. He flicks on the torch, sets it between his teeth, slips a letter from the folder and opens it. An ornate script.

> The Hawksbury Hurricane Restoration Society invites Flight Lieutenant Kingi Heremia, DFC, DSO, to attend the commemoration of the fiftieth anniversary of the Battle of Britain. The central theme of this commemoration will be the first official flight of …

The head of the letter topples over at its fold. He doesn't bother to open it out again but turns and looks out over the darkened ocean to where sea fades to sky.

In the morning, Kataraina steps onto the old jetty, raises her face to the new sun. She walks to where the rhythm of complete boards is broken and gaps begin to appear like the black keys on a piano keyboard, the sea foam dispersing and reforming beneath her toes. Beyond that the jetty ceases to have any pattern at all. Just a few posts, half submerged in the surf.

She picks her way back up to the shore. A sound raises her stare along the beach to where Kingi walks towards the estuary, sending gulls spinning aloft. She turns towards him, fording the stream to where he is crouched among the shells, studying a piece of driftwood. Birds' shadows circle on the sand and water around him.

At the sound of her steps in the water he looks up. She pauses midstream, takes a hand from the pocket of her jeans and waves it in a slow arc across her face.

'I have a long way to go,' he says.

'Who hasn't?'

'So why have you stopped here?'

'Reasons.'

Stillness, then, 'I can give you a ride into Te Kopu,' says Kataraina. 'You can arrange for a bus or whatever, to go and keep this promise of yours.'

'Thank you, no. I need to make this part of the trip by my own wings.'

'Reasons?'

'Yes, reasons.'

'Is there someone waiting for you?'

He lets the piece of driftwood fall and stands and brushes the sand from his hands.

'I don't know,' he says.

They breakfast on toast and jam, then Kingi goes back to work on the aeroplane. Kataraina washes the dishes then unpacks the rest of the contents of her case and hangs her clothes in the battered old wardrobe. She arranges her toiletries on a small table she drags beside the bed. When she is finished she walks up into the dunes, tugs a few sprigs of marram grass from the sand then stands scanning the sweep of the beach. To the south and north the dunes are sleeping figures. She imagines lifting off from one, sailing out over the sand, her shadow like the palest moon visible in a sunswept sky.

Mid-morning she walks down to where Kingi sits on the edge of the jetty, a handful of metal fragments catching the sun. She takes one, raises it, turning it over in her palm. The battered edges are multifaceted, like a diamond.

'I give up,' she says. 'What are they?'

'Number four piston. Well, what's left of it anyway.'

'So what now?'

'I have a comrade-in-arms in Auckland. He can cast and machine another. He makes replacement parts for old Moths.'

She stares. He nods towards the aeroplane.

'It's a Tiger Moth,' he says. 'De Havilland, D.H. 82C, version C.'

'OK.'

Kingi adjusts his position so his back is against one of the jetty poles. 'You know, the older I get,' he says, 'the closer the past seems.'

'Will I find that too?'

'Perhaps. If you're lucky.'

'Lucky? Shit! I'm trying to head in the other direction.'

He laughs in a woodwind voice, a faint whistle within it as if someone plays a tiny flute within him as he speaks. He runs a hand through his grey hair, looks along the length of wooden slats to the aeroplane marooned on the sand. Kataraina follows the line of his gaze.

'State of it,' she says, 'amazing it was in the air in the first place. Do you have to get warrants for those things?'

He squints his eyes at her.

'I'll thank you not to besmirch the good name of my aeroplane, young lady.'

She grins.

'So what do you do anyway?' she says.

'I lectured at university in England. Aeronautical engineering at Cambridge.'

'*The* Cambridge?'

'Yes.'

'Whoa! I'm impressed. Real pointy head, huh. I've never been further than Sydney.'

'I've never been to Australia. What did you do in Sydney?'

'I was an exotic dancer.'

He raises his eyebrows.

'You don't want to know,' says Kataraina. 'Trust me. So what was England like?'

'It was as good a hiding place as any.'

'Hiding place?'

He doesn't answer. She reaches down and picks away a fibre of rotted wood from a jetty board. She glances back at him. He is looking out across the waves, a distance now in his face, retreating from the present. He stands and raises his arm and sends the metal parts flying into the surf. The shards flame for a brief second, a tiny, fleeting squadron lit in the sunlight.

In the afternoon Kataraina walks up into the dunes and sits. She thumbs through the flaking leaves of her diary to where a blank page lies fallow. She takes a plastic biro from her jeans pocket and raises it against the page, tapping its tip against the faded paper.

Auē.

Nan, I know you'll never get to read these words, but that doesn't matter. I heard that when you were a kid they whacked you with a cane just for speaking your own language, so you just decided never to learn to read theirs and that was that. Done. Your own personal utu.

Kingi dips an enamel mug into the bucket of water. He takes the Tiger Moth's oil drain pipe into his hand, rests one end against his knee, and tips some water into the other end, frowning when a couple of seconds pass before any moisture lands on the fabric of his overalls. He shakes the pipe, a few drops of oil-stained water blooming among the shells. He crouches, runs his fingers over their indentations in the sand.

On the island the sky was black with parachutes, some suddenly flaring like torches as men flung themselves from burning aeroplanes. Then came the cry of the dive bombers, like some venomous insect. But strangest of all were the gliders, soundless, just a thin, transparent shell within which men with guns waited, counting the seconds until the tow planes would cut them loose, the rope vanishing in the dawn sky. The men on the ground stared long beneath the brims of their helmets, straining to believe what they were shooting at. Some of the gliders took hits and pirouetted in mid-air, moths singed by the heat of a bulb, tipping forward to nosedive into the tarmac, spilling men like eggs.

Kataraina

All the good little girls kept diaries. I didn't write much in mine, but I stuck things in it. We had this jar of paste, where the lid came with a sort of ice-block stick thingy attached to it. Smelt like sea water.

I used to cut pictures out of magazines: Diana Ross, Dionne Warwick, all cosy in my little book. Like those displays of butterflies you see in museums, hanging there with pins through them.

I read somewhere that when Vikings died, their whānau would put their body in a little boat and set it on fire and push it out to sea. When I used to come down here in the holidays, I used to imagine that old boat was mine and if I wanted to I could just push it out to the sea and sail away. But then we'd head home and the boat would still be stuck. Just like me.

Home, yeah, home. Sleeping with Matty. He would start off in his own bunk but end up in mine. Then when his dreams came he would start kicking out. Ten knees and elbows and twenty bloody feet. 'In the city, kids got rooms of their own,' I'd say to Mum, and she'd say, 'Look around you, nei. Does this look like the city to you, Miss High and Mighty?' And then, 'When you win the Golden Kiwi you can buy yourself a big house with a dozen bedrooms,' she'd say.

Yeah, yeah.

I bet city girls didn't have to sleep with their little brothers.

We moved away from you, when I was still a little kid. After that bust-up you had with Mum. I never knew what the bust-up was about. I only saw you a few times after that, when Pop would take us up to you, without Mum knowing. Dion would moan and want to leave, and Matty would just stare. First time Pop took us up, I didn't even recognise you.

After Dion headed off for The Smoke it was just me and Matty against the world. Pop made Matty a treehouse. Treehouse, hell, it was three feet off the ground. Pop wouldn't build it any higher cause they were afraid Matty'd fall out and hurt himself. And he'd go there and sit, staring out at the world, like he was at a bus stop but the bus never came. We'd have to drag him out for his kai or he'd starve.

There was the time me and him were lying on our tummies on the floor watching that movie *The Sound of Music*. Julie Andrews comes running up the hill and starts singing away. Matty jumps up and starts spinning with his arms whirring around and yelling his head off. I got up too, and there we were, both of us spinning like helicopter whatsits and shouting.

Then Pop came in from the woodpile with that Dobermann voice of his and we shut up.

Nana, you reckoned when Matty was born, all of him never came out. The part of him that thinks stayed behind in the place where babies are made. But you sensed him, more than any of us.

'That boy's not dumb,' you said. 'He's special, that's all.'

Dion would make a face, but only behind your back.

'Anyone make fun of this boy,' you said, 'they'll have to deal with my walking stick, nei.'

Eighty-five years old. And still with that big move-mountains voice. There've been times when I could've done with that voice.

When the holidays came we'd all pack into the car and head down here to the motor camp, the hill of our ancestors watching over us. The others would kick up a ruckus on the beach, but I'd head upstream to where the river fanned out into a pond, almost circular, pulsing with the raising and lowering of the river's flow. Like a heart. In the afternoons I'd stretch out on an old fallen tree and lie still. Draw my knees up and sit staring at my reflection in the water, so still the image was perfect, painted almost. 'Hey,' I'd say, 'you ain't so bad. You could pass for OK looking.' Then some bird would land on the water and I'd shatter.

Sometimes I used to wait until everyone was drunk or asleep, then sneak out and go back in the dark. I'd lie on that tree trunk again, an old cardie over me, or a blanket if it was real cold. Looking up at the moon shining. I'd imagine it was a spotlight, just for me. The pool was a stage and the sound of the water was people clapping. I'd lie there, wrapped tight in the blanket. But inside I was dancing.

Then we'd head home at the end of the holidays, back to a yard polluted with cannibalised cars. Wading the creeks for watercress, sometimes eels. Pipis at low tide. I bet none of the models in the magazines had to dig in the sand for shellfish. I used to dream of the day the moon would vanish beyond the trees and so would I.

I starved myself to stay slim, take my dinner back to my room, and hide it in my dresser drawer until Matty came in to go to bed. I'd sit on the floor and watch him wolf down every last scrap. After I'd tucked him in he'd lie there in silence, his doll fingers picking crumbs off the blankets. Those huge eyes, too big for his tiny face, staring at me.

When I told Dion, over the phone, about how I was going to be a famous model, he just laughed. 'They'll pay for your black arse to be in magazines?' he said. I don't reckon I ever saw him as my brother again.

The last time I saw you, I hitched up to your place. You were so frail then. I remember I didn't say much. We sat on your veranda and you looked out towards the hills and started to roll off a bunch of names of people I'd never heard of. You were telling me my history and I never knew it. I didn't want to know.

When I left there, I left you my diary.

The night I went, just slipped out the window, Matty was playing on the floor with his toy trucks. I wanted to hug him or something, but he'd just start kicking and clawing. Words were no use – he never did know what to do with words. I closed the window behind me. I looked back once and he was standing there, staring. He raised a hand. I raised mine too, to wave back. But he was just reaching for a moth on the glass.

In the city I got a job in a takeaway, had some photos done and put into a fancy portfolio which I lugged around the agencies. The first line-up I went to, turned out they just wanted hands, for a soap advert. But not mine. The guy took one look at me and said, 'You don't have the right face.'

'But you only want hands,' I said.

It was always the same routine. Blokes standing with their legs planted, scratching their chins like a butcher looking for the best cut. Wanting to poke at you. Hours waiting for line-ups, seconds taken to make the decision. Then the blonde got the job.

If the magazines didn't want my black arse, others would. And they'd pay. That's what Angel said, the first time I met her. Angel. Leaning into the shop doorway out of the rain, lighting her ciggy off mine. She stepped back against the glass and looked me over.

'Pay top dollar,' she said. 'If you're smart. The ones in the suits pay the best. The ones that don't roll their car windows down more than an inch to gawk at you. If they could screw you through that little bitty window opening they would. They wouldn't even have to touch you.' She blew a smoke ring. 'Top dollar.'

I told her to get lost.

She laughed. 'You will,' she said. 'I seen your kind a hundred times. Every bus from the sticks brings a couple more. But if you try and work this street I'll kick you all the way back to Te Nowhere.'

I got some work, in shopping malls. Bikini in the middle of winter. Sucking my tummy in until my muscles hurt and I had cramps. All that stuff I used to carry around in my handbag, like a soldier going to war. A bit of blusher, vanishing cream. Eye drops because the bloody lights stung. Eyeliner, seven different lipsticks ...

There was a guy – there was always a guy. 'You've got talent,' he'd say. 'You could be something.' They knew it off by heart. Polyester suit, strands of thinning hair plastered flat across an empty scalp. A couple of flashy rings or maybe a medallion. 'Come with me and you'll go places.'

Places. Yeah, I went places.

A year making myself up, then four years making myself down. Way down. You could always say you were only doing the other stuff just to pay the bills, until the next modelling job came up. Or the big break. But next can be a hell of a long word. Just four letters. I reckon one letter for every year I ended up waiting to be discovered.

'What kind of massage do you want today?' I'd say. 'We got "The Gentleman's", "The Deluxe" and "The Super Deluxe".'

Always the same question: 'How much for the Super Deluxe?'

They'd never look at my face. I could have had a bag over my head. And they always wanted a shower afterwards, before they went home to the missus, the 2.4 kids and Lassie.

Once I even got out. Yep, got brave and packed it all in and took off with my savings to Oz. Gonna head up north, Queensland maybe, where the wild horses are. Become a sugarcane cowgirl.

I got as far as Kings Cross.

When the punters were on top of me, they'd let out one last grunt and then go all limp, like a rag squeezed out. I'd be staring at some speck on the ceiling, imagining I was in an ocean or a river somewhere. Maybe just that pond. You see, it wasn't me they dumped into. 'Me' didn't come into it. 'Me' still lived in my mangy old diary. Like Matty's inside self, 'me' stayed hidden. I'd locked the door long ago.

Did you ever catch that moth, Matty. Sometimes I think *our* boats were burned the day we were born.

Then, Nana, you sent me that box of stuff. Buggered if I know how you found me. Must've had one of the cuzzies look for me, I guess. There was a single sandal I'd left at your place when I was tiny. A dry old piece of a biscuit I'd bitten into when I first got teeth, which had these puny little teeth marks. A tiny, broken half-moon.

And that old diary.

I stuck the tiny sandal on the mantelpiece of whatever dump I was staying in at the time and then forgot about it when I moved on. Wish I could remember what happened to the biscuit.

But I kept the diary.

What little writing there'd been had just faded away and the pictures were falling to bits. But there was a faint set of muddy footprints, from a cat I'd once had, back home. She'd just shown up on the doorstep one day. I'd fed her, loved her even. Not for long, but so what. I don't remember her walking across my page, just finding the paw marks and being pissed off. The rubber on the end of my pencil wouldn't get rid of them, just scratched the paper. Then one day she was gone, just like that. I don't even remember what I'd named her.

I wonder if Julie Andrews left footprints in the grass.

Nana, the last time I saw you, you told me about slaves, in the old days. About how you're not a slave because of what you are, but because of what you hold on to or let go. And how people can't take your heart, you can only give it away to them.

Then you laid them crumpled old hands over me.

'Wherever you go, mokopuna,' you said, 'don't you ever forget the road home. You promise me now.'

'I promise,' I said. Yeah, a kid's promise.

I must've lost track of that last bit somewhere.

The grapevine tells me that Matty and even Dion went to your funeral. But I didn't. I didn't even know.

So the weirdest thing happened, I started writing in the diary again, on the blank pages I'd never got to. So:

Hey diary it's me. I've found you again. Moth-eaten old thing you are. (The diary I mean — not me. Although, have you looked at yourself in the mirror lately, girl?)

So ... well ... here goes, just a buncha random thoughts, the thoughts I couldn't put down a million years ago when I closed you for the last time.

1) I think the cat's name was Truffles, or Ruffles, or Muffles, or ...

2) Maybe you were wrong, Nan, people can take your heart away.

3) Paste now comes in little plastic bottles with a soft rubber titty thing on the top.

4) I used to hate Julie Andrews.

5) The cat's name could have been Muffet. Or Buffet. Or Tuffet.

This morning, when it was still dark, I walked up the beach for half a mile or so. Then I sat in the sand, waiting for the light to come up behind me, looking back along the sand at my footprints. When the first light came I walked down to the shallows and scooped up a couple of handfuls of sea water, then carried them up the sand and tipped them into my footprints. Leaving a speckled pattern, like words on a page. I knelt, taking the wet sand onto my fingertip.

Sometimes I dream: I'm sitting cross-legged in front of you, holding one of your hands like it's treasure. Looking into your face, moving through the lines of it, the creases. Like the lines tattooed into your own Nana's skin. But not ink, just years. I reach out, run a finger down across them. You don't say a word. You just let me touch, feel, on and on. Like a little baby in a crib, feeling its own skin, feeling the air, the world, for the first time. You just sit there, letting my fingers find every inch of you. Every second of your life, carved into your skin, your pale grey hair. Painted into your grey eyes.

Then I stand and you stand with me, not old anymore, but any age, or no age at all. You slide your arms around me. I can't feel your hands, the end of your arms, there's just this hugeness to you. No corners, no edges. Like the reflection of the moon I used to watch, lying there in my blanket. Something I could slip into and float within.

I walked back into the sea until it was up to my waist. Lifted off my dress and tied it around my neck and walked on, letting the ocean find me, all of me. The bits that people paid for and the bits that no one wanted.

I looked at my face in the water, just glimpses. The sea was way too alive to leave my face still like it had been on that creek. I let myself sink. And I thought of that cat and lifted a paw, began to lick off the taste of the sea. I stood washing myself, letting the sea wash over me.

6) *The punters with the best suits were the worst. It doesn't mean the punters with the worst suits were the best.*
7) *The cat's name was Huffy, no, Puffy. Muffy? No definitely not Muffy.*
8) *Some things can't be bought and sold like paste. I don't care what kind of bottle they come in.*
9) *I don't hate Julie Andrews any more.*
10) *Nana was right, actually. You can give your heart away. You can lose it. Leave it someplace and forget where you put it.*

The cat's name doesn't matter. I think I'll just call her … me.

Hello Me. Nice to meet you. My name is Kataraina, and I'm coming home.

II

The Invisibility of Water

Jordan lifts his tattooed chin to the air, opens his lips to taste then slides once more beneath the waves. He dives, kicking with his feet, cutting through the sea's skin and into its veins. He twists, rolls over and over, lets the oxygen drain from his lungs. Then he rises above the surface again, drawing in the scent of salt on the wind, opening his pores to the air.

A half hour later he sits on the beach, a surfboard wedged in the soft sand beside him, its form casting a spearpoint of shadow. He glances up the beach to the dunes. Nowhere is there any evidence of other people. Neither a fence, nor marker post. Even the few tyre tracks have been blown over by the sand-seeded wind. A lone pohutukawa has a foothold on a small ridge, its overhang painting the gold of the beach a darker hue, as if a shadow tree, attached like a Siamese twin, grows in the sand. He sits away from it, avoiding even the suggestion of leaves on his skin, wanting only the invisibility of water.

He stands and jogs down to the tide, carrying his surfboard, entering the waves without slowing. He takes aim toward the north, where the high and low tide lines parallel each other to the horizon.

An hour's walking then a run into the ocean to surf, then another few kilometres on sand, an alternating road of land and sea. At the sight of the hill with its broken face he quickens his pace, peeling off through the shallows to arrowhead out to the deeper water, riding the current back in, looking for that one homebound wave. When he finds it he grabs its tail: breaker, board and rider a single figure. He aims for the line of dunes, a halo of surf breaking around him. He is almost to the shallows when he glances up beyond the jetty to where the shape of a vintage aeroplane sits in the sun.

Kataraina climbs the ladder onto the boat, goes into the cabin and lifts the guitar from the bed. She carries it outside, sits cross-legged on the deck and begins to play. Again she fumbles at first, but then begins to reach out along the breakwaters of her memory, her fingers seeking sanctuary among the frets. Her movements are slow, allowing each touch against string, each fretted tone to ring. She pauses, raises her hand to wipe away a few strands of hair which the sea breeze has blown over her eyes, then goes back to her music, unaware of anything peripheral to it until a shadow crosses the skin of her arms. A hint of footfalls on creaking wood. She glances up, expecting to see Kingi, but instead it is a young man, wearing only a ragged pair of shorts. She looks up the length of his muscled frame to his face where tattooed wings of ink rise from the bridge of his nose, half circling his eyes. The arcs of ink echo around his lips, his stubbled chin; their deep forest tinge matches the pounamu pendant on a string around his neck. His eyes search not her face or body but the fall of her fingers on the strings. She tries to meet his gaze, but he will not meet hers. She slows her playing, an arpeggio filling the empty space between them.

He glances to where a surfboard stands staked in the sand. She looks at it, suddenly conscious of the touch of sea water on her toes, dripping from his body. He crouches in front of her, still looking at her hands, his rust-coloured eyes seeming empty of any greeting, but bearing no anger either. They hold nothing but her reflection. He makes no move to claim the guitar from her, or even speak. He stands again and climbs back down the ladder onto the sand.

Kingi fingers the oily surface of the bearing, wincing when a torn shard cuts into his fingerprint, oil mingling with the sudden bulb of blood. He flexes his hand, reaches with his other hand into his breast pocket for his handkerchief. He spits into the cloth then dabs at his finger, looking up when a young man's figure appears on the dunes, the line of his body fractured by Kingi's view through the wing struts. The man pauses in front of the open engine compartment, glances down at the propeller resting on the right lower wing. He lifts it and runs his palm along the edge of one blade, its surface angled like an oar. He walks the length of the fuselage to the tail then crouches behind it, looking up its length.

'Another traveller,' says Kingi, 'or would you be the landlord?'

'Neither. Just looking after the place till summer.'

'What's the going rate?'

'Rate?'

'For accommodation.'

'Beats me. No one's been by until now.'

'I might need to kip here awhile, to work on the Moth.'

The man nods, still looking at the aeroplane.

'Whatever,' he says then walks away up through the marram grass.

Kataraina wades the shallows to the south of the stream, carrying the diary in her clasped fingers. She glances towards the horizon where a cluster of dark clouds pass, far out to sea. She opens the diary and raises it to the sun, taking a single page between her fingers, looking through the weft of the paper. She brings it to her nose and sniffs. Dust, perhaps a dim trace of grass. She closes the diary, turns to look back to the north where the surfer lugs an old dinghy out onto the sand.

He drags it through a tangle of driftwood, tails of seaweed forming a wake. He steps inside it, sits on the cross member, reaches into the hull and lifts up a small wooden block about the size of a fist. He takes a torn strip of sandpaper from his jeans pocket and wraps it around the block. Kataraina picks her way through the shells towards him. He glances at her sandaled feet. The etchings in his skin radiate in the sun, as if a stone has been dropped into the pool of his face.

'I remember when old Pōrangi Sam had that boat you're staying in,' says Kataraina.

He runs the sandpaper along the hull's lip.

'My granddad,' he says.

'Te Awa? Shit, you're one of them?'

He looks up at her for the first time. 'Yeah,' he says. 'What of it?'

She blinks. 'Nothing,' she says. 'Just wondered sometimes, where you all got to.'

He goes back to his sanding. 'Scattered all over the place,' he says. 'You know how it is.'

'Yeah. I do.'

She steps sideways among the seaweed, folds her arms. 'That's a beautiful guitar you've got,' she says. 'Did you carve the lettering on it?'

'Nah, bloke I once knew.'

'Once?'

'You're a big one for questions, huh.'

She turns to the trees, then back to him. 'You want us to leave?' she says.

'Us?'

'Me. Him.'

'It's up to you.'

Jordan spends a couple of hours sanding the dinghy. Parts of it are worn so smooth with countless waves that they are the texture of bone. He lifts his hands every now and then and shakes his fingers free of dust, then carries on. He glances up along the beach to where the old man tinkers with his biplane, oblivious to the passage of a four-wheel drive that slows to look at him, fishing rods and a dog hanging out of the rear tray.

Jordan watches the ute pass, the driver flicking a hand in a casual wave. He makes no gesture in return.

Mid-afternoon he stands back, aware now that the wood dust hazes about him when he shakes it free, an onshore wind building. He drops the block and sandpaper on the floor of the hull, steps out and walks to the riverbed and collects his surfboard. Within minutes he is in the waves, entering them with the gentle timing and ease of a lover slipping within the skin of another. He rides one crest then goes in search of another, a balance in the line of his body, from his toes to the tips of his fingers.

Kataraina stands in the dunes, watching the surfer's shadow captured within the fabric of the water. His outline as fleeting as a wavetip. She bends and scoops a handful of sand, then opens a slight gap in her palm to let it slip free as she walks from dune to dune, the sea-wind blowing the falling sand against her. She raises her hand high, letting the last of it go, looking through a curtain of sand at the surfer losing himself in the waves.

She had sat in a bar in Kings Cross in Sydney, her elbows on the beer-stained table, staring at the strobe lights reflected in her margarita. She'd never qualified as a true alcoholic, though she'd tried pretty hard, really just for dramatic effect. Poets and painters who became drunks were known as bohemian. She liked that, it had a nice ring to it. But even that she managed to screw up. Only Kataraina could try to have a lost weekend but end up remembering every tedious minute of it. Right about then it struck her that Kings Cross, which had never brought her happiness, was also a lousy place to be miserable.

When she sighted the first hint of coastline from the 767's window she'd leaned forward, watching the folds of sea turn to lacings of whitecaps. She had wondered if the first explorers had stood in their canoes and marvelled at that same sight. She turned to the other passengers, some reading newspapers, some packing their papers back into their bags. Mothers wiping the faces of infants. She was glad no one bothered to look up and see the wetness at the edge of her eyes.

She'd picked a spot and drawn an X on the window with her lipstick and watched its tilted cross drift over the land. When the ocean and pasture gave way to cityscape she leaned back and closed her eyes. She wasn't interested in the shadows of buildings.

Kataraina walks up the twilit stream bed to the boat and climbs the ladder. Jordan sits on the deck. Next to him is an old beer crate with some books in it. There's a jumble of other books around him. He has a large hardcover book open in his lap, his stare lifting up from it when he hears her footsteps. His hand is palm down on a page, a couple of fingers poised mid-sentence, as if sensing the voice in the words.

'Interesting?' she says.

He flexes his fingers against the paper. 'Yes,' he says.

'Looks a bit big for me. Was never much of a book reader.'

'Neither was I.'

She pauses for a moment then reaches down to his lap, stopping with her fingertips an inch from the page. She draws them back.

'What is it?' she says.

He flips over the cover and she glances down at its thick wad of pages and hardbacked cover. A stylised figure of a tree, leaves embossed above a trunk flowing like a waterfall. A large letter A beneath its roots.

'Whoa, heavy stuff. You got the rest of the set?'

'No. Just this one volume. I found it on a rubbish dump.'

'So what happens when you get to the end?'

He sits silent for a moment, then: 'I fall off, I guess.'

She reaches for another of the books. A much older volume, its cover is leather, worn thinner than skin. There are words embossed into its hide. *Paipera Tapu*. She opens it, the pages faded to the colour of sand. The ornate script is all in Māori. '*Paipera Tapu*,' she says. 'A bible?'

He nods.

'You speak te reo?' says Kataraina.

'A little.'

'Same here. Most of them swear words. Reckon we kind of got out of the habit.'

'Was there something you wanted?' he says.

'Just to tell you kai's ready.'

'Nah, it's OK.'

'I made enough for the three of us.'

He looks at her for a moment then goes back to his book. She puts the bible down on top of the pile.

'Well, I asked,' she says, then goes back to the ladder.

'Hey,' he calls.

She turns.

'Thanks anyway,' he says.

She nods her head and steps down onto the sand.

In the morning Jordan sits on the deck of the boat, a leg each side of the bow's tip, the guitar against his torso. He loosens his fingers against the strings, building a chord melody. There is a rustle of water and he looks up to see Kataraina at the head of the stream bed, stepping from stone to stone. The pale blue of her jeans is soft against the sharpness of the light on the water. Her steps seem wary, as if she needs to seek a sureness before she will plant another foot on earth. She doesn't once turn her head towards the boat.

He looks down at the guitar's strings, plucking only every third or fourth note, letting his left hand's fingers slide or hammer their way through most of the notes. In the spaces between the notes he senses the touch of this woman who has stepped into his water. Her body had huddled against the guitar as if trying to squeeze something from it, or keep it from slipping away. There was a hinted history in the slope of her shoulders, a hint he knows from glances at his own eyes in a mirror, or the nakedness in the pupils of men sitting on bunk beds staring at a ten by five room, knowing it has become their whole universe.

A breeze comes from the ocean, carrying a voice. Feminine. A humming. The texture of it is alien to him after these months alone. Now he has a woman and an old man as scouts on the edge of his territory. Just when he had become used to being the camp's ghost.

He stands and goes into the cabin and brings out the hard-covered book. He sits on the deck, leaning against the cabin door. He steers the cover open with a finger, finding a paragraph at random.

A

Archaeology
In a museum in Paris sits a carved
stone tablet from the broad plain
between the Euphrates and Tigris rivers.
The tablet is a depiction of the king of
Lagash and his sons. If one seeks the valley
of the Euphrates on a modern map, there will be
no Lagash, for it is a name written in dust.
The stone tablet is 4,500 years old.

His fingers settle on the guitar's strings, and while he plays he begins reading again, not realising for a half page that he is reading aloud, underlining the words with music.

Kataraina stops thirty yards upstream, hearing the guitar, the echo of the accompanying voice. The pluck of strings trailing each syllable like a lost child. She stands listening, thinking what a strange poetry it is that he recites. A monotone of facts punctuated only by staccato snatches of melody.

The rain blankets the courtyard, the grass circle. She sits at the small table in her cabin, watching the glass misting with her warmth against the cold beyond. The table has a wonky leg and rocks whenever she sets her coffee cup down. She goes to the wardrobe and opens an old box full of comics, trash magazines. She takes one, raises the table leg and sets the comic underneath. Mickey Mouse's smiling face stares up at her from the faded page.

She reaches for her diary on the bed and flips it open, shuffling through the pages to find an empty one. She takes her pen and begins to doodle, accompanied by the clatter of the rain on the corrugated-iron roof. She sketches a cat, a guitar, a boat. An aeroplane that she redraws as a bird, then again as a wave, surrounding the wave with others of its kind until the whole page becomes an ink sea. She takes another sip of the coffee now, cursing when it leaves a dark circle in her ballpoint sea when she sets it down on the paper. She tries to wipe it away with the edge of her hand but it won't budge.

All through the worst days on the game, the smoke-stained mornings when she'd lean over the toilet and spit, trying to chase away the taste of cigarettes and whiskey and some fifty dollar stranger's cock from her mouth, she would close her eyes and imagine the moon. She'd glance up at the tiny, louvered window, the skeleton of streetlight it cast on the walls. She'd blink hard, only opening her eyes to reach up and pull the lever to flush. Watch the water circle in the bowl.

A rap on the doorframe. She looks up to see Kingi's silhouette among the rain drifts. She gestures with her head and he enters.

'Can I impose on you,' he says.

'What can I do?'

'I need to get to a telephone. Set things in motion.'

'Give me a few minutes.'

'I thank you.'

When the rain eases she walks up the streambed to the boat and climbs the ladder. There are wet, sandy footprints on the deck leading to the cabin's open door. The rain paints the cabin's overhang with threads of silver. She unwinds their fibres with her eyes, sensing at the same time a drift of guitar from within. Then it stills.

'Don't stop,' she says. 'I was listening.'

He leans from his bed in the lower cabin, into the opening. His skin glistens with water. As if – not only outside but here in his house – it is raining.

'I'm heading into town,' she says. 'Do you want me to pick up anything?'

'Nah, I'm OK.'

'How'd you get out here, without a car?'

'One of the tribe brought me up. When …'

'When …'

'What do I win if I answer all your questions?'

'The pleasure of my company.'

He turns away, a half smile. She thinks of mentioning it, but doesn't.

Kataraina drives Kingi into Te Kopu and sits on a small picnic bench opposite the superette while he uses their phone to contact his comrade-in-arms in Auckland for the replacement parts. He steps out of the shop into the sun, glances up and down the highway.

'It'll take at least two weeks,' he says when he joins her. 'I trust our host will be amenable.'

Kataraina shrugs. 'I'm not sure he gives a toss.'

Kingi opens a bag of nuts and they sit delving into them, one after the other. He has shed his customary overalls and is garbed in dress trousers and a jacket at least twenty years old, perhaps thirty.

'So where are you en route to?' he says. 'If I may be so bold. Or are you planning on staying here?'

A cattle truck shapes itself out of the road dust. They turn their faces away as it passes.

'I think I'm going home,' she says.

'You don't sound as sure as you might be.'

'I'm not as *anything* as I might be. Does it matter?'

'I don't know if I'm in a position to answer that.'

She holds a hand up against the sun, a sudden eclipse. She moves her hand from side to side, breaking the light, like the flocks of flamingos she has seen in magazines. She has a vision of the Tiger Moth's propeller fading to stillness.

When they return to the camp, Jordan has the dinghy balanced over two sawhorses, planing the outside of its hull. A fine dust decorates his tattooed arms and hands, his bare feet.

'I'll need to stay here a fortnight or so,' says Kingi.

Jordan glances up, then goes back to his work.

Kingi and Kataraina sit with their toes in the stream. The wind carries snatches of the surfer's guitar across from downstream, the gaps in the melody suggesting someone trying to assemble an object without knowing what its final shape looks like.

'We used to come here every school holidays,' says Kataraina. 'Our grand tour of the backblocks. One pokey little dump to the next.'

'It's not that bad. I've been in far worse places.'

She lifts water in a cupped hand, lets it fall against her bare shins. 'Nah, it isn't,' she says. 'Ignore me. Just blowing smoke. Actually this was a kind of refuge for me. I guess we all have somewhere.'

'Indeed.'

'Your mate's family ran this place back then.'

Kingi stares.

'Him in the boat,' says Kataraina.

'Ah. You knew each other?'

'Nah. Don't remember him. There was a million of them. Sorta like a plague.'

He grins.

'So where are you headed?' she says. 'To keep this promise.'

'There's a Battle of Britain reunion.'

'You mean like an annual event?'

'No. Well perhaps some are. I've never been to any.'

'Not one?'

He shakes his head.

'So that's your promise?' says Kataraina. 'To finally go to one?'

He cups his hands in the water, just as she had. He sits staring at the tiny lake held in the bowl of his palm. 'I cut a trench a cubit long and a cubit broad,' he says. 'And around it I poured a libation to all the dead, first with milk and honey, then with sweet, sweet wine, and lastly with water.'

Kataraina turns.

'Homer,' says Kingi.

The guitar stops. Kataraina looks up, listening for it.

'The ancient Cretans believed that life is not a road but a dance,' says Kingi.

'Then I think I've lost the tune.'

Kingi smiles. 'And their feet move,' he says, 'rhythmically, tender feet danced once around an altar of love, crushing a circle in the soft smooth flowering grass.'

'Homer?'

'Sappho.'

Kingi flexes his toes in the water, the refracted light distorting their shapes. 'There *is* a theory that Homer never existed,' he says. 'That his poems were composed in snatches by dozens of people, later being assembled into one body of work.'

'Like one of those quilts you hear about, where all the women of the town get together to each make a bit.'

'Yes.'

'That's a cool idea. I like that.'

'The quilt or the stories?'

'Both.'

She goes back to listening for the next chord. 'I remember my dad talking about Crete. We had some uncles there, in the war.' She turns to him. 'Were you there?' she says.

'Yes.'

'A pilot?'

'No. I had traded in my wings before I got to Crete.'

'You didn't crash again did ya?' she says, grinning.

He looks up beyond the tiny delta of the river mouth with its momentary islands of sand, out to the open ocean.

'We used to go out sometimes,' he says, 'when the Jerries were scarce, off committing mayhem on some other part of the island. In one of the village houses there'd be candlelight and laughter. Usually wine, ouzo, to rinse away the fear and terror of the everyday of living life within rifle sights. Someone would have a mandolin and we'd light a small fire in a courtyard and sit warming our hands around it, me wrapped up in the garb of a Cretan peasant.

'And sometimes she'd dance, an electricity between her bare feet and the earth. She'd move within the veil of smoke, not just with the music but within it. Perhaps *beyond* it. Beyond anything in the world I'd known. I remember the rhythm of her bare feet against the stone; the tiniest gesture with her hands, as if she could sketch in smoke, grasp the mandolin's song in her fingertips. Her eyes, those eyes the indigo of grapes. She'd glance up, the tiniest inkling of a smile. More than anything else I'd ever wanted, I wanted that inkling to be for me.'

A few moments silence, then: 'Wow,' says Kataraina. 'Who was she?'

No answer.

'Touchy subject?' she says.

'No. It's just …'

He stands and dusts the sand from his overalls.

'So what's all this got to do with the Battle of Britain?' says Kataraina.

He picks his way midstream.

'Damn,' says Kataraina. 'I'm going to grow old waiting for answers if I talk to you two any longer.'

Jordan lies on his bed, the guitar beside him. He reaches up, flicks on the cabin's overhead light and picks up a book.

The Sumerians were builders of temples which they called ziggurats. Large pyramid-like towers, constructed as high as possible in the hope that they would reach all the way to heaven. At the ziggurat's crest was a shrine, with an image of the city that had grown up around the ziggurat. Priests collected grain, wool and silver to offer to the gods, to appease them and bring mercy and kindness. Each Sumerian city had a ziggurat dedicated to one particular deity. The city of Ur for example, built a ziggurat for Nanna, the god of the moon.

He closes the book and goes out into the sunset. He climbs down the ladder and walks up into the dunes overlooking the camp, stopping when he sees Kataraina's outline within the nest of light emanating from her cabin. She steps into the doorway and stands, backlit, looking up towards the dunes. He is suddenly aware of the retreating sun framing his own figure. He stands watching her for a moment then turns and walks down to the water.

In the morning he wakes to a knock. He stands naked, pulls on his shorts and opens the door. Kataraina sits on the stairs, a smile on her face.

'I was listening on the car radio,' she says. 'People in Berlin are taking the last of the Wall away. Piece by piece.'

He stares.

'What people?' he says.

'Just people. Ordinary people.'

'You walked over here just to tell me that.'

'I suppose so, yep.'

He shuts the door. Goes back to his mattress and sleeps.

The Berlin Wall. Kataraina lies back in centre of the circle of grass, raising an arm against the background of trees. She tries to picture its height, its miles of concrete topped with barbed wire. She remembers seeing it on television, guesses it was the height of that tree, the smaller one with the crooked branches. Doesn't matter. With a bunch of soldiers with guns surrounding it, it could have been six inches high and still impassable.

She wonders now how they must be celebrating, those who predated it seeing the city once again, as they remembered it from childhood. Like the sudden rediscovery of a favourite toy.

What it must be to have the world stop for you and start again.

He appears at the edge of her vision, his long hair tied in a pony tail. He is wearing the patchwork leather shirt she had held in the boat's cabin. The darkness of the hide seems to darken his own skin so that for a moment, when he stills, he is lost in the background of trunks and leaves. His moko is almost a camouflage.

He turns towards her.

'When are you planning on moving on?' he says.

'Is that an eviction notice?'

'Do you always answer a question with another question?'

'Why do you ask?'

He shakes his head, walks on into the shower block and closes the door. A few seconds later she hears the water running. She rolls over, lifts a clover leaf and sets it free on the wind.

Jordan has the hull of the dinghy laid over the sawhorses again. A tin of aquamarine paint sits in the grass. There are droplets of paint on the grass stems, on his bare feet and calves. When Kataraina passes on her way back from the showers, he turns to her.

'You look like Geronimo,' she says, pointing to a couple of spots of aquamarine on his cheeks. 'You painting the dinghy or yourself?'

She takes the sheets from her bed and washes them in the concrete tub in the shower block. She hangs them on the strands of wire strung at the building's rear then walks to the open tool shed, takes a broom and a small brush and dustpan, and goes from cabin to cabin, twisting down cobwebs, sweeping dust out onto the grass. She makes a pot of tea and takes it and a couple of mugs out to where Kingi works cleaning the oil from the inside of the engine cowling with a rag. He takes a cup and thanks her, and she goes back to where Jordan stands painting. He fills the other mug.

'I could get used to this,' he says, sipping.

'Hmmm … cupboard love, huh?'

He smiles, the surprise in his eyes hinting that it was unintentional. She looks into his half-drained cup and pours more tea in, filling it to the brim. She goes and gets another mug from the kitchen, fills it and walks up into the dunes.

She finds an old Marmite jar in the dunes, filled with sand. Probably left from a picnic long ago. She empties it, walks down to the shallows and fills it with sea water. She returns to her vantage point, tugs out some marram grass from the sand, plants it in the jar and places it at her feet. She looks back down to Jordan at the camp, lost in his painting. His silhouette against the sunlit grass, a dark finger moving against the frets of a guitar. So total is his immersion in his work she senses that if she was to call him, to shout his name, he wouldn't look up. Perhaps he wouldn't even hear her.

In her worst moments she had filled herself with noise, with movement. Dancing or singing or shouting or even screaming if that was all she had. Some song lyric she remembered, resurrected to drown out all other sound. But *his* silence seems to carry both without and within. In her silence she was *filled* with sound.

He pauses, steps back and runs his stare along the length of the hull, one hand raised a half inch above its tired grain. She lies flat in the sand, rolls over onto her tummy and places the glass jar in front of her, between she and he. He goes back to painting, captured now within the walls of the jar, his body bent, misshapen in the broken light, as if he is being disassembled then put back together – incomplete.

III

Zeta Orionis

Jordan

I suppose it's – what do they call it? – a statement of the obvious – to say prison makes your world smaller. But it's not that simple. Your world was small *before* you went into prison. You just leave yourself with nowhere else to go.

I was never much one for thinking outside the square, as the suits say. 'How it is is how it is is how it is …' was my motto. I reckon I got surviving mixed up with living. Easy to do.

Some people even say prison is an education and you come out with more than you went in with. Unless they're talking about scars, nightmares maybe, then I'd say it's a bunch of crap. The only thing keeps you from dying of boredom is the fear maybe you won't live long enough to die of boredom. Stuff I could've done without learning.

I remember one day a priest (priest, vicar, whatever) came. He didn't much talk about God, just talked about us. He didn't know stuff-all about us, but he wanted to talk, so what the hell. Then a couple of minutes later someone turned on the radio and we drifted away to listen to the footie.

Later, though, I thought about what he'd said. You get a lot of time to think, after you've counted every paint bubble and stain on the ceiling. But he set me thinking about what I had to do with God and what God had to do with me. And the answer was – nothing. I tried hard to be worried about it, but I couldn't.

'I don't reckon there is a God,' I said.

I figured he'd come up with all sorts of answers. Except for the one he did. 'Why?' he says.

Buggered if I could answer.

When I first got locked up, I told a couple of people Jacqui ditched me because I went inside. That's the kind of stuff you tell yourself, but it's not true. She'd ditched me long before; going inside just meant she didn't have to say it to my face. I'd at least spared her something. I reckon the kid was supposed to be some kind of last stand for us, a bridge, sort of. But I never crossed it. I was never one for building or crossing bridges.

I once read that New Zealand is slowly drifting north and in around thirty million years we'll be crossing the equator. Thirty million years, maybe I should mark the date on my calendar. And if it's true I'm planning to kick back on a hammock strung between a couple of coconut palms, sipping on one of them fancy cocktails with an umbrella in it.

There was an astronomy book I found in the library at Parry. Half the size of the table and mostly a bunch of maths stuff I couldn't figure. But there were them amazing photographs. Hell, I could never take photos of people without cutting half of them out, but these dudes get clear pictures of stuff thousands of light years away.

I sat there for hours, looking at the photos of new galaxies, solar systems being born. There were waves of pink dust, floating like sand in shallow water. And the stars like the tiny flecks of sun you see when you open your eyes beneath the waves. And most of all, the sculpture of the Horse's Head Nebula, astronomical number Barnard 33, in the quadrant of Zeta Orionis. I'd imagine myself drifting in the pink sky, rolling my body over like a swimmer taking a breath. Then turning onto my back, putting my hands behind my head. I'd wave, a tiny gesture no one was around to see. I'd smile. 'See ya around sometime, eh,' I'd say.

I thought about the ultrasound Jacqui had done when we went see the doc when she was five months gone. Before my sentencing, the last time. Squeezing the milky stuff over her then running the camera across her, like he was drawing the little one's shape on her skin. And there it came out on the TV screen. This tiny figure, delicate, almost transparent. Like a tiny horse, drifting among a field of stars.

'It's a little scary,' she said, 'seeing something alive inside you.' And it *was* scary. I hadn't thought about it until then. How you could be inside someone, part of you, you and not you. They gave us the photo. I wonder if she still has it.

The doc asked us if we wanted to know whether it was a boy or a girl. Jacqui squeezed my hand and said, 'No, we don't want to know yet.'

I still don't know.

I ripped the page out of the book and put it up on the wall of my cell.

'What's that?' the fellas used to say.

'The Horse's Head Nebula,' I'd say, 'Barnard 33, quadrant of Zeta Orionis. And it's a part of me.'

The red giant star Antares in the constellation of Scorpius is two hundred times the diameter of the sun. Astronomical name Alpha Scorpii. You could fit the earth inside it a couple of million times. Everything: the continents, the ocean, the people, everything. What is it can create something so huge, and so far away no one will ever reach it. But it's dying, like those giant trees up north. Nothing bad, just the dying part you get after the living part. One day it will go supernova then the only thing left will be darkness. A black hole.

I wonder if he/she ever thinks of their father. I wonder if *you*, wherever you are, ever think of your dad. Maybe even just once in a while. Or is whoever Jacqui's living with 'Dad' now. Maybe you don't know anything else. People think when someone goes inside, freedom's the biggest thing they give up, but it isn't. Not even close.

So you'd be seven, no, eight years old now. Time enough to forget everything. But how can you forget what you never knew? And how long will I be able to remember?

What would I say anyway, if I did see you. What is there to say. I could start at the beginning, the happy times, then just skip everything else. Why not? Yep, my life, pages ripped out, the good times measured in minutes and the bad times measured in years.

You'd think in eight years I could've thought up a name for you. Even just a make-believe name. But there's this hole in me that just won't let me. As if I'm not supposed to. Astronomers have thought up names for eight thousand different stars and then some, but I can't think of one child's name.

So I reckon I'd just say:

Hiya, do you know who I am? No? It's OK. It's not important. Wow, look at you, all grown and everything. Got your own bunch of friends. A person needs friends, and family too. People to look after you. And more important – people for you to look after. That's what everyone needs. How's Mum … does she ever say anything about me? No, no need to answer. I don't want to know. I just want to see you and you know, just sit and talk for a while. Hey, don't go …

On Mars there's a volcano named Olympus Mons, three times the height of Mount Everest. Astronomers once thought the streams of colour visible in the telescope's eye were canals. One dude even took a stab at the population there. Came up with twenty million or some such. Twenty million what?

No it's OK, like I said, I just want to talk. Tell me the names of your friends. Nah, no heavy reason, I'm just interested, you know. What do you like doing? What's your favourite kai? What's the icky stuff you dooooooon't like to eat. What do you like watching on TV? I'd just like to know. No big thing.

The 'canals' on Mars turned out to be sandstorms.

If you don't mind, I'd kinda like to stick around a while, not real close, but you know, close enough just to be able to see you every day. Wouldn't even have to be every day. Just now and then. Nah, you wouldn't have to talk to me or anything — well, not unless you wanted to. And then it'd be sweet. Just you and me.

There's a space probe named *Voyager*, been sent out to the end of the solar system and beyond to send back info. Only, you see there's no program in it which'll make it turn around and come home. It'll keep sending photos to earth until it either goes out of range or just runs out of juice and dies.

No it's OK. I'm not a stranger. Not really. I just haven't been around for a while. Been away. But I'm here now and that's all that matters eh … You know I could maybe walk you to school, no it's OK. I don't want to crowd you, just want to see — to be — a little piece of your life. Like I said, it's no big thing.

The *Voyager* space probe will never reach Zeta Orionis, never even come close. It's just too far away. But I can see it, now I'm out. Now I got more than just a piddly little window or a wire fence to look through. On a real clear night, I just have to wait for the right time and I can hold my hand up next to it. My tiny hand against something so big. I can see it, walk my fingers around it, do everything but touch it. And with my bare eyes the whole nebula is just a smudge.

No it's OK. I don't have to walk you to school. I understand. It's not cool, with your mates. No, really. It's OK. I'll just stand back here a bit and watch. I just wanted to …

I still have the photo from the book, all crumpled and flattened out and crumpled again. Stuck with Sellotape to the ceiling.

Antares, Aldebaran, Alpha Centaurus, Beta Persei, Cygnus … I can think of a hundred more names, but not yours.

No, it's OK. Really. You have your own life. I understand. See ya around some time, eh …

Horse's Head Nebula. Astronomical number Barnard 33. Quadrant of Zeta Orionis.

The closest I'll ever come to knowing you.

IV

Music from the Moon

Jordan

Ma used to work at this place that made clothes. She was stuck in the corner of the building where they fobbed off the things that didn't come out right. The 'seconds'. Sometimes they were damaged just a little, or damaged somewhere you had to look real hard to find. Maybe an inside pocket somewhere. It was a game we used to play sometimes, when I'd walk to her work from school, wait for her to finish, then walk home with her. 'Spot the damage,' we'd call it. I'd take something from the rack and sit, listening to the sound of the sewing machines, running the fabric through my fingers, trying to find whatever it was that made the garment wrong. Sometimes I'd find it, but only sometimes. Then Ma would smile, nod just a little bit and I'd sit there with my chin raised. The times I couldn't find anything she'd screw her eyes up and say, 'Keep looking.' Sometimes I never could find out what was wrong and I'd just sit there, going through it again and again, my fingers getting heavier and heavier.

A

Astronomy
Astronomy is the oldest of all the sciences, born from the first moment a human figure turned his face to the night sky and its tiny points of light and wondered. The earliest star charts were carved into Babylonian stone tablets more than 3,000 years ago. Some of these charts were used to catalogue the seasons, or to predict solar eclipses …

Jordan closes the book, stands, walks to the edge of the boat's deck and looks down into the stream. A few leaves float on the mottled surface, a pine cone bobs in the current. He climbs down the ladder, wades midstream, lifts out the pine cone and stands holding it, tiny scales of water drifting through the gaps between his fingers. He looks up into the pine trees beyond, themselves strangers here in this land that was once knitted together by kauri roots. He goes back to the boat, sets the pine cone on the small dresser beside the bed and takes the encyclopaedia and his guitar and goes back upstream. He sits on a ridge of sand, bare feet in the stream. The book is beside him, a fine spun wind unsettling its pages.

Art of the Ancient World

A pair of figures stand in relief against a wall, their mosaic bodies enlivened with yellow ochre. Note how the first figure carries a lyre. (Sumerian temple wall c. 2800 B.C.)

He studies the first figure. Some finer details are still visible. A long skirt, like a lavalava. Serrated at the base. A sash tied around his waist. His right hand beneath the carved figure of a bull that serves as the lyre's body, his left hand on the strings. Even with the dust and wind of thousands of years there is a hint of a smile on the musician's face.

He looks down into the water, his fingers shifting across the mother-of-pearl lettering between the guitar's frets. He doesn't look up until the sound of Kingi's footsteps reaches him. The old man reaches into the stream, cleansing a thin ribbon of oil from his hands. He looks up.

'Kataraina was telling me she knew your family.'

'Everybody knew them.'

'Te Aupōuri?'

Jordan nods.

'The people of the smoke,' says Kingi. 'In the musket wars in the old days we had to leave our homelands and head further north. So we lit fires all around the harbour's edge, in the hills. Lit them as cover and just drifted away with the smoke.'

'Seems we been doing that for ever,' says Jordan.

He taps his fingers against the guitar, lets loose an eerie distant sound, like a muffled voice from the far end of a street.

Kataraina appears behind them and sits in the marram grass. 'So what's all the whispering about?' she says.

'We were just talking about smoke,' says Kingi.

'Well ain't we just the peach,' says Kataraina. 'The sum total of the evolution of the tangata whenua. Sitting by a piddling stream west of nowhere talking about smoke.'

Jordan flips the guitar over, runs his fingers across the strings. His right hand moves into a strum, then an arpeggio. It's the same broken circle of melody he seems always to seek.

'What *is* that tune?' says Kataraina.

'Don't know its name,' says Jordan.

'Where did you hear it?' says Kingi.

'Old bloke taught me.'

'Old bloke,' says Kingi. 'Tō matua?'

'My father didn't teach me anything worth a damn.'

'Well, whoever he was,' says Kingi, 'he was a man of refined taste.'

'Why's that?'

'That piece, it's Ravel. *Pavane for a Dead Princess.*'

'Pavane?'

'A dance. A pavane is a kind of slow dance.'

'So who was this princess then?' says Kataraina.

Jordan stops playing, sits staring into the water.

'Helloooo?' says Kataraina.

He doesn't look up again, and he doesn't resume his playing.

Jordan walks from tree to tree with a rake, sweeping the fallen leaves into heaps then dragging them together into a larger pile. They crackle like ancient papyrus. He heaps them into a cairn on a piece of scrubby ground next to the camp's circle. In the late afternoon he lights it. Kataraina approaches, her forearm raised above the bridge of her nose, shielding her eyes from the rising heat.

'You've mentioned this "old bloke" a couple of times,' says Kataraina. 'Who was he?'

He looks up from his raking, stares through the heat haze of the flames. 'Why?' he says.

'The generosity in your voice when you said it.'

'Generosity?'

'Yeah. So I was just wondering.'

'You sure do a lot of wondering.'

'My only fault. Otherwise I'm pretty well perfect.'

He lifts the rake, twists the handle in his fingers, the teeth shedding another few flakes into the fire. 'Just some old bloke, been in a long time.' He lifts the rake out of the grass. He bends once more, lifting another wreath of leaves out of the grass.

'You didn't have to burn the leaves,' she says. 'They make good fertilizer.'

'So does ash. And I like the smell of burning.'

In the morning Jordan stands from his bed and takes his wetsuit from a hook on the back of the door. He lifts his surfboard out of the sand and picks his way beneath the trees to the beach, slowing when he sees Kataraina sitting on the sand. He carries on past.

'Where did you get those scars on your back?' she says, behind him.

He doesn't answer, just walks on through the shells, down to the tide.

Kataraina watches Jordan walk away, his scars changing colour with the shifting light. As if he was born with his veins on the outside of his body. She remembers seeing a strange-looking fish once in a tank in the corner of a tropical theme bar. A Mexican Walking Fish. You could see right inside it, see its heart beating. It gave her the creeps.

She goes to her cabin, takes her diary from her bag, walks back up into the dunes and begins to sketch. A radiating head of hair, like her own, but knowing no ends. Perhaps not hair, but veins. She stops sketching, sits tapping the pen's tip against the paper.

Jordan spies a wave building behind him and stands just in time to catch it, the horizon beyond the land falling as he raises himself up. A shuffle to get his feet placed to balance his weight. The wind whips against his face, the waves scuffing into fountains of spray, veiling anything more than a few inches from where his toes front the board.

At Paremoremo Maximum Security Prison he had been interviewed by a Corrections Service psychologist, a vague and distracted woman with a stare that never moved far from the door, a hand always hovering at the edge of the table, fingering – he guessed – the hand-held alarm. She arrived armed with a black imitation-leather folder with several sheets of questions spilling from its mouth. Each question seemed innocuous but stood ready to tip into the next, like dominoes. It struck him then that his whole life was interpreted by what was recorded on pieces of paper. An A4 human being. He had become a series of lists. Inventories. A charge sheet, a register of extenuating circumstances, a count of his meagre possessions that fitted into a cardboard box. A catalogue of days, each the same as the one before. He glances towards the dunes where Kataraina sits with her knees raised, writing or drawing in her own little book. Chin propped on an upraised palm. Now and then her stare rises out to sea. Perhaps she sees her own dominoes falling, like the old trees on the now-naked landscape beyond the hill where once forests had grown.

The wave begins to break at its edges and he corrects too late, suddenly upended as if launched from a ramp. A glimpse of sky, then nothing but spray. When he raises his face out of the water she is standing on the dunes, looking towards him, her book hanging from one hand. She is digging her feet into the soft hillock to stop herself from slipping. He pulls on the tie rope fixing the board to his left ankle, draws the fibreglass shell towards him and moves on into the shallows. He walks halfway past her, then stops.

'I got some of the scars at a gang initiation,' he says. 'Others in fights. The tracks on my back are cigarette burns. I got jumped by a couple of clowns in the boob. It was a warning for going against their Sergeant-at-Arms.'

Kataraina stands still, the diary hanging open in her fingers, pages skittering in the wind.

Jordan glances down at her book then picks up his board again but doesn't move away. He looks out towards the waves.

'What?' says Kataraina.

'You don't have to go.'

She nods.

She walks around the hill, looking for wildflowers. She finds a couple of handfuls and takes them back to her cabin and sits some in the Marmite jar with the marram grass. She fills an old chipped mug from the kitchen with water, places the rest of the flowers in that and sits them both on the windowsill. The tiny water garden sits in the afternoon sun.

'You don't have to go,' he'd said. Until then she hadn't entertained the possibility of *not* going, of not heading home from this, her waystation. But what *is* home? Or perhaps *why*. She reaches for the jar, dipping the end of a pencil in the water, sending his words swirling around in her mind. Each time she emphasises a different syllable, settling in the end on the *have* as the sentence's heart.

She walks outside, taking in the scent of grass, a faint tincture of pine needles. She leans back against the wall of the cabin, draughting his face in her mind, the way his pupils remain expressionless but the map carved into his skin moves. When he seems happy the lines of ink curve into a smile, even though his lips stay still. His eyes betray no tenant; just hibernate like dark eggs, only the swirls of his moko moving.

She turns a hand over, palm up, reading it as if it is a mirror. Are they so different, she and Jordan, she and the old pilot. She and Kingi are in the midst of either coming or going, but the surfer seems to be neither. Seems almost to be hanging, like a swing bridge across a river.

Jordan appears on the dunes, sketched against the sky, carrying a fishing rod and a plastic bucket. He steps free of the paleness of the sand, just as he emerges each morning from the sea's grasp. If she tried, she could care maybe a little. If he signalled to her that caring was a language he understood even just a few words of. When did she forget how to care? Was there a time, a date, an hour, a minute? When *did* that part of her die, exactly? Was it a single moment, when she stepped through the window and looked back to see Matty, reaching for something he couldn't capture any more than she could. Or was it a hundred tiny moments, the passing of bills of sale into her palm, the sound of her clients running the shower, the swirl of her mouthwash emptying down the plughole.

He disappears over the horizon, trudging back to his one confidante. The sea. His only intimacy seems to be with the waves, those blankets he beds himself within, where his body turns to shadow alone.

She rummages through the kitchen cupboards, eyeing the various tins. The pinging of rain on the metal roof is interrupted by the sound of scuffing feet on the flax mat at the door. Jordan stands with a bucket in his hands. He sets the bucket on the table, reaches into it and lifts out a couple of terakihi, already scaled.

'Whoa,' says Kataraina. 'A feast fit for royalty.'

He looks down at the pale pink flesh. It is still half liquid from the fishes' life in sea water. He reaches into the leather sheath on his belt and withdraws a jagged-edged knife.

'I got it covered,' says Kataraina, reaching for the knife. 'You go and unload some of that beach you're carrying.'

He stares. She brushes one of his bare shoulders, a few flecks of sand slipping down his tattooed arm to his bare feet. She flexes her fingers a few inches from the knife he still holds. He pauses for a moment, then turns it around in his palm, reaching towards her with it handle first. She takes it and he steps back, dislodging more sand from his body.

'Hey!' she says. 'You're trashing up my kitchen!'

He almost laughs, the closest she has seen him come. He leans against the door jamb.

'Out!' she says. 'How many times do I have to tell you.'

'It's pissing down!'

'Great, then you can shower on the way.'

The three of them eat mostly in silence, Kingi's cigarette smoke softening the light from the naked bulb. Then Kataraina stands, stretches, puts the plates in the sink and makes a pot of tea. Jordan runs the taps over his hands, picks up the guitar and begins to play a few sparse-sounding chords. He moves into melody, still passing through a hint of each chord now and then. He stops and reaches for his mug of tea, and Kataraina extends a hand towards the guitar. He looks at her, refilling his mug, then hers and Kingi's from the teapot. Then he lifts the guitar across the table to her. They pass the guitar back and forth across the table, each laying a hint of themselves into its wood, the echo of its strings. Kataraina's playing is rhythmic, a pulse that moves through her shoulders and her tapping foot. Jordan's playing is single notes or partial chords, three- or four-string arpeggios, nothing held for more than an instant.

'I was thinking maybe I might stay here a while longer,' she says.

'I thought you were headed someplace,' says Jordan, twisting the tuning peg on the high E string.

'I am,' says Kataraina. 'But it'll still be there in a couple of weeks. After twenty years, another few weeks won't make much difference.'

He looks up, then back down at the strings. 'Everybody seems to be delaying,' he says.

'True,' says Kingi.

'You got an excuse,' says Jordan.

'And I don't?' says Kataraina.

'Do you need one?'

'I don't need anything. It's not your business.'

'You made it my business, by landing here.'

'He's the one with the aeroplane, not me.'

'You know what I mean.'

'I came back for …'

'For what?'

'Because this place was the last place, the only place, in my whole fucked-up life where I ever felt free. Alright? Is that what you wanted?'

She glances at Kingi. 'Sorry,' she says.

He lays his gnarled hand over hers. She looks back up at Jordan.

'I don't expect you to even remotely understand what I mean,' she says.

He goes back to playing his guitar. 'Actually I do,' he says, looking down at the fretboard.

After washing the dishes they bid each other goodnight. Kataraina heads towards her cabin in the dark, startled by a sudden light from two bulbs set in the overhanging trees. She glances back towards the kitchen, realising he must have hit a master switch.

'Thank you,' she says, and walks on down the path.

Jordan opens his eyes to daylight and slips on his wetsuit. He blinks his way into the first of the waves, reading the undertow like a blind man following signposts etched in Braille. A touch of the sea floor against his palms. A handful of sand then a kick away.

When he steps up out of the waves he sees her, walking out along the jetty, arms outstretched, a tightrope walker. It's as if she puts total trust in the touch of the wood beneath her toes. She reaches the end where the jetty crumbles away and steps onto the first of the old posts. At the last one she stops, arms still raised.

Her feet are bare, toes curled to grip the wood. He walks across the shallows to the edge of the jetty, then up onto the boards behind her. Her eyes are closed to everything. Even his footsteps seem to inhabit another atmosphere, and he senses that wherever she is, it isn't in *his* corner of the universe.

At the jetty's end he stops, stands watching her, realising then that he recognises that look, that stillness. Like a photograph, a moment with no before and no after. He has seen it many times. 'If I stand still enough they won't see me, not even my shadow. Then I'll just slip out of them bars or that piddly little window and be gone.'

She turns in a slow circle and he hears then an echo from somewhere. He studies her impassive face, her lips not moving, just a tiny pulse in the skin of her throat. She is humming, faintly, like a tiny bell. She glances up once, along the horizon, then her eyelids angle towards her feet again, perhaps sensing now the transience of her balance as she stands on a single strand of wood above the ocean, a divining rod between sea and sky. He steps back to the edge of her voice's territory, then turns and walks back down the slatted road of boards.

It had been the first flicker of the page turning from child to something weightier, more burdened *by* weight, that last summer before Pōrangi Sam died with his old boat still landlocked. The camp had been full of shouts, running feet, laughter. The smell of sea-wetted bodies. In the last few days before heading home to go back to school only a few of his cousins and one other family, the Reihanas, remained. A time of increasing gaps, a winding down of the clock. The Reihanas had a girl, much older than he, a branch between the giggling girls he was used to being swept up in and someone different, someone whose eyes held secrets, like his mother or aunts. He had found two sand pebbles among the dunes and set them in the stream bed. Smooth, with restless faces that changed as they read the changing light, read the currents and where they were going. A faint harmony of colour beneath their surface, out of the reach of a fingertip. A couple of times when he came upon her, rounding a corner of a cabin or on the path beneath the trees where the kids would dare each other to climb the hill, she would glance at him, just for a second, and another page would turn.

He had sat upright in his bed, remembering he'd forgotten to put the rubbish in the sack for Uncle Hemi to take away, hearing a portent of his father's beer-sodden voice rasping in the coming morning air. So he'd slipped his feet into his jandals and picked his way along the line of cabins to the kitchen block. But he'd never got there.

She was walking along the path, looking now and then up at the moon. He watched her pass then moved up through the trees behind her. She seemed oblivious to the half light, moving with a certainty that carried him with her. She cut all the way upriver to the large pond where the stormflows gathered, then stopped at the pool's edge, looking into the water. He stepped out of sight, into a stand of toetoe. She stood at the water's edge for a long time, her moonshadow on its face. Then she climbed onto a fallen tree trunk and sat, her chin on an upraised knee. He looked up at the moon, its grey eyes carrying the depth of Pōrangi Sam's smile when people ridiculed him for taking forever to build his boat. Something wise beyond being smart. As if its secret would always be a fingertip away.

She sat for an hour, now and then a hand running over the fallen tree's bark, a glance up through the clouds, with those sand–pebble eyes.

Jordan

Atoms

As children some of us may have looked at a favourite toy or a clock and perhaps had the desire to see inside it, to take it apart piece by piece and see what it consists of. So it was with the process leading to the discovery of atoms. The Greek philosopher, Democritus, posited that there existed something so small that it was the building block of everything else in existence. He named this entity 'the atom'. Though his efforts were pure speculation, with a total absence of instrumentation to test his theory – he was not far from the truth.

The planet Venus was named after the Goddess of Love. They look at this little pinprick of light and call it a goddess. For centuries there was this theory that whenever people looked up at Venus and wondered what was there, maybe others were up there looking back. Until the Russians landed a spaceship there and found it was just desert, metal rain and poisoned sky.

But maybe once it really was sweet as up there.

Course then they have to wonder if one day Earth will end up like Venus. That if anyone *had* ever lived on Venus before it was poisoned, well maybe the last thing they seen before they choked to death was this blue ball floating in the dark.

Atmosphere

The earth is housed in a thick blanket of air that we call 'atmosphere'. The roots of the word are ancient Greek, meaning 'a sphere of vapour'. This sphere colours everything we perceive from our vantage point on the earth's surface. It also protects the planet, houses the gases that give and sustain our life. Other planets have atmospheres but not like earth's. Some are made of gases not conducive to carbon-based biological life, or any form of life as we understand it.

My old man used to have this way of walking, heavy footed, almost stamping in the ground, like he was boring post holes. Like he was a much bigger bloke than he was.

You could hear him coming from a mile away. 'Here comes Big Des,' they used to say, half joking, because he was usually the shortest dude in the room.

We used to fight all the time, as far back as I can remember. He had this set of rules that acted like a jail. Like the world had stopped changing the day he was born and he was around to make sure that it never changed again. It got to where just the sound of his voice made me hate. The old man's prison voice, I used to call it.

He'd come from the backblocks, but there wasn't much work. So just after I was born him and Ma took off from here and headed to town and moved into a state house. None of the houses had any fences or any trees in the front. They were just bare, like one big section with houses dumped all over it. Like emptying the dust bag of a vacuum cleaner. So everyone used to grow something in the front lawn. A little bit of garden maybe, just a few plants with some bright flowers. My mother, before she got sick, would get out there on her knees with a dinky little red spade and clear all the stuff around them so there'd just be this little patch of sunlight almost in the middle of all that sameness. They were probably just weeds, but does it matter? Colour is colour. I used to help her sometimes. She'd show me how to renew the soil, give it a bit of moisture from the hose, then empty the seed packet into the little crater.

When I was inside guys used to stick anything with a bit of colour up on the walls. Anything. As long as it had colour. If it had girls or cars then all the better, but if you couldn't find anything like that then whatever you could lay your hands on that had some colour. One dude had a photograph of a cheesecake with (I think) a passion-fruit topping on it. Bright orange, with little seeds in it. He used to stare at it for hours. He wasn't the only one. Funny what you hunger for when you don't have it.

There was this guy who'd made a little motor/generator thing on the sly, and he'd set it to run off a bunch of batteries, so it gave out light. A little blue bulb about the size of a sparrow's egg. When lights out came he'd start her up, and we'd sit, watching the filament brighten, till the whole cell was bathed in this faint blue glow. Like we were underwater maybe. Or maybe sitting on Venus looking up at the earth and wondering.

Most nights here Big Des would end up getting blotto with the other fathers, then go at it with Granddad. As crazy as he was supposed to be, old Pōrangi Sam could spot a bullshit artist a mile away. I guess cause he was one himself. At the end of each barney Big Des used to swear he'd never come back up home, but he always did. Then they'd get to working on the boat – the only times I ever remember them together without wanting to kill each other. There was silence between them, just the odd question about dimensions, about the colour of an inlay. Maybe in a way the boat did sail after all.

I used to wonder if there was some little corner of that for me. That silence. No, not silence – it was more like a quiet. A peace. I used to think maybe there was something of that crazy old man that I could maybe steal a tiny bit of: that fingers-to-the-world sense that drifted around him like the smoke from his roll-your-owns. Something that Big Des would catch sight of and say, 'Hey, is that tabletop gonna be inch and a half or inch and three quarters?' and actually hang around to listen to the answer. But there never was. Except for this one time.

One morning he comes tapping on the edge of my bunk bed, a little torch in his hands. It was still dark, but he half drags me down to the river's edge and we go out in this rickety old dinghy, just him and me. I had to hold the torch for him, highlight the passage out of the estuary. After a while we were out on the open water and he says, 'Flick the light off, tama,' and I do and the whole world goes dark. He rows for an hour or more, not saying anything. All I hear is the water trickling off the end of the oars.

Then he stops and just sits. Lifts the oars back into the boat. I start to ask what we're doing but he just says, 'Shhh', real gentle-like, without that prison sound in his voice. So I sit still, running a piece of fishing line through my fingers, and he just sits, rocking with the boat, his outline against the greying sky. He raises one oar and moves us around so we're side on to the horizon where the light's starting to grow and we sit looking over our shoulders. There's no sound now, like all the sound has given way for this moment. And then it comes, a faint gold light, appearing in an instant. Boom! Just like that. It grows like sheet lightning and the whole horizon is gold now. I look to the old man and he's still sitting and I watch the sunlight as it moves down his body from his face, down his bush shirt and jeans to his bare feet. The light shows lines, cracks, colours in his face that I'd never really noticed before. When it hit his eyes he looked down on the water, half turned towards me. And I saw the colour of his eyes, a faded brown, like tōtara bark. And the red stains at their edges, like he's bleeding somewhere inside. And I thought of those little patches of flowers in the bare ground.

Nothing I planted ever grew. Never did figure it out.

Alphabet

Modern western societies use the alphabet designed by the Romans 2000 years ago. The Roman letter names and forms were based on those of the Etruscans, who had adapted their alphabet from classical Greece. But the father of all of those systems of lettering was that developed by the Phoenicians over 30 centuries ago in a city at the eastern edge of the Mediterranean named Gebal. The name of

Gebal was later changed to Byblos — literally 'City of Paper' — City of Books. The first two letters of the Phoenician alphabet were Aleph and Beth …

There is music coming from Kataraina's cabin. Some R n' B, gospel tinged. Jordan doesn't recognise the exact song. Al Green maybe. Her door is half open and he can see her every now and then in the rectangle of sun in her door. He sits in the dunes, with his back to the camp. Looking out to sea. The music stops. He turns to see her appear wrapped only in a sarong, heading to the shower block. He goes back to watching the ocean.

Kataraina closes her eyes to the droplets. Balancing within its nest, she leans against the shower wall, focusing on the sound of the water. Then she leans her head back, her hair coursing down her back, heavy, as if she carries a child between her shoulder blades. She raises her palms beneath her breasts, her thumbs slipping up over her nipples, pressing them into her then flicking away to let the water run off her. A sting of electricity on her skin. Not erotic, just alive.

Dusk finds she and Kingi sitting at the broken end of the jetty, Kataraina with her toes dangling down over the water, now more sound than view.

'Tell me more of that ancient stuff,' she says.

'A budding historian in our midst?'

'I like hearing about things that are actually older than me. Doesn't make *me* feel quite so ancient.'

'Hey! I'm almost twice your age.'

'Oops.'

'Oops indeed.'

'Are there any stories about finding your way home?'

'The labyrinth, I suppose. Theseus.'

'I'm all ears.'

There is a splash in the shadows beneath them. The sound of footfalls in shallow water, a figure moving in what little moonlight there is. Jordan stops, raises his tattooed face to look up at them for a moment, then away.

'Theseus was sent to find and kill the Minotaur,' says Kingi.

'Like a monster or something?' asks Kataraina.

'After a fashion. But he was only half monster, half beast.'

'What was the other half?'

'Human. The other half was human. It … he'd been set loose by King Minos, sent to kill all the young men and women of Athens.'

'Shit! Nice guy, huh.'

'King Minos has lost a son to the city –'

'Lost?'

'He was killed. Fell in with the wrong crowd, I suppose one could say. So King Minos, in his sorrow and anger, called forth the Minotaur, but the beast went out of control. Such is the *lot* of beasts. It went on killing. So King Aegeas of Athens sent his own son Theseus on a mission to enter the maze in which the Minotaur hid – the labyrinth – and kill him. The labyrinth was always in darkness, and once entered could never be escaped. So to find his way out again Theseus unwound a ball of thread that his love, Ariadne, had given him. He found the Minotaur and killed him, then rewound the spool, the path guiding him back to daylight.'

'Why'd the beast have to die?' says Jordan from the edge of the waterline. 'Wasn't he *made* to kill.'

Kingi leans over the edge. 'Indeed, yes.'

'Who gets to pass judgement?' says Jordan. 'Who gets to say?'

'You're losing me, e hoa,' says Kingi. 'Are we still talking about the Minotaur?'

No answer, and no sound now but for the waves.

In the night Kataraina wakes and rolls over a couple of times, the blankets tangling around her. She flicks on the light and lies reading flakes of the past from her diary, her eyes straining to decipher the faded writing broken up by tears of paper where the pages lay stuck together and she has prised them open. Then she stands, raises the faded curtains to the bright moonlight frosting the grass. She tugs the blanket from the bed, wraps it around her, steps through the rectangle of her doorway and walks up into the dunes. The moon is huge, its silver troughs and valleys almost tangible. Reachable. Its glow casts pale sheets across the wavetips towards her. She pauses at a flicker of movement, her eyes slowly composing Jordan's imprint against the edge of the moon's circle. She moves on again, the blanket pulled high around her shoulders, angling herself so the light is behind him, his legs dangling from the jetty over the lighted water as if he could leave his footprints on its surface. His hands reach to the edge of the moon's pale orb then slip back towards his body. Like a harpist, plucking melody from metal, from vibration alone.

She leans against the wood of a jetty pole, watching his hands act on their pale stage. A part of her is saddened that his eyes, his whole body, aren't possessed with their eloquence. This 'stone' man whose irises give away no hint, no betrayal of human touch, but whose hands can draw music from the moon.

Jordan kicks open the door to the implement shed and stands waiting for his eyes to adjust to the inner darkness. The mower, a cardboard biscuit-carton full of nails and screws. Some concreting trowels, an open bag of cement. Some tins of paint and a couple of paint brushes. He lifts out the brushes, tosses them on the grass, brings out the paint tins and sets them up in a semi-circle, crouching to open each lid with a screwdriver. He uses a twig to stir the paint, most of it thick with age, breaking slowly like pack ice. A couple of weeks earlier he'd stripped the far cabin of its flaking husk, ready to repaint. Renew. He walks around the front of the kitchen block to the outside tap, crouches to run the brushes beneath the water. He glances up at the sound of Kataraina's footsteps on the grass. She turns to him. Her shoulders are covered in freckles, as if she stands beneath a filter of leaves.

'Morena,' she says. 'E pēhea ana koe?'

'E pai ana,' he says.

He looks around the camp.

'Where's Von Wreckedoften got to?' he says.

'Eh?'

'Himself.'

'You better not let him hear you call him that.'

He smiles.

'Cheeky bastard ain't ya,' says Kataraina as she turns to walk away.

'Hey,' says Jordan.

'Yup.'

'You planning to head back into town any time soon?'

'Why?'

'Might bum a lift. Need some more paint and bits and pieces.'

'You got the home handyman bug, huh?'

'Promised I would.'

'Promised?'

He turns off the tap.

'Well, said I would, anyway,' he says. 'No big thing.'

'Is anything ever a big thing to you?'

He stands, shakes the brushes dry.

'You OK?' he says.

'Why?'

'You seem to want to bite my head off. That's all.'

She looks down at the brushes dripping, then back up.

'Sorry.'

'I'm not your enemy,' says Jordan.

'I know. I know.'

She starts to head towards the dunes, then stops.

'Give me an hour,' she says. ''Bout that lift.'

'Cool. Thanks.'

She walks on up the beach, through pastures of driftwood and shells, following a line of footprints from the Tiger Moth. She stops, crouches in a pile of seaweed, uses a stick to raise a few strands, watches drifts of sand fall. She holds the seaweed against the sun, turning it over on the tip of the stick, the light changing it from deep forest green, to jade, then to emerald. She drops it and walks on.

A few hundred yards up the beach she stops again, where the footprints sweep up over the high tide line. There is an outline of bones in the dunes, a dark, burned copper. She moves on.

It is the rusted frame of a boat. The hull is like the skeleton of some huge, dead creature. She paces the visible half of its perimeter, counting the footsteps off in her head. So intense is her concentration that it takes her a full minute to notice Kingi sitting on top of the dunes, high above her. As if he sits in the creature's eye. The ghost ship's bridge.

'Hey,' she says when she reaches him. 'Whatcha doin'?'

'Just thinking.'

'About?'

'Why aren't you heading home?'

She stretches out her legs on the sand, brushes away an insect with a flick of her hand. 'I *am* heading home,' she says.

'So this is just a pregnant pause.'

She turns away from him, looks out over the waves.

'Did I say the wrong thing?' he says.

'You could say that.'

'Apologies.'

She scoops a handful of sand, raises it to her lips and blows some of it away.

'This place is a killer on shipping,' she says.

He raises his eyebrows. She nods towards the shipwreck.

'And Pōrangi Sam's boat,' she says. 'Jordan's boat.'

'Ah, yes. And my Tiger Moth, I suppose.'

She blows away another thimbleful.

'Yeah, but you'll be gone soon,' she says.

'Indeed. And you?'

'I'll be whatever.'

He fidgets with the trouser cuff of his overalls. She turns to him. He is shaved, his grey hair combed with attention and care. A sense of order. She has seen that need for order before, though not with his gentleness of gesture. Seen it in the counting of coins and cards, her clients making sure everything in their wallets and shirt or trouser pockets was complete. Then a comb run through their wet hair, a shake of a cologne bottle and a sniff at their own skin, making sure *their* smell only left the room with them. Their minds perhaps rewinding to erase the previous hour. A moment's self-conscious chatter, nothing-speak. 'Yes. OK. No. What was agreed. I can't. Well then.' If there was any glance at all at her it was at her hands or feet, the tips of her. Or a point a inch beyond her body. Her nakedness suddenly a shock to them, an affront.

But not Kingi. He looks full into her eyes and nowhere else. His fingertip reaches to brush strands of hair from her eyes, the bridge of her nose and she senses something in the angle of his hand. A hand that doesn't seek to weigh her, to calculate her cost. A hand than seems to neither take nor even to give – but just open.

'I'm giving him a lift into town,' she says. 'You want to come.'

'No, but I'll walk you back to camp.'

'Ever the gallant.'

'Ah, if only.'

Kataraina sits her handbag on the backseat of her car. She lifts off her sandals to shake them free of sand, pivoting onto the driver's seat. Jordan appears over the dunes, dressed in his patched shirt. He clutches a small leather pouch in his fingers.

She drives up the track to the metal road then out onto the highway, Jordan beside her. He seems somehow out of place in the passenger seat of a modern car with his moko, his second skin of scars and stitches. She grins to herself. He glances at her.

'What?' he says.

'Nothing.'

'Come on. What?'

'You ever wonder sometimes, if people think you're crazy?'

'No.'

'Liar.'

He smiles. 'I wonder sometimes if *you're* crazy,' he says.

'Oh that. Nah, there's no wondering about that.'

'So when are you getting back on the move?'

'Jeez, not you too!'

'Eh?'

'Kingi was just asking me that.'

'And what was the answer?'

'Don't see *you* in a hurry to get going anywhere.'

'That's cause I'm not. You never answered my question.'

'I thought you didn't like questions.'

He fiddles with the pouch in his lap.

'No hassle,' he says. 'Just that you seemed all fired up.'

'And now I don't?'

'Well, no. Not really.'

'You don't actually have to be going anywhere,' she says. 'To still be running away.'

He stretches his legs.

'I never said you're running away,' he says.

'I'm talking about you.'

'Shit. I'm not running away either. You're tying me in knots here, girl.'

They drive in silence. Then, 'Well,' says Kataraina.

They pull into Te Kopu. Kataraina eases the car over onto a patch of stones opposite the general store, stops and switches off the engine. A youth does circles on his skateboard, the board clattering into the stones as he tries to leap off and back on.

'This dude you hate,' says Jordan.

'Which dude?' says Kataraina.

'I don't bloody know. Whoever he is. I can see it in your eyes sometimes.'

She looks across at him. He stares out through the window.

'This dude,' says Jordan. 'He isn't me. I'm not him. Get it? I don't have anything to do with him, either real or imaginary. And if it's not just *a* dude but *all* dudes then it still doesn't have anything to do with me. You don't know me.'

'Didn't say I did.'

'You don't have to.'

'So, mister mind reader, what do you see in my eyes now?'

He turns to her. 'You think I don't know shit?' he says. 'Bad shit? You think I grew up with a glass of gin in my hand at the local country club maybe.'

'No. I'm not stupid.'

'No. You're not. You're just scared, that's all.'

'Oh, you think so, do you?'

'You'd already be back with the whānau.'

'Maybe I have other reasons.'

'And maybe you don't.'

She glances back across the street. The skateboarder has gone. 'Maybe we have that in common,' she says.

'What, being scared?'

She nods.

'Sure,' he says.

She looks back at him. 'I'm surprised to hear you admit it,' she says.

'Fear?'

'Yeah.'

He opens his door but doesn't step out. The door hangs open. He looks forward, through the windscreen.

'Sure I'm scared,' he says. 'Got no reason not to admit it. I live in a boat that'll never go to sea, out on the edge of fucking nowhere, no one but seabirds for company. I've spent ten years of my life in borstals and prisons. There's no need and no one to bullshit out here. Everyone I ever had that meant anything to me is as far away from me as is humanly possible.'

She reaches out a hand, runs it down the length of his arm. Clasping him just above the wrist. He nods, then steps out of the car.

They walk across the road. A general store. A clutch of houses, a few year-rounders and some holiday homes. In the shop he picks up a metal carry basket.

On the rear wall of the store is a handyman bar of sorts. Stop leak, rust paint, crack filler. He lifts up the few tins of house paint and takes his time comparing the colour keys. He puts three tins in the basket and carries it, like a beer crate, in front of him. Kataraina comes from the other side of the shop carrying a basket of her own. Crackers, cheese, bread, a couple of magazines and two bottles of wine. Jordan glances at the wine.

'Only the cheap stuff,' says Kataraina. 'But then I'm a cheap woman.'

'No you're not,' he says.

'Oh, my knight in shining armour.'

The two of them pay for their shopping and walk out into the sun. Just beyond the doorway a kuia appears. She looks him over.

'You're Des Te Awa's boy, aren't you,' she says.

Jordan nods.

'How's your brother?' she says. 'Him that owns that bank.'

'He doesn't own the bank,' says Jordan. 'At least not last I heard. He works in one. Serving at the counter.'

'More than you do,' she says. 'You never were much good.'

'Hey!' says Kataraina.

Jordan shakes his head. 'Leave it, Kat,' he says. 'Long past the point of bothering me.'

Kataraina gives the kuia a dirty look, pokes her tongue out. The kuia shakes her head. They put the groceries in the boot and get into the car.

'Don't worry,' says Kataraina. 'I saw her off. You get in any more trouble you just let me know.'

She raises her arm, poses in a mock bicep flex. She puts the keys in the ignition but doesn't turn them, just sits looking out over the steering wheel.

'And don't you go thinking I was serious about being cheap,' she says. 'This lot couldn't print enough money to buy me.'

'I know.'

She twists the key in the ignition and the motor sparks into life. She sits fumbling with the keys for a moment, then switches the motor off again.

'You know what I was,' she says.

He nods. 'Does it matter?' he says.

'Does it?'

'Not to me.'

She closes her eyes.

'Nobody sets out to get fucked for a living,' she says. 'And I don't just mean the sex.'

'I know.'

She opens her eyes. The boy on the skateboard reappears through the windscreen. A soft rain has begun, hazing his figure in the glass. He looks skyward, raising his face to the drops. Jordan leans back in his seat, folds his arms.

'When I was on remand in the Mount,' he says. 'Dude in the next cell slashed his wrists. Just some smart-arse kid who'd been acting tough, got in a fight and bopped someone. There wasn't much to it, from what I heard, but the other dude died while the kid was on remand. So now it's murder. Real prison. There was a young officer on the wing, just new at the job, not much older than the kid and me. So this new officer goes to give the kid the wake-up and starts slipping and sliding in all the blood on the floor. Runs out of the cell, gasping, hands and shoes covered in it. The next day there were two new faces, one on each side of the bars.'

Kataraina stares into the rain.

'I remember thinking,' says Jordan, 'maybe not then but later, that I wasn't going to give them my blood. That they couldn't have it. It wasn't the blood so much, but what was in it. That every blood cell – like every prison cell I stayed in, I suppose – carried just that little bit of *all* of me. They could cut it out, piss in it, but there'd always be more. Always be me. That even if my body was totally jacked up, there'd still be my mind. Mine. Free.'

She swallows hard, reaches up and wipes the tips of her eyelashes.

'Will you let me,' she says. 'Will you let me care?'

Jordan unfolds his arms, lays his palms flat against his thighs.

'I need to,' says Kataraina.

'Will you let *me*?'

She reaches for her eyes again but he leans forward, a hand rising against her cheek, his fingertip finding the wetness. He rubs it into his palm, taking this tiny piece of her into the lifelines in his skin.

An hour later Kataraina steers the car back down the metal road, then the dirt track towards the camp. Jordan leans forward in the seat, looking through the window when he sees Kingi sitting at the picnic table, talking to a young woman with a small child. She is dressed all in black, sweatshirt zipped up to the collar. Her flaxen hair is tied in a bun behind her head and topped with a pair of wraparound sunglasses raised high over her forehead. The child walks to Kataraina and shows her the green stuffed–elephant she carries. Kataraina takes it from her, examines it in the sun.

'This is Moana,' says Kingi.

Kataraina looks at the young woman. 'And you are?' she says.

'Leonie.'

'Where're you from?'

'Auckland.'

'Long way from home.'

'I was, yes.'

She looks at Kataraina. Jordan stands watching them both. No one seems motivated to speak. Jordan turns and walks towards the kitchen block. Kataraina follows him, turning back once to glance at the girl. The girl stands, the child's tiny hand interwoven with her own.

V

Rainsongs

Leonie

In my last year at high school, we went on this class trip to the aquarium. I'd been hassling Mrs Cleary the day before so she got mad. 'Leonie,' she said, 'when are you going to learn you're not the only person in the world.'

I thought about it, about being the only person in the world, and I liked the idea. Just me, lying back in a huge bath filled with water that never goes cold. Nah, not water – milk. Warm milk. Oh yeah and a million videos and CDs and no one to hassle me. Bliss.

That night I woke up to the sound of rain on my window. I lay listening for a while, then lifted my blankets off and moved out the door and down the hall, pausing at Mum and Dad's room. I didn't go in, just leaned my head against the door, one hand on the handle. I stood there for ages, listening to my breathing and theirs, mingling with the rain. I thought about going in, but I didn't.

Then, out of the corner of my eye, I saw a face. Well, sort of. Like when you're looking at something and then close your eyes and there's just a ghost of the image, half formed. A sketch on the inside of your eyelids. And it was singing, not words, just a wave sound, like wind or water. Or it could have just been the rain. A rainsong.

At breakfast Dad and Mikey and me sat at the kitchen table while Mum bustled round. And I knew – I suppose for the first time – their faces weren't *my* face. My face had been drawn from somewhere else.

Oh, I knew I was adopted – sure – but what had it ever meant? Adopted. Mikey used to tease me about it, but so what. It was just a word. Like matchbox or elephant or Bulgaria. And I'd always known I had another mum and dad somewhere, but your mum and dad are the people you can hear breathing at night, not someone who makes a fingerprint then leaves. But sitting at the table, among faces which weren't mine, and never had been, I realised adopted wasn't just a word. It was a someone. A me.

It rained all the way to the aquarium. I leaned back in the big, cushy bus seat and turned my face to watch the drops trickling down the window. I sat staring at my face in the glass. I scrunched up real close, so close our cheeks touched. Like, for a moment, we were sisters. And I began to sing, real soft, my breaths steaming the glass. Circling both of us.

At the aquarium the sharks were beautiful but scary, and the penguins were cute, but there was this one tank that captured me. Some rocks, a plastic coral reef, and a sea horse, just hovering there. And the closer I got, the more he seemed to be looking at me. He began to drift, head nodding, as if there was music in the water.

'Hey there,' I said. 'Where do you come from?'

I blew onto the glass, misting it. He went on dancing, in my little halo of breath. I moved my hand down, so he was almost in my palm.

'You and me have something in common,' I said. 'Cos I come from somewhere else too.'

And I think then I could hear his music. So I began to sing, sing him my rainsong.

In the night I had the dream again. There it was, looking down from the ceiling, and I suppose I knew then it was my own face. I got up and walked to my door and out into the hallway, and there it was leading me all the way. When I stopped at Mum and Dad's door the face kept on moving, moving away.

His name was Leo and he had the softest voice. Delicate, like something hidden away in a jewellery box. When I first saw him, he looked like just another rugby hero type. All swagger. But his voice didn't fit. So I'd watch him – out of the corner of my eye of course – to see if it was his swagger or his voice which didn't fit, because they just didn't go together. I couldn't make up my mind. It wasn't much of a secret his Dad was in prison and Leo had been shuffled from home to home, but if any of that was in him somewhere, it wasn't in his voice, or his eyes.

I was sitting under a tree when he came wandering up, then stopped when he saw me. He raised his eyebrows and stood there, so I shifted further into the shade and he sat down.

'The aquarium was cool, huh,' he said.

I nodded. 'Did you see the sea horse?'

'Yeah. I thought it looked sad.'

'Sad?'

'Yeah, you know. Like it didn't belong there, stuck in a little glass case.'

He picked up a leaf, cradled it in his fingers. 'Sorry,' he said, 'that sounded kinda dumb. But it just got me thinking.'

'It's not dumb. I thought the same thing.'

'Some stuff's just hard to understand,' he said. 'That's all.'

And he said it in his 'jewellery box' voice. I reached out, held my hand beneath his. He looked at me, smiled, and dropped the leaf into my palm.

When I was little Mum used to bath me, and tell me all these wild and wonderful stories, which I was always the centre of. I'd be a princess in Arabia, or maybe Guinevere or even some-one she made up. She'd soap my tummy and walk her fingers over my skin and tell me about all the things I'd do. All the handsome princes who would come searching for me. I'd lie back in the bath and giggle and she'd touch the tip of my nose with soapsuds and I'd blow them away. Princes, hah. Looking for me. Princes with castles and servants and white horses and whole countries named after them.

'And whole rooms filled with ice cream?' I'd say, and she'd nod and say, 'hokey pokey.'

I guess I never thought that somewhere there was another mum who maybe wanted to tell me stories about princes and touch the end of my nose with soapsuds.

The first time Leo and I lay together there were no skyrockets going off and waves rolling in to the shore, but there was a rightness about it. Like something missing had found a place to be. We were both scared, I suppose. Scared of ourselves, of what we were capable of. So I just listened to his voice. Held it against me, inside me.

Afterward we laughed at our fumbling. We'd been like two little kids trying to play the piano or something, maybe with boxing gloves! Hitting all the wrong keys. And I think I loved him for that more than the warmth and fullness of his body against me. That he could laugh about it, about himself. About how we both knew yesterday and today and tomorrow were not now the same and never would be again.

When I missed my time I got scared and made the appointment to see our doctor, on the quiet. She was cool about it. No heavy adult trip. She said I should just call her Jill. We did the test and then she took a plastic lunch box from beneath her desk and we went out behind her office to this little garden with benches and some shady trees and we sat.

'Can I tempt you?' she said, offering me one of her sandwiches.

'Nah. It's OK. I'm cool.'

'Salad and French dressing?'

'Nah. It's OK.'

We sat.

'What's on the other one?' I said.

'Peanut butter.'

'Peanut butter?'

'I like peanut butter.'

'Sprung!'

'What?'

'It's OK. Your secret's safe with me.'

She laughed and slipped her feet out of her shoes and sat with her bare toes on the grass, wiggling them in the sun. We talked for ages, about me, about the future.

Then she said 'six weeks' and I nodded and we talked some more. And amongst what she said I remember hearing the word 'adopted.' I looked up at her. Not really seeing her. Just hearing the word and looking up at the leaves and the sky. The pale smoke trail of a jet plane against the blue.

I wanted to tell Leo first. I tried to think of the words. We were walking down by the stream and every couple of minutes I was going to say it but I couldn't.

He crouched next to the reeds above the water's edge.

'When I was little we used to fish down here,' he said. 'Dad used to bring me. Just me and him. He was OK back then.'

'I didn't know there were any fish in this river.'

'There were then. Don't know where they went.'

'You caught them all.'

He laughed.

'I wish,' he said. 'I never caught stuff-all.'

'Do you think much about your dad?'

He looked down at the grass, then nodded.

'Sorry,' I said.

'It's OK. I can't change what is.'

'Maybe we can.'

He lifted a stone from the path, sent it skimming across the water. I stepped in front of him. He looked up. I tried to tell him, but the words wouldn't come. So I reached down and took his hands and lifted them up against me, under my T-shirt. Running them across my tummy, against my bare skin. Bringing them together and holding them to me. He raised his eyebrows and smiled. I held his hands tighter. His face was beginning to blur. I tried to blink him clear again. Then I saw through the tears that his eyes were huge.

'Really?' he said. 'Wow.'

I nodded and he moved close against me, touched his lips against my wetted cheek and we stood there, rocking. I could hear footsteps of people walking by, the sound of cicadas. The running water of the river. We just stood there for ages. Never letting go.

Jill came and sat with me when I told Mum and Dad. Dad picked up his teacup and stared into it. He put it down then picked it up again and put it back down. I don't think he even took a sip. Then he got up and went out. Mum sat down on the couch and just said my name over and over, like I'd got lost somewhere and she was trying to find me. Then she looped her arm under mine and we sat, no one talking. Listening to Dad getting out his gardening tools and his footsteps on the path.

Jill said there were some questions to think about and I heard the word 'adopted' again. I got up and went out to where Dad was lost among his roses. He sort of glanced sideways, but not at me. He reached out to drop some weeds into a pile on the grass. But when the weeds had fallen he left his hand there, just hanging. I walked up behind him and slid my fingers into his and they closed around mine. He didn't say a word. Then with his other hand he lifted the hose and pulled the trigger and a spray came out over the roses and we just stood there, listening.

I raised my index finger and wrote the word 'adopted' into the falling water. Invisible, unheard. Never to be spoken or written again. And I began to hum. Hum my rainsong.

VI

All God's Chillun Got Guns

Kingi

There was a windmill half a mile or so from the farm where I grew up. It didn't power anything working, just some eccentric farmer's fancy. Perhaps that need for proof that men sometimes become consumed with. A monument to 'what if'. It stood on the crest of the hill, arms circling in concert with any current of wind the day had gifted us. I used to walk to our boundary fence and sit on the old stile, staring up at it. I'd raise my hand beside it, walk my fingers from blade to blade, my steps powered as the windmill was, needing only the grace of the wind to stay alive.

Sometimes in combat in the air, over Folkestone or the Channel, the scream of the engine would vanish and I'd just hear that windmill, like a creaking of branches, a hint of leaves. There I was, top-side at 22,000 feet amid a swarm of fighters – while around me propellers death spiralled into the sea or turned to ashes in an instant with the ignition of a fuel tank – and all I could hear was a windmill. All through the aerial battle, the times when the sky was afire or black with AA smoke, I could sense that sound on the wind. That was my only constant.

A windmill.

'Dowding's Chicks' we were called, after the air chief who sat at his desk with his maps. Perhaps it was meant in jest or even derisively at first, but later it became an ironic form of respect. The young men of Fighter Command. At twenty-two I was almost an elder statesman. So many of them were little more than boys and many would stay that way, the clock's hands breaking off in their adolescence. A generation weaned in the clouds. When a new chap would join I'd look to his eyes to read what lay there, who was crouching within. I was always comforted when I saw a touch of bravado or the glint that revealed a larrikin smirking from beneath the goggles. It was better to die laughing. When a flyer's first need in the morning was to soak in the wealth of the new dawn sky – rather than listen for the puttering of the billy boiling, or seeing to the urgency of finding a pot to pee into – he was gone. When one suddenly found himself looking long at the sunrise with the realisation it might be his last, it usually was.

I shared the luxury of a currant bun once with a red-headed chap from B flight. He gave me one of his du Maurier filters. Some base wallah was prattling on in the background about morale or some such. The red-headed chap leaned back in his deck chair and said, 'My one remaining ambition is to watch my hair thin and my belly thicken.' I smiled, sat chewing my half of the bun. He was posted missing the next day. The operations clerk scratched the word on the blackboard then did his simple subtraction exercise so the numbers would tally and everything would be pukka for official records.

When I became a squadron leader it was down to me to write to the families. I came to hate stationery. The smell of paper and fountain-pen ink. On fine days I had a little fold-out table that I'd sit just outside the doorway of the hut. I'd park my backside on the step and pull out my workings. Whoever was about would see me and make themselves scarce. Flyer's superstition, I suppose. Amid all the carnage the one sight that reminded everyone of their mortality was me fluffing about looking for pages with an RAF letterhead. I once ran out of ink, looked up at one of the squad who was squatted on a small cairn of bricks, smoking a pipe. 'Lend us your pen?' I said. He glanced up, took his pipe from his mouth and said, 'With all due respect, Skip, go fuck yourself.'

A pilot on his first sortie was known as a 'sprog', but you were only a sprog once. Men became veterans in a week. Those who survived repeated sorties, sometimes up to seven or even ten in a day at the peak, developed an economy of movement when not scrambling. As if to allow us to sleep on our feet. In social company many bore the expressiveness of crocodiles. Perhaps just the merest movement of an eyelid or a chin in recognition. Everything else, every other expense on the energy or emotions was deflected. Others would step out of the cockpit at the end of a day's last scramble and straight into a bottle. A nasty concoction would be presented to them at daybreak, to take the fur off their tongues and give their eyes some semblance of clear vision. The only intrusion we allowed was the sound of the bell. 'Scramble.' We grew to divine the sound out of any background, the innocent pinging setting off the triggers the battle had installed inside us. Never to be exorcised. I knew a man who flew into a rage at the ring of a telephone, another who silenced the doorbell mechanism of the local tavern with his service revolver. Any sudden jolt, but only a *sudden* jolt, would elicit some hint of expression in the crocodile's eye. At Biggin Hill I stepped from a lavatory, stood fumbling with the buttons of my fly, when a hint of a running figure cut across my line of vision. In an instant I was sprinting, crossing the fifty yards to my Hurricane before I noticed no one else had moved. The running figure was a dog chasing a stick.

The windmill spun on. At Hawksbury I pulled a man from a downed Hurricane in a field of barley where I had crash-landed only a minute before and under his tunic and trousers he still had on his pyjamas. I saw a youngster with a Saint Christopher medal burned a half inch into his chest after a shot had caught his fuel tank. They unwrapped his shredded skin like Christmas paper. Children played hide and seek in the skeletons of downed Dorniers or Junkers 88s. I heard of one pilot who crashed and died on the cobblestones of the street he grew up in. So many others' last address would stand forever as M-I-S-S-I-N-G.

Conversations never plumbed any depth; you didn't want any thoughts intruding into the mechanism of brain to hand on control column, brain to trigger finger. I once had a fractured dialogue with a mess cook over the delights of Walls ice cream that lasted for two weeks. The only reading material in the pilots' room or the huts was magazines. No one ever bothered to begin on a novel.

Hawksbury, Kent, England

August 1940

I leaned against the wooden wall of a makeshift hut, in actual fact the body of an old fruiterers' lorry, its frame sitting on piles of bricks. The tyres had been spirited away to roll beneath an ambulance. Anything not serving the purpose it was built for *at that exact moment* was transported to serve that purpose elsewhere. That was our lot too as pilots. When the balloon went up most of the RAF were professionals, but professionals die like anyone else, perhaps just evade death a little longer. Experience gained a fraction of a second here and there, an instant's decision to bank left instead of right. Into empty air or tracer fire. But by August the training time for an RAF pilot had been cut from four months to six weeks, such was the toll. In a way it was the Somme all over again, only the battlefield and its nameless shadows lifted from the trenches and sprinkled like dust in the air.

I shifted my position against the wall, looked up at each passing figure, nodded to those I recognised, gave no more than a glance at those I didn't. It wasn't poor humour, just expediency. Too many names to remember, and for how long? At the height of the battle a mess-supply sergeant casually mentioned that most new recruits didn't stay alive long enough to warrant their first change of sheets.

If I attracted a longer glance than most it was perhaps due to the shadows from the overhanging roof echoing the darkness of my skin, a photo-negative image of the others. Perhaps I was a curiosity to them, a son of 'savages' come to their civilisation to help them destroy the sons of another civilised nation.

There were a number of Kiwis in the RAF. I came across a few at various stations, but I never met another Māori. I stood out only on the ground, when we gathered for a photograph or a formal dinner. In our aircraft we were all colourless, as if our skin had taken on the metal sheen of the planes themselves, our arms assuming the bone structure of wings. In the strange robotic cackle of our radio conversations even our accents vanished. Radio silence achieved a momentary equality that all the pomp and pomposity of politics never managed.

I glanced at my watch, then walked across the scales of concrete tarmac to the CO's office and knocked. His voice barked and I stepped in. He stood from his desk, walked to the window and looked out. A few moments of silence then he turned to me and told me I was squadron leader now. Everyone who had been senior was either in hospital or an unknown grave. I stood watching him, this veteran not only of this war but the last, a man who'd lost his cherry in the days when pilots lobbed bombs out of the cockpit by hand.

'How many times did you go up yesterday?' he said.

'Five. You have my reports, Sir.'

'It's all a numbers game.'

'In the end, I suppose it is.'

'Good thing you're a bloody mathematician or some such. That's where we went wrong, we should've drafted only mathematicians.'

'I'm not sure there'd be enough to go round.'

'There may not be enough of any of us to go round.'

He stiffened, his silhouette against the window glass, the grey of the tarmac beyond. 'You didn't hear me say that, did you,' he said.

'Say what, Sir?'

He nodded.

S/L HEREMIA

COMBAT REPORT

Date:	12/8/40
Flight, Squadron:	C Squadron
Number of Enemy Aircraft:	20–25 bombers (approx) and numerous fighters
Type of Enemy Aircraft:	JU88, ME109, ME110, HE111
Time Attack was delivered:	0930 hours
Place Attack was delivered:	Channel, off Dover
Height of Enemy:	12,000 ft
Enemy Casualties:	2 HE111s destroyed, 1 ME109
Our Casualties – Aircraft:	1 Hurricane
Personnel:	1

GENERAL REPORT

Scrambled from Hawksbury at 0930 and rendezvoused with 7B Squadron. Our 12 Hurricanes and their 20 or so Spitfires. Bombers were reported S–SE at about 15,000 ft. We lost time searching for them in the murk. Visibility was rubbish, thick grey cloud and rain. We climbed above it, topping out at 22,000 plus. Saw a group of Spitfires below us, heading west through the rain, missing the bombers now visible well to the south. They were mostly HE111s who seemed to have lost their fighter cover. We dived. A couple of the gunners spotted us and it was all on. We lost Red 7 (F/O Kerrick) straight away, caught a shot from a Heinkel tail gunner. Two of ours engaged the HE and it went up like a burst balloon. I had clear sight of a HE111 and hit it from midships to tail. There were small puffs of smoke and it wobbled a bit. I had another pass, the tail gunner marking me now with fire. I gave it all I had and saw some shrapnel fly off the port fuselage and wing. Then the engine blew, taking the whole wing with it. Just sheared off. The HE flew straight for a few seconds then just rolled away to starboard and dropped. The rear gunner's fire rose away into the clouds as it disappeared …

I found a seat in the mess hall, on one of the deck chairs dragged in to provide extra seating for the full house waiting for the film to start. I sat at the edge of the conversation, listening to the chinking of metal plates and enamel mugs, the occasional slap of hand on shoulder. It struck me then: the irony of how the British had sailed their ships into the midst of my father's people, and how I'd now made the journey in reverse, a spool of wool rewinding against gravity.

The projector whirred into life, sending skittering figures across the makeshift screen. A cheer went up and conversation faded for a moment as eyes adjusted into synchronicity with the rhythm of the film's frames. The Marx Brothers in a farce comedy of international politics and brinkmanship. I lit a cigarette and crossed one leg over the other, glanced along the rows of pale foreheads illuminated in a jerky vaudeville by the flickering on the screen. Some were peaked with RAF caps, some bare, some bandaged. This strange mishmash of young men, tossed together like survivors clinging to a life-raft.

Though the film was funny all the way through I recall laughing just the once, at a chaotic chorus-line number in full military regalia whose axis turned on the line,

They got guns, we got guns. All God's chillun got guns.

COMBAT REPORT

15/8/40

GENERAL …

Joined with No. 3 Spitfire Squadron from Lympne and headed E–SE where a squadron of Dorniers and fighter cover had been sighted. There must have been 60 or more ME109s and Spitfires between 20–25,000, fighting over the bombers. We had a few seconds in the open while the 109s were diverted so went straight in. Caught one HE111 napping, without forward fire. Saw the nose turret shatter like a dropped glass. Red 9 and Red 6 later said they finished it off. Took on another HE but it fought back, nailing Red 4. Saw his fuel tank explode and just a glimpse of a chute (yet to be confirmed). I went back in for the HE. Started firing at 500 yds, all the way to 100 when I veered away, my fire catching a piece of the port engine. Saw smoke and then a flash, but lost sight of it in the cloud. Swung round and dropped to 12,000 to reccy. Damndest thing … a sudden burst of colour and an airman landed on my nose, slammed up against the cockpit windshield, bits of parachute falling away. Possibly one of the crew from the second HE. He had one leg missing, the other hanging off, a boot tapping against the Perspex. His face was bashed about. All I could see was his mouth, gasping like a goldfish. I did a slow barrel roll and he was gone. For a second, just that one boot remained. Then it went too.

My father's eyes never saw much beyond the wind drifts of Te Paki Sands. The broken crescent moon of Parengarenga Harbour was the edge of the earth for him. We were islanded on a spit of land only a couple of hour's walk across, little more than the prow of a canoe. He was a horse wrangler, bushman, shearer, then a small land-owner, accruing – with his marriage to a local – a small parcel of pasture. As a young man he had walked among the skeletons of the former forests of the far north, a land cut and burned and buried and ploughed over. My earliest memories are of the smell of pipi in sea water, circles of brown feet and laughing faces, drifts of waiata breaking, reforming in the air. I sat always at the edge of the circle, looking in. The tattooed chins of the old kuia framed the words of songs already ancient when they were infants. A couple of the oldest men had been boys in the time of the wars against the Pākehā. My great-great-uncle Tamehana had a wound in his hand where a musket ball had gone clean through, the vanished tendons rendering three fingers useless. None of it stopped him from hauling in kahawai and hāpuka for the next seventy years.

I was something of a riddle to everyone, a stranger among them, always with my eyes lost in some book, nary a thought to stock or fishing or fencing. Sitting on a stile staring at that windmill, sketching its outline with a butcher's pencil on the back of an apple box. My younger brother, Eruera, was the glove fit for my father's hand that I never was, and we all knew it. Hands hard like weathered fence posts even in childhood. They were a set: Pap's first glance when the two of us approached always sought Eru, his eyes moving in an instant beyond my own borders. To them both I was a hole in the world, a place where puzzling thoughts gathered like clouds: mathematics, geometry, fractions. I couldn't tell a nag from a horse worth taking the time to train. They could read approaching weather hours, days away, as if it were a text book. I had other things that bothered me and – in a way – *that* bothered them. Perhaps only my mother understood, though she knew and cared nothing for the intricacy of the schemata of numbers and technical sketches I left lying around the house. She understood my need to find answers.

There were two more brothers after Eru. Tame and Paora were both boys who could sense the soil's bloodlines in a way I never could. We would gather sometimes on the sands at twilight, after the day's work was put to bed. The other three would dare each other to dive off a sea cliff into the tide. I showed little interest, so they wrote me off as a 'scaredy cat'. Instead I stood skimming shells in the shallows, not so much interested in how many times I could make a shell skip, but what forces, precisely, kept the shell airborne, and what forces made it fall.

For all that, my father's hand was not denied me: it was me who declined it and his whole world with it. He once said to me, or half said to me with a withering glance in my direction over someone else's head: 'He was born an old man, that one.'

'You sure he's yours,' said someone, to a burst of laughter.

'No,' said Pap, then fired off a kick in their general direction, just for good measure.

Other children might have been shocked. I was relieved. It had nothing to do with parentage.

My exit pass travelled under the name of Father Dominic, the only visiting priest who circulated by aeroplane. He'd had a Tiger Moth shipped over from England, piece by piece. Brand new. A few years of harsh Northland sun had weathered its canvas, so its skin much resembled the people of the land. He had fought in Palestine in World War One, trying to steady his rifle from the back of a camel. He followed the British he encountered there back to England, to Cambridge University, mucking out stables for two years while studying to pass the entrance exams. He took me up in the Moth, relenting after months of my badgering. I sat ensconced in the forward cockpit, my twelve-year-old eyes framed with an old pair of goggles. It was a wordless flight, other than one shout from his bass voice behind me, when I raised my arms perpendicularly, echoing the spread of the Moth's wings. My fingertips grasped nothing but air.

Being of an analytical mind himself he would set me mathematical conundrums which I'd answer with ease, to a raise of his eyebrows. His letter-writing campaign began, and at fifteen I stepped from my last year in the one-room schoolhouse at Te Hapua and into boarding school in Auckland, the recipient of a scholarship. That was 1933. The next time I saw Parengarenga Harbour was in 1982.

When the news of my scholarship came through, Father Dominic landed his Tiger Moth on the beach at the eastern boundary of the farm and walked up the hill with the letter in one hand, its edges flapping in the wind.

At university in Auckland I was still the curio. My dark skin was like a foreign passport, something to try and figure out without knowing the language. There was nothing overt, just that sudden glance I became used to, a surprise at my presence between bookshelves. It was only among the most 'civilised' of society that I first heard the expression 'a slap of the tar brush, eh?' I entered rooms to the sound of conversation ebbing. For a while, I thought that if I stood on an equal footing in academic terms I would balance the ledger everywhere else, but that extended only to the answers I voiced or presented on paper. In person I was still the stranger, a man stateless in his own backyard.

I studied mechanical engineering, the edge of a blade cutting through the cobwebs of history. A century that had begun with the horseless carriage as a sideshow exhibit had rapidly progressed to intercontinental aircraft. I lost myself in hydraulic systems, equations tabling force and inertia. Newton's voice was in my ear. He was almost a comrade, a confidante. Then one day the horizon shifted a few thousand miles further away, leaving a vast field of the imagination glistening like shell drifts at low tide. I had gone looking for a book on aerodynamics, a satchel over my shoulder, my scarf caught up in its strap. Three books in my right hand, my left hand fumbling among the spines for the title I sought. In haste I brought half the shelf down and stood balanced, an open page at my feet. I set my own books down on a bench and stood staring down at a faded volume with some diagrams copied out of Leonardo da Vinci's codices. The words were in Italian and written backwards to boot! I didn't care, just focused on the sheet of rough sketches, catching each fleeting moment of a bird in flight.

S/L HEREMIA

COMBAT REPORT

19/8/40

GENERAL …

We are down to two experienced pilots. The newcomers get in each others' way as much as the enemy. Sighted Heinkels east of Dover, steady at 14,000, approx 20 ME109s in escort. I wanted to wait for No.1 Canadian so we'd each have a semblance of a top guard, but one of the new arrivals got trigger happy and dived. I went after him. A 109 spotted him and hounded his tail. I strafed the 109, another 109 had a go at me. In seconds we were surrounded. Took out one, had a go at another but couldn't snare him. Trying to shake the one, then two on my tail. Saw a patch of cloud east of the coast and headed for it. Took hits on both wings and the fuselage, why she didn't go up I don't know. The bombers had vanished, it was fighter against fighter now. Caught another 109, but left it only limping. Still had the two tailing me. I headed back towards land, used the cliff faces to bank right. A hard 180 to turn and face the MEs. They were virtually touching wingtips, coming for me. I dropped below the level of the cliffs, low enough that I saw sea spray on my windshield. Climbed up towards their bellies, shooting. One took hits to the underside of his wings and cockpit. The other I missed and he scarpered. The wounded one just sort of hovered, engine stalled. Fuel exploded just as the canopy broke and he popped out, on fire. The chute snagged on the tail and he was dragged along behind the plane as it spiralled downwards. His burning figure jerking about, flaming hands fighting against the ropes, trying to break free.

From Auckland the next ticket was a scholarship to Cambridge. Emmanuel College was already 350 years old when I arrived there and stood with my suitcases against my knees, looking up at the chapel designed by Sir Christopher Wren. A couple of years before, a chap named Whittle had been tinkering in the labs with his ideas about a jet engine that he envisioned would render the propeller obsolete. I settled into the rather grand sounding Department of Aeronautical Engineering, fending off quips about 'whether they knew of the existence of the aeroplane' where I came from.

Halfway through my first year I rode a bus to Great Chesterford where another student was staying with his family for the weekend. I was invited to stay the night but was keen to get back to my books. I stepped back onto the bus and sat in the rear, my shoulder against the window. The villages we passed by and through seemed so self contained, like eggs that could never be cracked open, and it struck me then that the buildings that looked aged were juvenile compared to structures they'd been built over. Hooves of knights' horses had probably rutted these lanes before the cobbles went down, perhaps the leather sandals of centurions before them.

It was a sign that drew me back to the now. A sudden suction of time, like air escaping from a closed room when a door flies open. The bus stopped to offload a mother and child by a farmer's gate. I leaned forward then stepped out into the twilight and walked across the stones of the road. Looking at the open fields beyond, then back up at the sign. Aero Club, it said.

It lay among fields criss-crossed by dry stone walls that looked half a millennium old. Grass shoots grew up through cracks in the runway. A control tower that looked borrowed from a country horse-racing track. I stood at the end of the runway, the windsock like an arrow above me, an uncertain arrow, buffeted by the changing breeze. I fingered the metal draw-wire, tapping it against the pole. A faint metallic metronome lost in a second in the wind. I let go and walked on up the tarmac.

There was a Sopwith; behind that, a Vickers Vimy. At the end of the small row of parked planes I paused, a smile taking me all the way back to the edge of the Parengarenga where an old man's wheels had hazed the sand of a beach, his right hand holding the envelope in whose crumpled opening I began my travels. There, in the low light of the retreating sun, sat a Tiger Moth.

I circled its boundaries, my shadow mingling with its own. The delicate doubling of the wings was like a bird's reflection in water. I ran the edge of my palm down its spine, looking up only when a mechanic appeared, clad in overalls, wiping his hands on a rag, a lopsided grin on his face.

They were hardened men, pilots in the Great War who had never shaken the cumulus out of their hair. I entered their conversation easily, like a refugee from the same village, stranded in a new land. Discussions on the correct gauge of aileron linkages could occupy an afternoon. I was soon flying with them in every free hour I could scrounge away from my studies. While other students courted a pint glass or the shimmer of a summer dress I took to the air, earning my aerial time by working on the engines, suggesting adaptations of the fuel mixture or a reworking of the cylinder pots to get more lift.

All around us a dark sun was rising but I was on the outer edge of its reach, engrossed in equations about the relationship of horsepower to velocity. The names of Hitler and Mussolini were becoming regular guests at dinner tables, sidling their way into every conversation. Within a few months the Munich accord seemed to clear the air above us – for a while at least. In the summer, between classes, I'd wander through one of the colleges that backed onto the river Cam. I'd take a punt and steer it midstream then lie down, looking up through the overhang of leaves to the clouds. The branches painted the sky like black vapour trails. I did my degree in two years, achieving a first. But by then the dark sun could no longer be ignored. One early autumn day I awoke to a hubbub in the hallway. It quietened as I dressed and shaved. When I went looking for breakfast I was almost bowled over by a chorus of backslapping first-year students. I wagged a finger.

'Haven't you heard?' one said.

'Heard what?'

'It's on, for Christ's sake. It's on!'

S/L HEREMIA

COMBAT REPORT
27/8/40

GENERAL …

Caught up with the enemy just east of Shakespeare Cliffs. Inbound, which was a bit of luck. Mostly Dorniers, with a few HEs. Their escorts had drifted too high. Perhaps they lost sight of them in the glare of the rare sun. We had at most a couple of minutes clear so attacked immediately. It was 120 seconds of slaughter. I saw two Dorniers go down and have been told of two more. We fired at 500yds to 200yds but broke off before 100 as they were fully laden. Red 5 (P/O Watts) mistimed his last burst and was caught when their bomb load went up. Took his tail right off. With the total loss of stabilisation he went end over end like a boomerang.

Late September, 1939. I took the train down to London for a long weekend. I had my degree; I had an enrolment for post-graduate work. With the chorus of violence welling up around me, academia seemed trivial. A forest of barrage balloons had sprung up over London. I stood in Trafalgar Square watching the skeletal shapes of birds against the metal mesh cables holding the balloons aloft. Everything not chalk- marked for war seemed to be shrinking, becoming invisible. There were queues outside recruiting offices, not just young men but some with grey hair half hidden beneath the brims of hats pulled down hard on their scalps. Women pushing prams had to detour around piles of sandbags. A car's backfire would send people scurrying into doorways.

I rode home on the train, took off my walking boots, laid them on the floor beside my satchel and leaned back in the seat, looking out at the fields warming beneath the late summer sun. The last war had been fought over inches, but with my aeronautics background I already knew that this one wouldn't. Miles would vanish in seconds. The sturdy soldier, kitted out with enough gear to sink a fence post, would be a carnival duck to men travelling at half the speed of sound. Back at digs I lay on my bunk, listening to laughter from the courtyard.

I took my place in a cinema, arriving early for once, early enough to catch the newsreels. Poland had been flooded, like a pasture set too low to drain. Five-hundred-year-old churches staggered, toppling like midnight drunks. There seemed to be little individual prejudice: the Germans were flattening any-thing and everything. The air was the key. The air. I heard a mention of *lebensraum* and asked a colleague familiar with German what it meant. Living space, apparently, and the Luftwaffe had claimed their own living space, above the clouds.

On Christmas Eve I took a walk at dusk, past Front Court on the south side of the chapel, into the gardens, barren now at winter's insistence. Many students had cleared out, heading home to families circled around wirelesses, waiting ...

I pushed the punt away from the shore, standing to set the pole into the river bottom. I had my collar pulled up high against the chill in the wind. This was neither the sense of wind nor water that I'd carried from home, from the bowl's edge of Parengarenga where the tide could withdraw hundreds of yards, leaving footsloggers with the illusion that they could walk across the entire ocean. Here the river was a fault line, a tear in the landscape. I lay the pole down across the punt's width and stood, the current taking me downstream, my arms extended out from my sides, the shadows of leafless branches on my skin, itself the colour of bark.

I looked up through the empty branches. The air. The air would be the doing or undoing.

The Lent Term would begin on January fifth. I had twelve days to decide. I didn't take them. The day after that was Christmas Day. The day after that I joined the RAF.

S/L HEREMIA

COMBAT REPORT
5/9/40

GENERAL ...

Had word of Junkers 88s at 12,000 and wasted no time. Low on fuel. Only our leading half dozen got in some blows. One of the JUs was off course and limping, one engine smoking. I debated just leaving them as they weren't going to make it back across the channel. Then I took fire from the gunner. I pulled back a bit but he kept firing so I attacked. The first pass destroyed the wounded engine and she began to roll over. Then Red 2 (P/O Neil) finished it. We dropped down to head home but ran into a quartet of 109s. I immediately took fire along the port side. My left arm all pins and needles, bits of shredded Hurricane having ripped off my tunic right up to the shoulder. I could spot sea water through the holes in the fuselage. Red 2 dropped, I don't know why. I couldn't see any smoke. He just dropped. I banked away, fuel warning doing a merry dance. The battered canopy was fused to the cockpit. I bashed it with my good arm but couldn't budge it. I climbed to 3,000 feet then flipped her over, unhitched the harnesses and hung upside down, kicking at the canopy with both feet, suddenly feeling weightless. I pulled the chute. Red 2 had also baled out. His open chute was way below me. So were the 109s. They saw him and opened fire. The chute folded up like a discarded toffee paper. I didn't see him after that.

I had a letter from the fiancée of one of the new chaps. Morton his name was. She asked me, 'Did he fight bravely?' It was a common question.

He had come back from his first combat sortie with the shivers, and stinking of shit. After his second he reeked only of urine, but moved like a man encased in broken glass. I took him by the arm and led him to the shower block. It seemed like all I could do. He nodded. I made a mental note to check his condition when he returned from his third sortie, but he never did.

'Yes,' I wrote. 'Yes, he fought bravely.'

I've been asked a few times, 'What was it like?' I'm never quite sure how to answer, except perhaps that it wasn't like anything else. That's not much of an answer, granted, but it may be the only one I possess. Perhaps in the end it was just a succession of heartbeats, of lives measured not in months or years but in tiny, human heartbeats. That was the real sound of the Battle of Britain, of the 'Few', not someone singing 'White Cliffs of Dover' or a shout of 'Tally Ho!' but the silent pulse of blood in arteries, glycol in the coolant lines of Hurricanes and Spitfires.

In DaVinci's codex on the flight of birds he examines every bone, every muscle and tendon, reading each individual strand like the streets or relief lines of a map. I had gone to England to study what would cause force A to move object B, to see why the shell skimmed over a handful of waves before it fell. A shell. The empty, silent house of a creature that once lived, that once made a claim to an inch of territory. Before the war was over I was to see whole cities emptied, blown bare neither by sea water nor wind, but fire.

In the first week of September 1940, I took the three days' leave I had accrued. I was going to head back up to Cambridge, if for no other reason than to see if it still stood, if such things could weather this. I never got there. The train was full of soldiers. Somewhere in the Kentish countryside we slowed and everyone rushed to the right-hand side of the carriage. I followed, craned my neck to look up. In the air above us there was a dogfight, perhaps a dozen fighters, 109s and Spitfires I'd surmise. But all we could see were vapour trails, hundreds of them, circling, radiating like some vast network of arteries. The train slowed to a crawl and I pushed my way to the carriage doorway and out into the sunshine, then off the steps altogether. I walked down into a field, still looking up, oblivious to the retreating spool of the train.

I took off my RAF cap, stood looking up at the trails. The signatures of the moment, the autograph that would speak forever of the summer and autumn of 1940, signed on the parchment of the sky. I sat, then lay in the grass, my arms out from my sides, just another cross in the grass, in a field where others would be raised or fall. Staring up the tattooed sky. And I knew then that that was my moko, the Battle of Britain moko.

S/L HEREMIA

COMBAT REPORT

14/9/40

GENERAL …

On our fourth sortie of the day we spied a group of HE111s inbound, and attacked. We caught a couple before their escorts surrounded us and then there were three of them for every one of us. After that it was just good or bad luck. I didn't make a kill but wounded one Dornier and a lumbering ME110 that seemed to be in the wrong battle. Took fire on both wings, and perhaps also the tail as I lost 70% of stability. Dropped down to 500 feet to spy a landing site. I belly flopped in a field of silverbeet. Saw a burning Heinkel hop skip and jump right through a farmhouse. The local ARP tried to fight the blaze with a single bucket.

I hitched a ride back to Hawksbury on the back of a lorry carrying firewood. I lay among the cut and splintered blocks, the scent of wood. Sap. Earth. I was well past exhausted and could've lain there all afternoon. The lorry shuddered to a stop, a cloud of foul smoke rising. I stood, looking up at the fields surrounding the airfield. Pitted by bombs, the odd crash-landed Hurricane.

In an hour, in a borrowed plane, I was back in the air.

We sighted the wave of incoming fighters just off the coast, the twilit sky so riddled with them it looked like a sieve. A giant watering can. There must've been a hundred plus. I picked one and four others came after me. A couple of our chaps pursuing 109s ran mid-air into other 109s or maybe one of our own cutting across their path. It was a pheasant shoot. I took hits aft and on my port wing. I knocked out two 109s, only one of which I was focusing on. The other just got in the way. I swear within only a few minutes the sky began to clear, just from the carnage. There were smoke trails everywhere, planes falling on top of each other. I climbed, shook off a gadfly on my tail and found some open air for a moment's reccy. Then I went back in, low on ammo, likewise fuel. The fuel-gauge needle was dropping too fast. Must've been a ruptured line. Still they came at us. One shot took off my cockpit canopy, the next my oxygen line. The next a hunk of my shoulder, then one cut into my thigh. I dropped down below 10,000, my cheeks numb with the cold. I fumbled with my bloodied hand to rip the now-useless mask off my face and it vanished out over the channel. I headed coastwards, sighting the familiar chalk cliffs through the smoke. I spent my last cannon shells trying to hit a low flying 109 but got a piece of a wingtip at best. I turned away to scout some flat ground to belly down. Parallel with the coast I reached to clear a speck of oil from the front windshield, but it wouldn't budge. It began to grow, coming at me at 350 miles per hour. Shooting with all it had. I remember seeing, in the flash of the cannons, a sudden stop-motion film of Da Vinci's birds. Each frame divulged the secrets of the miracle of flight. I hugged the column to me and aimed straight at the 109. Neither of us veered away until the last second when his belly rose over me, my propeller's tips slicing him open just before they disintegrated. I was frozen stiff, too stiff to bale, so I just hung on, eyeing a strip of mudflat, a few ribs of surf. At the last moment I lifted the nose, skimming the wavetips, allowing myself a tiny smile, seeing my brothers' faces jeering at my endless skimming of shells in the shallows.

Then everything went black.

VII

Ships in the Dunes

Kataraina stands above the hotplate, an egg in her hand. She taps it against the edge of the pan and lifts it to let the yolk and white fall. She glances back towards the table then up to where Leonie stands a few paces beyond the open doorway, looking back at her with a steady, even stare. Moana is beside Leonie, trying to attract her mother's attention by climbing against her legs. Kataraina holds Leonie's stare for a moment then turns back, reaches for another egg.

Jordan tugs at the cable of the electric sander. He stands with each foot on a paint tin, reaching beneath the eve of the roof. Wood dust flies away from his hands. Every now and then he stops and runs his stare along the boards. Their nakedness is more stark with each sweep of his arms.

Kingi makes up the bed in the next empty cabin while Leonie unpacks her sports bag, then a second bag with Moana's clothes. She sits and taps her knees and Moana climbs up on the bed next to her.

'How about you nap for a couple of hours, eh?' says Leonie.

'Nope,' says Moana.

'No? No? Who's this talking?'

She looks up at Kingi.

'Are you guys family?' she says.

'Not that I know of.'

'All on holiday, then.'

'Not as such. I'm unavoidably detained.'

'How come?'

'Crash-landed my aeroplane.'

'Aeroplane?'

'Yes. It's on the other side of those dunes.'

She smiles, her eyes narrowing.

'You're just razzing me,' she says. 'You don't have an aeroplane.'

'As if I would fib to a young lady.'

She shakes her head, turns to Moana.

'This man says he has an aeroplane,' she says.

Moana struggles with the word. Leonie says it again, emphasising each syllable.

'Come on, Bub,' she says. 'Time for a nap. We've had a long trip. Noooo arguments, huh.'

'I'll take my leave,' says Kingi.

'Thanks for setting us up.'

Leonie watches him go then takes off her basketball shoes and swings over next to where Moana lies yawning.

'See,' says Leonie. 'I told you you were tired.'

She lies watching the sliver of green and grey and blue through the opening she has left in the doorway. She blinks herself awake a couple of times then unzips her sweatshirt down to her breastbone, peels off her socks and slips the blanket over her. The child stirs, reaching an arm out across the blankets, fingers flexing. Leonie draws her into her chest and lies with her palm rising and falling as Moana inhales and exhales. Listening to the rustle of wind in the leaves.

Jordan stands in front of the cabin's wall, a paintbrush poised in his fingers. He runs the bristles against the bare wood he has stripped, paints a square a metre by a metre then steps back. He dips the brush back in the paint and runs it across the wood.

He spends the afternoon painting, flecks forming a fine mist over his T-shirt and cycle shorts. He watches Kataraina come from the scrublands, walking beneath the trees, a small bunch of wildflowers in her hand. She has changed from her jeans to a dress. Pale blue, paler than the sky. She walks to the kitchen and comes back out with the flowers standing in an empty milk bottle. She goes towards her cabin then stops and turns and heads towards the stream instead, towards the old boat. A few minutes later she returns without the bottle or the flowers.

At sunset Leonie and Moana walk the track to the ocean, Moana stopping to pick up leaves and twigs on the way. To the right, a small stand of trees; to the left, dunes. They pick their way through the marram grass, stopping when Leonie sees the old aeroplane.

'Look,' she says. 'Just like the nice man said.'

Moana stares.

'Aeroplane,' says Leonie. 'Can you remember how to say it?'

They descend the track and walk around the Tiger Moth, Leonie marvelling at the smoothness of its metal frame, the balance in its architecture. She turns to Moana and raises her arms out from her sides.

'Whrrrrrr,' she says. 'That's how they fly.'

Moana laughs.

Leonie lays her open palm against a wing, then peers into the rear cockpit. Moana reaches for her hands, pulling against her, pleading.

'Up!'

'Oh alright, miss bossy-boots!'

Leonie bends and lifts Moana up from the sand to look over the rim into the cockpit. Moana's hands scramble for a hold, her eyes staring at the gauges.

'You're getting way too heavy for this!'

She braces Moana between her own body and the aeroplane, pointing to the various pieces of equipment and trying to guess what they are.

'And what about … that one?'

There's a flicker of movement beyond the aeroplane. Kataraina walks among the driftwood. Leonie draws Moana down and leads her up into the dunes, lifting her over the softest sand when her feet begin to sink. At the crest of the dune they stop and Leonie sits Moana at her side.

'Windy, huh,' she says.

'Cold.'

'Not cold. Whaddya mean?'

Moana grabs a sprig of marram grass and sits examining it. Leonie leans forward, sand sieving away beneath her. The waves are as tall as a person, peaks exploding in a roar, white foam misting like a smoke trail unwinding.

'Noisy, eh.'

Moana nods.

Kataraina walks down to the wet sand and takes the hem of her dress in her fingers; draws it above her knees, opening herself to the sea wind. She stands just beyond the surf's reach, each wave a messenger, her own body curving like a wave tip. She takes a few long strands of her hair and coaxes them down across her chest. A sweep of copper sunlight draws across her, as if an artist painting her among the scatterings of seaweed and shells, the broken pieces of driftwood.

Leonie draws her knees up and loops her arms around them. She rests her chin on the point of a knee, not taking her eyes away from Kataraina.

Kataraina turns away from her sea. Her fingers let the cloth of her dress fall free, acknowledging once again the lure of gravity as she walks back through her audience of driftwood and up across the marram grass and out of sight.

Leonie rises and takes Moana's hand, and they walk down across the scattering of shells, finding the trail of Kataraina's footprints.

'Can you stand in those?' she says.

Moana puts a foot in one, has to stretch to the next and almost falls. Leonie takes her hand again and they bookend the prints, following the record of Kataraina's passage down across the wet sand to the water's edge where Leonie crouches and draws Moana back against her knees, looping her arms around her, watching the waves build and rise and die.

It rains again in the night, the whole camp taking on the scent of ocean. In the morning Leonie feeds Moana then goes to the car and comes back with a folded-up pushchair. She lifts it apart, puts Moana in a turquoise jumpsuit and sets a white woolly hat on her head. They walk though the trees, Leonie pausing when she sees Jordan sitting on the upturned hull of his dinghy with a guitar across his lap. A fishing rod and flax kit-bag sit in the sand.

He stares seaward, his right hand drifting across the strings. The ripples of the waves beyond echo the swirls of the tattoos in his skin. She is almost to him when he turns to her.

'Hi,' she says.

'Hey there. How is it?'

'Your moko is amazing, like looking down into the ocean.'

He looks at her for a moment, then back to his guitar.

'How old's your daughter?' he says.

'Moana.'

'Moana.'

'Two and a bit.'

He looks up at her, the bronze-green of his tattoos mirrored in the tints of sun in his eyes.

'Is this your place?' says Leonie.

'A tiny bit of it has my name on it, yeah. Couple of grains of sand.'

'I suppose I must have some somewhere too.'

'Somewhere?'

She nods. He slips off the dinghy and crouches next to the pushchair, looking into Moana's tiny face.

'Hey there,' he says.

'Hello,' says Moana.

'Whoa. So formal.'

Leonie laughs. 'Do you have any kids?' she says.

Jordan looks up at her, but doesn't answer. He runs his fingertip along the edge of Moana's cheek and she eyes him with suspicion. Her hand reaches for his finger, closing around it. He stands and sits back on the dinghy's hull and picks up the guitar, his fingers casting a gentle melodic swell.

Kataraina comes from beneath the trees. They both look up.

'You three having a powwow?' she says.

She sits in the sand on the edge of the stream, dangling her feet in the water. Jordan begins playing again: a sweet, simple tune. Kataraina looks up across the stream, begins to hum within it. She starts to sing.

Baby mine, don't you cry,
Baby mine, dry your eyes …

Leonie sits listening, then crouches next to Moana's pushchair and takes her hands and begins to move them to the music. When Kataraina stops singing, Moana claps her hands together, Leonie following, laughing.

'Thank you, thank you,' says Kataraina. 'For my next number …'

Kataraina stands and sits on the dinghy's hull next to Jordan, shouldering him further along its length. He shakes his head, complies.

'El Maestro,' she says.

He begins to search the frets for an opening.

Leonie sits at the edge of their circle in the sand, watching the steam rise from the two kahawai that Kataraina has fried. There's a taste of driftwood smoke from their small cookfire. Leonie moves her feet forward among the shells, drawing their fragments like a blanket over her bare feet. Moana sits between her mother's outstretched legs, as if she has come to pilot her through the sand. They pick at the fish with their fingers. Kataraina licks her fingertips clean, then walks down to the shallows and crouches to wash her hands. She comes back and lifts Jordan's guitar from the sand, begins plucking at the strings. Kingi finishes his fillet then wipes his hands on a rag sticking out from his pocket.

'First-class fare,' he says. 'Compliments to the chef.'

'And the fisherman,' says Kataraina.

'Indeed,' says Kingi. He stands. 'Think I'll go walk this off. Need to check and see if my piston has arrived.'

Kataraina looks up. 'I'll give you a lift,' she says.

'Thank you, no. The walk will do me good.'

He walks up to the track.

Kataraina looks over at Jordan. 'And you, Kemosabe,' she says, 'how 'bout you show me that stuff you were picking out this morning. The run.'

'The blues scale?'

'Yeah. It's kinda neat.'

He crouches in front of her and places his fingers on the frets. Her fingers follow him, starting on the A on the fifth fret of the bass string and working all the way to the A on high E and back down again. She frets each note he points to and plucks it. They repeat the process several times, Kataraina's head nodding as she begins to sense the pattern in the voice.

'That's it,' says Jordan. 'You got it.'

They run through it again, Kataraina picking up speed. Then Jordan lifts his hand away and Kataraina plays on alone.

'You're a fast learner,' says Jordan.

'Haha! I wish.'

He laughs, an inside laugh. It's as if they share the edges of a language not drawn, not spoken into the air. Leonie burrows deeper into the sand, Moana against her body. Jordan sits at

Kataraina's feet, his bare toes against hers. He begins to whistle along with her notes. A delicate sound, echoing her notes like a harmonic. She slows, leaving a gap that he fills with another whistled note and she follows this time. She looks up from her fretting hand, into his eyes.

Leonie reaches down, taking a couple of handfuls of sand, letting them sift over her legs. She draws Moana closer to her, wrapping her arms around her. Then she turns away, towards the ocean, closing her eyes to the music.

Kataraina walks across the grass to where Jordan stands with his paint tins. He dips the brush in a tin of light blue and raises it against the backdrop, looking from the stripped cabin boards to the trees beyond, the sky beyond that. She steps behind him, borrowing his line of vision, watching the colours seep from one level to the next like a raindrop.

'Hey you,' she says.

He raises his eyebrows.

'Von Wreckedoften back yet?' he says.

'No, why?'

'Seemed a little far away this morning.'

'Got stuff to think about, I guess.'

'Sounds like you know some things I don't.'

'We all have our little histories.'

'Ain't that the truth.'

Kataraina moves next to him, leans against his shoulder, looking at the blank cabin wall.

'So?' she says.

He steps forward and begins to paint.

'You remember when Kingi was talking about that monster? In the maze thingamy?'

'The labyrinth, sure.'

'And you said, "Who gets to judge? Who gets to say?"'

'Yep.'

'What did you go inside for?'

He pauses mid-stroke, paint dripping from the brush.

'You don't need my story in your head,' he says. 'Believe me.'

'Let me in.'

'Not there, Kat.'

She stands behind him, loops her arms around his waist. Feels him inhale, hold it for a long time. She reaches up under his shirt, her fingers spreading against his bare skin.

'Murder,' he says. 'I went down for murder.'

'You didn't kill anybody. You're just saying that to scare me away.'

'Right for statement number one. Wrong on the second count.'

He turns, blinks hard, then opens his eyes. The lines of his moko seem to tremble.

She places her chin against the pounamu pendant around his neck. His pulse is against the tip of her nose as he swallows.

'Sometimes you think you've pissed off and left everyone behind,' she says, 'and sometimes you think everyone's pissed off and left *you* behind. But *I'm* not going. I'm standing right here and if you want to get rid of me you're going to have to fight me off, cause I'm not leaving you. Not today. Not this time.'

He lets the paintbrush fall and she feels it slip down her back, shedding its tears against her. She closes her eyes.

'You didn't kill anybody,' she says.

'Just myself,' he says. 'Just me.'

Kataraina steps onto the boat's deck. Jordan walks through the doorway, bending as always to fit. He pauses at the foot of the bed. She runs her hands up the edges of his torso, her fingers dragging at the fabric of his T-shirt, then on up over his chest and neck, across the ink lines on his cheeks. Moistness beneath her fingertips.

'It's OK,' she says.

She moves her whole body against his back, sliding her hands down level with his heart. Her palms slip down the ladder of his midriff to his belt.

'I haven't been with anyone since before I went in,' he says.

'Like riding a bike.'

He laughs, she glances over his shoulders to where his wet eyelids are closed.

'That's not what I meant,' he says.

'I know.'

He nods. She turns him to face her, tilts her face up to take his lips against hers. After they've kissed he takes a half step back, taking her wrists in his hands.

'You don't owe me anything,' he says. 'You don't even know me.'

'It's not about owing.'

A pause.

'Clean slate?' she says.

'Clean slate.'

He seems ready to say something else, but raises his chin in silence. He turns, guides both of them onto the sheets.

If it has been years for him, there is no hint of it in the grace, the ease of his body against her. His hands are huge, all around her, all over her at once. She closes her eyes to his touch and he takes her through the rooms of his life. Through one doorway his broken guitar playing, his sideways glances. Through another, his loss. In another room his music comes together and he draws her away with him, across the sheets, a tiny patch of sunlight catching her eyelids as his breaths echo against the sensitive skin beneath her navel. His eyes rise to look over her breasts, catching her flickering glance. He nods, closes his eyes to her trembling body. His arms loop around her, her skin afire with his touch. She eases down the bed, slipping her arms beneath his shoulders, raising him, bringing his face up over her. He stills and she traces a circle among the wisps of hair on the dunes of muscle between his nipples. She hears him chuckle, the sound fading to vibration alone, as she touches her nose against his collarbone and kisses him, inches above his heart.

She clasps him to her, their limbs interwoven like branches. His body remains still, not seeking to enter her, but just savouring her warmth. Their warmth. Her eyes find his irises that she had thought rustcoloured, but now seem a mirror to the colour of her skin, the tone of the wood of the ceiling, the soil of the hill beyond the windowglass. She looks through them, seeing not only Jordan, but the whole outline of the ship in the dunes, the aeroplane being reclaimed by sand. Then the strangest thing, a girl sitting beside a swimming hole, staring at her face in the water.

She wakes in the dusk, his body now just a pulse beside her. She leans over and runs her cheek across his chest, feeling him shift beneath her. Not without, but within. As if she can hear the streams of his blood, listen to the story that he keeps away from her.

She looks along the lines of his scars, navigating them. One beneath his ribs, like a skeleton of a leaf burned to ash, the other a couple of fingers' width from his left nipple. She runs the tip of her little finger over it, as if it is a socket into which she can press a plug. Some electrical connection that will flicker him into life. Or as if someone has tried to pull out his heart from the *inside*.

Jordan stands in front of the partly painted cabin wall. He crouches, opens the tin lid and uses the brush to stir. He glances across to where Leonie sits in the grass, Moana running, chasing real and imaginary insects. She finds a pine cone and begins to pick at it, rubbing one of its broken bristles against her palm, looking to see if it leaves an imprint.

'Give her a paint brush,' says Jordan. 'Maybe she could give me a hand.'

Leonie laughs. 'Not sure of her level of artistic ability,' she says. 'But I could.'

'You want to?'

'Sure.'

She stands, wipes grass from her jeans and walks to the hut. 'I await your instructions, maestro.'

He hands her the second brush. She looks back to check on Moana then dips the brush in the paint and runs it along a wood panel a few feet from where Jordan works. She turns to him and says in a mock Cockney accent, ''Ere, what's the hourly rate, Guv?'

'Ummm …' He moves to the second cabin and begins to apply the primer over the bare wood.

Kataraina appears from the laundry. She glances at Leonie, then Jordan.

'Slave-driver,' she says.

Jordan smiles. 'You're next,' he says to Kataraina.

Leonie raises her brush in a gesture of defiance. 'Oi!' she says to Jordan. 'Power to the people! Workers of the world unite!'

Kingi comes through the trees.

'How'd you get on at the shop?' says Jordan.

'It wasn't there,' says Kingi. 'So I phoned Auckland. Young Terrence says the piston has been cast and just requires machining.'

'How's the bore?'

'The bores are alright. Good enough to get me to Auckland at least. You know something about engines?'

'Holden engines,' says Jordan. 'Mark I Zephyrs. The odd Jap car. As long as it's nothing too complex. Never had much call to work on aeroplanes.'

Kingi reaches into his breast pocket for his cigarette case. 'You know,' he says, 'when the parts arrive; I could use a hand fitting them.'

Jordan pauses for a moment, then, 'OK,' he says. 'You're on.'

'Count me in, too,' says Leonie. 'There's nothing I don't know about aeroplane engines.'

'Aha,' says Kingi. 'A woman of many parts.'

Jordan reaches over, dabs a snatch of paint on the tip of Leonie's nose. She grimaces.

'Hey!'

She menaces him with her own brush and he shapes himself into the pose of a western gunslinger, brush at the ready by his hips. Leonie joins him in his pantomime. Kataraina shakes her head, begins to whistle the tune from *The Good, the Bad and the Ugly*.

'Alright pardner,' says Leonie. 'Go on and makes ye move.'

In the twilight Leonie takes Moana for a walk in the pushchair. The track is too stony and rutted for the pushchair's wheels so she skirts its edge and goes back down to the beach again. Kataraina sits on the sand, her back against a pale log, its skin bleached to bone. Her open diary is in her hand. Leonie steers the pushchair towards her, raising her eyebrows when Kataraina hears the squeak of the wheels and glances up.

'Hey,' says Kataraina.

'Deep thoughts?' says Leonie, glancing at the diary.

'Nah,' says Kataraina. 'Just laughing at myself.'

Leonie sits looking at Kataraina. Kataraina notices the eyes on her, turns and raises her eyebrows.

'I just want to get to know your face,' says Leonie.

'Really? Wish I did.'

'Don't say that.'

'A reflex, honey. You'll know what I mean when you hit my age.'

'Tell me,' says Leonie. 'Tell me about … you.'

'Shit! How long have you got?'

Leonie laughs

'Where are *you* from then?' says Kataraina, changing the subject.

'Well, born in Auckland, lived in Remuera most of my life.'

'Remmers, eeee gad! Hoity toity, huh.'

'Dad … well … the man I call Dad, is an accountant. Spends most of his time with his rose bushes. What's your whānau like?'

'Now? I don't really know.'

'What do you mean?'

'It's been a while.'

Leonie looks down into the sand. 'Yeah, for me too,' she says.

Kataraina puts down her diary, glances up at Leonie. 'You OK?' she says.

Leonie smiles, nods her head.

'Jeez girl,' says Kataraina. 'Don't go drowning yourself in secrets. It's not worth it. Trust me.'

'Trust you?'

Kataraina gives her a look of mock indignation. 'And why not?'

Leonie takes Moana against her, slips her hands up under Moana's shirt. The child a warm pillow against the cold sea wind on her hands.

Tonight Leonie volunteers to cook dinner and drives into town, returning with two large bags of groceries. With the supplies unpacked she ushers everyone out of her space. She is all action in the kitchen, which soon looks like the aftermath of a tornado. Pots and pans and plates everywhere. Moana sits in the children's sandpit with an old plastic bucket and a garden spade, spooning the sand into the bucket's belly. Jordan comes up from the streambed, raises his eyebrows at Kataraina sitting on the edge of the tabletop.

'Mutiny!' calls Kataraina. 'When's the food coming?'

'It'll be worth the wait,' says Leonie.

Jordan leans back against the table. 'What do you make of her?' he says.

'She seems a good kid,' says Kingi, placing his cigarette case on the table.

'There's something about her,' says Kataraina.

'Something … what?' says Jordan.

'Don't reckon I could describe it,' says Kataraina. 'And I don't reckon I can wait much longer for kai either. Hey you!'

A shout comes from the kitchen. 'Alfuckinright!'

Jordan begins to laugh. 'The youth of today,' he says. 'Man, I dunno.'

'Why, thank you,' says Kataraina.

'Not you!'

She leans forward and takes Kingi's cigarette case and raps Jordan over the head with it.

'Ouch!'

'Serves you right. Show more respect to your elders and betters.'

'Did someone call my name?' says Kingi.

They feast on lasagne with Bolognese sauce, arranged on a

bed of fancy lettuce with a halo of capsicum, slices of Spanish onion. Jordan takes a mouthful and nods his approval.

'Wow,' he says. 'This is serious.'

'Turncoat,' says Kataraina.

She takes a bite.

'Damn, this *is* good,' she says.

After dinner Jordan volunteers to wash the dishes, but Kataraina dismisses him from her presence with a tap of her upturned foot on his rear. He stands regarding her with mock disdain then heads away through the trees. Leonie looks towards the south, expecting him to return, but he doesn't. She turns to the kitchen where Kataraina is framed in the window, sponging the plates. Leonie helps Moana down from the seat and walks across the grass with her, pausing a few inches beyond the square of windowlight on the grass. Her eyes follow the shells of Kataraina's cheekbones up across her freckled nose to the dark cocoons of her eyes. Leonie imagines for a moment Kataraina's pupils showing not only the flickering droplets, or her own face in the glass, but something else – the face of the young woman and child standing beyond her water, beyond her light.

Kataraina runs the tap over her hands, then raises them, letting the water sift through her fingers. She catches droplets with one hand, then raises it so the water slips into the other. Her hands are like a loom weaving thread to fabric. Kataraina tilts her head back and lifts her wet hands to her cheeks. Her eyes close. Her face is tattooed now, like Jordan's. Not with ink, but with water.

She tilts her head forward and looks through the window and Leonie lifts Moana into her arms and steps from the shadows, her daughter's face beneath her own. She raises one hand to the glass. Kataraina stares for a moment, then raises a hand against the glass also. The two women are a mirror. Kataraina withdraws her hand, leaving her liquid imprint, but

Leonie doesn't move. She looks through this lens, this five-fingered teardrop into Kataraina's eyes. Women and child caught for a moment within the sound of falling water.

Jordan stands at the ocean's edge, the fishing rod casting a hairline shadow in the morning sun. He digs his bare feet into the sand and raises the rod higher, across the face of the sun. Out beyond the breakers a windsurfer cuts towards the north. Jordan pauses, lifting the rod aside, watching the sail furl and unfurl, stitch itself through the pale blue, the surfer's body taut against the wind, buffeted but not bent. He glances over his shoulder to where Leonie comes steering the pushchair through the shells towards him. She stops and raises a forearm over her eyes, spying the windsurfer.

'Wow,' she says. 'That looks like fun.'

'That's just what I was thinking.'

She comes on, then stops behind him.

'Those stars under your eyes,' she says. 'They mean …'

'Yep.'

He looks at her, then back towards the windsurfer. She changes tack.

'Are you and Kataraina close?' she says.

'Close? Why?'

'Just wondering. Just looking to get a feel for her, you know, her "world".'

She scuffs at a sand rib with the toe of her track shoes. He draws the fishing line towards him, alerts her with a sweep of his hand, then pulls the line over his head and whips it, cracking into the surf.

'Make sure you don't snag that windsurfer,' says Leonie.

He grins. 'He looks awfully scrawny eating,' he says.

'Reckon. Do you live out here by yourself?'

'Used to, yeah.'

'Until we came along.'

'I'm getting used to it.'

'Were you a gang member?'

'I was mostly a one-man gang. So what are you doing up here?'

'I'm looking for someone.'

Jordan raises the spire of the fishing rod high above him, pauses at the peak of his swing.

'Moana's father?' he says.

'No. I know where he is. Waikumete Cemetery. He came off his motorbike.'

He lets the rod drop onto his shoulder, the wind dragging the line over the wet sand, leaving a tiny snail trail. He searches for something to say but Leonie turns with the pushchair, Moana leaning forward to scout the unfolding sands.

Leonie halts the pushchair in the shade of the trees behind the camp and pushes the brake lever forward. She opens the tin of sky blue, dips the brush into it and begins to paint. Jordan comes up the track, a small necklace of assorted fish slung from a string.

'You OK?' he says.

'Yep. Thanks.'

'Looks like you have plans.'

Leonie winks.

'Plans afoot,' she says.

Jordan looks at the next cabin, garbed only in primer.

'I'd like to get that one finished today too,' he says.

'I've got this one covered, skipper. What colour were you thinking of for the other one?'

'Same, why?'

'The green'd look cool.'

'Reckon?'

'Yup.'

'Tell you what. I'll finish the one you're working on and you have a go at the next one, with the green instead.'

'Sounds like a good deal to me.'

In a couple of hours Jordan finishes the first cabin and in that time Leonie has covered one whole wall of the other.

'Not bad,' says Jordan.

She raises her brush in salute.

'Wind's up,' he says. 'Might go for a surf. You cool here?'

'Yep.'

The wind whips the waves into sheets, unfurling above and around Jordan as he lies on his stomach on the surfboard. He raises his head, the swells such that he can't see more than a few metres in any direction. He closes his eyes, navigating his way through the maze of waves by instinct. He hoists himself up, raises his arms outward. A cross of shadow on the waves. A shout wells up inside him and he lets it out, his voice vanishing in the hammering surf.

Leonie rocks back on her heels, looking at the wall. She crouches, opens the tin of blue and stirs it with the stick. Then she raises the brush, tapping its handle against her chin. She looks down at Moana.

'Whaddya reckon?'

She goes to the shed and brings out all the paint tins she can find. Another blue, a lighter green that she doesn't much care for and a somewhat insipid gold. She sets Moana down with her bucket and spade in the sandpit and moves to the next cabin, where she begins to trace out the skeleton of a tree. In half an hour the wall has been transformed, as if she has unclipped it from the cabin and carried it into the trees. Her brush strokes cast a line from board to board, linking the wooden frames with bowers of blue branches, green and gold leaves.

She steps away, folds her arms. Then she moves around to the next wall, begins to map out an ocean within the grain of the wood.

When Jordan comes back through the trees from the stream he slows and stops. Not only the second cabin but the third also is covered in sprawling branches of trees, leaves and vines. There's a sweep of ocean with a gold sun shining above.

'Holy shit!'

Leonie is sitting in the grass with Moana, reading to her from a picture book. She looks up at Jordan. 'What do you think, skip?' she says.

'What happened?'

'Thought they needed a little pizzazz.'

Kataraina comes down the path. Jordan circles the new-painted cabins. She stops and gapes.

'Whoa … radical!'

Jordan looks across at her, his eyes wide and staring. Kataraina dissolves into laughter.

'Something funny?' says Jordan, smiling now.

'Yeah,' says Kataraina. 'The state of the cabins was priceless, but the state of your face just topped it off.'

Kataraina walks to him, her eyes wide in challenge to his. Her face is still racked with laughter. She puts her arms around him, moves behind him to look over his shoulder, tracing the lines of the branches with her fingers in the air.

'What do I tell the whānau?' says Jordan.

Kingi appears, drawn by the sound of laughter. The others stand and wait for him to speak.

'Shows some flair,' he says. 'The perspective is good, perfectly to scale.'

'Trust you to come out with that,' says Jordan.

'Interesting use of colour too, the tree blue instead of the customary brown. Metaphoric perhaps?'

'Meta-something,' says Jordan.

Leonie stands and sits Moana back in her pushchair.

'Well, I like it,' she says.

Kingi walks over and stands next to her.

'Mind if I give you a hand?' he says.

'Not you too,' says Jordan.

In the last light Kingi and Leonie step away from the fourth cabin. Leonie's arms and neck are sprinkled with paint drops. Kingi reaches with his brush, aiming for the tip of her nose, but she steps away, wagging a finger at him. They stand looking at the mural they have fished from the boards, its spine running from one hut to the other; in the gaps between the huts the painted leaves give way to the pine trees beyond. Leonie turns a half circle towards the dunes, the path between them. Beyond that there is only ocean. Except for the aeroplane.

Jordan stands at the skillet, chewing on a piece of bread while frying eggs, lifting them out with the slice and dropping them onto a plate. Kataraina stands beside him, slicing some tomatoes over lettuce leaves. She lifts a bottle of French dressing and turns to the others. They all nod and she pours the dressing, then begins grating cheese.

Leonie sits at the table with Moana in her lap. She raises her hands over her face, then pulls them away. Moana giggles. Kataraina puts a plate down in front of them.

'Can you do me a favour and pass me the bananas from the cupboard,' says Leonie.

Kataraina opens the cupboard and lifts two out. Kingi takes a bowl and fork from the centre of the table, gives it to Leonie. He lifts a plastic bottle of milk from the refrigerator and sets it on the table. Leonie takes the fork and begins crushing the banana in the milk. She lifts a spoon and settles it in Moana's fingers.

They eat in silence. Jordan reaches over now and then to wipe the child's mouth or chin. Kataraina glances at him. He looks up, meets her eyes. She smiles then shakes her head in exaggerated disgust.

They lie on Jordan's bed, listening to the wind. The wood of the boat creaking beneath and around them. He turns, reaches with a hand to roll Kataraina over onto her tummy. He takes the sheet in his fingertips and draws it away, baring her to the night. He stretches an arm, flicks on the lamp.

'Hey!' she says. 'This is a private show!'

'Oh yeah,' he says. 'I forgot the dudes in the apartment building across the street can see us.'

He runs two fingers across the curves of her shoulder, bends and kisses the ridges of her shoulder blades. Her muscles stir beneath him.

'I love these freckles here,' he says.

'Glad someone does.'

He kneads the softness of her skin with the tips of his fingers, bends again to kiss a path down the faint traces of her spine. He senses her tense then release beneath his touch. He draws his hand lower, brushing her as if she is a board or canvas. Down across her cheeks to the tops of her thighs. Brushing her skin with a touch so slight her hips have to rise to seek it.

'When you go,' he says. 'It's OK.'

'Who says I'm going?'

'You're going home.'

'Maybe I'm starting to think about what *home* means.'

'I been thinking about that most of my life.'

'Really?'

He smiles. 'Nope,' he says. 'I wish I could say that. But for most of my life I haven't thought about stuff-all.'

'But you are now?'

He kneads the tops of her thighs with his fingers, then pushes down hard with his palms, moving his hands all the way up to her shoulders again.

'Yeah,' he says. 'Suppose I am. It's you. I blame you. You came along and complicated everything.'

She laughs. He coaxes her over onto her back and lies next to her. She looks up at the ceiling, at the crumpled photograph.

'What *is* that thing?' she says, pointing.

'The Horse's Head Nebula.'

'Er … I'll take your word for it.'

She rolls towards him, puts her chin against his chest.

'I've never been much good at keeping things,' she says.

'Meaning?'

'A warning, I suppose.'

'This could just be a moment. With no before and no after.'

'Could be anything we say it is.'

He lies still, the distant waves the only sound. She sits forward again, her profile seeping into the horizon of the darkness beyond.

'Troubles?' says Jordan.

'Nah.'

'It's OK. Shoot.'

'It's Leonie. She looks at me like I should know her.'

He raises his eyebrows.

'Oooooookay,' he says, grinning.

'Shaddup you! It's true.'

'Something you haven't told me?'

She turns to him. There is shock in her eyes.

'Jeez, girl,' he says. 'That was a joke.'

She looks forward again. He curls his hand around the curve of her shoulder, looking to draw her back down to him, but she is a stone in his hands. He crawls across the bed, sits cross legged in front of her. His hand moves against her cheek and she closes her eyes to it.

'All I need to know about you is what you choose to give me,' he says.

She nods.

'If there's more, then there's more. If there isn't, well ...'

'You're easily pleased.'

'No. I'm grateful. Man, I was a desert here.'

'There's something to be said for deserts.'

'Yeah, if you're a Bedouin.'

He smiles.

'This is amusing?' she says.

'No. Yeah. Well, yeah.'

'Covering all bases, huh?'

'Just seem to recall that you and I had a couple of conversations like this before. Only we seem to have swapped sides.'

She offers her hand, strangely tentative for her. He takes her fingers within his.

Leonie rises early and feeds Moana then puts her in a clean blue and white jumpsuit and sits her in the pushchair. She takes the stuffed elephant from the bed and sets it in Moana's lap. Moana begins to wrestle with it, knocking it onto the floor. Leonie shakes her head.

She goes to the shed and lifts out a tin of paint and a brush and puts them in the carry rack behind the pushchair's seat. They move across the grass to the track and down onto the sand where Leonie stops next to the aeroplane, sets the brake on the pushchair and opens the tin. She crouches, stirring.

Then she stands again and lays the first brushstroke on the aeroplane's fuselage.

The air is cold when Jordan lifts his head out of the waves, colder than the water itself. He turns and watches a wave come to him, over him. He stands treading water, his hands and fingers radiating outward, casting lines of droplets. He waits for the next wave and leaps into it, letting the wave's body carry him for a second, doesn't attempt to fight its muscles with his own. He turns back towards the horizon and awaits the next wave.

Leonie taps the brush's wooden tip against her cheek, squinting her eyes to seek connections in the half light between each of the lines she has drawn. She steps back from the aeroplane's fuselage and smiles. She checks Moana, sleeping in the push-chair, then heads back up the track towards the camp, looking for more paint and brushes.

Jordan clasps the surfboard beneath his armpit and walks up the sand through the drift of shells. He sees Leonie and the push-chair further up the beach, next to the Tiger Moth. He walks towards her, puzzling when he spies the strange new motifs etched into the aeroplane's skin. He smiles, laughs to himself.

'What do you think?' she says.

He raises one eyebrow. Kingi appears on the track, walking at his usual brisk clip. When he sees them he slows and stops, then comes forward again. They stand waiting for his reaction. He walks along the plane's length, then steps back a few paces. He crouches, running a finger across his chin. A branch sweeps along the fuselage's length, leaves sprouting. The branch itself is blue and the leaves gold. A fine background of green, the brushstrokes no more than wisps, like the paintings on Japanese pottery. He stays on his haunches for a moment then stands, walks to Leonie and holds out his hand. She passes him the brush. He dips it in the tin, the blue, and walks around to the other side of the aeroplane and begins to paint. Leonie reaches for another brush. The two of them move around the aeroplane, tattooing its parchment with new life.

Jordan meets Kataraina on the track back to his boat.

'Where's everybody got to?' she says.

'Not sure you'd believe me if I told you.'

'Huh?'

'Long story.'

'You're not going to start keeping a bunch of secrets are you?'

'Start?'

'Touché.'

'Jeez, now you're sounding like him.'

'Madame Von Wreckedoften, eh?'

He laughs.

'Go down at have a look for yourself,' he says.

'Where?'

'The old fella's aeroplane.'

She steps in front of him, kisses him on the cheek, then walks off towards the track down to the beach. He goes to the kitchen and makes himself a sandwich then sits out on the picnic table. An hour later he notices that Kataraina hasn't come back. He walks over to the track and down through the dunes, stopping when he sees Kataraina with Kingi and Leonie, all painting the aeroplane. Kataraina is crouched beside one wing, running a small brush across the sheeting. She glances in his direction and winks at him. He shakes his head and walks back down the sand towards his boat.

Jordan reaches up to the clothes line he has strung between two trees, unclips a peg and drops a T-shirt over his arm. He glances up at the sound of a car engine from the camp. He clears the line then goes into the boat's cabin, folds his clothes and puts them in a drawer. He leans against the bench, looking around. In six months here the only change he has made is the clothes he has in the drawers and the picture of the distant nebula pinned to the ceiling. Other than that, his torch on the shelf, and the small snatch of wildflowers Kataraina has put in a milk bottle and placed next to the torch. He sits on the bed, lifts the bottle and its flowers against the window, the petals tiny, almost transparent against the pale sunlight. He lifts the flowers out and sniffs them. They have no real scent he can make out, maybe just a hint of rain. He carries them outside and down the ladder, the bottle held aloft like a lamp. He walks to the estuary and crouches, emptying the bottle, then refilling it with stream water.

He spends the afternoon with a bucket and mop, swabbing sand and grime from the boat's cabin and lower mast and deck. He is almost to the stern when he hears footsteps on the boards and looks up to see Kataraina.

'Oops,' she says. 'You missed a spot.'

'Yeah, yeah.'

'Just been into the metropolis. The bits and pieces for Kingi's engine were there.'

'Really?'

'Yep. Dude at the shop was minding them. Big box of stuff.'

'Things are moving then, huh.'

Kataraina sits, looks out across the estuary. He stops his swabbing, leans on the mop handle.

'He was always going to go,' he says.

'I know.'

'But you're thinking that his going is going to kick *you* into going?'

She doesn't answer. He pushes some sand towards the edge of the deck with the mop, then coaxes it off into the air.

'People are always leaving,' he says.

'Yeah. But it was usually me that was doing the leaving.'

'Same here.'

'I never really had anything that …'

She looks at the stream.

'That … what?' says Jordan.

'Anything that the leaving of – if you know what I mean – would matter.'

'I did.'

'But you left anyway.'

'Yeah. No glory in it. I'm not some cowboy stranger dude out of the movies. The whole "who was that masked man" thing. Just my dumb stupidity. Or lack of caring. Or maybe even caring for the wrong things.'

She leans forward. He sets the mop against the cabin wall, walks to her and crouches in front of her. Her gaze is angled down past his feet.

'Hey,' he says. 'What is it?'

She doesn't move. He raises her chin with his fingertips and sees now, for the first time, that she is crying.

'Kat, what is it?'

'I'm full of shit,' she says.

'So am I. Big deal.'

A painful smile.

'No jokes,' she says. 'Not right now.'

'I'm not joking.'

She blinks, holding her eyelids closed.

'I did have something once,' she says. 'Something that was worth not leaving.'

He stares.

'I had a kid,' she says. 'A baby I gave up for adoption.'

He runs his hand along the edge of her cheek and up into her hair. Her eyes are still closed.

'I gave her up,' she says. 'Gave her away.'

She opens her eyes, looks full into his. He searches beyond her tears for something else. Even his own face.

'Girl,' he says, 'don't cry for her. She'll be somewhere. Be someone. She doesn't need your tears.'

'It's not her I'm crying for.'

He shifts onto his knees, then leans forward and draws her towards him, so she straddles his thighs. He closes his arms around her, taking the weight of her body into him.

Kingi crosses the stream bed and walks on a couple of miles to a fan of sand reaching into the scrublands. He follows it, finding its tip a full half mile inland. It's as if the sand is attempting to cross to the other sea. He turns and heads back to the west. Mid-morning a wind comes up and hazes the sea spray high above the tide line. He pulls up the collar on his flying jacket and stands staring at the waves, searching for the colours of other seas in the face of the water. He crouches and runs his fingers through the shallows, then stands and walks on down the beach.

An hour later the wind brings a steady rumble within ear-shot and he looks to where a shape forms, skimming the pools of phantom water the light paints on the sand. A bus, decorated in a kaleidoscope of colour. He walks into the dunes and waits for it to come level with him. Eager faces, cameras. He sits without moving. A couple of miles up the beach the bus slows, at the point he guesses it passes the Tiger Moth. It stops for a moment then moves on into the cold of the wind.

Jordan opens his eyes in the predawn and reaches for Kataraina, but finds only her indentation in the sheets. He sits up, trying to reassemble the landscape. He leans over the other half of the bed, where the scent of her still sleeps. He lies back, draws a handful of sheet over his bare legs, then the whole sheet over his torso.

She.

He had thought once, as a young man still naked of life's scars, that fucking someone, being fucked by someone, meant ownership, but that was just loose change that 'experience' empties from your pockets. She had spoken, in the car, of how people couldn't pay enough to buy her. How much does *he* have, hidden away in his caves?

He stands and walks out onto the deck and down onto the sand to the ocean, still naked, still carrying her scent on him. He meets the shallows at a run, dives headlong into the breakers, not washing her from him but taking her with him. Into his place. Into his water.

A half hour later he lies on his back deep in the dunes, out of sight to all but birds. He looks to the sky to the north.

All them miles. In prison you think in inches, because that's all you've got. Whole continents could fit in match boxes and you'd still appreciate them. But out here you get a sense of … what? Scale? Distance? No, more personal than that.

Out here you get a sense that everything's part of a string. Even if it's a few million light years away. A sense that you can reach out and touch the air that touches the sand that touches the sea that touches the sky that …

He closes his eyes, feels his body slipping against the dunes, against the pull of gravity. He digs both hands into the sand beneath him, trying to halt his slide. Then he lifts them out again, allows himself to slip further. A lost cause. It's only sand after all.

Kataraina clips the last peg on the arm of her blouse on the clothes line and brushes her wet hands on her jeans. She walks through the trees, cutting around the foot of the hill to the stream. She stands in front of the boat's prow, calls his name. No answer. She climbs the ladder and goes into the cabin, struck now, as she was on that first day, by the clinical neatness, the sparse furnishings. She smiles: this must be the best kept rickety old boat on the whole coast. She sits for a while, then lies back on his bed, staring up at the old wood of the ceiling, at the strange shapes swimming in the photograph that seems to have significance to him. She has settled her mind on the bright patches of light being stars, the clouds being some kind of smoke. The figure in the centre so dark, so vague against the shifting background. She closes her eyes to the picture, to the sound of the rising wind in the toetoe outside the window.

When he sees her curled asleep in the blankets he pauses then bends over her, his lips an inch above her face. His whole being is suspended, as if she is perhaps an element, a fire for him to thaw something inside himself with. He touches his lips against her cheek, then across her lips. Her eyelids rise. She blinks, once, twice.

The old wood of the boat creaks as they explore each other. The wind has turned to rain, echoing against the glass of the cabin windows. A few traces of it come in through an open louver. His hand across her thigh, his fingertips, then his tongue drawing the stiffness from her nipples. His ponytail slips across her collarbone and she takes it in her fingers, draws him in, lifts her own shoulders off the blankets and up to him. They pause, held by his limbs, bodies entwined a few inches above the bed, a note held and bent into vibrato. He lowers her, then pulls her to him again, still inside her, still a part of her in this moment, this one endless moment, while the touch of raindrops mingles with her fingerprints on the skin of his back. He stares at the wall, the boards turning to bars, then to nothing at all. She takes him by his hair, drags his face back into her orbit. He dips into her again and again, as if she is a wave. Her teeth are against his cheek, her voice whispering words he does not need to unravel into whole speech. Into logic. His body is held now – between heartbeats – by this woman who says she's going home. To this man who has no home but the ocean.

Her arms close around him, unwinding his orgasm in a shiver he suddenly fears might break him into pieces. He presses his cheek against hers, whispers in her ear. 'Are we free?'

In a boat in the dunes, in the rain.

VIII

Islands of Birds

Kingi sits on an upturned apple box, shining the torch beam up into the Tiger Moth's cylinder chambers. He follows the line of the beam with a bare finger, running its tip around the lip, then into the smooth metal well. He lowers his hands, the muscles in his arms tiring so much quicker than they once did. He turns off the torch and lobs it over onto the blanket where his tools sit. He takes a rag from his overalls pocket and wipes his hands.

They have rebuilt an old Hurricane that once bore his hands on the controls. A group of enthusiasts who were probably not even born when it last flew in anger, aero-archaeologists picking over and theorising about the bones of some ancient race of creatures. The Hurricane was reclaimed from the mudflats in November 1940 and taken in pieces to an old hangar on an aero-club's grounds, there to be forgotten along with the other flotsam and jetsam of war. The odd wing from a Vickers, bits and pieces of German wreckage. England in 1941 was an elephant's graveyard for downed aeroplanes. They lay in farm fields alongside forgotten scythes, the rotted wood of old cattle troughs. Most downed RAF planes were cannibalised to build or repair others, reborn over and over with reclaimed wing skinnings or spars, rebuilt engines, a new tail, a replacement set of Hispano MKI or MKII cannons set into the wings. A new pair of eyes would strain through the cockpit canopy or into the reflector gunsight. Even the tiniest parts were saved, handed in by farmers, housewives, children on their way to school. A piece of an aileron, a wheel hub, a shattered compass. Only the pilots were irreplaceable – at least until the next one came along.

The letter from the Hurricane Society had come to him via a route as circuitous as those he had once flown to hide his trail from enemy eyes. To the RAF, then the RNZAF, then a Battle of Britain enthusiast in Auckland for whom he had once corrected some technical details in the text of an article on World War Two fighters. The envelope had arrived on the front porch of the old house out of Te Hapua along with the electricity bill and an invitation to attend a dramatic production of the legend of Rangi and Papatūānuku at the local school hall. He sat on the steps, reading it, running his fingers through his grey hair. At first he had dismissed the idea, dropping the letter into a box in his roll-top desk along with a few other invitations to reunions and celebrations that he had never answered.

His walls were sparsely hung with family photographs, a few sepia-tinged windows into his childhood, into the decades that had passed within the house that he had missed. He was the first son to arrive and would be the last to leave. Eru was killed at Mersa Matruh. Tame at Cassino. Paora was too young for the war to claim and rarely ventured south of Te Kao, propping up his father's bent bones about the property then taking their place when they were consigned back to the soil. He and Kingi had exchanged no more than a half-dozen envelopes in thirty-five years, the last – in 1982 – being notice from a niece of Paora's death from a horse's kick to the temple and a call to come home. Kingi had sat back in the old leather chair in his professor's rooms at Emmanuel College at Cambridge and looked up at the floor-to-ceiling bookshelves, realising, perhaps for the first time, that he shared a greater intimacy with each title than he did with his own family. A month later he leaned back in another chair, this time in a Boeing 747, glancing up when he heard the voice of the stewardess, her hands pushing a drinks trolley.

He brought nothing home with him but for a few books, mostly about birds. Of Cambridge he had transported little but memories and a few personal notes from colleagues. Of his RAF days he carried even less. The Distinguished Service Order sat in a glass case at Cambridge's School of Aeronautical Engineering, the Distinguished Flying Cross hung pinned to a wall in the Auckland War Memorial Museum, no name or photo accompanying either (at the donator's request.)

On the first evening back he'd walked across the paddocks, down to the water's edge, and sat among the driftwood. Two men walked at the water's edge, the younger raising his hand in a wave.

Kingi walked along the beach to an estuary, wading across it to where the sand drifts bordered a field of crimson blossoms, their colours layered like the weavings of a wreath. He had stood in such fields of crimson before, on another continent, in another time. He bent down to lift a stem and flower away from its womb of soil. He closed his hand around its colour, sensing some of that passing through his own skin, painting him. Soil and root and petal. He dropped it into the estuary water and walked back up along the high-tide line.

There were horse's hoofprints cut into the sand, smaller prints of children, tiny indentations of heel and toe. He stood next to them, following their longitude down to the shoreline where the blue Pacific lapped in the shallows of his childhood. He walked to the water, stooping once to pick up a toheroa shell, flicking it from one hand to the other, looking out into the spread of Parengarenga Harbour. The tap, tap of the shell against his skin like the ticking of a distant clock.

He stopped and glanced up to where a gull stood perched on a sand outcrop, eyes swivelling at each hint of movement in its field of vision. He searched his pockets for something to tempt it closer, but they were bare. He sat watching the gull, the way it balanced its body against the wind shifts, a child of the air currents even when on the ground. He smiled, thinking of the 747 and its drinks trolleys, feeling now a stranger to what the aeroplane had become, knowing inside he was more a brother to the seagull.

In September 1940 the zig-zagging fury of the Battle of Britain dissolved into a creeping terror. Battalions of night bombers crossed the channel like a foul-smelling wind, invisible but for the faint heat glow from the engines, perhaps a spark as the bomb-bay doors grated open. Not having succeeded in paralysing the airfields, the Luftwaffe switched to pulverising the cities. Squadron Leader Kingi Heremia missed the opening incisions of what became known as 'The Blitz', his battered body lying unconscious in a military hospital, the bones of his Hurricane half-buried in sand, a footnote to the giant pages of chalk cliffs rising hundreds of feet above it. An eight-year-old boy had sighted his Hurricane going down. The boy had pinpointed its whereabouts to a recovery team consisting of a couple of farmers, a butcher and an undertaker. They pulled at the twisted metal with a crowbar and bare hands, digging his slumped form free from its sinking cocoon and passing him from hand to hand like a message. When he regained consciousness wrapped in white linen sheets he had few visitors, and those that did come to see him didn't stay more than a few minutes. His temporary surrender to gravity was nothing special: after all, men were falling from the sky everywhere.

A month in hospital, another two convalescing, catching moments of angry sleep beneath the drone of Junkers or Heinkel engines. When he could walk with no more than the aid of a crutch he haunted RAF training tents and hangars, helping new recruits up the rungs of airmanship like a teacher easing wary five year olds up the steps of a playground slide. He stood at the front of the small corrugated-iron-roofed shed that served as a flight school, half leaning on his blackthorn walking cane, taking hours with the students over options that in the air would have to be weighed in seconds. By March 1941 he made the arrangements to try to get back into the air, but then a chance conversation in an officer's mess turned his head. He picked a familiar accent out of the general hubbub of knives and forks on tin plates. An adjutant from the New Zealand Expeditionary Force. A raise of the eyebrows and a smile, then a quiet word that the 28th Maori Battalion were in Egypt and rumoured to be heading for the Aegean. That night he lay on his bunk, looking up through a hole in the tent roof where faint stars drifted in the flapping canvas. At sunrise he swung his strengthening legs onto the wooden boards of the floor and pulled on his boots, pausing to lift a stray sprig of grass from the toe. Ten minutes later he stood in the CO's office. Within two weeks he was on a troopship.

He arrived in Greece among the reinforcements for the 2nd New Zealand Division, just at the moment they were being driven back into the sea. The Germans rolled down the Balkan peninsular like a railway wagon broken free from its coupling. Nothing could stop them. When the allies found they were backed only by the sea they assembled a hasty flotilla and, like a hundred armies before them, cut across the straits to the south.

Many of the Expeditionary Force had never seen action. It was a bullet-holed baptism. In the last week of April 1941 over 40,000 were evacuated to an island whose name meant little at the time outside of the ranks of scholars of antiquity – Crete.

For a few weeks they swam in the surf under spring sunshine, between unrolling coils of barbed wire and laying seedbeds of landmines. The German bombing was methodical, designed to squeeze the defenders out of their positions or to destroy the new landscape they had woven. It was designed to soften the soil for the real invasion.

When the first parachutes dotted the sky not only the New Zealanders, Australians, British and Greeks armed themselves, but the islanders as well. He saw young women and girls armed with rifles already ancient at Gallipoli. He saw a priest carrying a flintlock pistol standing at the door to a crumbling stone church;

an old woman attack a Luftwaffe paratrooper strolling through her garden, her gnarled hands holding only a frying pan.

On the first day German parachutes floated like leaves, some holed, some jerking with a sudden electricity as shots tore into the paratroopers from below. Some intact, but with a still-born figure spreadeagled beneath. Amid all the carnage, enough landed still alive to turn the olive groves to skeletons of fire. For a week the Luftwaffe flew in supplies and reinforcements unmolested by planeless Allies, the defence force crumpling under the weight of technology their own commanders couldn't get their hands on. In the end the defence collapsed, the defence force's resistance as fleeting as summer rain upon the parched soil. On the south coast, their last bulwark, their hierarchy issued orders from caves, every man's face burned khaki from falling dust and dirt shaken free by German artillery or Stukas' bombs.

When the borders of the military battle moved on, sweeping the destroyed landscape back behind it like enormous footprints, the villagers still fought on, rising with the night shadows and moving through the vineyards like a ghost army. Farmers and bakers. A postman, a stonemason, perhaps a carpenter. A woman might bid her husband a nervous adieu and an hour later an ammunition dump would erupt into fire, staining the summer dark. The next day, Germans would walk from house to house, shouting, guns waving like barbed wire in wind. A group of old men would be dragged from a cafe and casually beaten beneath the olive trees as if they were carpets clogged with dust. A group of women walking would be stopped, the shoulders torn from their dresses. If a dark stamp tarnished their skin – signifying the bruise from a rifle's recoil – they would be loaded into a truck and taken away or just shot where they stood.

It was a land where wars past and wars present layered over one another. Tanks replaced chariots, aeroplanes instead of arrows. General Freyberg had promised no retreat from Crete, so the rocks and stone ramparts and vineyards of the island became, for a few weeks, the centre of the war. An axle running between two wheels turning in opposite directions.

After Crete's western airfield at Maleme fell the New Zealanders had turned inland, towards the mountains. In official terms it was a rearguard action, but in reality they were running as fast as the terrain would allow. The Germans unleashed cloud after cloud of their armies onto the island's north side, spreading like a dust storm into the central highlands, choking the New Zealanders against the ocean. They were caught in sun-soaked canyons, they bled into the rutted tracks of donkey carts. There was fighting in doorways, in pigsties and creek beds. Bullets passed through bone or flesh and then through sheets hanging on clothes lines. Bodies burned in fields laced with dandelions. Exhaustion and dysentery claimed as many men as artillery did, sickness or gunfire stripped the flesh from their bodies by turns. Snipers' bullets found men's skulls as they squatted to shit diarrhoea into the dust.

At Sfakia on the south coast they huddled against the rocks, slept in caves, lay littered about beneath the trees, waiting for the ships to take them back to Egypt where they had begun with such fanfare only a few weeks before.

Then one morning a sharp conversation ensued on the waterfront as the horizon claimed its last boat. An officer turned to the assembled men and told them they could fall out and do as they wished until the Germans arrived. It was over.

Lieutenant Kingi Heremia raises his left forearm over his eyes, looking at the stitchline of hills against the cobalt sky. There is a drone of aeroplanes. Hundreds of heads turn in unison, scouting the sky to the north. By the time the first burst of machine-gun fire kicks up the stones at their feet, Kingi is already running towards a rocky overhang.

He heads up into the foothills, the waterfront obscured now by clouds of dust and smoke. Shouts echo off the rocks. He has a .303 rifle gripped in his hand, his service revolver in its holster banging against his ribcage.

No time to get bearings, he has to just keep climbing, the waterfront is now a shooting gallery for the Luftwaffe. Kingi knows this game well, though in another guise. Don't present a stationary target, make a decision on direction – any direction – just make it and do it. He presses himself into a small crevasse, signals to the others seeking shelter, directing those lying prone on open ground to trees, bushes, large boulders. Anything that hints at cover. He turns to his left, looking through a jittering spider's web where its maker works in unruffled diligence. Stepping from his hiding place just as a Messerschmitt finds a groove in the air above, bears down on him like a monstrous hawk. He dives to the ground, spitting out a mouthful of dirt, watching the bullets build a hedgerow of dust. Noticing only when he rises and his hand is soaked that he has been caught in the arm.

He rolls onto his back, takes his knife from his belt satchel, and tears a strip from his trouser leg. He raises the wrapped arm against the sun, his blinking eyes examining the path where the bullet went right through. He leans over, spits out a mouthful of dust, blades of grass. There's a shadow on the dirt. A soldier looms and squats against the hillside.

'You need to remember to duck,' says the soldier. 'That's where you went wrong.'

Kingi looks up. 'Now you tell me,' he says.

A hand, rough. A bricklayer's hand perhaps, drawing Kingi up onto his unsteady feet.

'Now that wasn't so hard, was it.'

'Hang on,' says Kingi. 'I'll shoot *you* then help you up and we can compare notes.'

'I'm starting to like you.'

'I wish the feeling was mutual.'

The Kiwi soldier eyes Kingi's water bottle. Kingi loosens the strap and hands the bottle to him. The soldier takes out the stopper and drinks. His helmet is pulled down over his forehead, masking his face. The sun finds only his jaw, a couple of drops of water on his chin. His open tunic is torn and faded, and beneath that he is bare-chested. The only halfway regimental thing about him is his boots, which appear new, hardly marked. He notices Kingi's glance at his footwear.

'They were well shod, those paratroopers,' he says. 'I'll give them that.'

Kingi takes a mouthful of water then replaces the stopper, watching the soldier all the while. He extends his good arm. 'Kingi Heremia.'

'Zeke.'

'Short and sweet.'

'Nice of you to say. I have a feeling the last bus has gone.' Kingi nods.

'Well,' says Zeke. 'I'm not spending the next few years learning German.'

'Nor me.'

They watch the sky for a moment, beginning to walk, then breaking into a run when wings drop down out of the clouds.

They move westward all day, from one sparse island of shelter to the next. In the night they hear the echo of voices skittering off the canyon walls, never knowing whether they are near or far. Even the wind shifts are tricky, bringing the sound of trucks they know can't be within miles, but silencing the path of a drover and his sheep a mere thirty yards beneath them on the bank of a stream.

They sleep a couple of hours each, spelling one another on makeshift guard duty. Kingi has the shivers from loss of blood. His arm is swollen, more numb than painful. Zeke crouches in the streambed, raising cupped handfuls of water over Kingi's wound, then pausing to drink. He fills Kingi's canteen. Kingi has given him the rifle but still carries the service revolver.

With the dawn the lead German ground troops appear, a small squad of perhaps a half dozen, voices like the cutting of knives. The two hunted men ease down behind the low wall, wait for the voices to fade.

They spend the day in a small cave cut into the hillside. The landscape is too filled with Wehrmacht to risk moving. With the dark they begin to head west again. Zeke vanishes into a grove, returns with a pocketful of figs. At dawn they crest a hill, staying low so they're not silhouetted against the skyline by the new light. Below and to the west is a village. There are a few sleepy houses, hints of candlelight in a couple of windows, the tinkling of a goat's bell. A man emerges from an outhouse, lifting his suspenders over his shoulders. They skirt the village, moving above a winding road to where the canyon walls steepen. Below them rows of vines hug the hillside, their tendrils stretching to the edge of the visible. A jumble of ancient stone buildings. Looks like an old villa, perhaps a vineyard.

'Wonder if the restaurant's open,' says Zeke.

'You read my mind.'

They cross the road and move down the slope. There is no sign of life. No sound save the first calls of the birds, an occasional rooster. They walk around the exterior wall, seeking an entrance. Zeke tries a couple of ground-level doors, turns to shake his head. Kingi moves towards the house's west wall, finding a cobbled path, staying against the wall, flaking mortar crumbling into his hair. He stays within the grasp of the shadows: the light is no friend to the hunted. A stone path leads to an arch, shadows beyond. He stops, listening to a sudden wave of melody, drinking it in. He opens his eyes when he realises it is a woman singing.

He moves towards its source, like Theseus following his thread. Disoriented now, fatigued, weak from blood loss. He doesn't know nor care. Here, in this desert of dust and guns, he can taste an oasis of music.

He claws his way along the edge of the stone wall, steps out of the shadows and into a smaller courtyard where a woman looks up from where she treads in a grape barrel, not missing a note in her song. Her indigo eyes watch him, shadowing his movements.

He raises his good arm.

'I'm not German,' he says.

She stares.

'Anglos,' he says.

She glances at the arm he holds cradled in the other. She lifts a hand, runs it across her forehead, grape juice dripping onto her cheekbones.

'I speak English,' she says.

'Ah, good. Please don't be afraid.'

Her eyes widen and she smiles, her chin rising in defiance. She reaches down into the barrel, lifts a rope from a peg, takes an old rifle into her hands and turns its muzzle towards him.

'I think it is *you* that should be afraid,' she says.

She wipes her grape-stained forehead with the back of her wrist, keeping her rifle steady with other arm, the stock braced against her hips. Her dress is soaked, as if she has stepped from a sweet-scented sea. The faint swirling of the juice beneath her feet is the only sound.

'I'm not afraid,' he says.

'Yes you are,' she says. 'Yes, I think you are.

'I must compliment you on your English. Where did you learn?'

'America.'

'Good God. Learning to speak English in America. Is that not an oxymoron?'

She tilts her head. 'I don't understand,' she says.

'A joke, and a rather feeble one at that. How long did you live in America?'

'Seven years.'

She reaches to take the rifle in both hands. 'I should have shot you by now,' she says.

'Yes, you should have. Why haven't you?'

'I'm not sure. Why are you so dark?'

'Dark?'

'Your skin. The English are not dark.'

'Ah. I'm not English. I'm a New Zealander. A Māori.'

'So why are *you* fighting the Germans?'

'I tend to regard those who take pot shots at me as the enemy.'

They stare. She glances either side of him, perhaps studying the distance between him and the doorway, between the two of them.

'So why have you come into my vineyard?' she says.

'Thought you might rustle up some tea and toast for us. At what point did you decide not to shoot me?'

'You're assuming I have?'

The gaps between her eyelids narrow.

'Us?' she says.

Kingi nods towards the rear alcove where Zeke leans against the edge of the opening.

'Someone mention tea and toast?' he says.

She glances half over her shoulder, at the haze of Zeke's shadow on the wall. Her rifle is still raised towards Kingi.

'If you've come here to steal —'

'We haven't,' says Kingi.

'I could still shoot you,' says the woman, looking back at Kingi.

'Go ahead,' says Zeke.

'Thank you, Zeke,' says Kingi.

'I don't think he is your friend,' says the woman.

'Put the rifle down, Zeke,' says Kingi.

'It'll be your head on the block if she shoots first,' says Zeke.

'Put the rifle down.'

Zeke lowers the rifle and leans it up against the wall. The woman turns to him for the first time, then lowers her own rifle and steps out up out of the barrel. She looks back at Kingi.

'I shall look at that arm,' she says.

They sit at a wooden table. A jug sits boiling over a wood range. Her name is Alissandra. She bathes Kingi's wound first with water, then with iodine. He widens his eyes, exhales in a hiss. She squints at him, biting her lower lip. Zeke begins to laugh.

'I'm glad someone's enjoying this,' says Kingi.

Ointment for his wound, then tea, vegetable soup, and bread seasoned with oreganum and turmeric for their hunger. She sits tilting her head from side to side as they speak, perhaps seeking some other angle into them, searching for a three-dimensional drawing of these strangers and the altering landscape they bring. Kingi smiles, sensing her attempt to disentangle some sense of their character from the way they move, rather than their words. It is a habit he himself has picked up – the sine qua non of survival in the air – to take nothing at face value; to always look for the shadows where danger might prowl, half hidden; to look for any hint of thought given away by the eyes, or move-ments – be they of fingers or wing tips. She leads them upstairs to a long corridor where a few small rooms hover in half darkness. 'These were my brothers' rooms,' she says and leaves. Kingi sits in the window alcove, lifting the curtain a couple of inches and looking at a thin sliver of the valley. Zeke appears in the doorway.

'Not bad,' he says. 'Not bad at all.'

'The accommodation or our hostess?' says Kingi.

'Take your pick,' says Zeke. 'Maybe I will.'

Kingi turns to him. 'I told her we didn't come here to take anything,' he says.

'When did you become CO?'

Kingi lets the curtain fall closed. 'Am I going to regret giving you that rifle?' he says.

'Am I going to regret dragging you out of the dirt?'

Kingi wakes to music, flexes the fingers of his wounded arm, still feeling like he has sandpaper trapped in his veins. He listens to Alissandra's voice, as he had in the courtyard, recognising the tune but not the words. It's Gershwin, 'Summertime'. He sits up, straining to grasp the words, smiling when he realises she is singing it in Greek.

In the kitchen she looks up from the pot she is stirring, then turns her back to him to reach for some sprigs of wild garlic on the bench. Her long hair is loose now, over her shoulders and down past her waist. He pauses, watching it, then looks up through the window at the silhouettes of the cypresses against the dusk.

They eat at the kitchen table. Zeke stands a couple of times to go to the jug and pour some more hot water into the thick, black coffee.

'Are you here alone?' he says.

'I was,' says Alissandra.

'We should go,' says Kingi.

'Let me finish me bloody supper,' says Zeke.

'After that, we should go,' says Kingi.

'Should you?' says Alissandra.

'The Germans will come looking.'

'Are you that special?'

He looks across the table at her. There's a stillness, a straightness in the line of her shoulders. She places her elbow on the table, rests her chin in her palm. A grain of challenge is in her dark eyes.

'We'll go when it gets darker,' he says. 'Or tomorrow.'

She shrugs. 'You will or you won't,' she says.

Kingi leans back in his chair. 'When the Germans come,' he says. 'What will you do?'

'Do?'

'Will you fight them?' he says. 'That old rifle won't put up much resistance.'

'I'm not leaving. It is *you* that is leaving. Remember?'

Zeke stands and walks to the range and opens the door. Its fire is the only light in the room. He lifts another log from the pile and pushes it inside. It hisses, sparks dancing against his shadowed skin.

'You might have to,' says Kingi. 'We hear … things.'

'Things?'

'About Greece. The Germans.'

'I told you. I'm not leaving.'

'Perhaps the choice isn't yours.'

'Leave the lady alone,' says Zeke. 'It's her flamin' homestead.'

'I left Kriti for America,' says Alissandra. 'Then I left America for Kriti. I have done all the leaving I intend to.'

The night is warm for May. Kingi stands from the bed and walks down the hall to where Zeke's bed lies empty. There's no sound from where Alissandra sleeps down the hall. He goes back into his room, climbs out the small window and moves across the tiles of the rooftop. He wears just his shorts, his braces loose about his waist. The distant ocean lies silver-grey and still. He walks to the edge of the tiles, where the roofs of the smaller buildings form a series of steps to the dirt. He moves with deliberation, aware of his incomplete balance with his left arm in a sling. In a few minutes he is in the vineyard.

He moves down the slope, down through the rows of vines until he stands at the banks of a small stream. He undoes the buckle and steps out of his shorts and underwear and – holding his wounded arm raised – slips between the river's sheets.

He lies back in the water, hearing the buzz of distant aeroplanes. Gathering in Iraklion, in Suda perhaps, or at the airport in Maleme that was theirs ten days ago. Since he landed in Greece all they have done is retreat. At this rate he will be back home in a couple of weeks. Unlikely. Somewhere rather less hospitable perhaps.

There is a swish of sound in the reeds on the riverbank. He sinks back into the river, even his wounded wing, fingers tingling and not from the cool of the stream.

He watches the faint stains of night shadows on the water. In the retreat from Greece they had hidden in the hills like some lost tribe. The sound of shooting filled the valleys, jolting sleepers and dreamers to attention. He had sat on a rock reef beneath a stand of silver birches with the leaves' shadows masking his face. He couldn't help thinking of his own people, Te Aupōuri. He had become a rarity among them, a scholar, denizen of university courtyards. The taste of pipi and watercress was drowned by sauvignon and mint cake. But for all that he was still hiding from men who would burn his brown skin from his body and never know nor care who he was.

'You shouldn't be out here,' says her voice.

He blinks a touch of water from his eyes.

'Should you?' he says.

'It is my stream,' she says.

He lies, still, aware now of the deflection of his breathing back off the water, warm against the sunburned skin of his cheeks.

'We used to swim in this stream when we were children,' she says.

'Sounds like home.'

'Home.'

The whisper of her footfalls on grass already wet with dew. He thinks for a moment to call after her, but lets his voice vanish, with the rest of him, deep into the water.

In the morning he walks through the house, touching open doors with his fingertips. In a small room he finds a tub and a pail of water. He lifts off his singlet and bends over the tub, dipping his hands into the water then lifting them against his cheeks. He slaps a few handfuls of water against his bare chest, leaving his palms against his skin, feeling the water squeeze out and run down his abdomen. When he glances to his right she is standing framed in the doorway, a bunch of herbs held in the crook of her arm. She watches him for a moment then steps into the room, opens a cupboard on the wall, lifts out a cake of soap and extends her hand towards him, the soap in her open palm. He takes it from her, letting his fingers linger over hers without touching. She turns and leaves. He soaps his hands and runs them over his chest, up through his hair.

Zeke is sitting at the table in the kitchen, sipping from a cup. 'Finally,' he says.

'Beauty sleep,' says Kingi.

'Not surprised. Going for midnight swims and all.'

'Where were you?'

'About.'

'What did you do in peacetime, Zeke?'

'Peacetime?'

Kingi walks to the open back door, looks out to the alcove that leads to the hidden courtyard. He moves to each side of the door, checking the oak and chestnut trees for any sign of movement, then moves across the cobbles.

She is shadowed beneath the arch, treading grapes in the vat. There is a cadence in each lilt of her hips, echoed all the way to where her legs vanish in the grape juice. A rhyme, from shoulder to shin.

A shimmer of her eyelids. He waits for her stare to rise but it doesn't, and he realises he is not a part of this moment. He can only guess at what she sees, this lone tenant of a sanctuary of sweet-scented vines balanced on a precipice of violence. He looks away. The silence in her statued face is too intimate for his intrusion. He leaves, turning back only when a sudden rumble of artillery circles the far end of the valley. She glances up, away from him, towards the hills, the greying sky telling them both at the same time that it is not guns, but thunder.

When the first scent of rain hits her she looks up at him at last, her background painted in sheets of water and he sees now – for the first time since he arrived – she is smiling.

In the evening, she taps on his door. He is sitting in the dim light, perched in the window alcove looking out over the valley.

'Yes?'

'Can I come in?'

'Yes, of course.'

She steps inside, just another shadow in the lightless room. 'Your friend has gone off again,' she says.

'Seems to be in his blood.'

'I hope he will not bring attention.'

'I wager he's well versed in keeping incognito.'

She steps towards him. Everything in the room that isn't her, disappearing. There is warmth on his skin, not from the night air. He turns back to the valley.

'You are wishing you were …?'

'Home?' he says.

He taps a fingernail against the glass.

'Yes, I suppose so,' she says. 'Home.'

'No, it's not that,' says Kingi. 'In a way I wish "home" was here. That civilisation could be superimposed over all this.'

'Civilisation? You are in one of the oldest civilisations in the world.'

He smiles. 'Ah, touché,' he says. 'And I venture our lot have brought something less to these islands now.'

'You didn't make the Germans come here. No more than I did.'

'Didn't we. We're all just little boys with guns. Does it matter what colour cloth our uniforms are woven from?'

'I think that might be too big a battle for one man with a wounded arm to fight.'

'Touché again. You are perceptive. Where were you when I was losing the Cambridge–Oxford debate?'

A pause, then, 'Are you making a joke of me?' she says.

'No,' he says. 'Quite the opposite.'

She steps to the alcove on the far wall, leaning back into the shadows. Her voice comes from the dark. 'Your friend reminds me of many of the men I have grown up with. Looking at you from the corner of his eyes, as if he is deciding whether to wink at you or shoot you.'

'And me, who do I remind you of?'

'No one. No. I don't think of anyone.'

'Is that a good thing or a bad thing?'

'Does it have to be either? Or can it be both?'

Kingi smiles, then stops, his body's grip at the window suddenly feeling tenuous. She leans forward, into the last faint light, a slight smirk on her face, as if sensing his discomfort.

'Be careful,' she says. 'It's a long way to fall.'

'Don't worry,' he says. 'I've fallen further.'

In the night he rises and walks down the stairs to the kitchen where an inking of moonlight seeps in through the windows. He raises his good arm into its path, his skin a paler shade of shadow. He opens the door and steps onto the cobbles.

Zeke sits against the inner wall of the archway, smoking a cigarette.

'Another midnight walk,' says Zeke.

'Speak for yourself.'

'I was thinking of checking the lay of the land. Care to join me?'

They skirt the edge of the road, the bushes, keeping out of the moon's sight, cutting beneath the overhangs of the olive trees. There is no movement in the village. They take to the scrub-covered hills, in an hour coming upon a larger town sitting silent in the crook of a valley. They peer down at the empty lanes then negotiate a precarious stone wall and drop into a dusty lane. Zeke waves a hand and Kingi steps back into the shade of a birch.

There is a staff car in the town square, a couple of motorcycles on their stands. A lone German stands in a doorway, smoking a cigarette. He reaches to shake some ash from the cigarette's tip, leans back against the door jamb.

There are some muffled voices from within, one rising. Then a gunshot.

Kingi and Zeke move back through the shrubs and up into the trees of the hillside and away.

They sit in the kitchen sipping strong coffee. Alissandra enters from the yard, carrying a small ceramic pot with some small shoots poking over the rim.

'Where did you go?' she says to Kingi.

'Go?'

'Last night.'

'Tumbled,' says Zeke. He looks up at Alissandra. 'He led me astray again,' he says.

'We did some reconnaissance,' says Kingi. 'Habitual for us pilots.'

Zeke turns to him. 'You're a pilot?' he says.

'Yes,' says Kingi.

'You were flying a bit low when I found you,' says Zeke.

'I transferred out.'

'Who were you with?'

'The RAF.'

'Were you in that business last year?'

'Yes.'

'Gawd. A genuine hero in our midst.'

Zeke looks up at Alissandra. 'Another coffee for the fly boy,' he says. 'If you please, Madame.'

She pulls out a chair. 'What were you looking for last night?' she says.

'Just the lay of the land,' says Zeke. 'Don't appear to be any Jerries in the village. But there are a few in the town.'

'Which town?' says Alissandra.

'To the east,' says Zeke, 'three or four miles.'

'Elysse,' says Alissandra.

'Well, we're all behind the lines now,' says Kingi.

'We?' says Alissandra.

'I'd guess the whole island's fallen,' says Zeke. 'We're stuck. Might as well be in Hitler's local watering hole. Now *there's* a good idea.'

Alissandra narrows her eyes. 'I'm not sure I —'

'He's rambling,' says Kingi.

Alissandra leans back, brushes traces of her hair back away from her eyes. 'My whole family left for America. Except for my father. My mother died when I was a child. I have four brothers and they all live in New York. Only I came back, when my father was ill. Dying. Then it was just me.'

The men stare.

'It's been a long time since I was a "we",' says Alissandra.

They sit eating, no one speaking, then, 'If you are going to go out walking,' says Alissandra, 'you will have to get rid of those uniforms.'

She goes to the stairs and looks back at them. They follow her to the large room at the end of the hall. She opens the door and goes to the window and closes the curtains to the daylight.

'In the wardrobe,' she says. 'I never got around to throwing them out.'

Zeke opens the wardrobe. Shirts, a vest, a leather jacket. A few pairs of trousers sitting folded on a shelf. Old but well aired.

'My father's,' says Alissandra.

'You sure about this?' says Kingi.

She nods.

After dinner they sit at the table, the day retreating around them. No one rises to light a candle. Alissandra raises the ceramic coffee pot and pours Zeke a cup.

'Ah, you're an angel,' he says.

'Wait until you taste the coffee,' she says. 'Those were the beans I was going to throw away yesterday that I forgot to throw away the day before.' She toys with the handle of her cup, then looks up at Kingi. 'And you,' she says. 'What will you do, when this is over?'

'Go back to my schematics, I expect.'

She sips from her cup. 'None of my brothers wish to return from America,' she says. 'I have written to them, but nothing.'

'How long have you been running it alone?' says Kingi.

'I had two helpers, local men. But they joined up with the Partisans when the fighting in Greece began. Your people will send more soldiers, to run the Germans away?'

The two men look at each other. Neither answers the question.

Kingi rises in the pre-dawn darkness and walks to the shuttered window, his frame cloaked in his new Cretan garb. He dips his good hand into the water bowl Alissandra has left for him, raising his wet fingers to his face. He flexes his injured arm. He has more control over his grip now.

To reach freedom they'd have to first reach the sea and to reach the sea they'd have to walk through the German army. He is now an island in another island within an ocean of fighting. If they leave the vineyard he might find only a bullet or the tip of a bayonet. If they stay they endanger her, this woman who brings water for his broken flesh, her dead father's clothes for them to wear.

He uses his strong arm to lever himself onto the ledge and climbs onto the freedom of the roof, conscious, in these last few days, of the nakedness of daylight. How war, even in its stillest moments, reconstructs reality, turning the sun into a searchlight. He wonders if he will ever again be able to take a few steps in it without pausing to scout the horizon or glance over his shoulder.

But with the darkness comes a sense of mooring ropes cut, and he comes alive on its current. He picks his way across the tiles, bare feet delicate against the terracotta, his internal gyroscope keeping him in balance. He could close his eyes now and spread his wings and be back in a heartbeat over English pasture, performing his deadly ballet in the sky, that pas de deux with ammunition. He stands, commanding his squadron of roof tiles, no scent of oil or benzene, only the caress of the wind.

He drops to the next ledge, then into the courtyard, stopping at the border of light from the kitchen door. Her outline is etched within the frame. With the sound of his feet on the cobbles she turns.

'I thought you were still asleep,' she says.

'I was.'

'You should be more careful. Your arm.'

'It's still attached.'

She glances down at his bare feet and he is conscious then that beneath her long skirt, hers are bare also. They stand in silence, neither seeming to want to take the gamble to speak next. She lifts the candle in its cup from the bench and walks out into the passage. He pauses, then follows the sound of her footsteps.

She moves into a large room with a tapestry on the walls and goes to the grey stone fireplace. An ornate silver candlestick sits on the heavy wooden mantle over the opening. She places her candle within it and walks on, announcing the outline of shapes in the room. A leather settee appears then vanishes and a painting of a Greek man in full national dress comes into view. Defiance is etched into the man's eyes and his shoulders are straight.

'My grandfather,' she says as she passes.

They move on through the house, her candlelight ushering ornate canvasses from the dark corners, moments of her history appearing like painted thespians, making a single bow then slipping behind a curtain. He walks behind her, his toes at the edge of the light's tide.

He senses a sanctuary in these walls: not the transient guard of guns or armies, but of stone, of masonry. Ceilings that have watched over centuries. And in that moment he senses generations; their sum total now embodied in the singular symmetry of a barefoot woman bearing a candle through the shadows. She stops, turns to him, the flame a teardrop glistening above her hand.

'Is it true,' she says, 'that the Germans are killing people just because they are Jews?'

'It has been said. They're killing people just because they're in the way. That much I know.'

A pause.

'Are you Jewish?' he says.

'No. Am I in the way?'

He stiffens. 'When the soldiers come,' he says, 'I'll stay with you.'

She glances into the darkness beside him.

'Don't make me any promises,' she says. 'You don't have to stay. Not for me.'

'Then I'll do it for me. I need to promise something to someone. For my sake.'

She shifts her bare feet on the stone floor, the candle flame twisting with her movements.

'It always seemed so simple from the air,' he says. He looks down at the flame. 'We share one thing,' he says. '*My* people have also died in these hills.'

'And are you guilty that you are alive?'

'Ah, I've been guilty of that for a long time.'

She stares, perhaps waiting for some further joust, but he does not speak again. He raises his hand to his lips, wets a forefinger and thumb, clasps them over the flame, and the light goes out.

The Germans appear mid-morning, not even bothering with stealth. A couple of trucks and motorcycles on the road at the foot of the vineyard, perhaps two dozen soldiers. Kingi sees them from a second-story window as he lifts a razor to his cheek. They have, at best, five minutes. He has not seen Zeke since breakfast. He puts the razor in his tunic pocket and tips the water out the window onto the grass. He takes the revolver in its holster and his officer's belt with the ammunition hidden beneath the mattress and loads cartridges in all the chambers as he walks down the hall. Alissandra appears at the head of the stairs with her old rifle. He holsters the revolver and takes the rifle from her. She grips her hands over his, pins him with her stare.

'Come with me.'

She leads him into the kitchen, into the walk-in pantry. She lifts a couple of spice jars off the shelf and puts them on the bench then lifts away a small panel and a handle appears. She pulls it and the shelf and then the whole back wall begins to move.

'Good grief,' says Kingi.

It is an alcove, a passageway beyond. She replaces the panel and jars and steps into the passage. Kingi draws the shelf and wall back into place.

There is no light and no candle to guide her. She takes his hand and moves down the passage. They are close to the left-hand wall. She uses its solidity to maintain her bearings. He does the same and they drift down this lightless river, their bodies nudging against the stone. They are about twenty yards into the passage when the crunch of boots sounds above them.

He feels the wall draw away, her hand now the only messenger. He is islanded, as if in an aeroplane, immune to all but gravity. But this time he has a co-conspirator, he who normally flies alone. He feels her stop and he stands, transfixed by the sudden silence. It isn't until her breath touches his cheeks that he realises she has turned to face him.

She moves her arms down the length of his body, guiding him down, the wall cold against his back. The muffled echoes of footsteps, voices, are all around them. She slips the rifle from his fingers and he hears the safety catch click. He removes the revolver from the holster and lays it in his lap, a finger poised above the trigger.

The clatter of boots echoes from room to room, but losing urgency. He is not aware in any way of the size of this tunnel. The far wall could be six feet away or a hundred. She could whisper that there are another dozen people sitting against the wall opposite and he cannot dismiss the possibility, such is the darkness.

She shifts against him, and he focuses on listening to the ebb and flow of her breaths, trying to read them, know them, as he would his altimeter.

He feels her fumble for the rifle and reaches for her hand, twines his fingers into hers. A clasp of recognition in return. Her cheek touches against his shoulder and her fingers flex against the skin of his palm, the gentle pulse of waves at dusk. He tilts his chin into her hair, closing his eyes within it. Discovering it from scent and sense alone. Perhaps leaving some sense of him, of this moment, like tracks in sand, smoke spoors in sky. All the ground and air he has covered, not an inch of it as precious to him right now as this stranger's hair. She he knows only by glances, her gossamer trails of grape juice on the cobbles of the courtyard. He thinks of all the aeroplanes his fingers have sent spiralling into the ocean or farmers' fields somewhere. Of the men he had breakfasted with, played cricket with on the aerodrome lawn. Smoking woodbines in the dawn light with companions who would be ashes by nightfall.

He thinks of the women he lay with in London or in the villages bordering the airfields. Investing only a few captured moments, a few coins from his pocket for their drinks, but never anything of his self. Or theirs. Love among the air raids. Love, such a transparent word, a naked word, and he was never transparent in love. His body was, his skin against their skin, but nothing of his core was ever naked; it was always hidden by the shell he wove about himself like the frames of his aeroplanes. The sudden release of bullets or his seed perhaps no more than a muscle reaction. His lovers knew no more of his heart than the men he had gunned down from the glare of the sun.

He slips his face down against her cheek then suddenly turns away, over his own chest. Hoping that in the moment before he moved she didn't feel the touch of wetness on her skin.

There is no kick at the hidden doorway. No sudden burst of light or angry voices. The bootsteps fade. They wait until it stretches for an hour, then two. Then they stand and she lets go of his fingers, and they walk back through the darkness.

At twilight Alissandra sits on the wall at the edge of the small courtyard, her feet dangling over the drop. Kingi walks beneath the arch, still wearing the holstered revolver. He can see the opening at the far end, to the valley below. See the outline of her back against the light, the confetti of trees beyond. He steps past the grape barrel, stands just beyond the reach of the sunlight.

'Why weren't you afraid?' she says without turning.

He doesn't answer.

'Are you never afraid?' she says.

'Yes. But I stopped.'

'When?'

'There was a time, when I was going up every day and not knowing if I'd come down, that I suppose I just ceased to care.'

'That is what you want? Not to care?'

'I don't know.'

'You must.'

'Must I?'

She turns and looks up at him, then looks away.

'I will not play games,' she says.

He shifts his position, still standing within the portico, camouflaged from the daylight.

'It seems you do not wish me to ask any more such questions,' she says.

'It's not that.'

'Then what is it?'

'I just don't have any answers for you.'

A rustle of movement on the stones. Kingi takes the revolver, turns with it pointing into the archway behind him, clicking off the safety just as Zeke steps through the aperture.

'Crikey!' says Zeke. 'Don't shoot, cowboy.'

'Sorry,' says Kingi. 'Had a bit of fun earlier.'

'A visit?'

'Yes.'

'Saw them hanging round,' says Zeke. 'Going from house to house. A truck passed not twenty yards from me.'

Alissandra turns, her eyes wide.

'The village?' she says. 'What happened?'

'They stopped to buy apples.'

'You're joking,' says Kingi.

'Scouts honour,' says Zeke. 'Apples from a roadside stall. A dozen soldiers lolling about, armed to the eyeballs with MP38s. Standing there chomping on apples while the young fella selling them was singin' out for his mum to bring more.'

Zeke leans against the grape barrel, pulls out his tobacco pouch. 'Hang about,' he says. He glances at Kingi then looks to Alissandra. 'How did you explain his ugly face to Fritz?'

'We made ourselves scarce,' says Kingi.

'Alone or together?'

'I suppose we were together?'

'Really?'

'Ezekiel.'

Zeke wets his cigarette paper, clasps the two sides together around the stalk of tobacco.

'Ezekiel,' says Kingi. 'Smirking is against the Geneva Convention.'

Kingi comes from the slope above the main house, carrying an armful of kindling. The holster is shunted around to his back. He pushes at the kitchen door with his boot. He lays the wood down on the stone floor next to the range then lifts half of it again and walks down the hall to the library. He eases the stash into a metal drum next to the huge slate fireplace then stands brushing his hands above the ashpan on the hearth. He pauses, leaning against the bookcase. There's something he hadn't noticed before, at one end of the bookcase: a Box Brownie camera. He walks to it, picks it up and peers down into the tiny window, catching echoes of the various shapes in the room. A shadow passes the doorway. He calls out. Alissandra leans through the frame. When she sees the camera she raises her hand in front of her face.

'No! I never look well in photographs.'

'Look well?' says Kingi, smiling.

'You know what I mean.'

She backs out through the door.

He follows her, still holding the camera, steering her through the kitchen and out into the light of the courtyard, just as Zeke appears on the path from the vegetable garden.

'She doesn't seem too keen, mate,' he says.

'Just one?' says Kingi.

'No,' says Alissandra. 'I don't like my photographs.'

'Tell you what,' says Zeke, hand reaching for the camera, 'I'll take one of the both of you. Fly Boy here can keep you company. Can't say fairer than that. You can save it for posterior.'

Alissandra eyes him. She turns to Kingi.

'Alright,' she says.

Kingi shrugs. He walks over next to her, backing almost beneath the arch.

'Closer,' said Zeke. 'That's it. That's … got it.'

'I think I blinked,' says Kingi.

Kingi steps down from the Tiger Moth and walks down the sand, flicking his torch into life. In the other hand he holds a photograph, its weathered face soft against the skin of his palm. He sits among the driftwood and spreads it against his knee.

He has carried it for almost fifty years, the white borders dulling to twilight. But her face hasn't paled. If anything it has purified with the years, distilled itself from the fading parchment like rainwater from a grey sky.

He puts the torch between his teeth, pushes the photograph as flat as its ancient skin will allow. A man and a woman beneath an arch. The woman with a rueful smile, the man's eyes caught in a blink. A blink that has lasted half a century.

Smoke trails in the Cretan sky. Kingi and Zeke laze in a stand of chestnut trees, their backs up against trunks, their weapons beside them. Kingi eyes movement through the leaves. The transport planes are now a constant at the airfield at Maleme, lumbering in off the sea to dip behind the spine of hills.

Behind them the mountains rise stark against the cloudless sky. He looks east to where the orange-tiled roofs of the village sit nestled in the trees. The church commands the highest aspect, its dome like a rising sun. Beyond that a green hill hovers, topped with a stand of pines. Beyond that, the mountains themselves, their higher slopes a speckled grey beneath the deep blue. Kingi glances over at Zeke, snoozing beneath his hat. He lifts a fallen twig and flicks it at him. No sign of movement.

There must be other New Zealanders in these hills, future exhibits in this archaeologist's Pandora's Box. He closes his eyes and they come to him: exhausted, shambling men, scuffing the stones with their boots, hands held high. Hungry, ragged. Stumbling through the mountain tracks at gunpoint. Closing their eyes against the shadows of barbed wire on their skin.

'They can look after themselves,' says Zeke.

'Ah, Sleeping Beauty wakes.'

Zeke sits up. 'They don't need you fretting over them.'

'Is mind reading among your many talents?' says Kingi.

'Afraid that's a military secret.'

Kingi lifts a pebble, flicks it in Zeke's direction. Zeke leans away, watching it fly past.

'Tsk tsk,' he says.

'So what am I thinking now?' says Kingi.

'A very large, very cold beer.'

'One out of two, not bad.'

'Alright then … our hostess.'

'Who said you get another guess?'

Zeke rises to a crouch, looking down into the valley.

'Starting to feel like three's a crowd,' he says. 'Way she looks at you.'

Kingi doesn't answer.

'It's that dickey arm that did it,' says Zeke. 'Master stroke, getting yourself winged like that. Works every time – the wounded warrior. Should've thought of it meself.' Zeke reaches into the pocket of his shorts, lifts out his tobacco. 'If the Huns catch us here,' he says, 'chances are they'll shoot her too.'

'And the good news?'

'There isn't any. Good news died September third, nineteen thirty-nine.'

'If you get any more perceptive I'll shoot you myself.'

'Fly Boy, you wouldn't know which end of the rifle to shoot with.'

'I'm a fast learner.'

'Fritz will be back,' says Zeke. 'You know that.'

Kingi nods.

A leaf crackles on the slope behind them. Both men shift behind the trunks, weapons drawn, relaxing when Alissandra whistles. Kingi stands from behind the tree.

'Talk, talk, talk,' she says. 'Typical men.'

'I've always fancied myself the strong, silent type,' says Zeke.

'You've always fancied yourself, full stop,' says Kingi.

'All my life,' says Alissandra, 'listening to men go on and on and on. And the more wine, the more words. And the more words – the less sense.'

'Blame him,' says Kingi. 'I was just sitting here minding my own business.'

Zeke stands and dusts off his trousers. 'That's it,' he says. 'I'm going hunting for that beer.'

Kingi boils the kettle on the stove and tips the hot water into the basin. He throws Zeke a tea towel. When they've finished Zeke goes outside, under the archway to light a cigarette. Kingi walks down the passage from the library, pausing when he hears a soft, hummed refrain of 'Ol' Man River' coming from the doorway to the cask room. Alissandra is standing before a cask taller than she is. A candle burns on a ledge above her. Her eyes are fixed on a thin tube of glass with stoppers in each end, a ribbon of wine held in equilibrium between her fingertips. She lifts one hand, then the other, the liquid slipping from side to side like mercury. Kingi leans against another cask, watching her, the dark plum of her dress echoed in the wine. Liquid and lady resonate with the intimacy of lovers.

For a moment Kingi thinks of something jocular to say, but lets it pass, realising that at this moment he could produce a rabbit from a hat, do handstands on a unicycle and Alissandra would not notice him, such is her communion with the figure in the glass. She raises both hands now, an arch, perhaps a rainbow. All her movements halt at the arch's apogee. And for a moment the war and the world it profanes cease to exist for her. For him. A woman and her tiny river of wine. A man standing in the shadows, realising there is nothing he wouldn't give for a passage across that river.

He turns and walks back up the stone stairs, pausing when the smell of Zeke's cigarette smoke reaches him.

'Mind how you go there, Fly Boy,' says Zeke. 'If you leave her in misery I *will* knock your block off.'

'And I would deserve it.'

'If I thought you were joking, I'd do it right now.'

'Is this about the time you *do* regret pulling me out of the dust?'

Zeke drops his cigarette butt on the stone floor, crushes it with his German boots. 'I'll let you know,' he says.

In the late evening Kingi stands over the stove, spooning some slices of steaming marrow from the pot onto three plates. He wraps his hand in the tea towel and takes the handle of a pan, sifting waves of rice frying in olive oil. A shuffle of footsteps in the courtyard. He lifts the edge of his vest, raising the revolver from the holster beneath it. He steps back through the doorway leading to the hall, just as Zeke appears behind him with the rifle. A gruff voice from outside, calling Alissandra by name. She pushes past the two men and goes to the door, motioning them to stay where they are. She turns the handle.

'Konstantis,' she says through the opening. 'Theos.'

She glances back into the kitchen.

'Friends of my father,' she says.

A brief conversation in Greek, still at the door opening. A silence, then Alissandra nods and draws the door open to let the two men in. Both are middle aged with grizzled chins that jut forward. Kingi reaches to shake hands. The taller of the two, Theos, regards him with a smiling disdain. Both are garbed in loose shirts and woollen vests and have the robustness of farmers.

'Englezakia?' says Konstantis.

'Not bloody likely,' says Zeke, stepping from the doorway. 'If you scout yourself an Englishman on this island tell him he can salute my colonial backside. Leaving us in the lurch.'

'Now, now, Zeke,' says Kingi.

Konstantis prompts Alissandra to translate Zeke's words which she does. The two visitors stand puzzled, then burst into laughter. Suddenly their whole posture changes and they begin shaking the two New Zealanders' hands with vigour. Konstantis produces a carafe from somewhere about his person and lifts off the stopper and offers it to Kingi.

'Now we're getting somewhere,' says Zeke.

Alissandra smiles.

'They know that if they bring something for me to drink then I'll give them a bottle from the cellar when they go.'

'Bush commerce at its finest,' says Zeke, reaching for the carafe. 'Thank them on our behalf, will you.'

'You won't thank me when you've tasted that,' says Alissandra, making a face.

'Missus, you'd be amazed what I've drunk,' says Zeke.

The frying pan has begun to smoke, so Kingi lifts it off the heat and turns the rice over with a fork. Alissandra takes two more plates from the shelf and the meal is divided between five. They all sit at the table, the two men speaking to Alissandra between mouthfuls, and she translating back and forth. Where is New Zealand? Are there more soldiers in the hills? When is the invasion force coming to take back the island? Theos speaks of a makeshift prison camp in Galatas, of columns of men marching across the mountains to Suda. There is a short-wave radio in the village and the men sometimes sit in the café and listen to the broadcasts from the BBC. There is talk of submarines sited off the coast, of British aeroplanes coming and going in the night.

'Submarines?' says Zeke. 'Strewth. Got your water wings with you there, Fly Boy?'

Kingi grins.

'Germans have been seen only sometimes,' says Alissandra, translating the men's conversation.

'Are they looking for escapees?' says Kingi.

'Yes,' says Alissandra.

Theos raises his arms, forming them into an imaginary rifle. He aims it around the room.

'Phut, phut phut,' he says.

'That one came through loud and clear,' says Zeke.

After an hour's talking and drinking the two Cretan men leave, Theos tarrying by the door until ushered out with a tap of Alissandra's foot.

'That chap seemed to wish to stay a while longer,' says Kingi.

'He wanted to stay, to protect me,' says Alissandra.

'The cheek!' says Zeke. 'You're safe with us.'

'It is you two he wanted to protect me from,' says Alissandra.

Kingi's eyes bulge in mock horror. 'I really don't know what to say,' he says. 'They have impugned my honour as a gentleman.'

'Oh, sod off,' says Zeke.

The next day is Sunday. Alissandra warms the iron in the morning and spends an hour on her best dress. Then she walks up the hill to the road and heads towards the church in the village. Kingi and Zeke slip up into the hills above her, keeping to the scrublands, small stands of brush dotted with cypress.

In an hour the villagers emerge from the church service and gather in the square to talk and laugh. Kingi and Zeke step from the trees into their midst. The Cretan men are in their Sunday suits, some with a single bright flower tucked behind their ears. The young girls sparkle in their white dresses.

A couple of hours of trying to pick up threads of conversation, a few swigs of ouzo. Then Alissandra bids her friends goodbye and walks arm in arm with the two strangers, back down the road. Three Cretans out for a Sunday stroll.

Kingi sits on the ledge beyond the window, his fingers toying with a leaf from the bougainvillea covering the west wall. There's a trace of dirt still in his fingerprints. He turns to watch the sun begin to set beyond the mountains. He imagines for a moment flying over the aquamarine waters clear to Gibraltar, then the storm-drenched channel beyond. He lifts a potted anemone into his lap, the sun's warmth in the terracotta welcome against his body.

He looks skyward now to where a gull soars on a cushion of wind. Then another. Still more, each echoing the first. He smiles, places the potted plant back on the ledge and draws his hands up behind his neck. If he is not to leave this place, at least his last stand would be on an island of birds.

Dusk finds him still on the ledge.

'What are you doing up here?' says Alissandra, the light so weak now that she is sound only.

'Thinking.'

'Do you wish you were back with your aeroplanes?'

'I'm not sure any more.'

'Sure? What is it to be sure?'

'I fear you're asking the wrong person.'

He is up in the clear Mediterranean dawn, rearranging the books in the vineyard's library. Their covers are stacked row on row, like the bottles in the cellar. He sits on the wooden armrest of the settee, remembers his first steps into the Auckland Public Library, his body dwarfed by the rising tiers of spines and covers. Then again at Cambridge, where whole buildings and quadrangles echoed only with the silence of thoughts. Each page a new landscape, open country where the ink dust settles into fields. Into architecture.

He begins to arrange the books into alphabetical order. Most of the titles are in Greek, quite a collection for a family of winemakers. He tries to arrange the wording into some sort of meaning in English, thinking that he should have taken languages for at least a year. He remembers at Cambridge, hearing young men in tennis outfits having entire conversations in archaic Greek or Latin. Overhearing once a dialogue in Sanskrit, which he had to ask the name of as it was as alien to him as the skies of Saturn.

Alissandra appears in the doorway, showing puzzlement at his sudden demonstration of the librarian's art. He raises his eyebrows to her.

'Needed a sense of order this morning,' he says. 'Your father was obviously a reading man.'

'My grandfather was.'

She begins her singing again as she leaves. When she goes beyond the kitchen he loses the thread of her voice. He reaches for another book and leans to blow the dust off the cover.

He continues until he has finished the whole shelf then steps back, wiping dust from his forehead with the edge of his hand, realising then that he hasn't heard her voice for perhaps half an hour. He walks to the kitchen, glances down the path to the vineyard, then crosses beneath the arch.

A soft refrain echoes against the stone. Kingi smiles as he realises its source: her footfalls in the grape vat, a descant to her singing. He ducks beneath the inner arches, to where the cool scent of stone beckons. She looks up from the barrel.

'Your favourite place,' he says.

'It keeps me …'

'Sane?'

'I was thinking – home.' She pauses. 'Your people, how will they know where you are?' she says.

'I suppose I've been listed as missing.'

'No, not the army. I mean your family.'

'I don't really have a family. Not a permanent family, anyway. Perhaps a few transient ones.'

'Transient.'

'Comes and goes.'

'I know what it means. I was just thinking about how you mean it.' She glances down into the barrel, then raises her head again, a hint of mischief in her eyes. She extends a hand.

'I was never much of a dancer,' he says.

'Come on!'

He walks to the edge of the barrel and looks in, the liquid's spice tickling his nose. She is submerged up to her knees, dress tied around her waist, her legs bare. She nods to the right side of the barrel, to the ladder. A pail of water stands next to it. He removes his shoes, dips his bare feet into the pail then steps onto the first rung and pauses.

'Don't you trust me?' she says.

'Yes, actually.'

She reaches, grabs his hand and draws him over and in. She laughs, bends and dips her hand in the juice then touches it against the tip of his nose, running her wetted finger in a circle up over his forehead and across his cheekbones.

'Don't be so tense,' she says.

'I'm trying.'

'Let your body be relaxed.'

'I fear that might be out of the question.'

He steadies, feeling the grape flesh radiating beneath his feet, like sand beneath shallow surf.

'Show me what to do,' he says.

'Oh, it is very easy. I will make of you an expert. A Cretan!'

She raises her arms, then begins to shift her feet on the floor of the vat. He does the same.

'That's it,' she says. 'I think you *would* be a good dancer.'

He moves behind her, balancing a couple of inches from her body. A tiny step forward, his chin against her neck. He loops his arms around her chest, crossing them so his right hand graces her left cheekbone, his left against her right. A touch of each fingertip against her temples, the tiny pulse seeping into him. He slips down her length again, this time cupping his hands in the liquid of the vat, then he runs them – soaked now – up over her contours. The smoothness of sand dunes. He flexes his fingers over her breasts, liquid circles radiating beneath his palms, her nipples tightening in the circles' eye. He cups his hands again, this time not with grape juice but with her softness. Sensing that pulse again, he closes his eyes to the harmony of their bodies shifting in the well of wine.

It is Kingi's turn to make dinner. A lumpy soup, spiced with oreganum and turmeric from the garden. Some oranges Zeke has come across. Kingi and Alissandra sit in silence. An occasional glance at each other. The twilit shadows from the courtyard trees cast expressions on their faces that harsher light would blank.

'Cat got everyone's tongues?' says Zeke.

Kingi looks at him, turning away at Zeke's smirk.

'Oh,' says Zeke.

'No, not oh,' says Kingi.

'How about "ahhhh" then,' says Zeke.

After dinner Kingi and Alissandra stand at the tub, again in silence. Her hands lift from the soapy water to braid into his.

When they've finished she throws the cloth over a peg on the wall and walks down the hall into the dusk. He snuffs out the candle in the kitchen and sits in the doorway, a slice of moon rising through the cypress branches beyond. There is no sound of war tonight. Even the drone of supply planes has quietened. He picks out the first stars, calculating the direction of England. Then of home.

Her voice, far away. He walks to the blackened hallway, raising his arms like a cat's whiskers, negotiating the passageway by feel. He cannot place the melody, a Greek song perhaps. When he enters the cask room she is standing in front of one of the huge barrels with the glass measuring tube in her hands.

She raises the tube, passing it beneath her nose, her eyes closed to its scent. He watches her chest rise, hold for a moment, then he steps from the shadows.

'May I?' he says.

She raises the tube to him and he takes one end, her fingers not letting go of the other. She lifts the stopper from one end and he leans to take the fragrance in, the pungent alcohol turning his nostrils to fire.

'Rather potent stuff,' he says.

'But not finished. Another season, I think.'

Kingi raises the tube to his lips.

'No no,' says Alissandra. 'It is not ready.'

'Just a taste?'

She waves a finger at him, lifts the tube from his hands and lets the wine drain into a pail. She moves to another cask, adjusting the valve, sending a dark trickle into the tube. She takes both ends between her thumbs, a tiny overflow running down her wrist. Kingi lifts one of her hands away, replaces it with his own, and they stand, the liquid in the tube balanced like a dancer captured mid-step. She raises the tip of her other index finger against his lips and he opens them, tasting the spilled wine from her fingerprint. She raises the whole tube above his mouth and he accepts it all, closing his eyes to swim blind. Then he feels the glass slip away. Feels her lips against his.

In the darkness she is sound and scent and taste only, and he loves that. Having to navigate her by touch and instinct and faith alone. He rolls her over and over on the bed, her body balanced on an invisible string from his fingertips. Her laughter is muffled into the sheets whenever she flips onto her stomach. Then she is above him, orchestrating his movements with feather-light touches of her fingers or toes on his bare flesh. Her figure rising above him, slipping him beneath her, all the way until the bitter sweetness of her engulfs him. The scent of fallen leaves on the forest floor. Soil and root and bark. Then he is on top of her again, tensing his triceps to raise his frame up and away from her, touching her with his tip only, suspending himself for an exquisite, endless instant, before he collapses.

First light, calls of birds coming up the valley walls. Kingi rolls over on the sheets and reaches for Alissandra, but finds only her indentation, her scent in the fabric. He blinks himself awake, his eyes deciphering her nakedness, framed in the square of the window.

'Good morning,' he says.

She turns to him, her hair falling across her cheeks.

'Good morning to you too.'

'What are you doing all the way over there?'

She doesn't answer.

'We were beautiful,' he says.

A hint of a laugh.

'That did sound rather melodramatic, didn't it,' he says.

'I think I liked the "we", though.'

He raises himself up against the bedstead, opens his arms. She moves to the bed and sits against him, his arms closing around her waist.

'So quiet,' he says.

'I was thinking about my family.'

'This moment is ours.'

'Is it?'

'Yes, of course.'

'Does it change anything?'

'Should it?'

He runs his hands up across her forehead, lifting her hair almost into a bow, a cascade through his fingers. He leans against it, drawing strands against his lips.

'You know I can't tell you everything will be alright,' he says.

'I know.'

'I don't have that power.'

She nods.

'I wish I —'

'Shhhh,' she says.

He closes his eyes against her. 'Bugger them all,' he says.

'I beg your pardon?'

'I don't care about any it of right now. Not now.' He slides his fingers out beyond hers, then over, beneath her palms where he pauses. 'Not now,' he says.

Explosions puncture the morning air, echoing up the valleys from the coast. Kingi steps from the bed and into his trousers and pulls on his boots. Zeke is already in the hallway, dressed. The two men move out across the courtyard then wade across the stream to the hills. They climb through the light covering of cedars to the summit where they lie face down, watching bombers move in off the ocean and vanish behind the hills, attracting sharp stings of anti-aircraft fire from what they guess to be the German positions at Maleme airfield.

'Wellingtons,' says Kingi. 'Lancasters too.'

'Looks like your cobbers have finally called in the cavalry,' says Zeke. 'Mate, we couldn't *buy* tickets would give us a better possie than this.'

'You must send your commendations to the organisers.'

'I'll shake their bloody hands when I'm safely back in Alex.'

The fireworks continue, the bombers setting smoke rising beyond the olive groves. German return fire stitches the lightening sky with black ripples of flack. A second wave of bombers comes in from the west, then moves away. Silence. An hour goes by. The two men still sit, watching the smoke drift over the sea.

'Bit tardy with the follow-up,' says Zeke.

'I don't think there's going to be one.'

'I was afraid you was gonna say that.'

Zeke reaches into his pocket for his tobacco and papers.

'Where *did* you get that stuff?' says Kingi.

'Ask me no questions, Fly Boy, and I'll ask none of thee.'

'Meaning?'

Zeke gestures towards Kingi with the tobacco. Kingi takes it, unfurls a paper from the crumpled stack.

'You and our hostess,' says Zeke.

'What of it?'

'You got eyes for the whole layout? The vineyard and everything? And here was me thinking you were in a hurry to get back to your warm beer and maypole dances. What's the Greek word for "squire"?'

'I hadn't thought about any of that.'

'Naaaah.'

'Jealousy doesn't become you, Ezekiel.'

Zeke shifts his boots in the dirt. He reaches to sketch a couple of lines with his fingernail in a waft of dirt on his boot tops. 'This boy's got to get to a boat or a plane and get back into it,' he says.

'You sure that's it?'

'We going to get sideways over this? You don't have no Spitfire wrapped around you now.'

'Hurricane. And quit the posturing. I'm as anxious to get out of here as you are.'

'Sure you are.'

Kingi tips a needle of ash into the twigs and dead leaves. 'Are you accusing me of being a slacker?' he says.

'Calm down, Fly Boy. We're well aware of the survival rate of RAF pilots. It'd take a shitload of nerve even to go into that.'

'Then what?'

Zeke lifts a dry leaf, closes his palm around it. The leaf dissolves into nothing more than powder. 'Just don't tell me you love her.'

Kingi leans back on his haunches. 'Maybe that's what I need to know,' he says.

'Stop right there,' says Zeke. 'I do *not* want to hear it.'

Alissandra has made pancakes and a bowl of herb broth tinged with rosemary. She glances up as the men enter.

'I think it is a little light for you two to go exploring,' she says.

Zeke slumps in a chair. 'Wasn't much to see,' he says. 'Bloody Poms hardly got out of the starting gate.'

'Oh?'

'RAF air raid,' says Kingi. 'Not up to much. Unfortunately.'

'So you won't be leaving this morning?' says Alissandra.

'Not on an empty stomach,' says Zeke, reaching for a spoon.

Kingi stands and walks to the bench, lifts the plate with the pancakes. He leans over a jug sitting next to the sink, sniffs. 'Good lord,' he says. 'Milk?'

Zeke raises his eyebrows. 'That powdered sawdust stuff?' he says.

'No,' says Alissandra. 'Real milk.'

She lifts the jug from the bench, brings it to the table and sits. Zeke pours a thin stream into an old stoneware mug and raises it to his lips. He gulps the milk down in one slurp, a white moustache curling over his lips.

'Buggered if that wasn't some grade-A stuff,' he says.

'Konstantis brought it around while you two were on your adventure,' says Alissandra.

'My compliments to Konstantis' cow,' says Zeke.

'Cow?' says Alissandra. 'One day he hopes to be able to afford a cow. For now, his donkey will do.'

Zeke swallows hard, raises his hand to his face. The veins on his forehead pulsing. 'Shit!' he says.

Kingi smiles. 'Now would that be cow shit or donkey shit, Zeke?'

The twilight is quiet. Kingi spends an hour turning over the northern half of the vegetable garden, caking his boots with dust, dirt as hard as cement. He watches Alissandra walk up the small rise above him, behind a rocky outcrop, where a bird flies from the sound of her footsteps. A few minutes pass and she doesn't reappear. There's a hint of melody, but it's not hers. A sound of such delicacy, more spirit than substance. Kingi pushes the spade into the dirt and moves up the rise.

At the crest he sees her, sitting on the shaded hillside above a field of wild orchids, her cardigan over her shoulders. She smiles when she sees him, then raises her fingers to her lips. He approaches, craning his neck to follow the nod of her head down into the small canyon, where a shepherd boy sits among the rocks of the valley floor, playing pan pipes. Ragged, dusted sheep mill around him. Kingi crouches next to Alissandra. She lifts his hand into her lap.

There's a ripple of movement below them. Kingi's eye is guided to a tiny shape alighting on the pale gold tongue of an orchid. He leans forward.

'Look,' he says. 'A hummingbird.'

Alissandra leans next to him.

'No,' she says. 'It is a moth.'

'I don't think so.'

'It's a hummingbird hawk-moth. My father showed me, when I was a little girl.'

Kingi slides a few inches down the slope. He tilts his head, focuses on the creature's body as it hovers, wings oscillating faster than sound. A couple of inches in span, a grey body and black tail. He moves further, now only a couple of feet away, smiling when he sees a proboscis emerge and dip into the orchid's open heart. He pushes himself back up the hill.

'Well I'll be,' he says.

'We saw hummingbirds in America, but they do not fly here.'

'I've never actually seen one. Amazing the tricks the eye can play. Or perhaps the imagination.'

'I wish it could have been a hummingbird. Just for you.'

The shepherd boy plays on, neither looking towards his meagre flock nor towards the imposition of strangers' eyes on the hill. His fading form echoes the same sunset land as the notes from his pipes. The instrument seems to vanish, so that his body alone is melody. Alissandra closes her fingers over Kingi's as they sit, neither uttering a word, while the shepherd boy clothes his flock, the listeners, and the whole valley with his music.

Kingi moves out to the verandah, running his palm over the metal of the grated railings which are still warm from the day. Zeke appears from behind the large chestnut tree, stepping over where the roots have roughed up the pale cream paving stones. He looks up. 'Fly Boy,' he says.

Kingi stops at the head of the steps leading down to the courtyard. Zeke turns and sits on the bottom step. He glances back over his shoulder.

'I reckon it's time,' he says.

'And the method?' says Kingi.

'We steal an aeroplane.'

'From Maleme, presumably.'

'Yep.'

Kingi looks through the emerald leaves.

'Hear me out,' says Zeke.

'I'm listening.'

'We waylay a couple of Jerries from one of them convoys. For their uniforms.'

'We'd be bringing them snooping around here.'

'Then we do it somewheres else. It's a decent-sized island.'

Kingi looks down into the valley.

'You know about Jerry planes,' says Zeke.

'Only how to shoot them down.'

'Would have to be quick. In case they cotton on to us, once we're airborne. Two seater, obviously. What does that give us?'

'I saw some ME110s in Greece.'

'Are they fast?'

'You propose to just wander in and borrow one?'

'Got a better idea? I ain't waiting for no phantom submarine.'

Kingi walks down the staircase, sitting two steps above Zeke.

'Boat,' he says.

'All the way to Egypt?'

'Head west, skirt the coast then out towards Karpathos and Rhodes. Then on to Turkey.'

'Plane'd be faster.'

'But a plane doesn't seat three.'

Zeke turns, leans back against the metal pickets of the railing. 'Ah,' he says.

'Ah, indeed.'

'She won't go.'

'Leave that to me.'

A chestnut leaf falls, lands on Zeke's upraised knee. He flicks it away with a finger.

'I'll go with or without you,' he says. 'You know that.'

Evening finds Kingi in the library. He opens a cover, runs his fingertips across the paper, sensing each word, each character, as he might the pulse of an inamorata. He thinks of Alissandra clothed in her sheets last night, housing her scent and her warmth, inches that felt like miles from his body where he sat upright with his back against the wall. How her heartbeats had echoed inside him, across fields within him that have lain fallow for so long. Not just a pyxis of physical need, not just animal, but something residing in a deeper artery.

Alissandra passes by the door. She stops when she sees him.

'There you are,' she says. 'I've been looking for you.'

'Needed some thinking time.'

'Am I to know this thinking?'

Kingi taps his knuckles on the arm of the chair.

'It seems not,' says Alissandra.

'Have you ever thought of leaving again?' says Kingi. 'For good.'

'I told you. I've done all the leaving I intend to.'

'Things change.'

She kneels against the chair. Kingi raises his right hand above her, but doesn't touch her. She lifts a hand to grasp his.

'Lousy timing,' says Kingi. 'It's just damned lousy timing.' He stands and draws her against him, searching the weight of her for some answer, some tunnel straight to the equation's solution. She tilts her face and he kisses her, running the back of his fingers against the pulse of the vein in her neck, tracing its electricity down to where he undoes the top buttons of her dress. Lowering his face to drink her in.

In the night he hears Zeke pacing the hallway beyond her bedroom door. He lies listening, knowing that if Zeke wished it, he could probably run up and down the passage and not be heard. She stirs against him and he touches her cheek, her eyelids. Why couldn't this room be in Cambridge and she be some dean's daughter. Why here? Why now? He raises his arms out from his sides, casting a moon-shadow on the wall. A sketch of wings.

Zeke looks up from his breakfast. He wipes his mouth with the back of his hand. Kingi lifts out the chair from beneath the table, knocking Zeke's knee in the process. He sits on the front of the chair, leaning over the table.

'When?' says Kingi.

'As soon as you're ready?'

'And if I'm not ready.'

Zeke puts the spoon down in his half-finished bowl of porridge. 'Then you're not,' he says.

'*You* don't have any reason to stay,' says Kingi.

'That's true.'

'But I do.'

'True also. Now, tell me how any of that makes a blind bit of difference.'

'Do you have all day?'

Zeke swivels in his chair. He pulls another chair out from beneath the table and puts his boots up on it, one over the other.

'I was afraid you was going to say something like that,' he says.

'What do you expect me to say.'

'I'm sure I don't know.'

'Have you never had anything to lose?'

'Watch it, Fly Boy.'

Kingi fidgets with a crack in the wood of the table. He picks up the pepper grinder and wraps his hands around it.

'Tonight I'm going scouting,' says Zeke. 'Down to Kastelli, where the fishing boats head out west. Don't see why one of them couldn't forego fishing for a night and head around the back of the island to Karpathos.'

'And what would the captain of this vessel say?'

'Can't risk dealing with no captain. There are other ways.'

Kingi puts down the pepper grinder, a faint seasoned dust rising from it. Zeke glances down at it, his nostrils crinkling.

'Just after sunset,' he says.

They slip out of the vineyard, up over the hills and past the village, towards the town of Elysse. They can see no soldiers in the town or on the roads beyond. They are two hours walking the hill tracks and valleys to the sea, stopping in the lee of a hill crest and looking down over Kissamou Bay, with the fishing port of Kastelli in its apex.

They stay in shadows, avoiding street lamps as if their light is poisonous. A dog nuzzles a rubbish bin in a doorway, an old drunk stands in the middle of a square, arms raised in wordless praise to the night, or his stupor, or both.

On the dock a couple of cats scurry. The caiques sit moored in a row against the old wooden jetty. Zeke climbs aboard one, vanishing within its jumble of ropes and nets. He comes back and crouches in the lee of another caique's hull.

'We'd need to be here soon after midnight,' he says. 'The salties probably head out here around three-ish.'

Kingi nods.

'Is that a yes you understand,' says Zeke, 'or a yes you're coming?'

'We'd better head back.'

Another couple of hours in the hills, avoiding retracing their same steps. They reach the jagged herd of hills over Elysse just after dawn, keeping the new sun to the left. They are halfway past the town when there is a shout. The accent unmistakably German.

They duck down behind a thorn bush as a half dozen or so Germans amble out from a squat stone building. Then an officer. The officer recites a short speech, as if they are at a dedication ceremony, then more soldiers appear, this time dragging a line of civilians. Young men, a boy, a woman wearing a head scarf, an old man who struggles to keep up. All are tied together with a rope. The old man stumbles and one of the soldiers helps him up with the gentleness of a father to a son. The old man nods at him. The officer looks up at the rising sun. He recites some more of his monologue. The two guards motion the people towards a wall then step clear, one offering a cigarette to the other. The second man nods, strikes a match, the flame flickering against the cackle of shots from the half dozen other soldiers. Dust rises from the stones of the wall. The woman is the first to fall, the old man the last. He crumples rather than falls, like a page of abandoned newsprint blown against the stone.

Zeke swallows. Kingi grips the bush, aware a couple of seconds later than a thorn has penetrated his palm. Droplets of blood decorate its spike.

The German soldier who had earlier helped the old man up walks over to where he lies gasping and looks down at him. He turns and says something to the others then raises his rifle and shoots the old man in the face. He reaches over and unties the scarf from the woman's head and drapes it over his helmet. The other soldiers laugh as he poses with great ceremony. The officer grins for a moment, then wags a finger. The soldier tosses the scarf back amidst the pile of bodies and the Germans walk away.

In the night he wakes to shellfire, the unmistakable growl of naval guns, not land-based artillery. He walks to the window but sees nothing, the wind bringing the din from the far side of the island, echoing off the canyon's walls. He is surrounded by invisible armies. He goes down the hall to Zeke's room, but it's empty. He knocks on Alissandra's door, entering at the faint refrain of her voice.

There is minimal light, a pale moon dusting her bed, her outline beneath the blankets. He feels for the chair against the wall and sits, the creaking of the wood the only sound in the room.

'You cannot stay up in the air,' she says. 'Just reaching out and touching, now and then. Whenever you feel safe.'

'I didn't plan for it to be like this.'

'Plans, yes, plans. Everyone has plans. I have spent my whole life listening to men talk of plans.'

A ripple of fabric, her bedspread shifts. Her face is still unreachable by light.

'Forgive me for intruding,' he says as he reaches for the door.

'Wait.'

He hesitates.

'Yes?' he says.

A long silence. Only the curtain moves, shifting in the breeze.

'I won't leave,' she says. 'You know that.'

She walks among the vines. Kingi stands at the vineyard's edge, watching her. He creeps across the grass, shadowing her, waiting until she turns her back to check the condition of the vine leaves. He steps forward, puts his arms around her. She pushes back against him. He hugs her for a moment then steps clear, aware of the stiffness, the tension in his grasp. She turns.

'What is it?'

He stares. She waits for a moment, then goes back to her vine.

'When you go,' she says over her shoulder, 'don't leave me with any promises.'

'Who says I'm going?'

'Who says you are staying?'

'When this is over –'

'No. I said no promises.'

'You're not making this easy.'

'Why should I? If you escape, you have a somewhere to go to. I don't. *This* is my somewhere.'

'Only because you choose it so.'

'Oh yes, choose. Choose. Did you learn about such things in your university?'

'Don't do this. Not now. I just wanted to tell you –'

'Shhhhh.'

Her fingers against his lips. He takes her wrists in his hands, pressing them against his chest.

'I need you to listen to me now,' he says. 'They are shooting people in the towns. We saw them in Elysse this morning.'

She crosses herself.

'I've come to ask you whether you want me to stay. Whatever you say, I'll do.'

She stands for a moment, then pushes him hard in the chest, knocking him off balance. He stumbles back against the vines, leaves coming away in his hands as he tries to steady himself. Her eyes burn.

'Don't you dare!' she shouts.

'What?'

'You'd like me to tell you what to do. So you can get out of making the decision yourself. Then whatever happens is my fault.'

'It's not like that.'

'If you die here it will be because of me. Is that it?'

He moves towards her again.

'I'm not the enemy,' he says.

'Yes you are. You and all of your smart, strong men. You think I haven't seen you before? In my father. In my brothers. There is always some cause. Some *other* thing that must be caught and held, even if it means that the thing will break in your hands. Always.'

'I'm not the enemy.'

She curses him, a hail of words he has never heard. He drops his arms to his sides.

'I'm not *your* enemy,' he says.

She flails at him again. He stands, taking it. Closing his eyes to her rage. 'Look around you,' she says. 'See this. All of this. Do you think that the land cares about all our big ideas. Do you?'

'I don't know. I only know that I have found something I didn't think I had.'

She turns away, looking out over the vines.

'If you are looking for an answer from me,' she says, 'I don't have one.'

He nods, then turns and walks back up the hill towards the house.

He twists the handle of the tap in the kitchen and leans under it, takes a long drink. When he leans back, Zeke stands in the doorway.

'Tonight,' says Zeke. 'Before midnight. I won't come a-calling.'

Kingi reaches for a towel and wipes his hands. He goes up the stairs to his bedroom and lies down on the blankets. He puts his hands behind his head, stares up at the play of shadows on the stone of the ceiling.

At dusk she comes to him, closing the door with a bare foot and moving on top of him. She lifts off her dress and tosses it onto the bedstead. He reaches up, pushes her slip up over her shoulders, taking her breasts with his palms, her nipples between forefinger and thumb.

She leans over him, her hair flowing over his face and neck as she lifts his shoulders, dragging his vest and shirt off and sweeping them onto the floor. She sits naked on his bare abdomen, bending to find his mouth, covering it with her own.

His hands are against her bare back, her ridge of shoulder blades, then down to the softness of her upper thighs and cheeks as she flexes on her knees, rocking back and forth, her eyes closed to the visible world. He draws her closer, as if he can pull her all the way inside his life, bring his museum of order and certainty and logic to her life. But here, even draped in her scent, the sweetness of her, a stone is falling between them. He arches his back, needing to enter her, to push himself all the way through to some other place where they can be free. But he can't. Instead he wraps her against him, needing her weight, her warmth. Holding her as her breathing slows.

He closes his eyes, taking her tears on his eyelids.

'I don't have your answer,' she says.

'I know.'

They sleep with the sound of a soft rain on glass. The smell of wet leaves and soil. When he wakes it is well dark. He hears Zeke moving in the next room. A chair rattles as objects are placed on it, then lifted back off. A cupboard creaks. A long silence, then booted footsteps in the hall. Her face is against his collarbone, a flicker surfacing on her eyelids, perhaps from a dream. A flex as she swallows. He lifts a lock of her hair to his lips, kisses it as he hears the kitchen door shut beneath them.

When he wakes she is framed in the window, a Madonna of the grapevines. He blinks the sleep from his eyes, extends his hand towards her.

'No promises,' she says.

'No promises it is.'

He turns his reaching hand over, palm up. She steps from the window frame and comes to the bed. He spins her around, over onto her stomach, grabbing her bare feet and tickling her soles with his fingers. She shrieks.

'That'll teach you,' he says.

'For what am I being taught?'

'I'll think of something.'

He tucks her back beneath the sheets with him.

He sits at the kitchen table, his coffee cooling beyond his fingertips. She walks to the range, then the sink. Not touching anything with any forethought, just fiddling with various things. Then she turns, leaning against the bench.

'Zeke has gone for good, hasn't he,' she says.

He nods.

'You knew?' she says.

'Yes.'

'I'm sorry.'

'For what?'

She turns to face the sink, propping herself against it. She takes a towel from the wooden rack and sifts its fabric through her fingers.

'No,' she says. 'I'm not sorry.'

'Neither am I,' he says. 'Neither am I.'

He spends the day cutting more wood for the stove, pausing mid-afternoon by the stream. He crouches on the bank, dips a hand into the stream then raises it to drink, glancing up when her reflection appears among the reeds. He takes another sip, is about to lean back and stand when her bare foot pushes against his backside, upending him, face first, into the water.

He rises out, spitting weeds. She raises her arms like a prize fighter, dances a jig on the bank. He sweeps his hand across the surface, daubing her with the spray. She laughs, moves closer, tempting him with her eyes. He reaches up and she leans into him, clamping her arms around his shoulders as he pulls her, both of them, backwards into the stream.

Kingi crouches shirtless beside the outdoor tap and washes the soil from his hands and chest. He bends to take the water in his hair. There is a dandelion shining among a clump of weeds beneath the tap. He stays on his haunches, taking in the purity of its colour, its defiance against all the towering structures around it.

He eats supper still bare chested, bare footed. Alissandra stands to take the dishes to the sink but he captures her in his arms, pulls her into his lap. She turns and scratches her fingers through his damp hair.

'Is there any dessert, Missus?' he says.

'You have hands, don't you?'

'Indeed I do.'

He clutches her tighter, tickling her abdomen. She grabs one of his hands and pulls it to her mouth and bites it.

'Flamin' Nora!'

She laughs.

'Who is Nora?' she says.

A knock at the door. Alissandra calls out in Greek. Kingi recognises the voice as Konstantis'. Alissandra opens the door and Konstantis steps in, glancing at Kingi, surprise registering in his eyes. Konstantis says something to Alissandra in Greek and she narrows her eyes, asks him to repeat what he said. He does so and the two of them turn to look at Kingi, a curious chill seeping from the warm summer air, running along Kingi's bare arms to his torso.

He sets out soon after dusk, taking much the same route Zeke and he had taken. He bypasses Elysse by sticking to the hill tracks, the map lines cut by shepherds. The bay of Kissamou opens before him, a few lingering lights from the Kastelli waterfront mirrored in the harbour. He makes his way down to the cobbled streets. The bleached white walls of the houses are still stark, even in this quarter light. A couple of alleys take him to the harbourside, where he waits for a full half hour, scouting the shadows for any sign of movement.

Konstantis had said that he'd seen him when he came down to the town to barter for fish. On one of the scaffolds used to string the rare catch of a swordfish, perhaps a shark. Kingi darts across the road to the waterfront, dodging lamplight. He keeps the bay to his right, passing the moored caiques. On one an old man sits, smoking a pipe, looping a length of rope through his fingers. He nods as Kingi passes, then goes back to his work.

There. A jetty, topped with a sort of gantry. The body swings in the sea breeze, upside down. Bound at the ankles. The rope creaks like old, rusty door hinges. He presses his back against the frame of a cart, running a hand along the gnarled circumference of its wheel, feels a numbness again in his arm, the first time for days. Then he runs, half crouched, across the wharf, close enough to reach out and take Zeke's face in his hands. Close the dead eyes with his fingertips.

Alissandra finds him sitting on the edge of his bed. She kneels on the floor in front of him. He stares beyond her. Not even aware of the solidity of her shape, as if she has turned to glass.

'It's not us,' she says.

He doesn't answer.

'It's not to do with us,' she says. 'None of it.'

He stands and takes his holster from the bed beside him and walks to the door.

'Will you come back?' she says.

He turns, inhales the musk of old wood, stone of the villa. Of her. He stares long into her shadowed face.

'I thought you said no promises,' he says.

She stands still. That defiance in the line of her shoulders he had seen that first day, in the vat of grape juice. All his years of learning, his logic and reason. None of it has prepared him in any way for this moment.

'Will you?' she says.

He nods. 'Yes,' he says. 'I promise.'

He turns and walks down the hall.

It is an hour to dawn, a little less, perhaps, when he reaches the outskirts of the airfield at Maleme. Still dressed in the attire of a Cretan winemaker, as if he is all cultures in one. The skin of a Māori, the mind of western education and civilisation. The eyes of a pilot. The clothes of a worker of the land. A twentieth-century Everyman.

He skirts one edge of the airfield's perimeter. There is no security wire and only a desultory guard strolling to and fro. The Germans have total control of the island. A light flickers from a hangar where mechanics in overalls work, fragments of conversation drifting on the breeze. He aims for the far side of the airfield where the single-seat fighters – the interceptors – are most likely to be already fuelled. He ducks beneath a wing, then another. A couple of HE111s. A Stuka. Beyond them a small flock of ME109s. He crouches, looking to reduce his silhouette against the lightening sky, then steps out onto the runway.

He stops next to a 109, hoists himself up onto the wing and unlatches the cockpit canopy. The cockpit itself is familiar: steel tub seat, control column, the staring metal eyes of the gauges. He sinks into the tub, no comfort of a packed parachute beneath his bones. He fixes the harness over his body, fingers the leather grip on the column, closing his eyes for a moment, his mind opening drawers of schematics and diagrams. Takeoff velocity. Elevation. Then a fleeting image, a woman's face over him, the fragrance of grapes in her hair. He swallows, taking the scent within him, then fires the engine into life.

The noise is deafening after weeks in the vineyard, the engine's shudders vibrating his legs against the cockpit wall. He adjusts the control column, points the nose towards the north end of the runway.

A couple of overall-clad men walk, then run from the hangars. He ignores them, heads away from the town's lights, toward the dark of the sea, feeling the land let go. He pushes the throttle lever, then feels for the switch to retract the wheels. Allows himself a smile.

But: the perfume of grapes comes back to him and his hands fumble at the column, a dusting of images clouding his irises. A hint of moonshadows edge the window alcove, his nakedness sitting against the wall, her body leaning into the well of his, his arms cupped beneath her breasts. His fingers rise up to her face, exploring each pore of her cheekbones. He tries to blink her away, opening his pupils to the sea, trying to lose her face in the water. But he can't. The engine pitch changes and he realises he has eased the throttle lever back towards him, slowing him, the 109's nose neither headed towards Egypt nor the sea, but back inland. He floats, as if in water, or a vat of wine. His sketches and calculations slip back into their drawers. Velocity, elevation … what? He reaches for them, but sees them shatter. Closes his eyes to everything but her, what she has given him. What he has lost. Which is it?

He jerks at the column and the port wing drops, the 109 careening into the canyons, casting a hawk's shadow in the dust. A road appears, woven into the hillside. He follows it like a vein, an artery leading back inside himself. Egypt gone now. The Mediterranean vanished. He sights the village, the road leading to the vineyard, part of him aiming at its rutted surface. His fingers feel for the switch to lower the wheels. Then he pulls away. His body suddenly ice. Seeing his fingerprints in the sky leading guns to her doorway. He banks right, the church dome looming. He clears it, but clips the spire, sensing its spike puncturing the fuselage beneath him. The fuel tank. He looks at the fuel gauge, willing the needle not to drop. But it does. He taps his fingers on the column, the pilot now of a poisonous raincloud of 87 octane, awaiting just a single spark to turn him into a fleeting sun. He banks again, away from the vineyard and village, away from the island, the wind funnels from the valleys like tidal rips beneath him. Steering him out over the ocean.

A half mile offshore the engine gasps, then stalls and he becomes just one more wave. He braces. There are no sparks. Just water. He pushes open the canopy to feel the spray on his face.

He steps out onto the sinking wing, then slides down into the Mediterranean, the fuselage awash now, whitecaps building against the tail rudder. The island spins in his pupils. He can no longer taste the wine. Just salt spray. There is wetness on his cheeks again, though not from the sea. A glimpse of darkness, the inside of a secret passage, as she and he had hid from the sound of boots. His tears in her hair, when he'd known, for the first time in his life, the meaning of the word 'we'. He lies back in the water, as he had in that English meadow a million years ago, watching his moko etched in the sky. He reaches to touch his cheeks with sea water, then closes his eyes, opening them again only when the patrol boat looms above him, the man in uniform reaching to part Kingi's hair with the barrel of his Mauser.

Macroglossum stellatarum of the family *sphingidae* – sphinx moth. Sometimes mistaken for a hummingbird.

He looked it up, in the autumn of 1946, back in Cambridge. The day the photograph had arrived. A man a woman against a wall. A chestnut tree beyond. The man's eyes closed to the photographer, or perhaps something else. It had arrived in a cream-coloured envelope, postmarked Iraklion, Kriti. Just a photograph.

He had started a half dozen letters, few getting further than an address, a few formal lines. None of them sent, all of them ending scattered amid his equations, drawings of aeroplanes and birds.

IX

People of the Smoke

Jordan

They don't tell you about the pain and when you first get to know it you think that ... well one day it's going to end. That there's an 'other side'. It'll just go away like a cold or the flu or something and then you'll forget. And maybe if you forget then what you've forgotten won't live any more, or you'll be tempted to think that it never did.

That's how it goes.

But it isn't true.

Pap used to tell us to hang tough, to never let the bastards get us down. Me and Georgie and Tania too. I remember going up once to the hospital to see Mum after she got sick and swiping some flowers from our garden and carrying them all scrunched up in my fist then shoving them at her. She gave me this long look, a strange look, like I was standing a hundred yards away. Then she took them and smiled, I reckon more at the flowers than at me.

He wouldn't say much about it, just sort of nod and grunt. I remember the day she died. He walked in to where Tania and me were watching TV and just crouched there, saying nothing for a hell of a long time. He reached back and flicked off the TV and the screen shrank away and went black. We sat there, looking up at him, in the silence. Then Tania grabbed my arm and started pulling on it. Still he said nothing, so all there was was the sound of his breathing. Like running sandpaper across wood. He shook his head a couple of times, then stood and walked away.

For all his bellowing, when he needed to say something, anything, Big Des was a stone. I suppose a part of me hated him for that, for years. But maybe that stone had settled inside him and he couldn't talk with it there.

He never came to see us in Parry. Not once. Not that I wanted him to, but still.

Paremoremo Maximum Security Prison, 1987

I lay on my bed, the sound of snoring echoing off the walls. If I tried hard enough I could've translated that sound into something else. Wind in leaves. Even the ocean, maybe. Swap the stink of socks and dirty jeans and the pisser for sea water.

I used to think about what was maybe happening outside. You do that in the beginning. Like you're on holiday and you still have reservations for a place in the real world. But after a while the real world fades, and then you realise, you're *in* the real world. As real as it's going to be while your arse belongs to the prison system.

I'd been keeping an eye on the old man since I got in. Hepi Maniopoto. Been in and out all his life, so they reckoned. The first time I saw him he was sitting alone at a table, eating. Even among all the jail and gang tattoos, his moko dead-centred the eye. None of the brothers seemed interested in staring him down. Just left him alone. Then I heard the guitar in the night, well after lights out. The screws could've told him to shut up, but they didn't. And he was always playing music that I'd never heard. Said one time he was playing a fugue. 'What the hell is a fugue?' I said. The old man looked at me and said, 'There's encyclopaedias in the library. You've got eyes haven't you?'

After lunch I stood on the landing, looking down. The sound of his guitar started up and I leaned against the rail, listening to it. Then I walked towards it, his battered face looking up, prompted maybe by my shadow or the sound of my footsteps.

'It's Rodrigo,' he said.

'Eh?'

'Concierto de Aranjuez. Second movement.'

He went on playing.

'Rodrigo was a blind man,' he said. 'Did you know that?'

'Yep.'

'Bullshit.'

I smiled.

'How the hell would I know that?' I said.

'You forget what I told you about the library?'

Another ripple of melody.

'What's all that crap on your hands,' he said. 'That gang shit?'

'You screwing with me? You ain't too old to go sailing over the rail.'

'It'd be a waste of your precious energy. I'm about to expire anyway. Save yourself the trouble.'

'Thanks for the concern, but I'm still thinking about it.'

His hands moved into a classical-style arpeggio. A couple of the notes were false, his bony fingers stuttering.

'Friggin' arthritis,' he said.

'I got a guitar too.'

'I've heard it.'

'You reckon you could teach me some of that stuff?'

'In exchange for?'

'I'll lend you the keys to my Rolls Royce.'

He stopped playing for a moment and looked up. There was a little crinkle of laughter around his bloodstained eyes. 'Piss off,' he said. 'You made me forget what I was doing.'

I stood hard up against the rear wall of the cell, staring straight ahead. Not at the two prison officers flanking the doors, not even at the officer bent over my bed, kicking all my stuff onto the floor. A shaving brush, a tin of foam. A box of tea bags. A fifty cent plastic comb. He turned around, hands balled into fists, fingernails crunching into his palms. I smiled. He looked at me for a second then aimed a kick at the guitar sitting against the wall. He caught a bit of it and sent it spinning onto the floor. It lay there, echoing. He smiled this time, searching my face for some sign, some victory sign. He reached up and ripped a couple of photos from the walls, tossed them on the floor then walked over them as he circled the room, pushing over everything not fastened down, glancing up now and then at my face again. Like we shared something.

They found nothing, there was nothing *to* find. But that wasn't what it was about anyway.

When they'd gone I lay down on the bed, staring at the underside of the bunk above. The only thing I'd picked up was the guitar. I retuned it and lay back, picking at the strings. Then there was a knock at the door. I looked towards the opening, where the old man, Hepi, stood shaking his head. I was going to tell him to piss off, but he raised that beautiful guitar of his in front of him, with P-a-p-a-t-u-a-n-u-k-u inlaid into the fretboard. I nodded and he stepped on in.

'You going to shift your carcass,' he said, 'or am I going to have to rest my weary bones on the crapper?'

I swung my legs out over the floor and he sat on the puny mattress, looking around.

'I like what you've done with the place,' he said. 'They find what they were looking for?'

'Didn't find shit,' I said.

'Then I hope they weren't looking for *shit* then, or they'll be plenty mad.'

'Just a warning, someone whispered maybe.'

'Someone's always whispering.'

'Doesn't matter. I'm cool.'

'Good for you. Wouldn't want you to start blubbering over it.'

'Said I'm cool.'

'You get any cooler there'll be an icicle up your arse.'

I laughed, then began to pluck at my guitar again.

'That stuff you sometimes play,' I said, 'sounds like Gypsy music.'

'Harmonic minor scale. Little bit of eastern scales in there too, Arabic scales even.'

'I don't know any of that.'

'And yet you own a Rolls Royce,' he said.

He started to move his skeleton fingers against the strings.

'Follow me,' he said.

I was pretty much lost, but tried to suss where he was going and get there too. He was playing stuff I'd never thought existed, all kinds of classical stuff, some jazz. He stopped and showed me that harmonic minor scale, then just vamped on some minor chords and got me to stretch the scale over them, me feeling my way like a caver – sensing what handholds would stick and what would let me go. After a while I looked back up at him, this old man, lost in his music. Immersed. Shrunken shoulders giving way to his hollowed-out chest. The shape of the guitar's body the only hint of fullness. The outline of a teardrop almost, as if he was pregnant.

South Auckland, 1979

Jordan sits in the car, drumming his hands on the steering wheel. Dylan is in the passenger seat. Dylan reaches into the glove box, rummages around. Some brochures and scrap papers, a pen. A couple of cassette tapes. He takes out the tapes, leans forward to catch some of the light from the streetlamp.

'Stink,' he says. 'Roger Whittaker.'

'Don't even think about it,' says Jordan, looking at the car's cassette player.

'I wasn't,' says Dylan. 'Should've brought some of my own sounds. Why can't they have something decent.'

'They should've known you were gonna steal their car.'

'I got the munchies.'

'You always got the munchies.'

'There's a burger bar round the corner.'

'They all know us by sight. And they don't know the car. We'll head across town.'

Jordan drives a couple of blocks, coming upon the bright lights of a petrol station forecourt.

'Hang on,' says Dylan. 'Pull in here.'

'We don't need any gas.'

'Pull in, cuz.'

Jordan stops beside the air hose. Dylan gets out and heads towards the petrol station interior. Jordan leans back in the seat, looks up the street at the lines of telephone poles. Beyond them the neighbourhoods of Mangere East lie in darkness. He leans against the door, feeling the cold through the window. He glances left into the pay booth just in time to see Dylan pull a knife from his jacket and bring it up under the attendant's face.

The attendant stands still, his eyes visible even from this distance. Dylan walks around behind the counter, glancing now and then at the attendant. He rummages through the cash register, shouts something at the attendant and the attendant drops out of sight behind the counter. Dylan works his way back out of the shop, stopping to fill his pockets with chocolate bars on the way out.

He climbs back inside the car and looks at Jordan. 'Got Moros and some of them peanut bar things,' he says. 'Which do you want?'

Jordan pulls out onto the street, the car lurching across the road. 'What the hell are you doing?' he says.

'What?'

'Robbing the dude.'

'He family to you, or what?'

'He's got eyes, he can ID the car.'

'Well yeah. Since you pulled away like Mario Andretti he can.'

'Shit. You'll never learn.'

'Nothing to learn from you.'

A traffic light turns to amber. Jordan plants both feet hard on the brake pedal. Dylan lurches forward, banging his arms against the dashboard. Chocolate bars fly everywhere.

'What the hell did you do that for?' he says. 'You got a screw loose or something.'

Jordan steps out and walks around and pulls the passenger door open and drags Dylan out onto the asphalt. Dylan grabs at the last couple of chocolate bars he still holds. Jordan shoves him over onto his side and kicks him in the legs and backside. Dylan tries to speak.

'Don't,' says Jordan. 'You say one bloody word and I will stomp you here and now.'

Dylan looks up at him.

'Don't,' says Jordan.

Jordan goes back to the driver's door. He stands leaning against the roof stanchion, fist balled against the metal, then he opens the door and gets in. A couple of lights go on in houses.

A dog barks. Jordan reaches over with his foot, kicks the passenger door wide open again. 'You gonna lie out there all night?' he says.

Dylan stands and dusts himself off, then steps back into the car and sits. 'I ate the last of the Moros,' he says. 'You're gonna have to make do with a Peanut Slab.'

A factory car park. A rusting mesh fence coming away at the base. Rubbish blows in the wind. Jordan walks across the cracked concrete to where Jacqueline sits atop a stack of old pallets. He steps onto the stack and climbs up and sits next to her, looking out over the empty yard. Beyond it is a vacant lot, a mangy, rubbish-strewn creek running through its midst. A concrete pipe spills grey foam into the water.

'One day all this shall be yours, m'boy,' says Jacqueline.

'Thank you. I ... don't know what to say.'

She turns, shifting against him. He takes her head in his lap, runs his fingers across her long, dark hair. A thumb down over her right cheek, and across her lips. She closes her eyes to his touch.

His father sits at the kitchen table, cutting some slices off a cold roast. He spears the slices with a fork and holds them up to the light. Then he speaks, still staring at the meat. 'Don't get her knocked up,' he says. 'That's if you haven't already.'

'As if that's *your* business.'

'As long as you're standing here in my kitchen, it's my business.'

'Whatever.'

His father puts a slice in his mouth, sits chewing. A half empty beer bottle sits on the table. There's a sink full of dishes, some torn beer cartons stacked against the fridge. 'Beats me why you even stay here,' says his father.

'Beats me too.'

'Well then.'

'Remember when you took me fishing?'

His father raises the beer bottle, takes a swig. 'Nah,' he says.

Jordan pulls his jacket collar up against the rain. He pauses outside a shop window, a shoe shop with the latest running shoes. He looks at the prices and smiles and walks on. Just before he reaches the entrance to the street mall a car door swings open in front of him. A Mark II Zephyr coated in streaks of grey and black rust paint. He glances inside. A dark face, a mess of hair and wraparound shades.

'Te Awa,' says the face in the car.

Sandman. No one knows what his real name is, and no one asks him. He sits holding the door open, his sunglasses reflecting the shop windows and awnings, Jordan standing on the pavement.

'What you up to, Te Awa?' he says.

'Nothing much.'

'Nothing much.'

'Yep.'

'Where's that shit-for-brains cousin of yours at?'

'Dunno.'

'You dunno.'

'Nope.'

Sandman looks towards the car's passenger. 'He says he doesn't know,' he says.

Sandman looks back up at Jordan. 'Heard you did some stuff in Waikeria,' he says.

Jordan doesn't move.

'Heard you might've wasted some dude,' says Sandman, 'but they never got to pin it on you.'

'What are you, a nark?'

Sandman laughs. 'I like you,' he says. 'You've got stones.'

'I'm touched.'

'And so you should be. Tell that sister of yours that I'm looking for him.' Sandman sits tapping his fingers on his jeans. 'I don't care how big a man you were in Waikeria,' he says. 'That means nothing out here.'

He reaches and pulls the car door closed again. Jordan turns and walks up into the mall. An hour later he is buying some fish and chips when someone punches his arm. Dylan. He raises his eyebrows.

'Your gang mates were looking for you,' says Jordan.

Dylan smiles. 'They need me,' he says.

'Shit.'

'You won't be saying that when I'm patched.'

Jordan pays for his fish and chips. The two of them walk across the mall to where a wooden bench sits beside a water sculpture. A vertical stack of plastic scoops, tipping one after the other when a small jet of water comes out of a nozzle above them. Dylan stands looking at his reflection in the water, then spits into it. Jordan opens the newsprint wrapping. Steam escapes. He offers the parcel to Dylan who lifts out a couple of chips, wincing at the heat.

'You ever think of heading back up home?' says Jordan.

'What for? Everything I want is here.'

'You know that mates of *those* dudes end up inside, don't you.'

'So what. We survived Waikeria didn't we?'

'That was borstal. Next time, your arse goes into the Mount, Parry maybe.'

'I can do a serious stretch. If I have to.'

'What movie did you learn that line from? And who put the word out that I wasted somebody when I was inside?'

'Might've been me.'

'Thanks, cuz. Now I got nutcases thinking I'm one of them.'

'Aren't you?'

'So what did you tell them that you'd done?'

'Told 'em I wasted two boobheads and a screw.'

'You didn't.'

'Piss off. I wouldn't last five seconds. They'd kill me in advance. Just in case.'

'Think I might spread the word around then.'

'You think too much. That's your problem.'

'Man, I got a million problems, but that ain't one of them.'

Dylan reaches for another handful of chips. 'You're thinking I should quit prospecting,' he says.

'For starters, yeah.'

'Maybe become prime minister instead.'

'I'm getting tired of looking out for you.'

'I just want to do stuff,' says Dylan. 'Be someone.'

'I know.'

'Sometimes you sound like my mother.'

Jordan flicks a chip at Dylan but he bends away, dodges it.

'And a lousy shot too.'

There is a party every Saturday night. Somewhere. They buy what beer they can afford and steal what they can't. A scattering of old cars at the kerb, on the front lawn. Neighbours' blinds drawn. Jordan stands in the front-door alcove, drinking from a beer bottle. He has a roll-your-own cigarette in his other hand. A handful of people he barely knows push past him, walk out to the street. They stand on the footpath, laughing, staging mock fist-fights with each other. Dylan appears in the door.

'We're heading out soon,' he says.

Jordan takes a swig from the bottle.

'Could be a place for you, cuz,' says Dylan.

A car slows, stops in the middle of the road. He recognises the streaks of black over the grey rust paint. The car rolls into the glare of the streetlights. Sandman. Dylan moves down the steps. He glances back.

'You coming?' he says.

'Might have to tag along to see that you don't beat yourself up.'

They slide into the rear seat. Sandman turns with a look of exaggerated shock on his face. 'Well bless my little heart,' he says. 'Te Awa has seen fit to join our escapade.'

They drive around the backstreets of Mangere East, then Otahuhu. Another couple of cars slip in behind them. Sandman glances into the rear-view mirror. They stop a couple of times and Sandman has brief conversations with the streetkids hanging around, a familiar alky shambling along with his bottle. They head east towards Glen Innes, skirting the back of the town centre and veering down a sidestreet to where it ends in a large yard with containers stacked row on row. The car pulls in behind some trees and stops. Two silhouettes appear in the headlights and then vanish.

'Them,' says Sandman.

Dylan is out the door and gone.

'Shit,' says Jordan, stepping out the door.

He walks in the direction Dylan ran, the Zephyr inching along behind, the headlights casting his shadow twenty feet high. He stops and the car stops behind him. In the lee of a steel roller door five young men stand facing off against Dylan and some others from the following cars. Dylan walks along the line of faces then breaks into a little dance, arms aloft like an orang-utan. The boys against the roller door sneer. There is a full minute of posturing then it erupts. Fists, steel-capped boots. Someone pulls a chain from a jacket. Jordan walks towards them, keeping a wide field of vision to each side. One of the boys from the doorway goes down from a wild blow. When he rises a knife appears from his waistband. Dylan is blindsided, falling against a jumbo bin. One of the others lifts a bottle from the piled rubbish overflowing the lip and breaks the top off against the bin's metal edge. Jordan is on him from behind, grabs him by the hair and smashes his face against the peeling paint. Blood seeps into the rust. The bottle drops. He slips to the asphalt, fumbles for the bottle, but Jordan stomps on his hand, crushing it into the shattered glass on the pavement. The man tries to lever himself up against the bin but Jordan raises his foot and kicks him in the stomach, then again in the face. He folds over, his legs twitching. The knife wielder attacks, but Jordan sidesteps him, taking his empty hand and using it to twist his arm around in its socket. A scream. Jordan spins him further, forcing his arm back and up. A loud crack. He flails at empty air with the knife, Jordan circles away from his swipes, looking for the opening. He finds it, kicks the flailing hand. The knife clatters. He grabs at air. Jordan lets go of his arm and kicks him between the legs, the arm hanging loose, grotesque. He tries to stand once more but Jordan grabs the broken arm again and punches him in the eye sockets and mouth. Blood streams. The man falls. Still he attempts to rise. Jordan stands over him, raises his foot a hair's breadth above the man's cheekbones.

'You sure you're still in this?' he says.

The man closes his eyes. Jordan turns and walks away.

'Te Awa.'

Sandman sits on the Zephyr's bonnet.

'Piss off,' says Jordan.

'Te Awa. You need to be careful of what's inside of you, brudder.'

Jordan spits on the bloodstained ground.

'Ain't your brother,' he says.

He drags Dylan down a back alley, Dylan protesting all the way.

They sit in the park, Jordan, Jacqueline, Dylan and his girlfriend Mereama. Mereama fingers a new gold chain Dylan has around his neck. She coos in approval. Jordan looks across at him.

'Makes you look like one of those dudes in the Bee Gees,' he says.

'Just jealous,' says Dylan.

Jacqueline sits cross-legged next to Jordan. She reaches down, lifts a sprig of grass and tosses it into the air, watching it float on the wind. Jordan lies back, propped on his elbows, watching her. He reaches with a hand, toys with some strands of her hair.

'You coming out tonight?' he says.

'Got to study. Exams coming up.'

'School, shit,' says Dylan. 'Why don't you ditch that.'

'Shut up, man,' says Jordan. 'Just cause she's got a brain. Unlike you.'

Dylan makes a face. Jacqueline stands, looks over toward the children's playground.

'You coming?' she says.

Jordan stands and dusts off his jeans. They walk across the grass, to the children's playground, stopping next to the sandpit.

'The old man's still giving me grief about you,' says Jacqueline, 'about you coming round to the house.'

'I don't come round to the house. Hell, I park at the end of the bloody street. Where does he want me to park, Wellington?'

'You know what I mean.'

'Yeah. He doesn't want me no how no way.'

She crouches, sweeping a hand out over the sand.

'You still going to uni next year?' says Jordan.

She nods.

'That art stuff?' says Jordan.

'It's not "stuff".'

'Here, or out of town?'

'Don't know.'

Jordan leans forward, draws a simple stick figure with a finger in the sand. He begins to scratch down another figure beside it but stops.

'You know what I'm asking,' he says.

'Yes. But I don't have an answer for you.'

He steps into the sandpit, his track shoes leaving ribbed prints. He looks down at them. He turns, looks back towards the others.

'You're better than that,' says Jacqueline.

'He's my cousin. What do you want me to do?'

She looks out over the see-saws and swings.

'I can't make you any guarantees,' says Jordan.

'I know.'

New Years' Eve 1980. He goes with Jacqueline to a gathering of her university-bound friends, saying their farewells both to the decade and each other, before heading to various campuses around the country. He stands against a windowsill, drinking from a can of imported beer, a few inches beyond the reach of their conversation. Jacqueline dances to a Stevie Wonder song, her feet circling on the carpet. A couple of her girlfriends also lost in the music. A young man in a tapestry waistcoat sits tapping his fingers against a knee, smiling up at them. Jacqueline looks over at Jordan, gestures with an outstretched hand. He takes a sip from his can, looks up at a poster on the wall. A dreamscape, with clocks melting into the dirt. He glances back at Jacqueline, still with her arm outstretched. Then he turns and stares out through the trees, into the darkened street.

He knows Dylan is knocking over the odd dairy, maybe even some more petrol stations. Maybe on the word from the gang, who knows. Jordan has a job stacking boxes in the warehouse of a knitwear factory that makes clothes for children. Row upon row of cartons filled with plastic bags with teddy-bear faces on them, labels like Mr Lucky, Bobo, Sportygirl.

She comes to see him sometimes once she starts at the School of Arts. He takes a long lunch and makes the time up later. They sit in a coffee bar, Jacqueline with one leg crossed over the other. A portfolio and a plastic cylinder with her drawings and designs leaning against the table.

'Some of us are getting together on Saturday,' she says. 'Checking out the Impressionists exhibit.'

He stares.

'You never know,' she says, 'you might actually enjoy it.'

'Don't think I can make it.'

'Hanging out with Einstein I suppose.'

'You becoming a snob with your varsity mates?'

'You resent me going to uni? Maybe you shouldn't have just walked out in the fifth form.'

Jordan takes a bite of a sandwich.

'Any time you want,' he says.

'Is that a challenge?'

'Nope. Just the way it is.'

'I'm not quitting on you until *I'm* ready to.'

Jordan gets a Christmas bonus and shouts them a trip down to the central plateau. They stay a couple of nights at a fishing motel in Turangi, getting up before dawn on the second morning and heading up the mountain, empty of people in the off season. The rock faces rise above them, only the uppermost crags carrying a blanket of snow. They sit in the ski-field carpark, watching the sun rise over the bare valleys. Jordan raises a bottle of cheap wine to the sun, tapping the bottle against Jacqueline's champagne flute.

'Don't make any promises,' she says.

'I was just going to say, "here's to you". '

In 1981 she starts her second year at university. They have a small flat across the road from the railroad tracks, Jacqueline cursing when the fumes dull her washing. One day when she's at class he gets home early, sees a folder with the ends of various sketches and paintings she has done. He's aware suddenly that after screwing her for two years he's never even once looked at her art.

He spreads the various pieces of paper around the living room floor. He struggles to recognise anything. He remembers her telling him once about abstract art and expressionism, but he had one eye on the league on TV. He sits in the midst of her paintings, reaching out with a hand now and then, not touching them, just hovering a few inches above them. Realising that within her skin, beyond the immediate that he knows about her, is someone he doesn't know at all.

That night he sits up watching her, long after she has gone to sleep, trying – in the silence – to hear and know *her* language. Hear or sense it in the soft purr she makes whenever she moves. He curls himself around the shape of her back, as she lies facing away from him. Nuzzling his nose into her hair, an arm over hers, his palm and fingers around her wrist. Letting his breathing slip in synch with hers. Closing his eyes to the sound of her.

Dylan is a patched gang member now, but still drinks sometimes with Jordan. The two of them with a foot up on the rail, munching on reheated pies. Dylan goes to buy the next round, comes back and slams two jugs on the table. He raises his eyebrows.

'You still with her, cuz?' he says.

'Yep.'

'She still got big ideas?'

'She's got a zillion ideas.'

'Yeah.'

'Yeah.'

'It's cool. Don't worry. I'm not gonna get on your case.'

Jordan fills his glass from one of the jugs. A couple of Dylan's gang brothers come across from another table. They nod at Jordan. For some reason he thinks suddenly of how they were all in the primers together, all those years ago. Dylan lifts his glass to his lips, takes a drink. His eyebrows rise over the foam. Jordan nods. Then a sudden shift, to a vacant section behind his parents' house, two ten-year-old boys climbing among the stacks of rotting fibrolite with old broom handles for guns. A nail hammered into the wood and bent with a screwdriver, serving as a trigger. Rat-tat-tat-tat-tat. Dylan looking up, a trickle of blood coming from his nostrils, the bleeding he sometimes had when he became nervous. 'Sissy bleeding,' one of the other children had said to taunt him.

'You won't tell anyone about this?' said Dylan.

'Naaaah.'

'Promise.'

'Don't need to promise.'

'Still'

'OK, I promise.'

He blinks, back in the public bar. He looks across at Dylan. Dreads halfway down his back. A couple of hours of laughter, razzing each other, then Jordan walks home across the railway tracks.

He is about to step from the curb when he sees the Zephyr. It slows, next to him, holding up traffic. Horns beep. It pulls into the curb and Sandman smiles from the passenger seat.

'Well, well,' he says.

'Bugger off,' says Jordan.

'Still stuck up, I see.'

Sandman turns to the driver. 'Such a waste,' he says, shaking his head.

The driver sneers. Jordan remembers him from Waikeria. Calls himself Locust. He also remembers he doesn't like him.

'We're on the lookout for people to help protect our investments,' says Sandman.

'Investments,' says Jordan. 'You mean like in the stock market?'

'Maybe you could use some cash, shithead,' says Locust. 'Treat that honey of yours right for once. Before she takes up with a real man. Shit, might go round there and treat her myself.'

Jordan leaps onto the bonnet of the car and over to the far side. He has the door open in a flash and grabs Locust by the hair, smashing his sunglasses against the bridge of his nose. Into his eyes. Locust jerks back in the seat and Jordan grabs his collar and pulls him against the steering wheel. The horn blasts. He drags Locust out the door and into the street, Locust clutching at his bleeding face. Locust throws three or four wild blows, half blind before Jordan drags him to a potted tree and bashes his forehead against the trunk. Locust's face slides from knot to knot, leaking blood. Jordan pulls him away and drives his head against a raised knee, then kicks him twice and shoves him, face first, against a newspaper honesty-box. Locust lies in the grass, oozing vomit and broken teeth.

'Te Awa.'

Jordan turns.

Sandman sits on the Zephyr's bonnet, sawn-off shotgun aimed at Jordan's face.

'This could be it,' says Sandman. 'Here. Now.'

'What are you waiting for?'

'Not much of a way to go. Over some smart-mouthed wanker with a grudge against you.'

'You don't have it.'

'Oh come on. Think. If I was to kill you now, I'd just say that he did it.' He glances at Locust. 'Be walking round free as a bird while your cook's blubbering over your coffin. You don't understand the balance of power. You just don't understand socio-politics. I despair for the younger generation. I do.'

'I've had enough of this.'

Jordan turns and walks away.

'Te Awa. You will join us. One way or the other.'

Jacqueline sits in a wicker chair by the window. She doesn't look up when he comes in, and in fact is so still and quiet that he is surprised when she appears when he turns on the light.

'How come you're sitting here in the dark?' he says.

'Just thinking.'

She looks up. 'We're going to have a baby,' she says.

He leans back against the bench. 'What about your studies?' he says.

'I'll fit them in.'

'You sure.'

'About what?'

'About everything, I suppose.'

'Sure? Shit. Who says I get to be sure.'

He walks over to her, sits cross-legged on the floor next to the chair. He reaches for her hand, draws her down onto the floor with him. He leans back against the wall and she leans into him. Her fingers reaching for his.

'What happened to your hands?' she says.

'Dropped some crates on them.'

'You need to be more careful.'

'Ain't that the truth.'

She looks out the window again, then back to his face. 'Are you going to be around?' she says. 'Are you going to be around, for them?'

'Yes.'

'That's easy to say.'

'Yeah, I know.'

'I've seen enough bastards think they'll give it a go. Kids and that. Then remember their loyalties to their mates and go and do something stupid and end up back inside.'

'That's them. Not me.'

'I know. Trouble just follows you around.'

'I'm not going to sit here and justify my existence. Not even to you.'

'A child needs a father,' she says.

He lays his hand on her midriff. 'This child *has* a father,' he says.

She places one hand under his, one over. 'No lies,' she says. 'No bullshit. If you can't or don't want to be a part of this – tell me now.'

'I want it.'

She clasps his hand and doesn't let go.

Kokinia Prison Camp, Athens, 1941

Prisoner 42965, Lieutenant Kingi Heremia, stands a few feet from the wire, looking out at the dusty hills, the turquoise sky. A sudden arrow of movement and he looks up, capturing in his stare the outline of a petrel. He watches it float, suspended on a wind current, then pirouette and circle and vanish behind the cypresses.

A shout from a guard. He moves a few paces further from the wire. The guard approaches, anonymous beneath his helmet. The helmet itself somewhat redundant as – in here at least – the Wehrmacht have all the guns. He searches the sky for the petrel again, perhaps tracking a line in his imagination, back to the island.

'The bloody stuff's still there,' says a voice from behind him.

He turns his head. Another prisoner, Clark, an officer from the New Zealand force that was captured in the retreat from Greece.

'You can look at it,' says Clark, 'imagine with all your might that the wire just isn't there. But it is.'

'Thinking of home. Terrible habit.'

'Where's home for you?'

'Northland. Te Hapua. About as far north as you can get.'

'Canterbury for me. Ashburton. Where'd you pick up the accent?'

'Cambridge.'

'Ah. A scholar?'

'After a fashion.'

'You smart chaps shouldn't be dumb enough to end up in places like this.'

'You know, I was just thinking the same thing.'

He is kept in the camp for another four weeks, each day scratched with the end of a spoon in the dirt within the shadow of his tent, the marks having to be recut every couple of days after they've filled with dust. After his capture in the sea off Maleme airfield he had been interred at Galatas prison camp with other escapees gathered up from the hillsides, plus the last of the soldiers captured in the original surrender in May. Galatas camp was a scorched dust-bowl, run with a mixture of totalitarian efficiency and careless violence. Prisoners escaped with surprising regularity, sometimes prompting little action from the guards, sometimes prompting a 'stray' bullet to find someone walking too close to the fence. There was no pattern, no certainty. A prisoner might be stopped and screamed at on an innocent errand, with nothing more than verbal violence dished out. The next might be shot on sight.

One night Kingi lay in his tent, his dream scarred with rushes of wind. He reached up, ran his fingers across his forehead where a thin trail of blood slid towards his eyes. He sat up staring at the row of new bullet holes letting in arrows of light from the searchlight towers, the beams angled like surreal raindrops. There was no more shooting. He dabbed at the scratch with a torn piece of his shirt. Within a few minutes he was sleeping again.

He raises his eyes up from the horizon, scanning each sector of sky as if through the dirty glass of a cockpit windshield, watching for any change to the balance of things. A formation of clouds builds in a slow-motion scramble from plain cirrus into the shape of an infant thunderhead in ever-deepening grey, then black. He raises his head to an eleven o'clock position, blinking his eyes in joy as the first of the rain hits his face. All around him men leap up from their card games or turn away from their walks to duck back into their barracks. He alone stays, under the watchful eye of the guard in the tower high above him, taking the water on his cheeks. He opens his mouth, lets the rain take him.

Just after Christmas they board the vessel *Arkadia* which takes them to another camp at Salonika. The new camp is a shock after the relative ease of Galatas and even Athens. Acres of barbed wire, and guards who shoot for pleasure if no other reason presents itself. A couple of months later he peers between the wooden slats of a railway wagon, watching the Mediterranean woodlands give way to deeper grey – mountain and forest and cold that penetrates any layer of clothing – as they pierce the late winter snowdrifts of Poland. Behind him someone farts. A groan of dysentery. There's a shuffle of feet moving away from the culprit as Kingi puts his lips to the hole in the slat, happy to lose sight of the world just to taste the freshness of the air. A whiff of steam, burning coal. Any tiny strain of oxygen is a gift to him.

Kommando E535, prison work-camp in southern Poland. He spends long days burrowed underground, digging for coal to fuel the Reich's engine. The frontline war becomes remote to them, just the occasional drone of an aeroplane engine high overhead, the sound both muffled and echoing in the caverns as 1942 dissolves into 1943. Twelve hours a day entombed in a sunken ship. The change of seasons mocks them. Underground, even with the intense thirst, a trickle of water is viewed with suspicion, a weak flow viewed with outright fear. Soldiers practice their insolence on the guards, a couple of them roly-poly city workers detailed to the lowly ranks of guarding the 'filth of the Allied gangsters'. A couple appear fresh from the Hitler Youth, all pimples and pomposity. Now and then a prisoner plays a game with the wrong guard and takes a rifle butt in the teeth for his troubles, a boot to the ribs while he is prone in the coal dust. One man is shot for no known reason on the march back to camp one afternoon. The killer is no more than a child, prodding at the shivering lump bleeding into the snow beneath him. The Luger's barrel steams in the cold, the only warmth for miles around, as the prisoner's body – a Canadian from memory – begins to vanish beneath the snowdrift.

Jacqueline is five months pregnant. She has an appointment with the ultrasound clinic. Jordan takes her in the knitwear-factory van, driving all the way with her hand on his knee. The clinic is sterile. White walls, innocuous décor paintings. Muzak over the sound system. She sits reading a magazine, he walks around the room, stopping to prod at the artificial flowers. The nurse calls them, and they're ushered in.

A television screen sits among a bank of other electronic devices. A strange grey-blue haze, the shapes pulsing like a fish's gills. Jordan sits on a plastic chair, Jacqueline's fingers entwined in his. The doctor searches Jacqueline's skin, his eyes focused only on the screen. The event has the silent reverence of prayer almost, the doctor lost within the electrical conversation between the device in his fingers and the screen. He raises his eyebrows.

'Everything looks fine,' he says. 'Would you like to know if it's a girl or a boy?'

After the appointment they drive out to Beachlands, then on to Maraetai, taking the winding shoreline road to Umupuia. Jordan gets out, takes off his shoes and socks and walks over the grass verge to the sand, speckled with a million shells. The sand goes from fawn to a mottled grey with the setting sun, the last light burning on the highest ridge of the hills. Jacqueline appears at his shoulder with some cold chicken, a bowl of salad. A bottle of sparkling grape juice. They sit at a picnic table, looking up at the occasional passing car. Then Jacqueline goes for a walk around the bay. He watches her grow small against the retreating tide, then crouches in the sand, looking up the line of the bay. A sprinkling of sheep on a far paddock follow the passage of a farmer on a three-wheeled bike. The silver sky beyond.

He lifts a handful of sand, tiny droplets of it falling across his bare feet.

She comes back along the sand, holding her jandals in her hand. She stops when she sees him staring, does a twirl and curtsey by the storm-water run-off pipe. She does another twirl in the sand but slips, falls flat on her backside. He stands clapping. Puts his fingers between his lips and whistles.

'Seven, maybe seven-point-five,' he says. 'For the degree of difficulty.'

'Ouch.'

'What's next.'

'Oh, by the way, thanks for the sympathy.'

They go back up to the van, put the rubbish in an overflowing bin. Then they sit on the edge of the grass ridge, Jacqueline's feet swinging over the sand. The distant cries of gulls seem like the only sounds in the world.

'Should've brought the camera,' he says.

'We'll bring it next time,' she says.

By 1944 there is talk among the men of the Russian army advancing to the east. Talk of the prisoners being shuttled now into Germany itself. Bombers of every colour scheme pass overhead, a bizarre airborne League of Nations. Now and then they drop their lethal seeds within earshot of the camp. Kingi stands from the lunch of cold soup and mouldy bread and walks to the roadway a few paces away. He has heard a shuffling on the stones of the road. He looks one way to an empty stretch through the trees. He hears a shout in German and turns the other way, turning not into the eyes of the party's guards but a platoon of ghosts.

They are more ragged than the term 'ragged' can begin to hint at. Thin as broomsticks, covered in sores and blisters, hair flaking like paint on rotted timber. Eyes stare, not at him, not at anything discernable. The yellow and black stripes of their uniforms seem to run on into their cavernous faces. As they pass, the reek of them is overpowering and he gags. A small retinue of guards herd them with the mechanical efficiency of workmen in a slaughterhouse. A ragged form stumbles into Kingi and begins to retch against his chest. Kingi lifts him upright, setting his bony face pointed forward and away. He stands still, one scarecrow among a column of scarecrows. The last man turns to him and stares, his eyes like spinning coins. He manages a grin, a line of broken, yellowed teeth. Then he collapses, his limbs like kindling. He grapples in the stones, clawlike hands searching for a lever with which to raise himself. He cannot. Kingi walks to him, reaches down to lift him from the roadway. The prisoner collapses again when the first shot hits him. Kingi jumps, then tries to lift him again. The second shot pins the man to the road. The third takes off the top of his bald head, peeling away his skull cap like an onion. Blood sloshes onto Kingi's worn-out shoes. Kingi closes his eyes. Waits for the next shot. His. But it never comes. When he opens his eyes again the ghost platoon has dissolved into the background of snow. Not even the sound of their footfalls remains. Just the acrid smell of smoke.

The move comes in January 1945, the guards setting off explosives in the pit head to flood the mine shafts and deny the use of the precious fuel to the advancing Russians. They move out on foot, dressed in uniforms holed and patched and holed again and patched again. Each man's face is a shadow of his pre-war self. They speak in a half-dozen different accents or languages, but with a strange brotherhood reserved for such men suspended in time, between real life and death. They're like the crew of a ship in a bottle. Some of the men – the infirm, the injured – walk leaning on their comrades. The fitter men attempt to hide their condition on the assumption that if the more cynical of the guards find out, they will shoot them. Kingi walks with his arm looped around a prisoner named Illingworth, originally a big man and well fleshed, but now reminiscent of an aged and empty picture frame.

Any hint of a marching formation has vanished like desert rain. There is little or no chatter, not even among the guards. Kingi looks from one German face to another, eyes as empty as their prey. There are days when, at evening, curled up with the others in some barn stinking of cattle or horse urine, he cannot remember a moment of where he was in the morning. He has taken to reciting flight manuals from memory, using their structure to draw himself out of this tunnel. Engineering details, mathematical equations. $X =$ the product of $T \times Y$ to the power of H. Anything with a logic to it. He has seen hungry men crunch up a leaf in their palms and eat it. He has knelt, sucking at handfuls of snow for their tiny hint of sustenance. There are only four guards now, the rest having been picked up by a defensive unit. With their westward move towards Germany, he senses it could be another month before any 'friendly' army will overrun them. In his condition, in all their conditions, that is a month they don't have.

The sound of bombers overhead is a constant now. A couple of times bombs fall close enough for the men to be shrouded in snow or dirt, crouching behind tree stumps or ice cliffs, then emerging into the clearing light like some ancient race of bog men.

The next morning dawns with a hint of late-winter sun. After a couple of hours walking the guards call a halt, one complaining that his left boot has come apart. He sits on a boulder and raises his foot to examine the sole. Another guard, a greying, bookish-looking man, pulls a packet of cigarettes from his tunic and his comrades take one each. Kingi looks up through the thin sprinkling of trees, raises his stare skyward at the drone of aeroplane engines. Two of the guards head away amongst the matchwood forest, talking to each other. The grey-haired guard follows the line of Kingi's stare, shakes his head, smirking, then says something in a patronising tone. Kingi reaches to pick a few flakes of snow from a trunk, crushes it between his palms, watching the water drip through his fingers. He is still watching the water drip when he realises that he is now on his back on the ground, hands held aloft over his face, instinctively shielding them from the fire.

The body of the greying guard flies over him, crashes against a tree. The tree bends, its torso aflame. Everywhere there are clods of dirt, branches shattering and men's bodies cartwheeling. Whole trees collapsing like dynamited chimneys. Snow and mud everywhere. He crawls to the lee of a rotting trunk, his hands over his bare head, his ears screaming in a metallic whine. One moment he is flat, the next seeming to stand, then float. Then flat again. He burrows into the snow, pulls a couple of branches over him.

Silence.

A world of echoes, as if he is underwater. He stands, leaning against a trunk, trying to build some semblance of landscape about him. Two bodies, both German. One is whole, the other in pieces. He walks to them, rummages among their uniforms, lifts out a Luger. He sets a round in the chamber, then turns to look for survivors. He kicks at what bodies he finds, friend or foe. None stir, until he comes across a lone German out among the woods, lying with his trousers down around his ankles. Burned pieces of another body hang from a tree a few yards away. The German is puffing, his pupils huge in his pale face. His teeth are chattering. Kingi raises the Luger. The guard blinks hard then fumbles at his waist, perhaps realising suddenly he is half naked. He fumbles for his penis, takes it into his hand and begins to urinate down over his bare legs, the stream turning to icicles on his bony legs. He looks back up at Kingi.

'Kamerad?' he says still pissing over his legs. 'Kamerad?'

Kingi levels the Luger at the German's temple, takes a gulp of icy air and steadies his finger against the trigger. The German splutters a tiny bubble of blood from his mouth and lays his head back. His pupils seem to withdraw from the world, like leaves in a snowdrift. In the silence Kingi lifts his finger away from the untouched trigger of the Luger.

He takes a belt from one of the Germans, to keep his trousers fixed to his skeletal waist. Another has a map, another a rifle and a couple of cartridge clips. None have any food. He walks off through the barren glade.

He spends the night in a snow cave. The winter ice crackles around him as he debates his destination once again. To the east the Russians will be approaching, but to find them he'd have to go through the retreating scatterings of the German army. To the south, who knows? Is Czechoslovakia still held by the Nazis? The last snippet he'd heard of the Allies in the south, from a prisoner captured in late '44, they were stalled in Italy. To the West, the Brits or Yanks must be out there somewhere, but there's an awful lot of the Reich's land to cross before he'd be sure to run across them. After all, if Berlin has fallen, or is close to falling – and hence the Reich – there'd be no more bombing missions lighting up the night sky, pounding the bejesus out of the Wehrmacht's supply lines. So that option can be dismissed. He closes his eyes for a moment, searching for some thread to find his way out of this labyrinth. But within a minute he is asleep.

In the morning he raids a woodsman's hut at gunpoint and leaves dressed as a Polish peasant. The man stands complaining in his dirty underwear as Kingi walks away through the bare forest trunks. He continues west for a few miles, aware now that he should be over the German border.

The next day they appear before him on the road. At first he lurks behind, his eyes sketching their trudging shapes out of the misted light. Another few miles and he is among them, their meagre accumulations in carts, in baby carriages, anything with wheels. They pay him no mind, nor even acknowledge his presence. They are German in voice, but in visage something else altogether and it strikes him now that he has come full circle: from shooting them down from the anonymity of a Hurricane's cockpit, to knowing their callousness and confusion first hand; and now he is anonymous once again. But this time he is among them, among their children and mothers and grandmothers. The stencils of their Luftwaffe's toys flashed up on the briefing board at Biggin Hill never mentioned stumbling women in rags, snot-nosed kids shitting their pants while they walked, screaming at the emptiness of their bellies. He thinks of the stumbling, starving prisoners of the camp for 'undesirables' gunned down in the road, and for a moment he closes his eyes to it all. To all nationalism, to all pomposity, because this is where it leads.

He spends the night in an old shepherd's hut, hardly larger than a country outhouse. He has to sleep half-sitting up, but at least he's out of the wind. The next morning he is on the road again, pausing on a hillock to watch a column of men thread the same road the refugees were taking west. He is watching them for a full ten minutes before it registers that they're Allied prisoners.

He cuts through wooded glades, a few shoots of green threatening to appear through the grey. He stops, cradles a leaf in his fingertips. Tiny, fleeting perhaps, but at this moment soft, delicate as a woman's hair.

The buzz of an engine, turning into a whine. Not a bomber, a fighter. Or several. He stays within the glade, searching the sky for their profiles. A skitter of shadows in the snow, too quick to pinpoint as they pass overhead. The rattle of machine guns, small cannons. They are shooting at something on the ground, beyond the next hill. A German patrol perhaps, a convoy. He moves deeper into the wood.

Flights of bombers and fighters dip from the clouds off and on all day, suffocating him with the heartbeat of war. Blotches of smoke rise here and there. The odd burst of flame, then blackness. He keeps heading west, coming at dusk upon a clearing, still, almost serene amid the carnage. He should be wary, but he isn't. He strolls out into its opening, as if taking his ease in the high street on a spring evening. He is about midway across the clearing when the plane comes from nowhere, a hole opening in the sky above him, sucking a sudden swirl of smoke. He plunges into the snow, flat, like a swimmer caught mid-dive. His ears wait for the thump, the sudden ringing. But it doesn't come. He opens his eyes, looks up, just as the strange snow descends like feather-down over the clearing.

He stretches a hand out beside him, takes one of the snow-flakes, realising in its damp brittleness in the chill air that it is paper. He is awash in a field of paper. He blinks his eyes clear of ice. They are pamphlets, worded in both English and German, exhorting the 'defeated' Germans to surrender. He begins to laugh. Remembering newsreels of Chamberlain waving a shred of paper in the air, 'Peace in our time', and they're still bloody at it. He closes his eyes, even out here in the open. Bugger them, if someone sharp-eyed spots him they can have him. Wake me when it's over. Sleep, I just need sleep.

In a dream Alissandra hovers over him, her hair on his bare chest. The harmony of her shadowed smile. He has one arm in the water of the stream, trawling through the reeds, the tiny bubbles bred by the current. She dips her own hand in the water then raises it above him, a single finger descending out of the sun towards him, her eyes hidden by her cascading hair. Her finger finds the centre of his forehead. His pores accept the touch of the water. Grateful. She runs her fingertip down between his eyes, across the bridge of his nose then away, her fingers blooming like a parachute. He reaches for it, just out of range, he stretches but can't ... quite ... reach ... there. He has it. A piece of paper. He screws it into a ball, lets it fall away.

Jordan stops at the dairy and picks up the newspaper. A gang shooting at a traffic light. *Reginald Joseph Tomoana, known in gang circles as* Sandman ...

He pays for the paper, puts it under his arm and walks out to the van.

A week later he is in the back bar of the Eagle Tavern when Dylan comes in. He stands by himself at the bar for a while then comes over to where Jordan is playing snooker.

'Cuz,' says Dylan.

'How is it?'

'Cool. Cool.'

'The cops catch the dude that killed your mate?'

Dylan shakes his head. Jordan completes his game, loses, forfeits fifty cents.

'Another one?' says Dylan.

'Nah. Time I got back.'

'Cook's got your old fella on a leash.'

'What are you doing here? This isn't your local.'

Dylan stops smiling. He looks around.

'Just here for the beer, bro,' he says.

A man comes out of the toilet, fiddling with his fly. He doesn't have a gang patch, but here it's hard to tell. Almost everyone is aligned to something or someone. The man stands talking to a small group of people, mostly younger than he is. They seem to hang on his words. He laughs, says his goodbyes and walks to the door.

Dylan looks back at Jordan.

'Spot ya,' he says.

Jordan nods, reaches for his jacket. A guy at another table is selling some mussels in plastic bags. Jordan fumbles in his pockets for some money, goes across to him. He buys two bags then heads out the door. It has rained and puddles dot the asphalt. Iridescent streaks of petrol. He is halfway across the carpark when he hears voices. The street light profiles two figures, one of them Dylan's. Jordan opens the van's door, and steps in, throwing the plastic bags with the mussels on the floor. Shouts. He holds the key an inch from the ignition, but doesn't put it in. Instead he steps back out of the van and walks towards the two men.

'Everything OK, cuz?' he says.

'Get outta here, man,' says Dylan.

The other man, who Jordan recognises now as the guy who came out of the toilet, leans his head back then spits in Dylan's face. The street light illuminates the edge of the blade, only for an instant. Then it disappears somewhere within the toilet guy's ribs. He raises a hand, stares at Dylan, his body shuddering when Dylan withdraws the knife then shoves it back in. The two men in a tense embrace. Blood on their shoes. Dylan steps back.

Jordan closes his eyes, then opens them. The carpark is somehow darker now.

'What the hell did you do that for?' he says.

'Utu, bro. He wasted Sandman.'

A car pulls alongside. Faces stare. Jordan turns his own face away from them, pulls his jacket up over his head. He grabs Dylan and pulls him into the shadows. The toilet guy lies among the cigarette butts and dogshit. Bleeding into the rainwater.

The twilight is brief and cold, a counterpoint to the slow trudge of refugees slipping on from the east and south. As if Germany's borders have been pushed inwards on the map, sending all names and roads and railways sliding into its centre. He joins them, but pauses at dusk on the outskirts of a city, letting a few hundred footsteps of the haunted caravan pass on the road. He looks into the faces. Some show exhaustion, others show a hint of hope at the zigzag of buildings on the horizon. Even with the camouflage of the refugee column around him, he is wary of travelling into an urban area. Cities mean garrisons, possibly SS or Gestapo. He steps off the edge of the road, wades through a net of muddy wagon tracks and on into a field. He negotiates a stone wall, and walks up a farmer's road into a small wood. As he walks past the grey slate farmhouse a face appears at the curtains and vanishes. He imagines his own visage, his figure. What a fright he'd give the undergrads in Cambridge if he walked in the door of the common room right now, with all the appearance of a Palaeolithic man rescued from a peat bog. In a field he finds a small cache of turnips and puts them, half frozen, into his pockets. He uses a rock to shear off an angled piece of stone from the wall, creating a sharp edge. He crouches in the lee of a grove of elms, chipping away at a turnip, then eating it as slowly as he can manage, to make the taste – however awful – last.

Sometime mid-evening he drifts into sleep, opening his eyes once again to a Cretan sky. A flock of gulls circling, pushed inland by an oncoming summer storm. He stands watching them, somewhat disoriented when he sees they all sport leather flight helmets and goggles. He rocks back on his heels, watching them flow straight overhead, making the most hideous cacophony of squawks. He looks back down, forward again towards the ocean. Just in time to see the stormfront assemble like some great bulbous cabbage, sprouting tails and heads and tongues. For some reason he is frightened now and he doesn't like it. He turns, searches for a door back inside, but there is just the bare stucco wall of the villa.

He wakes to fire, scalding his eyelids and forehead. He raises a hand in front of his eyes, begins to back up the hillside, his feet scrambling. Stilling only when he realises the fire is miles away. In the city. Or rather, the city is in the fire. He stands. Towers of blood red rise against the black, turning his own hands as bright as daylight. He moves further into the tree line, the naked trunks and branches cutting across the night-mare theatre beyond like cracks in stained glass. Oranges and reds and golds and maroons. Sudden swarms of yellow sparks that must be as large as trolley cars give birth to a single creature of flame possessing the arms and legs of some monstrous puppet. A hundred-yard-high Pinocchio stomping around in a mad, drunken dance. Burning. Screaming. He lies back in the dirt, pulls his peasant's coat up around his chin. After a while he closes his eyes to the fire, letting it flicker against his eyelids.

The city burns all morning, then at midday more planes rip its bones to shreds. Not just bombers but fighters. Small cannon fire, machine guns strafing the streets. He looks up, not recognising the outlines of the fighters, but realising by their markings that they are American.

In the twilight he moves out. The streets of the city's out-skirts are filled with refugees. Soldiers guard the streets to the town centre. He skirts them, moving down backstreets, across the little cobbled squares. Here and there shops sit with their windows blown out. A haberdasher's, a tobacconist's, a milliner's. A confectioner's or butcher's would be rather more handy.

He passes across a couple of main thoroughfares, turning to where their inner reaches have been turned into caverns by sheets of smoke, buildings hung with individual fires, like hellish Christmas decorations. Streets blocked with smoking rubble, here and there a body out on the asphalt or cracked stones. A man, a child. A naked woman. A team of horses still tethered to a smouldering wagon, some metal pails, half melted, sitting amid a small pyre of bones. Shoes here and there, perhaps a suitcase. A woman's cosmetic bag spilled. A comb, a brush. A small cracked mirror. A pair of spectacles catching the strange, pulsing light. The closer he gets to the city centre the more wind blows through the bodies, the sparer they become, cavernous themselves. He steps with a wary tread, avoiding a hand, a foot, an infant's blackened face. Some of the mouths are open in shock, some merely surprise. As if photographed mid-gesture, then sculptured in clay and sent to the kiln. There is commotion around him, but no haste to it, like figures attempting to run through water, or quicksand. A bespectacled man with a long scarf walks through the dust, calling someone's name. And all around the blackened snow. Not snow. Dust. He stands, the world passing around him, just shadows now. He had thought to have seen death, in the ribbon of smoke of a falling aeroplane, an incendiary streamer, a wave farewell. But that was not death. That was not death. Or if it was, then *this* is something else.

He stands in silence, his feet spread wide to balance himself, like a man adrift on an ice floe, a raft of tethered logs. No certainty in the line of his body against the darkness. A sliver of masonry falls, dust circling at his weary feet. From somewhere he hears a scream, but he can't tell if it is human. Could be the wind rifling through a blasted doorway perhaps, or the open mouth of a burnt child.

They got guns, we got guns, all God's chillun got guns.

A bakery. Windows blasted out. A few loaves of bread sit on smouldering racks. The bread is dusted, half-scorched into charcoal, but he reaches through the window and takes it anyway, stuffs it in his pocket. He turns back to the street. A man faces him, eyes staring. Kingi reaches for the Luger but the man darts away, stooping at a splay of half-incinerated corpses around the skeleton of a tram. He bends. In a flash he has taken melted rings off fingers, slipped necklaces over hairless skulls. There is a shout. Two soldiers step from a doorway, call out 'Halt.' Kingi fades into the ruin of the bakery. The man looks around, pockets his treasure, makes for the shell of a department store. 'Halt!' He doesn't. They shoot. He falls. Kingi stands in the shadows, chewing the burned end of a piece of bread. Pumpernickel.

He moves through the rest of the suburbs in the cover of dusk. The air itself is like summer, scalding his throat. He walks along a riverbed looking for some clean water, but all sources of liquid are either burned dry or layered with steaming bodies. In their attempt to escape the fires tearing at their backs and hair, some appear to have actually drowned.

A fortnight later Kingi is in woodlands, patches of ground thawing in the first winds of spring. Now and then a flower, perhaps a bird. He moves south-west, towards the direction everyone else is fleeing. Moving against the tide of refugees escaping from the fronts, grime-covered soldiers slumped in the backs of trucks, on the turrets of tanks. At night he walks the roads, but in daylight he treads only the outlands, pastures wet with melting snow and ice, his identity still hidden within a woodsman's rags.

He wakes at dawn, wedged in the branches of a tree, a pain in his side from a new growing shoot. He gathers his gear about him and slips down into the slush. At mid-morning fighters appear from nowhere, strafing the fields, the roads, anything that harbours movement. The fighters swoop low enough that he can smell the aviation fuel. He stands sniffing it, loosens the collar of his coat, baring his full face to the wind for the first time in weeks. All around him figures fall, slaughter in the spring sunshine. The air shatters into dust, helmets, rifles, chunks of flesh and spurts of blood. He stops dead in the road, raises his arms out from his side, a scarecrow among the flotsam of retreat. Of defeat. He who had never seen the face of a single man he'd killed, a single death in flesh and blood, but has now seen hundreds. The bullets tear new furrows among the fields, send swarms of leaves howling in their wind. He stands for fully ten minutes, the river of boots and bodies and baby carriages passing around him as if he is a stone amid their current. After the second pass, the fighters swing around to the north and come back. A man walks past him, lifts a pistol from a shoulder holster and raises it to the planes, his whole body jerking as he fires, as if he has walked into an electric fence. A stray shot from a plane hits him and he falls. A woman next to him lets go of the hand of the little boy she is walking with, picks up the pistol and carries on shooting, her finger fumbling at the trigger. Misfiring. She curses herself, curses the pistol, curses everything around her. The fighters move away, the whine of their engines fading on the wind. The woman spins around on the dusty road, sending people ducking. Now facing Kingi where he stands with his arms raised. She points the pistol in his direction, the muzzle trembling from the shudders engulfing her body. The boy stands mute beside her, not so much silent as empty. He reaches down and pulls up his socks. Everyone else has ducked for cover so it is just the woman and the child and Kingi, islanded on a road, somewhere in southern Germany. She waves the gun in a crazed zigzag, her voice beginning to break. Her face tortured, terrified. Once it might have been pretty. Light blue eyes, perhaps turquoise in a kinder light. Kingi leans towards her, reaching his arm a few inches across the no man's land between them. She stares at him, blowing air out through her cheeks. Spittle wobbles on her chin. Her hair is wet, matted across her scalp.

We got guns, they got guns, all God's chillun got guns …

Statues.

Staring.

Her face softens and she begins to nod. As if she and he share something personal, something intimate. But there are skitters of shadows in her eyes, cracked glass. Her pupils widen and she begins to smile. Her teeth appear, bloodstained where she has bitten her lips in her rage. The boy steps to her, tugs the edge of her coat. She spins around, pistol in two hands, and shoots him in the torso. He sits back on the ground, the bullet raising a small tent of dust as it ricochets off the ground after passing through him. He jerks once, then lies back, as if it is time for bed. She spins around again, jerking the pistol towards anyone and everyone. Then at last, back at Kingi. She takes it in two hands again, the tip a spearpoint in the weak sun, focusing on Kingi's chest. Kingi reaches into his belt, lifts out the Luger and shoots her in the forehead. She spasms, a clod sailing from the back of her head, into the field. She falls at the feet of the boy, her arms jerking, then still. Kingi lowers the Luger, pulls the trigger again and again, emptying the magazine into the dust, stopping after a few seconds when he realises there's nothing left but clicks. He drops it on the ground and carries on down the road south.

An hour later there is a rumble from the trees and he stops. American tanks are coming across the field towards him. The refugees run for the opposite wood, for the treeline and the hills beyond. He watches them go then turns back to the tanks. Soldiers now appear, threading between them. He hears English for the first time in weeks. He doesn't move. The soldiers approach, wary, glancing over his shoulder, into every nook of landscape beyond. Their weapons are poised. He raises his arms, closing his eyes to the smoke.

The knock on the door comes as Jordan takes a swig of water from a glass at the sink. Jacqueline pokes her head out from the bedroom where she readies herself for bed.

'Not some of your vagabond mates wanting a nightcap,' she says.

He is halfway to the door when it shatters, toppling off its hinges. One policeman grabs him by the hair, the other two pinning his arms. He thinks for a moment of going for it, causing as much damage to them as he can, but then sees Jacqueline still standing in the doorway in just her bra and panties, her belly round and full. He bites his lip, looks up at the bulb hanging from the ceiling.

When he is dragged out of the back of the police van and into the remand cell he is still dressed only in his undies.

The trial is mostly stalemate. A couple of people from the car that slowed down in the carpark knew their figures well enough to place them. The police try to 'persuade' him to inform on Dylan; Dylan to inform on him. Both remain silent. Jacqueline comes to see him before the trial. They sit on opposite sides of a grey wooden table. Whenever he moves his chair squeaks, the only sound in the room.

'Just dob him in,' says Jacqueline. 'How hard can it be?'

'What? Where did you grow up?'

'*I'm* not there any more.'

'That's not how it is.'

'Oh, thanks for clearing that up for me.'

She lifts a packet of cigarettes from her jacket pocket, opens the lid towards him. He takes one, but doesn't look to light it, just puts it in his own pocket. She tosses the whole pack onto the table, it slides off and falls into his lap. He picks it up, sets it back on the table.

'Why won't you?' she says.

'Because.'

'Great answer.'

'Only one I got at the moment.'

'Should I come back, when you've got a better one?'

'Look –'

'I won't wait. Don't think I will. Maybe you've OD'd on some bullshit code but I haven't.'

'It's got nothing to do with any code.'

'You've got your own loyalties. Here. Sitting right in front of you.'

She stands, lifts her shirt out of her skirt, baring her pregnant belly.

'See.'

He closes his eyes.

'You don't understand,' he says.

'You got that right. First thing you've got right since we sat down here.'

He shakes his head. She walks around the table. A couple of guards take a step towards her. She stands in front of him, reaching out to take his head in her hands, drawing his face against her bare tummy.

'Listen,' she says.

'Don't do this.'

'Just shut the fuck up and listen. Do you hear that?'

'Jacq –'

'Do you *hear* that?'

He pulls away, tilting his head down and running his fingers across his eyes.

'I didn't mean for it to happen like this,' he says.

'Actually, that doesn't make any difference. Screw Dylan. Screw them all. It's about *us*. About you and me and the little one. No one else.'

'It's not that simple.'

She slumps back in her chair, her eyes closed.

'Nah,' she says. 'Uh uh. It's exactly that simple. How many times have I heard this shit before.'

'It won't be forever.'

'Yes it will. You and me just have different concepts of "forever".'

She looks towards the window. Her eyes have a hint of rain in them. They're like the iridescent puddles on the asphalt of the carpark. He thinks hard for something to say, but nothing comes out. She stares long into the window, as if it is she that will remain here and he that will leave when their time is up.

'You know what pisses me off?' she says. 'My dad was wrong about you. Dead wrong. I told him a hundred times. He's still wrong and he'll always be wrong. Wrong, wrong, wrong, wrong, wrong. But what pisses me off the most is that none of that actually matters any more.'

Accessory to Murder. Reduced to manslaughter on the vagaries of the law. Arguments back and forth. None of them coming to much. Life sentence. Good behaviour, out in maybe eight. He and Dylan are separated. He never sees him again, just hears on the radio a few years later – while he's sitting eating a bowl of Cornflakes in the prison dining room – that one Dylan Waaka was found on the floor of a prison kitchen with his head caved in. A bloodied frying pan was found nearby. He sits with a spoonful of Cornflakes held six inches from his lips. Droplets of milk dripping into the bowl. He puts the spoon into his mouth and sits chewing.

No one is ever charged.

X

Mare Imbrium (Sea of Rains)

Leonie

There were two of them standing on the path. Their blue uniforms looked hard against the grass beyond. A man and a woman constable. The woman was blond with lots of freckles, and she had her hair pulled back in the severest bun. Must be regulations or something. She was nice though, if a little scared. They asked my name, Leo's full name. The make and model and year of his motorbike – like I'd know. They said something about a car and a motorbike colliding, about how the road was wet. I don't remember what they said after that. They sat on the couch, stiff like figures in photographs, then the woman stood up, walked across the rug and sat next to me. She asked if she could make me a cup of tea. The guy just sat looking at his hands. The lady cop then asked if I wanted her to bring my washing in, because it'd started to rain. Moana was jumping around, making a lot of noise, twirling on the carpet with her arms outstretched. I reached out and touched her and her face seemed suddenly cold.

'Shush, Bub,' I said. 'Shush. OK?'

She kept on twirling.

At the funeral, Mum and Dad shuffled a little on their feet. I can still see them standing with their backs to the wind coming in from the harbour. Beyond them the little church on the far hill was so tiny against the bush rising on the hillside above it. At one point Dad's glasses blew right off his face and he stooped to pick them up, but the wind blew them further away, up against the mound of dirt. Moana snatched at them and I let her out of the pushchair to pick them up, but she forgot about them and instead crouched poking with a finger into the dirt, trying to make the shape of a happy face. It was a game we used to play. Leave each other drawings of happy faces. In sand, in spilt sugar or a spread of flour on the bench. Sometimes even in the soap suds in her bath water.

The guys from Leo's whānau were all dressed in black. Dark shades. His father wasn't there, but no one seemed to miss him. Except for the little tiny piece of him that was being lowered into the dirt, with his brothers and cousins dropping flowers into the hole.

Holes in the ground. Places where stuff goes. Sometimes it comes back out and sometimes it doesn't. I thought about that that night, lying in bed. My hand slipped down into the hollow in the mattress next to me. I flicked on the reading light, took off the engagement ring he had given me and rolled it across the sheet, watched it tip down into that indentation. It circled for a while then just stopped and lay on the empty sheet, at about the point where his heart would've been.

Moana has this way sometimes, when she suddenly stops her stream of questions and jumping at every dash of colour or movement she sees. She just stops dead. 'What's up, Bub?' I say. 'Cat got your tongue?' She stands, no part of her moving. And her eyes look older for moment. No, not just old. Older than old. I reach out a hand for her, but she's gone again, chasing some butterfly's shadow across the grass.

Sometimes I don't know what to do. What to tell her. Wishing that I could fast-forward the tape and she'd suddenly be sixteen years old and we could sit and talk about it, prise it open like a jar with a tight lid. I wonder what he is to her now, is he any more than just something that was on the other side of the door for a while but isn't any more. Like a colour faded or a taste that you remember, but can't find again.

I spent months with myself on the other side of that door. An exile in my own heart. It was so much easier to just concentrate on getting the jam or grass stains out of her clothes. Picking up the benefit. I got a waitressing job that gave us some extra to pick up an old car so we could at least head for the beach without having to fall between the cracks of bus schedules. When I'd collect her from a friend's place after work, sometimes she'd be overjoyed to see me and try to almost climb back inside me, and sometimes she'd be ice. That older than old look again. I could never tell what was coming, which part of her I'd see. In the end I gave up and just took care of the next ten seconds. Then the next.

The world might be a big place, but it's built of the tiniest pieces.

Moana sits with a plastic bucket wedged in the sand beyond her toes. Her spade scoops sand from the beach and it falls into the bucket. When it is full she sets down the spade, flattens the captured sand with the palm of her hand, then rises on her knees, lifts the bucket and tips it over. She taps on the over-turned base with the spade, then draws the bucket away, leaving a flattened cone of sand. She sits back and stares at the tiny hill, then stands and takes the bucket in two hands and walks down the beach towards the tide.

Leonie calls out from the dune, then trots over to her, taking Moana's hand in one of hers, the bucket in the other.

'What?' she says.

'Water,' says Moana.

'Sea water?'

Moana nods.

'It's a long way,' says Leonie.

'Don't care. Water.'

They walk down to the shoreline. Moana takes the bucket back from Leonie and crouches at the edge of the shallows, scooping up a half bucket of water. She looks back up the sand. They return to Moana's sand sculpture. The child kneels next to the cone of sand, reaches into the bucket and lifts out a handful of water, losing most of it among the shells. She tries again, quicker this time, setting loose a few droplets over the tiny tower of sand.

'Rain,' she says. 'Rain.'

'Who's clever then, huh?' says Leonie.

'Moana.'

Leonie laughs then kneels next to Moana, dipping her own hand into the bucket, sprinkling water, making tiny furrows in the face of the sand.

In Jordan's boat's cabin the books are usually laid out in a neat row, but today most of them are stacked in a tower reaching from the floor. Kataraina leans the broom against the wall and sits looking at them. The largest book is on the bottom, smallest on top, as if they are returning to the form of the tree they once were. She decides to take one out and read it, but which one? She reaches, runs her fingers from book to book, slipping like something fallen from a high branch. A twig, a leaf, a bird. Down the tower's trunk to the floor, to the book taking its full weight, which she recognises by its size as his single encyclopaedia volume. His one window into the world. She crouches, lifts all the other books away one by one and sets them on the floor around her, taking the encyclopaedia in her hands and sitting back on the edge of the bed. She opens it and brushes through the first few pages. She flips to the back and begins drifting from there, stopping on a page with two coloured drawings of spheres, one labelled 'Ptolemy' and the other 'Copernicus'. In the first the earth is in the centre, the hub, and circles radiate out for the other planets. In the 'Copernicus' sphere the sun is at the centre. She runs over each of the orbital ripples in her mind, wondering how Mercury, the nearest planet to the sun, stays on its journey without falling in. Wondering how Saturn, the last planet in both sketches doesn't simply go off track and fall off.

She flips the page and stops. The moon. A large painting, shades of dark and paler greys, a few explanatory labels, just as on a map of any other place. She smiles: no roads, no railways. No straight lines. She presses both thumbs into the moon's centre, then draws them outwards, radiating like the lines in Copernicus' solar system, stopping at a deep indentation, a vast bay, painted a darker grey than any other on the map, as if an opening to the sky beyond. She lifts the book up, searches the bay's rough circle for a name.

Mare Imbrium (Sea of Rains)

She presses a thumb into Mare Imbrium's indentation on the moon's face, smiles, thinking of the suggestions of human touch she had seen on the window glass the first day she arrived here. She goes to the small dresser, takes an old builder's pencil from the window ledge above it and writes across the blank space at the foot of the open page.

I didn't know it rained on the moon.

She closes the book, the last few millimetres of her thumb still lodged between its covers, then withdraws her hand and reassembles his tree of books and goes out onto the deck.

Leonie eases herself up the dune, digging her heels beneath the sprigs of marram grass. She looks over Moana's head up at the aeroplane, its mural alive against the backdrop of sand. Her paintbrush sits in the empty paint tin. She lowers her chin to touch it against Moana's cheek, the child's warmth pulsing in her lap. A smile across at where Kingi sits on the paint tin, running a cloth chamfer around the rim of the new piston.

She watches the vibration of veins in his hand as he works, his arms gnarled, their polish fading like the legs of an antique chair. He pauses, lifting the component to eye level, seeing perhaps a history or future kept secret from others. She had seen this before, with her father's – the man she knew as her father – roses. As a child she had wondered how something silent, unmoving, could catch his ear and eye. How she would call him from across the yard and wait for an answer that never came. She used to sit sometimes, when he was at work, a few inches from the rose bushes in the little bark garden, trying to unravel their language like he could. Sure, they were pretty colours, and she liked the way the rain gathered in their succulent inside folds. But he never showed in any other way that he was a man captured by colour. He wore the same white shirt and brown or black trousers every day, the same navy blue tie. Then as she grew she began to understand the cycle of growth in others, that some things couldn't be grasped and let go in an instant.

Kingi reaches beside him for a file, hardly bigger than a nail file, and taps it against the metal. He turns the piece around in his hands, searching for a keyway perhaps, an entry. He sets the file against it, his touch so light she can't hear its sound.

'You were a pilot,' she calls.

He looks up. 'I still am, young lady.'

'No, I mean, in the Second World War?'

'Gad, yes. A bit before *your* time.'

'Dropping bombs?'

'No. I was a fighter pilot.'

'Like *Top Gun*?'

'*Top Gun*?'

Leonie laughs. 'Never mind,' she says. 'Hey, must be cool to fly. Is it kind of like swimming?'

'A little. Yes.'

Leonie looks down at Moana, then spreads her arms parallel to the ground and begins to make whirring noises. Moana imitates her.

'Your left wing-tip's a touch low,' says Kingi. 'Your aerodynamics will suffer.'

'Oops. OK. How's that?'

'That's better.'

Leonie lifts Moana to her feet and stands also, her arms still out from her sides. She flits off across the sand in her aeroplane guise, swooping down over the shells and out towards the tide. Moana follows her, aping her every move.

Kingi stands smiling, watching them circle. When they approach again, Leonie winks at him and he walks out, raising his arms to lead her up into the softer sand, then down over the high-tide line to the edge of the sea's reach. He pivots, crossing a ford of shallow water then heading back up towards the dunes, the two comrades in his infant squadron tailing him across the sweep of sand.

Jordan pulls out a chair, leans its back against the kitchen wall and sits. He looks up at Kingi, overalls peeled down to his waist, a blackened hand buttering his toast.

'You still want a hand with the engine?' says Jordan.

Kingi turns.

'Are you offering?'

'You still asking?'

'Yes.'

'Then yeah.'

Kingi nods. Kataraina appears in the doorway.

'You're not going to trust this dufus with your precious engine are you?' she says over the rims of her dark sunglasses.

'Quiet in the cheap seats,' says Jordan.

'Cheap? Oh, I'm way too expensive for you, honey.'

They eat amid chatter. Kataraina leans back against the wall, raises her legs and stretches them over Jordan's. He turns and glares.

'Did I order your big feet with my lunch?' he says.

Leonie sits watching, noticing the ease between Kataraina and Jordan. They seem to have an unspoken pact, as if the pair of them are the two sides of a leaf. But there's something else between them, a jagged edge. She thinks of that leaf, how the two faces co-exist out of necessity but never see each other in their entirety. She has known that ease – and known the loss of it – even though she is only a couple of months past twenty.

Jordan reaches and takes a sip from Moana's glass of milk. The child sits back, horrified. Leonie picks up the glass also and takes a sip.

'Hey,' says Moana. 'Mine.'

She clasps her hands around the glass, staring at the both of them. She takes a swig and puts it back down on the table. Kingi leans and lifts the glass and sips, the circle now complete. Except for Kataraina, still with her feet across Jordan's lap, glancing at a magazine through her dark sunglasses. They turn to her. The conversation quiets. She flicks at the pages, then looks up over the rims.

'Oh for Pete's sake,' she says. 'Give it here.'

She raises the glass to drink. When she lowers the glass there is a tiny droplet of milk at the edge of her lip. Leonie reaches with a finger and takes it and rubs it into her fingers. Kataraina turns and looks at her over the black of the sunglasses' lenses. Her long lashes are like an inverted horizon above the bronze of her irises.

Kingi leans back from his plate. The sunlight draws out the rare streaks of black amongst the grey of his hair. Blackened twigs amid ash. Leonie reaches out and runs her fingers through it down to his crinkled brow, the scuffed sand of his cheeks. He looks at her with that sense of vast distance he carries. She remembers once seeing an old black-and-white movie about journeying to the centre of the earth, where the travellers came upon an underground ocean stretching as far as the eye could see. She moves her hand down the edge of his cheekbone and off into the air. He doesn't move.

Kataraina wakes next to Jordan and sits up, looking at the faint outline of the hill through the cabin's windows. The early evening has gathered itself around them. She leans and kisses his forehead and chest and he stirs and rolls over. She stands, slips on her jeans and shirt, takes the torch from the shelf and goes outside, down to the beach then up towards where the aeroplane sits, just one shadow among many. She flicks on the torch, reclaiming the Tiger Moth's body from the night, tracing the web of lines painted onto the aeroplane's hide, following each avenue, each tributary, seeking the source. She finds rows of painted leaves, a snatch of grass, tree roots. A pale structure appears, with a river flowing through its arches. Then a woman's face, her hair becoming the leaves, becoming the river. No, not leaves – vines. She douses the torch beam, seeing the face now only in her mind. Then she switches it on again. On and off, on and off. The face painted now in her memory. An image that can't be blinked away.

Footsteps on the sand.

'Promises,' says Kataraina.

Silence.

'You're not going to the Battle of Britain reunion, are you,' she says.

She stands still, aware now only of the rhythm of the surf.

'You're not –'

'Yes,' he says. 'I am.'

'But that's not your promise.'

'No.'

Her sandals crackle among the shells. She flexes her finger against the torch's switch. She could run the beam over the path, search him out. But she doesn't. She flicks it off again and stands in the dark.

'I never believed in second chances,' he says.

His voice startles her, as she realises he has moved to within inches of her in the dark, without making a sound.

'In the air, you neither gave nor were given second chances,' he says.

'Not everything happens in the air.'

She reaches into the dark, finding his back, running her palm up to a shoulder, then across his collar, his body turned away from her, leaning against the fuselage of the Tiger Moth.

'Come on,' he says.

'What?'

'Let's go for a ride.'

She puzzles for a moment, then senses him crouching in front of her. She turns the torch back on, aiming it down into the sand, catching his face at the edge of the beam's circle. He has his hands clasped as a step for her, his eyes signalling towards the Moth's front cockpit.

'You sure?' she says.

He nods from the shadows and she withdraws her feet from her sandals and steps barefoot into his hand, lifting her leg up in a long step onto the wing, then up into the opening, fumbling for a handhold to guide herself in. She sits on the leather seat, surprised at its snugness. She uses the torch to light the instrument panel. It's a forest of needles and numbers. She turns back to the shadows, holding the torch out over the wing.

'You need this to find your way?' she says.

'Not necessary, thanks.'

A creak from the frame and she hears him settle in behind her. She points the torch beam forward, a narrow tunnel of light reclaimed from the dark sand and sea.

'Who is she?'

'She?' says Kingi.

Kataraina taps her hand on the fuselage beside her, where the woman's face sleeps in the darkness of her fields and vines.

'Is she the dancer?' says Kataraina.

'Yes.'

'Is she your promise?'

A sheet of wind against her cheek, night air in her pores.

'Is she?'

'Yes,' says Kingi.

Kataraina leans back in the seat, reaches above her, her fingers flexing in the whisper of new moonlight. She closes her eyes for an endless second, opening them when his palm slips into hers.

'Orbits,' she says.

'Orbits?'

'I was looking at this book of Jordan's. At the chapter on astronomy. It had all the planets circling the sun. But no matter how far a planet went, it came back one day to the same place it had begun.'

She presses her thumb against the back of his hand.

'All my life,' he says, 'I've been a man who's seen the world in terms of geometry. Of structure. Angles and plane surfaces. Topology and topography. That the world could be explained if we drew enough lines, calculated enough degrees of rotation. Explain how one thing fits into another, how things connect or separate.'

'So did these rules of yours turn out to be true?'

'Yes. Everywhere there was no human touch.'

'And then?'

'Then I was lost.'

'Lost in a promise.'

'Lost in a promise,' he says.

'Tell me about her.'

So he does, this pilot whom she senses has always been the most private of men. In a grounded aeroplane generations older than the passenger who sits with him in the dark, taking in each stanza of his story amid a descant of waves. Of a priest who travelled by biplane, oak desks topped with scrawled treatises on flight, of aeroplanes folding up like broken children's kites. Of grapes and the woman who tended them. Drew nectar from their flesh; her own flesh and compassion drawing an essence from him he had denied he possessed. When the story is finished she opens her eyes for the first time in an hour, turns to look at the first hint of sunrise over the hill of her ancestors. His voice stills and he climbs out of his cockpit and drops to the sand, his muffled curse at the stiffness of his old bones bringing a smile to her face.

'Thanks,' she says, as she watches him walk up into the dunes.

He turns, smiles. 'Thank you,' he says. 'For …'

She nods at his unfinished sentence and he waves and walks on. She leans back, taking the new sun against her left temple. She settles back, closes her eyes to the double horizon of wings beneath and above her and glides away into a sky of dreams.

Jordan stops a few paces from the Tiger Moth, seeing Kataraina asleep in the cockpit. He pushes his sunglasses up onto his forehead, stands still, trying to assemble the familiar landscape. The aeroplane. A few scattered parts are strewn beneath the folded-over blanket. The old man – he can't see the old man. Instead Kataraina inhabits his frame. 'Madame Von Wreckedoften,' he had called her, the joke now evaporating as he suddenly senses its aptness. 'You know what I was?' she'd said, and he'd asked her if it mattered. He holds the canvas tool pouch against him, seeing in his mind, perhaps for the first time, the echo of each of the three of them in each other. A fleeting triangle on the edge of nowhere. A trinity.

He sets down the pouch and moves beside the rear cockpit, the lower wing stopping him from getting any closer to her. The wing itself looks too flimsy to carry his weight. He reaches, draws a few wayward strands of hair back from her shuttered eyelids. She stirs, her eyelashes rising against the sunlight.

'Hey,' he says.

'Hey, yourself.'

She smiles and he gestures for her to stand and she does, then steps out onto the wing. She sets her hands on her hips, glares at him to move, but he doesn't. Instead he steps right up against the wing, loops his arms around her and lifts her into his own arms. She squawks, then breaks into a laugh. He turns, still carrying her, and walks back through the shells. She throws her arms around his shoulders, her cheek against his collarbone. He walks all the way down to the streambed then up to the boat where he sets her against the ladder and she climbs, glancing once back at him. He smiles, gestures her up onto the deck and walks back up to the outlet to the ocean.

Kingi lifts the engine cowling away, revealing the Tiger Moth's workings. Jordan crouches, peering up into the piston chamber. He runs his middle and index fingers around the inside of the bore, his eyes closed, feeling for any ruts or snags likely to chew up the edge of the new piston's seals. He raises his eyebrows at Kingi leaning in from the other side.

'Whose idea was it to put the engine in upside down?' he says.

'The factory's.'

'Because?'

'So the pilot could see over the top of it.'

Jordan laughs.

'I'm serious,' says Kingi.

Jordan laughs again, louder this time. 'I can see my experience on Zephyrs and HQ Holdens isn't going to be much use here,' he says.

Kingi takes the new piston out of the rag he has it wrapped in and pushes it into the chamber. 'Like a glove,' he says then rocks back on his heels, stares up into the engine in silence.

'Problem?' says Jordan.

'No. Just thinking that …'

'That this means you have no further reason to stay.'

'I suppose. Yes.' He turns to Jordan. 'And where will *you* go?' he says.

'I've got nowhere to go. Least not somewhere you could find on a map.'

Kingi touches the upper rims of his spectacles with a blackened fingertip. 'Last night,' he says. 'Kataraina wanted to know some of my story.'

Jordan searches the blanket for the feeler gauge. 'And?' he says.

'And I told her.'

'And now you're having second thoughts?'

'No. I just wonder how many stories she can carry.'

'Probably more than you or me could come up with.'

'It wouldn't be fair of us to try.'

Jordan runs his thumb over the feeler gauge's markings.

'Yeah,' he says. 'I know. That was a dumb thing to say.'

'I'm just concerned that there's not room left in there for her own story.'

Kingi takes the gauge from Jordan and sizes the tolerance between piston and chamber wall. He nods and Jordan stands and peers down into the engine from the side, reaching at the same time to steady the crank shaft. He tries to rotate it a couple of times but it is too stiff.

'We have to oil it down a bit first,' says Kingi.

'Gotcha.'

'When I was in England,' says Kingi, 'in the war, they used to have these blackboards in the ops rooms, where the pilots names were recorded.'

'Yeah, I've seem them in movies. Like a darts scoreboard or something.'

'Yes. Very apt analogy. Well, there was a running gag in the flight, in the blackest humour of course, where some of the pilots started a sweepstake on whether the blackboard would ever fill up with names or whether there'd always be enough pilots dying to make sure the ops clerk didn't have to get a bigger blackboard. We each chipped in a few coins and whoever became the "one pilot too many" that sent the clerk scurrying to the supply depot would win everything in the kitty.'

'You won?'

'Nobody won. Not ever.'

Jordan crouches beside Kingi, the old man's stare still running up beneath the inverted head, checking every piston tolerance.

'You didn't tell Kataraina that did you?' says Jordan.

'No. Only came back to me just now.'

'How come?'

'The part I remember most, looking back, was that sometimes in haste the clerks wouldn't rub hard enough on the board, and ghost letters from the names of other pilots would still be visible.'

Jordan sits in the sand, brushes his oily hands against his bare knees.

'You're asking me if I'm going to disappear on her?' he says.

Kingi flicks the blades on the feeler gauge closed. A fine mist of rain has begun to fall. He reaches a hand out into it, then closes it into a fist, squeezing moisture through the gaps between his fingers.

'In the past,' he says, 'whenever anyone's upset you, what have you done?'

'Walked away. Or squashed them. Depending on how much they meant to me.'

'I either walked away or shot them down,' says Kingi. 'But without even the luxury of being able to say they upset me.'

'You don't strike me as someone who walks.'

Kingi lifts a small stone from the sand, rolls it around in his open palm. Jordan taps the mallet head against a shell, cracking its flimsy bones. At the sound of the crack, Kingi looks over at the younger man's hands.

'Did you ever think,' says Jordan, 'that the place you had to go to – to survive – was a place you could never come back from?'

'Not until it was too late.'

'And how do I know when that is?'

Kingi looks away through the strengthening rain.

'We become old men very fast,' he says. 'You won't even notice it happening.'

Jordan covers over the broken shell with sand.

'If I could change just one thing,' says Kingi, 'it would be that I *could* change.'

A trace of ocean in the breeze through the slivers of the window slats. Kataraina opens her eyes and turns her face towards the glass. The boat's cabin is silent but for her movements on the sheets. She stands, steps over to the window and peers out. Grey sky, the remnants of last night's rain.

She sits and draws a swirl of sheets around her waist and up her midriff, stopping beneath her breasts. Twisting the fabric against her, her body is a buoy buffeted by waves. She lets the sheets fall and lies back, running her palms from her forehead down across her eyes and on down each side of her neck. Then she peels them away, laying them flat, supine on the sheets. She looks to the ceiling but doesn't see it. Sees not the interior boundaries of an old boat but of the boat's sole passenger. Her stare works its way down the walls to the window pane, to the bottle of flowers on the ledge next to the glass, aware now that though Jordan has shed the envelope of the jailhouse from his outer body, the interior of his cabin still carries its markings. Aware now that the wildflowers and her body are the only shapes in this room not constructed of straight lines.

Where did he go, inside himself, before she came? Was he just a framework of boards and empty air, like the ladder that leads to the deck? He has loved her, physically, she's sure of that. His body an instrument of intimacy in the way his glance and his words always veer away from. If there is destruction in him, as he fears, then he banishes it to some distant ocean when he is with her. He makes love in silence, in absolute silence. Even his breathing almost vanishes. As if he is making love to her *from* his silence. Her only signal of his climax the tiny instant of suspension his body goes into, hovering like a fish in the ring of a tide pool, unsure of the way forward or the way out. Then she pushes up or back into him, craving the weight, solidity of his bones against her, anchoring her. Or is it she that anchors him?

She stands and walks, still naked, out onto the deck. The air is warm against her bare skin, a light dusting of rain. A paper-thin film of water graces the deck and she revels in its touch against the soles of her feet. She raises a foot, lets it draw back, her toes carving a fleeting circle in the water. She thinks of the morning she arrived here, shedding her sandals above the water's edge.

A few paces, to the boat's stern, taking the faint rainfall in her pores. She turns to face it, closes her eyes, seeking it only with her tongue. And in its succour she begins to move her hands, her fingers casting raintrails on the spruce boards beneath her soles. Her feet begin to move in concert, and she allows the rarity of a smile; a real smile, an inner smile.

Straight lines – how she hates straight lines.

Jordan walks back through the drizzle. Halfway up the estuary he stops, seeing Kataraina on the deck. He ducks into a stand of toetoe, seeking the anonymity of its feathers as he watches her, the fluidity of her body against the wood, against the world. Bathed in a music he is not party to. A look skyward to the rain, then back at her arms, hands alive as always, knowing her body is capable of conversation even in the faintest flex while she sleeps. A foot against his calf, toes drawing him to her within a well of sheet. Her legs opening around his hand, clasping his fingers within her warmth, her wetness, all while she dreams. Her lips grasping an ear or the dancing tail of his hair when he is within her. A montage of her comes to him now, through the lens of toetoe leaves, through the rain. Her entry into him, when it is he who thinks *he* enters her. Tasting him, slipping deeper within his private places, his denials, his secrets than any other. How has she done this? How has it seemed so easy when for his whole life he was a fortress, a pā on a hilltop, crowded with fences and guards. He smiles, a cold smile, knowing now that he didn't go into prison, prison came into him. A brother, a mother, a lover. Its womb of concrete had been perfect for him, for the cairn of stones he mistook for his heart.

But now, she has opened the door to his cell and marched on in. She who dismisses everything she does and is, everything around her with a flick of her eyelashes, but betrays that dismissal with the colours of her compassion. Clothing him with her eyelids, a tiny flex of her fingers or just a hint of her pulse as she shifts against his naked chest.

In prison you learn to value the tiniest things. A single tea bag or cigarette, a smile from someone who will only be your friend until the smile fades. You watch for the smallest details, like a map reader. Sense the shape of things in the most infinitesimal of snapshots, the axis of survival turning on the ability to discern the elements of a shifting landscape. A knife poised over a piece of pumpkin on a plate, or destined for your lungs. A shadow at the edge of the latrine doorway: is it a trick of the light or a fight to the death? But not here. None of that stuff belongs here, within the touch of stream water. Within reach of her music. A refrain of that moment in that long ago when a young boy had hidden in the shadows, watching a girl watching the moon. He closes his eyes for a moment, smiling somewhere deep inside. 'You become an old man very fast,' Kingi had said. No, he thinks. Not this time. Not here. He steps from the toetoe, walks towards his boat in the dunes. Toward the figure oblivious to the visible world, Kataraina dancing in the rain.

Leonie

When I was a kid I used to so look forward to birthdays, like all kids do. Mostly for the presents, of course. I was maybe ten or so before I even began to get some idea of what the word 'birth' even meant. It was hard to imagine that we come out of someone else on some specific day. I mean to us it's like we were always here, just that there's a point in the past beyond which we can't remember. It's hard to think of being nothing. When you see a little baby, a few hours old, you don't think you can say that 'yesterday you weren't part of the world.'

Birthdays.

A couple of days after my eighteenth birthday Moana was born. A couple of months before my twentieth birthday Leo was killed. Moana's dad would forever be the 'guy in the photographs'.

For my own mum and dad, my birth mum and dad, I didn't even have that.

So the day *after* my twentieth birthday I wrote away to the Central Registry to apply for a list of counsellors, one of whom would be my guide through the process of finding out who my *birth mother* was.

The counsellor, Patricia, was pretty nice about it all. Not at all 'official' acting. The counsellor's just there to act as a kind of bridge between you not knowing and knowing. They can't *not* tell you who your real mum and dad were, the law says they have to, but they're there to be a body in the room with you when you find out. When you hold this little piece of paper in your hand with a name on it that you don't recognise, and some medical stuff and the name of the hospital and you tell yourself that it's you but part of you won't believe. Then you realise it's the first time you've been in the room with your mother's name since you were born: *Kataraina Reihana.*

I stood and walked to the wall. There was a picture of a mountain and a river and some trees. I tried to see myself in the picture but it was hard. I don't know which mountain. I'd never seen it before. I looked back at the piece of paper.

She was hard to track down. The birth certificate just said she was from Auckland so I checked around the Reihanas in the phone book, but nobody knew her. The only other mention on the certificate said she was Te Aupōuri so my next step was to get a Northland phone book and I had my first bit of the plot. I finally got hold of an aunt who said she'd gone to Auckland yonks ago and never come back. They had the address of a flat from when her Nan had once sent a dude to look for her. Nobody knew her at the flat, but I left my name anyway. Then I had a phone call saying they'd found an old card on the mantelpiece from some club in town. The club was long gone, so I checked around every other one I could locate. No one wanted to talk, until I came across a manageress of a club, who seemed to know. She used the name Angel. She sat on the other end of the phone saying nothing after I mentioned Kataraina. She wanted to know who I was, so I just told her I was family. A long pause, then she said that Kataraina had headed for Oz a few years ago but she'd sent a postcard about once a year. No address or number, just a postmark from Bondi or King's Cross. I asked for a photograph and she asked me how come I didn't have one. I gave Angel my address and treaded water. I thought about maybe borrowing some money off Dad and heading over there with Moana. Then, weeks later, I received a card in the mail. Out of the blue. It had been forwarded, I guess, by Angel. She wouldn't answer my messages to confirm. Stuck to the back was one of those little square photographs, like at five-minute photo booths. Two women, laughing, partying I guess. One was Pākehā. The other wasn't. I read the card all the way through, then realised I was looking at *her* writing. I ran my finger over it, across the creases and smudges. I read the last line about a hundred times. It just said, '*oh by the way, hon. Ring the church bells, I'm going home.*'

Home.

Home.

Auckland? No. It said *going* home. Like Auckland – where the card was addressed to – couldn't be home. I phoned her aunt again. Nothing. So I took a gamble and headed up. Stayed at the caravan park in Te Kopu for a couple of weeks, showing the photo around. Nothing but shaking heads. Then I'm standing at the counter at the takeaway and the girl from the shop comes across the car park in her apron.

'The woman in your photo,' she says. 'The woman in your photo.'

But you haven't headed up home. You turned off the highway and came down here …

Out beyond the crashing surf lies calmer water, but more dangerous. It mists into a smoke trail on the horizon. Kingi stands at the water's edge, taking it all in, his senses mixing one scent with another, one sea with another. Ocean to sea. Waves to grape leaves. Sea wind speaking beyond words, as a woman in a grape barrel had once spoken with a single ripple of her body.

The water swirls at his feet, touching him for an instant then drawing away, leaving two small ridges beyond the tips of his shoes like a sculptor has carved the soft indentations for a figure's eyes. He lets the water's sound circle in his mind. The slipping sand is no more transient for him than the passage of half a century.

Footsteps. Not from his memory, but the present. Jordan stands a few feet away, his surfboard under his arm, looking to the horizon.

'We're not so different,' says Kingi. 'You and I.'

'Maybe.'

'It's just that you're young enough to still trust in certainty.'

'I'm not sure I trust anything.'

'You only think that. You trust in silence. Perhaps in anonymity.'

'Anonymous? Look at my face, dude.'

'Yes. An irony I rather appreciate in you. Kataraina told me that you admitted to being scared. That she loves that in you. Loves that most of all.' Kingi turns to face him, the withdrawing tide opening holes in the sand beneath his feet. 'Perhaps she used the breath of my story to blow away the dust in her own. But it was mutual. I used her also, as perhaps so many have, from what she hints at. Only I didn't use her body, but something more deeply hidden. Something tiny and frosted – but still alive.'

'And what use have *you* found for this hidden thing?'

Kingi smiles. 'Ah,' he says. 'I've used it to speak for me. I've used it to say goodbye.'

'Goodbye to who?'

Kingi turns to him.

'Goodbye to the part of me that never said goodbye.'

After lunch they sit out in the circle of grass. Jordan rolls his fingers across the strings. D major, B minor, F sharp minor seventh. G major sixth. Softening from full chords to a glissando arpeggio. Leonie lifts Moana from her lap and sits her on the table, her legs scrambling against the wood. Jordan looks down at the tiny toes, her fingers moving against the grain of the table top, her eyes focused on the skin of the wood, as if she has seen a fish in the current of a stream. Moana reaches back to her mother, and the two play patty cake for a moment. Jordan plucks the two bass strings of the guitar, reaches to a tuning peg, glancing up when Leonie turns from her game and stills, following his fingers, then his eyes. He holds the evenness of her stare, not a speck of her flinching. His imagination imprints for a moment a snatch of another face's outline at the edges of her eyes. Her own face reappears, skin with the shine of carved and polished whalebone, a paler gold than that suggested by her irises' unmistakable tincture of tangata whenua.

Back to his fretboard.

'Do you know how to play "Dancing in the Moonlight"?' she says.

'There's a couple of versions, isn't there?'

She squints, mulling over his question. A hummed melody, her arms circling Moana. Jordan searches for the chords within the pages of his fretboard, sifting major from minor. His fingers slip from change to change like water on a garden terrace. He rings her voice with his hands, the music echoing against Leonie's face. She moves from humming to singing.

'Everybody here is outta sight, they don't bark and they don't bite …'

Fingers move from B flat to C minor, then to F minor seventh …

'It's a supernatural delight, everybody's dancin' in the moonlight …'

He joins her for the chorus, their voices bringing Kataraina sashaying from the shower block in her sarong, her bare feet soft on the grass. Kingi follows, nodding his head to the rhythm. Jordan moves to a percussive beat with his right hand, syncopation flowing from his fingers. He closes his eyes, listening to the women sing.

'Everybody's dancin' in the moonlight, everybody's feelin' warm and right … it's such a fine and natural sight …'

Leonie begins to step around the table, Moana's hand in hers, the child a rustle of rhythm on the tabletop. Kingi beckons Kataraina with an exaggerated stretch of his hand towards her. She nods, does a rather rustic curtsey, takes his hand and they move together, over the dew-wetted grass.

Leonie stands at the open doorway, her eyes sketching Kataraina out of the shadows. Kataraina lifts a suitcase onto the chair and begins to take her clothes down from the racks on the rail in the cabin's sleeping alcove. A tap at the door.

'Going?' says Leonie.

'Not far.'

A pause.

'I'm shifting my gear into the boat,' says Kataraina.

'Did he ask?'

'He doesn't do much asking.'

Leonie leans against the wall by the doorway.

'You don't know who I am, do you,' she says.

'Should I?'

'National Women's Hospital, June 18, 1970.'

Kataraina stands with a blouse in her fingers, toying with a rose embroidered onto the chest. 'What?' she says.

'National Women's Hospital, June 18, 1970. One twenty-seven p.m. Me.'

Kataraina sinks to the bed, folds the blouse, then opens it out then folds it again. 'How?' she says.

'It doesn't matter, does it?'

'If you're screwing with me I'll rip your head off.'

'I've come back.'

'I swear –'

'It's me. I've come back.'

Kataraina stands and places the blouse in the suitcase. She arranges it so it is square with the case's lip. Straightening it with her fingers. Then she drags everything else from the rack and drops it all in and closes the suitcase. She steps forward past Leonie and goes on out the door.

XI

Hummingbird

Jordan

I stood at the edge of the road, not turning to look at Paremoremo's perimeter fence or the guard towers. I'd seen enough of them from the inside to not care about what they looked like from the outside. I held a paper bag in my left hand. Pretty much everything I amounted to. A comb, a brush, some coins, two T-shirts and two pairs of undies. I had on a two-dollar pair of sunglasses. In my right hand was an old guitar with ornate mother-of-pearl inlays in the fretboard. In my shirt pocket was a crumpled photograph of a distant nebula. Everything else I'd gathered in prison, a transistor radio/cassette player, a few tapes, a pair of cheap track shoes, I'd given away. I just stood waiting for an hour, not glancing once at the prison service cars coming and going. A woman walked past, pushing a pram. The wheels made a crackling sound on the stony edge of the road, like a distant fire. I listened to that sound for a moment, looking the other way.

A battered-looking ute came down the road, half-covered in mud. The other half was mostly rust. The driver pushed the door open. I didn't move.

'You gonna stand there all day, man,' he said.

Uncle Jimmy. The old man's youngest brother. Or second youngest, I can never remember. I stood looking at him and he turned forward, reached into his pocket for his ciggies.

'Take all the time you need,' he said.

'Thanks.'

We headed up to the Riverhead Coatesville Road then cut west to the motorway.

'Got to say you don't look all that overjoyed to be out,' he said.

'Just thinking.'

He nodded. 'Your old man hasn't asked about you,' he said.

'Should I give a toss?'

'Do you?'

I shook my head. He stared out through the windscreen. He set the wipers going for a moment to get rid of some dust.

'You want to head straight up or do some visiting round town?' he said.

'I'll head straight up. If that's cool with you.'

'Sure. Give me a good excuse to go do some fishing up there.'

I stayed with his family for two days, keeping to the local streets, playing with Jimmy's grandchildren. Then we headed on north, through Whangarei and up through the Mangamuka Gorge and on through Kaitaia then down onto the flatlands, the sandlands of the Aupōuri peninsula. Through Waipapakauri where the gumfields once circled, then further north still to where we turned onto a side road and headed down an old flaxcutters' track towards the setting sun, to the circle of open land amid the pines, some cabins, a concrete-block shower building. He turned off the engine, I stepped out – and it hit me. Silence. I thought I'd known silence in prison, but I hadn't. There were always doors slamming, someone's bunk creaking or footsteps on the landing. Even when there was no overt noise there always seemed to be the background discord of someone's pain. As if the men who had called your cell 'home' before you had left pieces of themselves there, stained or smoked into the rock. I walked across the grass and up onto the dunes, the silence retreating, dissolving beneath the voice of the surf. The tide was way out, but it didn't matter. I hit it at a run, kicking my clothes free on the sand. I dived under the water, keeping my face inside it for as long as I could. When I finally came out Jimmy was standing in the shallows, smiling.

'For all of it,' he said, 'I got to envy you one thing.'

'Envy? What the hell is there to envy?'

'The look on your face.'

He stayed for two days, the two of us fishing from the old jetty at high tide. Then I watched his ute roll away up the track to the road. When it was out of sight I walked up into the dunes and sat.

It had been a couple of weeks before my release when the old man, Hepi, had come and sat on the edge of my bed.

'I got cancer in my lungs,' he said.

'Bad?'

'Don't reckon there is any good cancer.'

'That's a tough break.'

We sat in silence for a long time, then he spoke again. 'Good to see you're controlling your overwhelming sadness,' he said.

'I'm doing it out of respect for you.'

The old man smiled, sat there wheezing. 'I want you to have my guitar,' he said.

'You ain't dead yet.'

'True, but you're out soon and if I see you back here I'm likely to smash it over your head.'

'What was the dude's name?'

'Who?'

'Your tohunga tā moko.'

'Tamehana Te Rangi.' Hepi took a gasp of air and there was a sound like there were steel plates slipping around inside him. 'Moko's not a plaything,' he said. 'You remember that.'

'I know.'

'You been thinking hard about this?'

'Yes.'

'Since when?'

'Since the day I died.'

He looked at me sideways.

'That's good then,' he said. 'And here I was, thinking you were going to give me some crazy answer.'

After a week in the camp I walked north out to the highway with a duffel bag and a change of clothes. Caught a lift further north with a milk-tanker driver, saying goodbye at Te Kao. I legged it from there. The house was old, maybe from another century, with a tōtara board and bark lean-to attached. A roof of thatched flax. A girl answered the door and went to fetch a woman who said that Tamehana would be back later. No one asked me why I wanted to see him or even who I was. They asked me in, but I thanked them and walked up into the hills and went to sleep on a small promontory overlooking the valley. The sound of a motor woke me, hours later. I sat on the rocks, looking up at the retreating sun, then down at the van parked in the house's yard.

I knocked on the glass pane of the door. A different girl answered and called out for 'Grandpa' and he stepped out from an inner doorway.

His grey hair was tied in a pony tail. The ink in his moko so ingrained in his skin it looked as if it had preceded him and he had just stepped into it. In every change of light he looked a different age, like he wasn't a single man but a gallery. A history. I reached back a zillion years to recite my whakapapa. He nodded, sat on the edge of the steps, looking up into the tree line, speaking only in stabs, like poking at ashes with a stick.

'What do your people think?' he said.

'I never see them.'

'Wife? Children?'

I didn't answer.

'What *do* you have?' he said.

'Myself.'

He squinted his eyes into the falling light. 'I need to sleep on it,' he said. 'Come back tomorrow.'

So I did. And the next day and the next. I ate with his whānau, listening to the lightness in the children's voices, the snatches of lives current and past from the tūpuna. Tamehana's daughter made up a place on a camp bed, but I wanted to sleep with soil against my back so each night I'd walk back into the hills. Tamehana prompted me with questions – nothing that required a yes or no answer, just little openings for me to tell some moment of my life. As if he was using them to map out a diagram for some structure he was building. I gave up moments from my childhood, the 'wild' Te Awa boys. Pieces of my life with Jacqui. The child I'd never seen. Even a few scattered sentences dragged out from behind the bars of Parry. He took it all with no change of expression. Except for once, when I mentioned, in passing, the old guitar player. Hepi. Then he smiled.

On the fourth day I stood by a creek, staring down into the water. I heard his footsteps.

'See how the water bends the rushes,' he said. 'Like they're about to break.'

I nodded.

'But the rush and the water stay what they are,' he said. 'It's our eyes that see the break. Things don't always stay what they are. Or things can be something without knowing it.'

'Is it the being or the knowing that's important?' I said.

'You tell me.'

'I think they're just steps on the same road.'

He picked up a blade of grass, dropped it onto the water. I watched it circle, then pick up the current and move off downstream.

'Come on,' he said.

The lean-to on his house was filled with sketches, stencils, rough ideas gouged in wood by seekers. There were even some old marks cut into the dirt of the floor. We spent the day sifting so in the end a pile of designs almost engulfed me. I picked up one sketch, done in charcoal on paper that had faded to the hue of sand. Half circles, waves, an inner core of solid ink, the rest radiating like mist.

I raised my eyebrows, held the paper up to the light.

'A fallen moon,' said Tamehana. 'A sea child.'

A week later I got a lift with some surfcasters, back to Te Kopu. I walked back down the track to the camp, moved my gear out of the cabin I'd been sleeping in and into my tupuna's old boat. I scrubbed out the inner cabin, nailed some loose boards, then walked to the stream, waded out into it, bending once while I washed the grime and borer dust away to glance at my moko in the streamwater.

Jordan pulls his fingers away from the induction manifold, cursing, rubbing the tips against each other. Kingi looks up.

'Occupational hazard,' says Kingi.

Jordan wipes his hands on a rag. 'Do you think about the stuff you did,' he says. 'You know.'

The old man looks at him, his eyes looming large in the spectacles' lenses. He looks down at his oil-stained hands. 'You mean taking a life,' he says.

'Yeah.'

Kingi reaches up to the flame trap, pushes it against the block. 'Yes,' he says. 'Sometimes.'

'And?'

'A wing commander once told me that conscience is the luxury of the safe.'

'You believe that?'

'No.'

Jordan tightens the bolts against the carburettor's casing. 'Dude I once knew said that I would need to be careful of what was inside me.'

'A friend?' says Kingi.

'Nope. Not even close.'

'Sometimes our enemies see us more naked than our friends ever do.'

'Or than *we* do?'

Jordan glances down at Kingi's shoes.

'Was he right then?' says Kingi. 'This chap you knew.'

'In a way, yeah.'

Kingi lowers his hands and crouches dead-still, looking across the sand. He leans forward over a small heap of shells, reaches and lifts a gull's feather in his fingertips.

'The story isn't written forever,' he says. 'Sometimes the Minotaur can walk free from the labyrinth.'

Jordan looks down at Kingi's hands. At the pale feather rippling in the sea wind. Kingi hands it to him.

'Or fly free,' he says. They work on into the twilight, tightening the last of the engine's fixing bolts in the dusk. When Jordan walks back into the camp, the cabins and the kitchen seem empty. The lights are off. Jordan flicks the switch, goes to the sink, runs a glass of water and drinks. He looks out at the vanishing circle of grass. He walks back out and looks up and down the row of cabins.

Kingi comes from the shed. 'They jumped ship?' he says.

'Don't know. Gone walkabout somewhere.'

'Might rustle us up some rations,' says Kingi.

'I'm gonna get changed.'

The boat is dark also. A suitcase sits on the table in the outer cabin.

'Kat?' says Jordan.

No answer. He descends the steps and pushes opens the inner cabin door. She is sitting at the head of the bed, cross legged. Blankets pulled up around her.

'Hey.'

She raises her face, the light too dim to see her eyes. 'She said she's come back.'

'Who?' says Jordan.

'That's all,' says Kataraina. 'Just that she's come back. As if it was *her* that left.'

He steps onto the bed, noticing when he touches against a knuckle that she is trembling. 'Shit, girl. You're gonna have to fill me in on this one.'

'I thought that if a child wanted to find the mother, that the mother would be notified or something. That's what I ... no ... I never thought anything. I never thought about it at all. Not bloody once. I never did.'

He tries to draw her against him but she is the weight of an iceberg in his hands. Her stare against the wall not moving with him.

'Slow down, Kat, and tell me.'

She looks up.

'I'm lying. Of course I thought about her. Everything about her. Except this.'

'Leonie?'

She nods.

'Kat, really? Man. Unreal. Un*real*.'

A look of anger at his smile.

'Damn,' he says. 'This is amazing. You've got a family.'

Challenge in her eyes.

'Kat,' he says. 'This is fantastic.'

'Why?'

'Why? Why? What are you, crazy?'

She looks back at the wall. 'I'm not crazy,' she says.

The flatness in her voice swallows his laughter. He braces himself against the wall and lifts her into him. She is all angles and ridges and edges, her fluidity lost. Even the sense of high tide that he loves in her breasts seems to have ebbed. She neither leans into him nor away. Just hovers within his grasp, somehow a thousandth of an inch out of reach.

He wishes now for Kingi's toolbox, for some device that can peel away the layers of her pain.

'I'm not crazy,' she says.

She raises her chin, stares into his eyes then through them into some landscape he doesn't tread. There are petals of blood on her lips and chin where she has bitten into her flesh. He touches it with the tip of his nose, then his tongue, wishing at this moment he could suckle her with it. With her own blood. He closes his eyes. The last thing he sees is the dark bloom opening on her chin, like the tiny rivers and roads and pathways of a moko.

She doesn't speak again.

At some point her eyes surrender to sleep.

Jordan raises his head out of the ocean, taking in the new day's colours. She had stirred several times in the night, as if unsure whether she had left a door open somewhere. A sudden sense of absence beside him, then footsteps in the cabin, a creak of the boards on the deck. Intermittent silence. He thought to go to her, to ease her away from the trench he'd seen in her eyes, but felt his hands had no means to lead her back. A stone had descended into him, down his throat and through his veins. A sinker, like the stone triangles he uses when surfcasting, transporting him back to a ten-by-ten concrete box where the old man, Hepi, had sat on the edge of his bed, cursing the petrified bark of his arthritic fingers.

Each time she returned to his bed, her body felt a year heavier.

He lifts his chin out of the water for an instant, as comfortable with the touch of waves as a child would be with its mother. He segues from freestyle to backstroke and back again, looking up once at the last of the fading stars. At the constellation Scorpius. Its body glides towards a different dawn, a more distant dawn, like the prow of a ghost canoe. He swallows another gift of oxygen, a glimpse of dunes, of the old man's aeroplane.

Kingi walks across the sand to the aeroplane. Barefoot, wearing just trousers and singlet. He looks down the beach to the trail of footprints leading to the distant shallows, the surfboard upended. The tide is well out, a good fifty yards from where he stands. A floating range of cloud mountains hovers, mirrored in the glass sheet of the sea's wash. He turns and walks the path of prints to where they enter the first inch-deep reaches of the Tasman, searching all the while for the printmaker's tangible form, stopping when at last he discerns the swimmer amongst the breakers.

A hand rises and Kingi waves, stilling the fan of his fingers when he realises the hand is just the beginning of another stroke. In this half light he thinks of the weightlessness of flight, the temporary defiance of nature by technology. Of mornings when the sky would suddenly clear of the trails of burning aeroplanes, when he'd realise his enemies were in retreat or downed. Never a silence so whole as that, so huge. Even the howl of his own engine seemed to fade, its purpose suddenly redundant. So beautifully redundant. A flex of the control column, the Hurricane slipping into a roll, as if within a giant chute in the sky. Rolling, rolling, over and over. His balance lost to all logic, to all earthbound intelligence. A windmill of fields and hedgerows and sky, a Constable landscape shattered by this visitor from the twentieth century, the aeroplane century.

He stands in the waves, letting the thin tips of the surf take his fingertips. What if he is just being an old fool? Almost fifty years on. How did the years slip by so quickly, as if he had left a gate open and a pet or a child had slipped out, never to be seen again. He slips out of his singlet and takes a handful of seawater in his palm, lifts it to his chest and wipes it across his neck, squeezing his skin as if he is a sponge, a sponge of history. Not flesh, not bone, but something malleable. The one thing he'd never allowed himself to be. Not Kingi the glacier. Kingi, the knight of nuts and bolts.

'Can you wash everything away?'

He turns. Leonie stands at the water's edge.

'Can you wash everything away?' she says. 'All of it?'

'I think perhaps you mistake me for someone who has an answer for you.'

'What does it mean to be born?'

'Child, I can answer a thousand questions, but what you're asking at this moment is beyond me.'

'I know.'

'Well, why do you ask?'

'I shouldn't have said it.'

'Said what?'

'I told Kataraina that I'm her daughter.'

He looks back at the surf for a moment. When he looks back Leonie has half turned, faces north to the thinning finger of land he himself had looked down over only a few short weeks ago.

'I assume she didn't have any idea?' he says.

'No.'

He nods.

'I shouldn't have,' says Leonie.

'You came all the way up here to tell her?'

'Yes.'

'And now you have.'

'Yes.'

'Then why the regrets?'

She sniffs against the wind. He clasps his singlet in one hand, droplets of water running down over his withered arm.

'Sometimes we mistake a moth for a hummingbird,' he says. 'We don't take the time to see all that the moth is.'

'I don't understand.'

He drops his singlet into the water, watches it twist and unwind in the wavelets. 'Where's Kataraina now?' he says.

'I don't know. I checked the boat. Her car's still here but ... I thought she might be with Jordan.'

Kingi looks back out into the waves.

'She could love me,' says Leonie.

'When did you last see her, before you came here?'

'The day I was born. She could love me.'

'Oh child, she's probably loved you every day of your life.'

'She ignored me when I told her.'

He shakes his head. 'That's not what I mean,' he says.

'She could.'

He extends a hand. She stands for a moment, then walks through the shallows to him. He takes her into her arms, turning her to face the open ocean with him.

'Where's Moana?' he says.

'Sleeping.'

'Would that we could all sleep through the hardest moments.'

She shivers against his bare chest.

'No,' he says. 'I shouldn't have said that. It's sleeping – sleepwalking – through the hardest moments, that destroys us.'

Jordan crouches beneath the trees, his hair still wet from the sea. He examines the network of wooden veins above him, searching for the source of a tūī call. Another whistle. He stands and walks through the pine needles. There, beyond that cradle of leaves. A flicker of movement. He smiles. When he looks back to earth Kataraina is standing at the edge of the trees' shadow. She glances up into the branches then back to his face.

'You must think −'

'No,' he says.

'But I −'

'No.'

Her eyes darken. 'You just gonna interrupt me all day,' she says.

He raises a finger to his lips. 'Shhhh.'

'Don't tell me to shush.'

He points up into the trees. 'Look.'

She steps towards him. He encircles her with his arms, his chin across her cheek. He puts a hand beneath her chin, tilts her head skyward.

'Look,' he says.

She softens against him.

'I see it.'

'Horse's Head Nebula. Barnard 33. Quadrant of Zeta Orionis.'

'What?'

'Sometimes we get a second chance.'

'We?'

'We.'

Jordan meets Leonie coming across the sand, her outline only half complete without the familiarity of Moana orbiting her passage from place to place. There is a neatness to her, a sense of strict borders. Like an envelope. Leonie is dressed once again in black from head to foot, hair swept back from her face. The zip of her sweatshirt is like a trace of bone, an X-ray cast by a trick of the light.

'Where is she?' asks Leonie.

'At the boat,' says Jordan.

'Can I go and see her?'

'I don't have the right of granting permission.'

'It's your boat.'

He smiles at her directness. Its lack of adornment is familiar to him now. Straight back, chin raised in gentle defiance.

'What's funny?' she says.

'You remind me of someone.'

Leonie swallows. 'I didn't show up here to hurt her, you know,' she says.

'I doubt if it was you showing up *here* that hurt her.'

Her hands move behind her back. She is as solid as a branch.

'What did you come for?' says Jordan.

'Are you judging me?'

'No. I just want to know.'

She squints into the wind. 'I don't know,' she says. 'I just needed to find her. I never thought about what I'd do when I did. Haven't you ever needed to do something, just because … just because it needed to be done? I'm not making sense. Haven't you ever had something inside you that you needed to get out?'

'Sure. But I reckon I've only just figured that out.'

'You're thinking that I'm upsetting some balance. That after I've gone, she won't be the same.'

'She's already not the same.'

'Isn't that a little selfish?'

'Selfish? Of me or Kataraina?'

'Selfish of you. Why are you coming between us?'

He looks out over the ribs of sand. Wisps of her hair have loosened from the bun tied behind her. Tiny shavings flick in the wind.

'We've made a pact,' he says, 'Kataraina and me. Nothing said, just something inside. Like two people standing on the edge between something and nothing. At least you're still at the beginning, you haven't reached the edge.'

'I'm not a kid. I'm twenty.'

'I'm not talking about that.'

'Shit, I don't reckon you're that much older than me.'

'I'm a lifetime older than you. But that's not what I'm talking about.'

'I have to do this.' She shapes to speak some more, then stops. Her hands unclasp from behind her back and she runs them down across her torso, her fingers flexing on her thighs. 'Moana will be waking up,' she says.

He steps to the side, not turning to watch her walk towards the track.

A knock against the frame of the outer cabin. Kataraina turns and looks up the steps. A shadow flickers against the edge of the bench.

'Hello?' says Leonie.

Kataraina closes the drawer and stows her suitcase beneath the bed. She takes the guitar from where it leans against the bedhead and sits with it across her lap.

'Hello?'

'I'm in here,' Kataraina says.

Footsteps, a glimpse of Leonie's track shoes, then Moana's feet encased in tiny sandals. Leonie sits on the bottom step. Moana moves around the cabin, staring up at everything.

'Guess I must be – *we* must be – a bit of a shock,' says Leonie.

Kataraina plucks a couple of notes, reaches to turn a peg head.

'I didn't mean for this,' says Leonie.

'What *did* you mean for?' says Kataraina.

Moana climbs up onto the bed and stands peering out the window. Kataraina moves into a minor arpeggio.

'We can just go,' says Leonie. 'I've seen you, I've told you.

We can just go. If you want, I'll leave you my address.'

Kataraina's fingers move up the fretboard. 'Ask away,' she says. 'Ask what?'

'Whatever it is you came here to ask.'

'I just want to know you. Just a piece of you. Like he does.'

'He?'

'Jordan.'

'That's different.'

'I know, but I'm reaching. At least he has a foothold. I don't have anything.'

'I don't know what to say to you.'

Leonie folds her arms, then unfolds them again. 'Stuff happens that we just don't anticipate,' she says.

She stands, moves to the edge of the bed and sits again. Moana kneels at Kataraina's side, reaches out with her fingers towards the guitar strings. Kataraina lifts her hand away, lets Moana touch them. Her left hand still fretting chords. Moana bangs the strings twice, Leonie opening her eyes and mouth wide at Moana's amazement when music comes out.

'Wow,' says Leonie. 'Who's clever, eh?'

'Me,' says Moana.

She knocks against the strings again. Kataraina changes her left hand fingering so a different chord rings. Moana is again amazed.

'Are you going to stay here?' says Leonie.

'I don't know,' says Kataraina.

'Do you mind if we hang around for a while?'

'That's up to you.'

Leonie watches Kataraina's fingers on the guitar, then looks down at her own.

'Were those the questions you were expecting me to ask?' says Leonie.

'Nope.'

'I didn't think so.'

Kataraina stops playing.

'I don't know who your father is,' she says. 'If that was your next question.'

'Was –'

'I said I don't know. I just don't know.'

Leonie turns to the window. Moana taps against the strings again, moving closer to examine them. She plucks each one in turn, seeming as much concerned with the texture of the metal as the sound. She looks up at her mother, her face twisting into a frown when she sees the tears.

'Stuff,' says Leonie. 'Stuff always gets in the way.'

'Do your parents … do your parents know you're here?'

'No.'

'You didn't tell them.'

'No, I didn't.'

Moana pushes past Kataraina, forcing her to lean back. She climbs onto Leonie's knees, a finger reaching to brush at the wetness on her cheeks.

'I like him,' says Leonie. 'Jordan.'

'So do I.'

'He looks like he has secrets too.'

'We've all got secrets.'

'Yeah. Don't we?'

Leonie takes Moana against her, her hands closing around her daughter's back.

'This isn't easy for me either,' says Leonie.

'Well, *I* didn't come looking for you.'

'No. No, you didn't.'

The men fasten the propeller mid-morning, then Kingi lifts the engine cowling from the sand, shakes it clean, and Jordan helps him lift it over the open engine bay. They fix the mounting bolts and step back.

Kataraina looks up from the bench when he enters the outer cabin. She raises her eyebrows.

'How is it?' says Jordan.

'You guys finished?'

'Yep.'

'Wow. So he's ready to go.'

'Yeah, I guess so.'

'We should have a party tonight.'

He steps around the bench, eases her against him. 'It's OK.' he says, 'if you want to bum out or cry or scream or smash stuff or whatever. No need to fake it around me.'

She nods. 'I'm alright,' she says.

He leans back, looks her up and down. 'That's what I've always thought,' he says, smiling.

She accepts his leer with exaggerated grace. 'I'm not faking anything,' she says. 'And thanks.'

She pauses, then turns to him. He raises his eyebrows.

'Can you put those two bottles of wine in the fridge?' she says.

He nods. 'Sure. You sure you're OK?'

'Yep. If you ask me one more time I'll brain you.'

'What's she going to do?'

'Whatever she thinks is right, I suppose.'

'Kat –'

'I know. I know you're here.'

He nods. 'I'll get that wine in the fridge,' he says.

She lands on the sand, lifts her skirt and crosses the stream to the dunes on the far side.

'I don't know who your father is,' she had told Leonie and it's true. She doesn't.

Father.

Mother.

Daughter.

Just words. Scratches and sounds.

No.

Not just words.

She reaches down and scrunches up the hem of her skirt, tightening it into a pillow against her, her legs bared to the wind.

My daughter was taken from me five minutes after she was born.

Nothing was *taken*.

She looks up. On the slope of the dune opposite Leonie stands with Moana. Skeletoned against a reef of cloud. If Leonie waves to her she will wave back. If she even smiles Kataraina will smile back. She thinks, suddenly, of that shiny metal dish in the operating theatre, realising that little by little over twenty years, she had come to see that bare metal face as her daughter.

Smile. Wave. Something. But Leonie doesn't. She just looks, for a long time, Moana pulling at her hand to go down onto the beach. Then she turns and walks down the incline, sand flowering from her footfalls.

I don't know who your mother is. Maybe I used to, once …

Jordan borrows Kataraina's car and drives into Te Kopu with a shopping list and buys sausages, some vegetables, a couple of loaves of bread and the handful of condiments and spices Leonie asked for. He finds only some, guesses at substitutes for the rest. He sets some kindling into the hutch of the barbecue, stuffs some paper in and watches the flame grow. The women usher Kingi from the kitchen and he – the guest of honour – uses the time to pack up his gear. He spends the late afternoon perched in the marram grass with Moana, showing her the insides of shells, driftwood knots.

Kataraina and Leonie commandeer the kitchen, working at the edge of each other's space without exchanging more than a few words.

Salt?

In the cupboard above the stove.

OK. I got it.

In the twilight Kataraina carries the bowls of salad out to the picnic table, clearing a waft of pine needles with the screwed-up apron. Leonie appears with quartered tomato, potato salad dressed with yoghurt and vinegar and black pepper.

They eat beneath the trees, Jordan raising the sausages on the end of a fork and placing them on everyone's plate.

'Are there any that aren't nuked?' says Kataraina.

'Shut up, you,' says Jordan, shaking his head.

Kataraina leans to Kingi. 'Where'd you find the chef?' she says.

Kingi opens the wine and they each sup, except for Jordan. The first bottle vanishes in minutes so they open the second. Kingi looks across the table at the group he has come to know to varying degrees in the last few weeks. The two women bookending the young man with the tattooed face. He smiles to himself, at another one of his life's detours, realising that the most personal threads of his life have been spent in accidental moments. Kingi who falls from the sky. Von Wreckedoften, as Jordan had called him.

Moana stands on the bench seat, scouring the plates of food. He helps her with her tiny chunks of sausage, taking her onto his lap. He cuts up a piece of newspaper with his knife, shapes it into a party hat and plonks it onto her head. She feels at it, then goes back to her food. He raises his glass in a toast to everyone present and they to him, the second bottle of wine emptying in the next hour. He smiles at himself, at the haze the wine has set going in his head. He shakes his head, trying to drag himself back to full equilibrium. He hasn't been drunk in years.

Jordan looks over and laughs, then stands and goes to the kitchen. When he comes back he sits next to Kingi.

'So where's first stop?' he says.

'After Auckland, straight through to London.'

'Then what?'

'The reunion and demo flight. Then on to Crete, should take twelve to fourteen hours all up.'

'What are you taking, the slow boat?'

Kingi shakes his head. Jordan stares, then his eyes narrow.

'What are you up to?' he says.

'I'm going to borrow a Hurricane.'

'Borrow?'

'Yes.'

'You're joking.'

'I'm serious.'

'You've teed this up?'

'Down to the last detail. A few old cobbers and I.'

Jordan begins to laugh. 'You're pulling my chain,' he says.

Kingi shakes his head. Jordan reaches for the wine bottle and refills Kingi's mug, a look of disbelief still in his eyes.

'Don't stay here forever,' says Kingi.

'Maybe I belong here. Maybe this *is* my forever. Every night I lay my head in my grandfather's boat, within a stone's throw of the pā of my ancestors. Every morning I swim in the waves they swam in, fished in.'

'And Kataraina? Does she still speak of going home?'

Jordan looks away to the dunes.

'Home,' he says. 'That's an awfully big word, isn't it.'

Kingi nods.

'You know,' says Jordan. 'I always thought that it came down to having things. That the *having* was what it was all about.

But not everything can be had, be possessed. Or needs to be. That somewhere you'd have freedom, and somewhere else you wouldn't. But it isn't like that for me now. At any given moment I have nothing and everything.'

Kingi reaches, places a hand on Jordan's shoulder, realising it is the first time he has touched him, outside of the web of the Tiger Moth's engine bay. Jordan nods his head, sits back against the table. He extends a hand to Kingi and they shake, Kingi laying his other hand over them. He draws Jordan towards him and they touch noses, the old man turning then, standing and walking away into the trees.

Kataraina takes the back of Jordan's leather shirt and leans over the table and kisses his cheek.

'What was that for?' he says.

'Do I need a reason?'

He smiles, then squints his eyes and reaches into his pocket and takes out the feather Kingi had given him. He opens his palm beneath her curious eyes.

'For me?' she says.

He doesn't move. Kataraina takes the feather and turns beside to where Moana sits on the table and inserts it into the child's hair. Moana feels at it, half takes it out then slips it back into her curls.

Kataraina stands and shouts. 'Music, maestro! I want music.'

Jordan lifts his guitar from where it leans against the table, begins to run his thumbs over the strings. Slipping into the adagio run he played the first time she heard him.

'No, not that,' she says. 'Not that dead princess dirge whatsit thingee. Let's have some soul!'

Leonie raises her glass. '"Dancin' in the Moonlight"!'

He plays the intro and Leonie stands and sets Moana on the grass, lifting the child's arms into a twirl. She begins to sing.

'We get it almost every night, when that moon gets big and bright.'

Jordan is leaning into his playing, shoulders swaying with the chords, foot tapping on the grass. Kataraina moves her bare feet on the grass in front of him, the flow of her hips and arms and hands an extension of his music. Leonie glances at Kataraina, moves to her, reaching for her fingers. Kataraina half turns, reluctance perhaps in her eyes, a tentative grip.

'Everybody here is outta sight, they don't bark and they don't bite ...'

Leonie's left hand is on Kataraina's hip now, moving behind her, the fingers of their right hands still entwined. Leonie begins to sway in concert with Kataraina, then the two women step away from the table, Kataraina's long skirt swirling. She looks into Leonie's eyes for a moment, then down towards where her feet tap a honeycomb of prints in the dew-wetted grass.

Moana eases between them, flailing with her arms, her feet rising and falling like a series of blinks.

'Dancin' in the moonlight, everybody's feelin' warm and right, it such a fine and natural sight ...'

Jordan looks up from his guitar, watching the three figures moving on the grass. Two women and a child. Strangers to him until a short while ago. He glances over his shoulder at Kingi half-shadowed among the pines. At the far edge. He thinks of smiling at him, perhaps inviting him back to the table, but they have said all they are going to. Now he wishes him only altitude.

Only altitude.

Kingi stands beneath the trees, watching the movement within the faint halo of light.

Accidents indeed.

He turns and walks away, taking the long route around the dunes, back to the Tiger Moth.

He will not sleep in a bed tonight, his last night with the Moth.

The two women slow as Jordan's fingers slow and step from the moonlight back to that strange, broken melody he plays. His pavane. Kataraina looks over at him, waiting for him to glance up so perhaps she can admonish him with her eyes. But there is something different this time; this time he plays it with a fullness she has not heard before. The arpeggio and melody interspersed, alternated, each adding strength to the other. As if another guitarist, unseen, sits with him in accompaniment. She stares long into him, waiting for his eyes to rise, but they don't. Just as they didn't rise that first time she'd seen him, standing on the deck of his boat, watching her own hands move on his strings.

Leonie steps closer, almost within Kataraina's breath. This child with her own child. A whole history strung like flax strands in front of her. A foot now above hers, an arm around her waist. Her head tilts to lay against Kataraina's neck, cheek against cheek. Breasts against her, against her own breasts, the child able to feel the nearness of them, the history of them, hers – for the first time.

Tomorrow. Tomorrow Kataraina will tell her about seeing a cat's face in the water.

'It's a girl,' said the doctor. 'You have a daughter.'

In the morning Leonie kneels next to Moana, attempting to do up one of the buckles on the child's shoe. Moana still has the feather in her hair from last night. Leonie tries to take it from her but she pulls away. Leonie shakes her head, glances towards where Jordan works again painting the hull of the old dinghy. Moana begins to wriggle.

'Stay still for a sec, Bub,' says Leonie.

Moana senses a game, lifts her foot away. Her mother glares in mock anger but the child sees through it and laughs. Leonie grabs Moana's midriff, begins to tickle her and she shrieks.

Leonie takes advantage of Moana's momentary distraction to slip the strap into the loop. She leans to tie the other shoe but a shadow crosses both the tiny foot and her hand. She looks up to see Kataraina standing above her.

'Let me,' says Kataraina.

She crouches, taking Moana's foot in her hands. The child leans against her, Kataraina's body supporting her. Kataraina stretches the strap, slips the latch in.

'There, Bub,' says Leonie. 'What do we say?'

'Thank you.'

Leonie looks at Kataraina.

'I don't …' she closes her eyes. 'I don't expect you to tell me anything you don't want to,' she says.

Moana is still leaning her weight against Kataraina's shoulder. She touches one of the long strands of Kataraina's hair, loops it around her wrist.

'I just want to know you,' says Leonie. 'To know who my people are.'

Jordan walks across the grass to the tap on the outside of the kitchen block. He crouches to run the bristles of the brush in water, then stands and goes into the shed. Leonie turns to Kataraina, seeming to search for something in her eyes.

'What?' says Kataraina.

'I'm just thinking about what I should call you,' says Leonie.

'I can't give you an answer on that one.'

Jordan comes back out of the shed and stands on the grass, flexing his empty fingers.

'Problem?' says Kataraina.

'Out of paint,' he says, with a sly glance at Leonie. 'Can't think why.'

Leonie starts to answer but he raises his fingers to his lips, then gestures with his hands to usher her stare back towards Kataraina. He turns and walks away.

'Our families used to come here all the time when we were kids,' says Kataraina.

'So you've known him all your life?' says Leonie.

'No. We never …'

Kataraina's voice trails off. Leonie draws Moana back to her, loops her arms around the tiny waist. Kataraina looks towards the path through the trees.

'Come with me,' she says.

'Where?'

'Come on.'

They walk up the path through the trees, Moana pulling at Leonie's hand whenever something catches her attention. A toetoe feather, a nest of shells. They walk on to a spot where the path curves around a marsh where a pond lies in the centre. The outline of a larger pond ghosts beyond its borders. Kataraina stops, looks into the still face of the water.

'You know what I said before,' says Leonie, 'about wanting to know.'

'Yes.'

'You don't have to say anything. Not a thing.'

Kataraina looks up into the clear sky where a faint moon fades against the deepening blue.

'When I was a little teensy kid,' she says, 'I used to think that if I climbed high enough, I could reach the moon.'

'Maybe you have.'

Leonie looks up the slope of the hill, the terraces weaving their way upwards, like rings in a tree. She moves a few paces down the side path, taking Moana by the hand. She turns.

'You coming, Mum?' she says.

Kataraina looks down from the moon, into the faces of her child, her grandchild. She nods, slowly, a nod that has taken twenty years to complete.

Jordan has trailed the three at a distance, stepping into their footprints in the sandy soil. Two women and a child, another trinity of sorts. He catches glimpses of them through the leaves, stepping off the path and into the trees when they pause at the edge of the marsh where Kataraina looks again at her moon. He picks his way forward, stopping at the touch of a nikau leaf against his bare arms. He smiles. Now the girl with the sand-pebble eyes of so long ago has a girl of her own, and she in turn a girl of her own. Mothers, daughters. Lifetimes of unshared memories between them. He eases his own prints between theirs, careful not to overlay Moana's, remembering for a brief moment, his cheek once set against a pregnant woman's body, sensing a tiny pulse within. He blinks his eyes to the warmth of the earth beneath his toes.

Perhaps Pōrangi Sam's old boat does get to sail after all.

They skirt the foot of the hill, then Leonie gestures towards the track leading up the edge of its body, with its soil the tint of the skin of the people who once cultivated its slopes. Its own skin is knitted with grass the hue of pounamu.

'I'm too old to play mountain goat,' says Kataraina.

'I want to see … everything,' says Leonie, 'and leave a little piece of me, of something here.'

'Like buried treasure, huh.'

Leonie smiles, her smirk turning mischievous when she spies the feather still in Moana's hair. She points skyward and opens her mouth in wonder. Moana follows her sudden stare. When she does, Leonie plucks the feather from her daughter's hair and holds it aloft.

Moana snatches at it. 'Hey!'

'Can't I keep it?' says Leonie.

The child puts her hands on her hips and glowers, then her face softens.

'What do you say?' says Kataraina.

Leonie laughs. 'Thank you,' she says and turns and walks up the path.

She follows the track upwards to where it fades into a jagged stitch a foot or so wide, perhaps trodden into existence by sheep or goats long gone. Or bare feet. To the north and south the endless beach, panes of waves stacked one over the other. To the west only ocean. The ragged triangle of the hill rises behind her. She negotiates the first terrace, finds an opening with sufficient rock and root with which to hoist herself to the second. In a couple of minutes she is within a few layers of the crest, the camp now fifty feet below her. She sees now that Jordan has joined Kataraina and Moana at the path's entrance. She waves at them, the feather clutched in her fingers.

A semblance of a path leads to the south-west, overlooking the estuary. She manoeuvres her way through the crumbling soil, roots exposed like old masonry. Above the boat now, its hull is a teardrop beneath her. She sets her toes at the edge, a hand gripping an outcrop of stone.

From this height the boat seems not to be on its framework, but poised on the sand awaiting a tide on which to float. She leans back against the hutch of grass, soil dusting her shoulders. Looking down at the boat, the stream, the beach stretching to infinity.

A gull cries, swooping down on a wind jet, hovering in the swirl of updraft around the volcanic cone. It is stilled a couple of arm stretches from where she lies pressed against the flesh of the hill. She reaches, halving the gap between them, the gull's eyes like needlepoints in its pale face. The wind rises and the gull begins to drift away. Leonie blows a long breath towards it, the wind change completing the gull's passage into exile. A sudden arrangement of its wings and it is fifty yards away in an instant. Over the tip of the boat's mast and across the stream and away over the dunes. She turns back towards the summit, tests the sureness of a rock outcrop with her foot, then steps onto it, raising the feather towards the summit's windblown soil. She turns it point forward, slips its arrowhead into the pores of the hill.

The gull squawks and she jumps, dropping the feather. She snatches at it, her weight jerking sideways. A second's disorientation as her foot, bare now with her sandal fallen away, searches for solid earth. Searches.

It is the suspension of time that is the greatest shock. The slow arc of her hand as it reaches for the feather, then the rock face, then just an old root from a long-dead tree. Like a view of a landscape from an aeroplane. Road and river and coastline. She feels her body begin to fold over backwards, a strange wind ushering her on. She balls her hand into a fist, suddenly angry at her carelessness. She crushes fingers against palms until they sting, then draw blood, her eyes now focusing on the long tail of a root she is gripping, holding her against the cliff face. She swallows, unwilling even to breathe, sensing the simple emptying of her lungs might be enough to break her bond with the earth.

Jordan is halfway up the track in seconds, his running feet in the dirt sending his vision skittering. He can see the broken edge of the hill, nothing but blue sky beyond. One instant she was there and then the picture changed. A new frame. An empty frame. He reaches the cutaway and shouts her name.

'I'm here!'

'Where? Where? Oh shit.'

He is on his belly, reaching for her, his arm aching in its stretch. She is shivering, shaking her head, her cheeks scratched with tears of dust and dirt.

'Can you reach me?' he says.

She won't move either hand away from the root. Running footsteps behind him. He turns. 'Stay back, Kat! I see her. Just got to get to her.'

Kataraina's gasps, Moana is beginning to howl. Hours seem to pass. What to do? Kingi's voice now. Jordan glances over his shoulder. Shouts.

'Hold them back! Keep them away!'

He shakes his head free of it all, looks back to Leonie where she hangs, suspended. He knows the end of root she's holding won't last, half rotten, attached to nothing but unravelling dirt. He feels the veins of the rest of the roots beneath his chest, beneath the eroding dirt. He blinks, swallows hard.

'Shit,' he says. 'There's only one way.'

He climbs over the edge, feeling with his foot for something to gain a momentary balance. The first rock breaks away, vanishes. So too the second. The next seems to be fixed to something. He probes it, easing his weight onto it, then finds an old buried branch with his other foot. Some more roots, all found with his feet, his stare never leaving Leonie.

'Just hang on,' he says.

Her eyes are closed now, tiny specks of dirt and grass slipping from her hair. He crawls against the hill's wounded face, downwards, so his head is level with her knees.

'Reach with one foot,' he says. 'Onto my shoulder.'

'I can't.'

'You have to. Go on, reach.'

Her toes uncurl, stretch into the gap between them, her heel settling onto his shoulder. He grasps the extension of the root she holds, its severed tail inches beneath her.

'When I say go,' he says. 'Take your weight off the root and put it onto my shoulders. Then bring your other foot across.'

'You're crazy!'

'When I say go.'

She blinks, her teeth chattering.

'Go!'

She steps sideways, her hands clawing at the edge of the hill, the larger roots coming into her grasp. He feels himself sink with her weight, digs his toes into the hillside. Suddenly her weight eases and he looks up to see her clambering up over the rim. A haze of dust. He shakes his head, trying to clear his eyes. He reaches again for the larger roots. Once. Twice. The hillside seems to rise against him with each movement. He looks at the stream of tree fibre clutched in his hand, puzzled, amused even, at its sudden weightlessness. The aches in his neck and shoulders and forearms slip away, as if he is back in his ocean, within his bed of water. His upper body opens out like a wing, his mouth gasping a last gift of air before he returns to his home in the waves.

Leonie's eyelids fall. Her hand reaches for Kataraina's, finding warmth even amid its trembling. Warmth enough to almost wash away the terrible jolt of Jordan's body hitting the deck of his boat.

Kingi drives Leonie's car up the track to Te Kopu to phone the ambulance. By the time it arrives mid-afternoon the sun is curtained in a film of rainwater. The daylight now almost a rumour. When the officers arrive Kingi does all the talking, the women communicating only with tiny gestures, then fading into the shadows. Now and then a shake of the head. Leonie sits with Moana and Kataraina, in Leonie's cabin, Moana scribbling with crayons in a colouring book. Kingi shakes the ambulance driver's hand, gives a final wave to the police constable and they drive on up the track to the main road.

Kingi knocks at the cabin's door. There is no answer. He pushes it open. Kataraina lies on the bed, her hair fanning over the pillow. One hand taps against the window pane. Her fingernails click.

'Footprints,' she says.

Leonie looks up.

'They look like footprints. On the first day I came I saw his footprints in the sand and the smudge of these fingerprints on the window.'

Kingi pauses within the door's frame.

'They tell a history,' says Kataraina. 'Like the old days. Tell where someone has been. What they've been up to. Where they're going.'

Leonie kneels beside the bed, laying her cheek against Kataraina's waist.

'It was a female cat,' says Kataraina. 'Moth-eaten old thing it was, only just alive. Funny how life sometimes just won't let go of us. No matter how hard we try to let go of it. Sometimes.'

Her stare hasn't moved from the glass.

'If you use more water and less soap you don't get the streaks on the pane. You just need to remember to rinse off when you've finished with the soap, or it goes all streaky.'

Leonie moves up onto the bed, lies next to Kataraina. She props herself on a shoulder, draws Kataraina's head towards her, taking her face against her chest. Kataraina closes her eyes to the rise and fall of Leonie's chest.

Hawksbury, England, September 1990

Former Flight Lieutenant Kingi Heremia stands on the tarmac, clothed in an RAF Battle of Britain replica flight uniform. The only concession to modernity is a contemporary flying helmet. He flexes his fingers within his leather gloves. A military band plays. He looks around, his neck clasped by his Mae West life vest. The packed parachute knocks against his rump whenever he moves. He looks up into the patchy sky, his mind travelling through storehouses of memories of English weather – cloud-ceiling levels, visibility parameters. He has been fêted and celebrated, dined with other former RAF pilots, none of whom he actually flew with. In his tiny corner of the remembrances of the summer of fifty years past. Events all over England, everywhere there was the smell of aviation fuel or glycol, vapour trails staining bower meadows and moors. He thinks for a moment of those he flew with and a kaleidoscope of names rushes by like low-level cumulus. Like flak. He has spoken little since he arrived, only when obliged to. And then only in thanks to the RAF and to the organisers and those aircraft archaeologists who had reclaimed the metal bones of the Hurricane from the mudflats. Then reclaimed it from history itself. The one thing he has not spoken of is aerial combat. And he will not again.

The first sight of the restored Hurricane was a shock. He had seen it from the back of a car, his hand moving to grip the rear of the front seat as they approached. He allowed himself a smile, relaxed against the seat and wound down the window. Hurricane Mark 1, vintage 1940. Crashed off Dover, September 1940. Rebuilt between 1982 and 1990. Wingspan a touch over 40 ft, length 31 ft 5 in. Powered by one Rolls Royce Merlin IIII engine, with an output of 1,030 horsepower. Range: 600 miles. An hour talking to mechanics, a couple of Hurricane enthusiasts from the aero club. He had requested at least an hour in the air with it before the show. He was given thirty minutes. It was enough.

The roar of the engine shocked him, the Merlin seeming to want to work the teeth in his jaw loose. He clasped the control column, easing it along the runway then accelerating into a murky sky. For the first couple of minutes he was a novice in the seat, his hands unsure, jittery. The Hurricane's body had the aerodynamics of a paving stone. But then he began to slip into a pact with it, a gentlemen's agreement of sorts, and it responded to the surer touch. He looked to port and starboard, down at the patchwork of fields, realising after a few minutes that he was altering his flight path every ten seconds, just out of reflex.

Never present a stationary target.

He looks around now at the grey tarmac, its surface veined with tyre streaks, as if children's skate trails on an ice pond. He thinks of another gathering, half a world away. Two women and a child, each carrying a clue to the others' identity, like the faint shapes on the glass pane that Kataraina had taken within her once Antarctic heart. And the fingerprint maker, the tattooed man whose moko threaded in and out of their lives.

'*At any given moment I have nothing and everything,*' he had said. *Nothing and everything.*

He draws his stare back from the beach, back to the tarmac. All the times he almost vomited with the stench of leaking fuel or oil, knowing a single spark no larger than a pinprick would turn him into a human flare. It could have ended so many times, any one of a thousand shots piercing his visor or finding its way up through the Hurricane's floor and tub seat. But they never did. They never did and he has never known why.

He sees them again, the women and child, standing against the backdrop of dunes. Their shadows form into a single shadow in the slanted light. Perhaps they carry a hint of the young man who had stepped so many times from the sea and stepped off the edge of the earth to return the woman's daughter to her. A child lost once, not to be lost again.

He had settled heavy into the cockpit, part of him not wanting to bring the Tiger Moth back to life, as it meant further breaking their circle. When he set the motor going he leaned back with a smile, sensing the young man's hand in a part of each revolution, each turn of the crank and propeller. He fixed his chin strap, looked once at the figures on the sand. Leonie with her arms looped around Kataraina, Moana against Kataraina's legs. He drew the goggles down from his forehead and waved once and steered the Moth away from its nest of shells and into the sky.

The band stops playing. He takes his cue from his hosts and steps forward, up into the cockpit, up into the summer of 1940. He blinks hard against the vibration of his bones, looks down at his trembling hand on the control column, eases the Hurricane out onto the tarmac.

He smiles, whispers into his chin strap.

'Sometimes Icarus doesn't fall to earth.'

Kataraina sits on the bottom step of the small staircase leading into the boat's cabin. A fractured light seeps through the windows. Everything in order as usual, except for his bed, *their* bed, her night-time wanderings in the blankets the only hint of chaos. She stands and walks to the dresser, his books now back in their library arrangement. She lays her hands on their bones, as if she can reawaken his eyes over them, just for a moment. The encyclopaedia that never got past the first chapter. The Māori-language bible he did not possess the words to read, as he believed perhaps he did not possess the tools to decipher so many things, human things, which she knows now wasn't true. She takes his battered leather shirt from the rack, slips it over herself, though she isn't cold. She walks back out onto the deck and down the streambed to the sand and on down to the shallows where she kneels and slips his shirt off again. She places it in the water, drawing it through the last of the falling waves, then raises it and opens it out again and sits it back over her shoulders and walks away.

The day of the burial the young men lift the coffin and carry it across the dirt track and through the rotted wooden gate onto the plateau. The ground is rutted with land slips, some of the headstones sitting askew. Most are just flat stones, faces bald like shells to the sea air. Around one grave stands a tiny wrought iron fence, above another a crumbling concrete plinth. A gull perches in front of a jar of fading flowers. The women stand with their backs to the sea, Leonie against Kataraina, now and then reaching to draw Kataraina's wind-blown hair back from her cheekbones. Moana is braced against their legs. Kataraina wears the leather shirt again, the collar pulled up beneath her chin. She glances over the coffin at the small circle of faces around the grave, none of whom she can recall. The minister struggles against the sound of the ocean and his words veer away, broken in the wind. Buried beneath the calls of the circling gulls. Kataraina steps forward once, as the coffin is lowered into the grave against the sound of singing. The sound of the sea. She whispers something, too faint for anyone but her to hear.

'I never knew it could rain on the moon,' she says. 'Thank you.'

In twenty minutes it is over and Jordan's whānau file away, none of them looking to the two women and the child. None of them knowing.

At sunset with the retreating tide they walk out across the sand, Kataraina and Leonie, carrying Jordan's surfboard between them. It is a hundred yards to the waterline, the glistening sand catching the last light like glass. Moana sits in the dunes with her bucket and spade. Kataraina moves up the beach to where the sea is flattest, to where Jordan had once pointed out the rip tide, where the water retreats fastest and sweeps the unwary away. She steps into the shallows and moves on until the weakening waves glance against the women's thighs. She halts, turns to Leonie, and they lower the surfboard into the water and begin to push it out, stopping, letting it go when the water is more than waist deep. It slips along the beach, bobbing, and they follow it, push it further out until the sea is up to their breasts. Then they turn, move back towards land, backtracking, shielding their eyes from the setting sun. Watching the board slip from wave to trough, become part of the skin of the sea. A last glimpse, the sunset blood red on the board's back. Then both the board and the setting sun are gone.

Kataraina turns to Leonie and Leonie bends to the shallows, takes a sea-wetted finger and runs it down across Kataraina's forehead, across a cheek and down her chest to her heart. Kataraina nods, blinks once, then they head back to the dunes.

Kataraina sits in the marram grass, her diary in one hand, a pencil in the other. Leonie stands at the base of the dune, reaching out to catch Moana as she comes rolling down the dune's face to land in her arms. She lifts her, holds her upside down, looking around in mock puzzlement.

'Where's Moana gone,' she says. 'Where's Moana?'

The child bursts into laughter, fighting to get at her mother's legs. Leonie flips her over, lets her go and she clambers up the face of the dune again, falling against Kataraina's feet. Kataraina puts the pencil between her teeth and leans forward and straightens Moana up, admonishing her with a raised finger, then ruffling her hair. Moana turns, takes a few wary steps then leaps over, letting herself roll over and over and over again down through the marram grass.

Kataraina takes the pencil from between her teeth, opens the diary.

Auē.

That's what you used to say, Nan, remember? Whenever there was something you couldn't agree with, or just didn't understand. Maybe you'd just seen some stuff, even if you wouldn't talk much about it. I reckon maybe I have now, too.

Auē.

She flicks forward to an empty page.

Nan,

I've found a friend, a girl who says she knows me. I met her a million times in my dreams but never stopped to say hello, never told her who I was. Who she is. I reckon all she wants is to come home.

I always thought that 'home' was a place. An address. But it isn't. It's not a 'what' or a 'where', it's a 'why'.

It's a reason.

Like I said, I've found a friend. I've also lost one.

His name was Jordan and you'd have looked a bit sideways at him at first, but you of all people could always see through things. Into things. So I think you'd know. Sometimes I think I saw into him too.

I'm sick of running, Nan. Sick of looking for that kid that sat by the pond and looked at her reflection under the moon. I thought she was my friend but she wasn't. No, that's not true. The truth is that I wasn't a good enough friend to her.

Kingi banks to the right, goes into a wide half circle, keeping an eye on both the altimeter and the visual horizon. He climbs again, the airfield coming into his vision at ten o'clock, the engine on song now, the sketch of wings a stranger in this land. Not a stranger to the place but a stranger to the time.

He straightens, checks his air speed, comes down out of the clouds and over the runway, this old man in a piston-engined fighter plane. He half flips, his wing vertical, his body sensing the channel in the air, the right place to be right now at this moment. He even allows himself a smile.

One more pass, a barrel roll, just for the hell of it, then a veer away to the south east, the airfield vanishing behind him. Within minutes he is over the water.

He cruises around 180 miles per hour, not straying above 5000 feet. Down over the pastures of France for a good three hours to the first refuelling stop at Gap-Tallard, fields of lavender spreading beneath his wings as he approaches. A handshake, a momentary embrace with a couple of acquaintances he hasn't seen in twenty years. A mathematics master from Cambridge, a former engineering pupil who now constructs bridges, both arranged to be out here for this old man's folly. Few words are spoken. Neither asks if he is sure of what he is doing.

Away, skirting the mountains. A night landing at a smaller airfield tucked away near Bari, flares laid on the concrete to mark his target. Another old acquaintance, a former RAF mechanic, dragged from his crumbling retirement in a terraced house in Gateshead. Kingi watches him with the fuel pump, realising that for all they are doing for him, he never really thought of any of these men as friends. He keeps his radio off to the chatter that must be circling his lone spearpoint towards the darkened Mediterranean.

A few hours rest and a final refuel at a backcountry airfield on Peloponnisos, rising again just before dawn and pointing the nose out over the Mirtoan Sea, changing course again with the sunrise. Steering towards the outline of a large island, an outline he has not seen in almost fifty years.

Kriti.

He raises a hand, slides the cockpit canopy back and lifts his helmet visor.

Leonie sinks into the sand at the foot of the dune, taking Moana against her. She rolls onto her back and Moana leaps on top of her, crouching, her bare feet on her mother's chest. Moana puts her hands on her knees and glares. Leonie raises a hand, pokes her on the point of the nose. Moana does the same in response. A stare down. Moana begins to drum with her hands on her mother's tummy, beneath her heart. Leonie glances up the slope to where Kataraina sits writing, smiles, seeing for the first time perhaps the echo of her in Moana's face.

Kataraina catches Leonie staring and pokes out her tongue. Leonie returns the favour, then turns away to look across the ripples of sand to the distant waves.

Kataraina lifts her pencil, leafs back a few pages. Tiny droplets of sand sifting from her fingerprints and into the grain of the paper. She begins to read.

Sometimes I dream: I'm sitting cross-legged in front of you, holding one of your hands like it was treasure. Looking into your face, moving through the lines of it, the creases. Like the lines tattooed into your own Nana's skin. But not ink, just years. I reach out, run a finger down across them. You don't say a word. You just let me touch, feel, on and on. Like a little baby in a crib, feeling its own skin, feeling the air, the world, for the first time. You just sit there, letting my fingers find every inch of you. Every second of your life, carved into your skin, your pale-grey hair. Painted into your grey eyes.

Then I stand and you stand with me, not old anymore, but any age, or no age at all. You slide your arms around me. I can't feel your hands, the end of your arms, there's just this hugeness to you. No corners, no edges. Like the reflection of the moon I used to watch, lying there in my blanket. Something I could slip into and float within.

She dips the pencil's tip into her mouth, then writes beneath:

I'm a Nan now too. Maybe the circle sometimes does join up.

The old pilot makes a wide turn to the south-west, Maleme appearing to the south, where a young man from another island had stood and watched those phantom rain clouds in that long ago. The Bay of Kissamou opens to his right. He crosses it then turns again over the sea. Straight ahead the White Mountains build from the horizon. He swoops in over the land, a backbone of green and grey hills, catching the sun. Air speed down to 120. Stands of cypresses, flecks of white and orange rooftops. The dome of a cathedral. He climbs, swings round again, coming in lower this time, heading west over his island of birds. Course bearing … it doesn't matter any more.

The hillsides, the valleys. Rooftops again, the road, and just for an instant, beneath his wings, at last – a vineyard.

Macroglossum stellatarum – belonging to the family of *sphingidae* – sphinx moths. Sometimes mistaken for a hummingbird.

Kataraina holds the diary open, where she has glued a photograph between her notes. A crumpled, grainy image of a figure swimming, in a starlit sea. A universal sea. She runs her fingerprint over the caption.

> *Horse's Head Nebula, Barnard 33. Quadrant of Zeta Orionis.*
> She bends and kisses the page, then closes the covers.

Acknowledgements

I am indebted to several people for their help in the gestation of this book and their general support:

John Huria for his editing nouse. Dr Susan Sayer, my agent. Robyn and Brian Bargh for everything Huia Publishers has come to be. Antoinette Wilson for her insightful suggestions for the short story version of 'Zeta Orionis'. Also the fine writers and good people of the Wilderness Writers Group in Auckland who gave me invaluable feedback on the initial drafts.

Several books were also crucial in my research: *Free Lodgings* by Peter Winter for an inside view of POWs in Crete and Greece. *The Few – Summer 1940, the Battle of Britain* by Philip Kaplan and Richard Collier for its evocative photographs and first hand testimony. *Moko – Maori Tattoo*; photography by Hans Neleman, from whose beautiful photographs I deciphered hints of the faces of Kataraina, Jordan and Leonie. And *The New Book of Knowledge* – published by Grolier – of which I possess only the 'A' volume, retrieved from a rubbish dump, just as Jordan does in the novel.